D1737298

Nadine Mutas
c/o Block Services
Stuttgarter Str. 106
70736 Fellbach
Germany
nadine@nadinemutas.com
www.nadinemutas.com

This is a work of fiction. Names, characters, places and incidents either are
products of the author's imagination or are used fictitiously. Any
resemblance to actual events or locales or persons, living or dead, is entirely
coincidental.

Cover by Orina Kafe

ISBN: 9798863360423

❀ Created with Vellum

TILL HEAVEN DO US PART

INFERNAL COVENANT ❖ BOOK TWO

NADINE MUTAS

For Mina, my beloved little gray hellcat. Your nine lives were used up too soon, but I am grateful I got to be your human for a little while. Happy hunting beyond the Rainbow Bridge.

PREVIOUSLY ON...

AKA A RECAP OF ZOE'S FABULOUS ADVENTURES IN HELL, FOR THOSE WHO READ THE FIRST BOOK A WHILE AGO. IF YOU JUST READ HELLISHLY EVER AFTER, FEEL FREE TO SKIP THIS. (IT'S KIND OF LONG.)

All right, my friend, get yourself a comfy chair, some hot beverage of your choice, and settle in.

sips tea

So, the whole thing starts on Zoe's twenty-fifth birthday, when the demon she accidentally summoned at the tender and hormonally challenged age of thirteen shows up in her living room, all broody and grumpy and unfairly hot, intent on completing the marriage contract she inadvertently trapped him in during that ill-fated séance twelve years ago.

To Zoe's great dismay, the whole thing isn't a joke, and she sees herself forced to actually marry and follow Azazel to Hell—where he promptly wants to deposit her out of

I

sight and out of mind, sequestered away in his grand mansion.

Zoe is having none of that, of course.

A few testy, banter-filled, and annoyingly sexually charged fights with Azazel later, she manages to slip out of her comfortable quarters and right into trouble, which is when Azazel's guest Zaquiel notices her, quite inconveniently so for Azazel.

In order to save face—if word got out that not only has Azazel been tricked into a contract by a human, but he's been forced to *marry* one, his reputation would go bye-bye—Azazel passes Zoe off as his "pet" in front of Zaquiel, though he has to negotiate with Zoe to get her to play along.

Zoe successfully barters for freedom of movement within Azazel's house and guaranteed visits to Earth, and then the games begin.

During the meeting with Zaquiel, the simmering sexual tension between Zoe and Azazel boils over, and something shifts between the two of them. Subsequently, Azazel makes his new intentions of ~~not being a dick anymore~~ wooing Zoe clear and proceeds to court her with, among other things, the indisputably romantic gesture of gifting her her own personal fearsome hellhound.

Despite Zoe not being a dog person, that move surprisingly works, and Zoe decides to test the whole "demon in the sack" idea, which results in several rounds of mind-blowing sex, the aftermath of which gets inappropriately commented on by Azmodea, Azazel's twin sister.

Azazel takes Zoe to Earth to visit her best friend Taylor and then her mom, but when Zoe realizes during her visit that her estranged father has died, she breaks down. Because feelings are hella complicated, and just when you *think* you don't care about a family member anymore, around comes some unresolved trauma.

To make matters worse, Zoe then finds out that her dad's soul went straight to Hell to pay for his ~~being a lying little shit to his family~~ adultery, and to raise the stakes unnecessarily more, it's Lucifer who has possession of him.

As in, Azazel's *grandfather* Lucifer, who delighted in watching Azazel get bullied at his court as a young demon in penance for the sins of his father, Azrael, whom Lucifer blames for breaking his favorite daughter, Naamah.

You see, Azrael and Naamah were an item, despite the fact he was an angel and she a demon, which is, like, the ultimate Romeo-and-Juliet thing, except, you know, they weren't horny and prefrontal-cortex-lacking teenagers who were ready to die for each other after three days of humping and—I digress.

When Naamah got preggers by Azrael, Lucifer orchestrated his fall from grace, so Azrael would join Naamah in Hell, but angel boy couldn't cope with the Dark Side and decided to skip. Probably didn't get enough cookies.

After Azrael abandoned his family to bleach his wings again, Naamah's mental health declined. Presumably to the point she lost the will to live and committed suicide...or so everyone believes.

Zoe, however, finds out the truth when she traipses around Lucifer's palace during the Fall Festival—a grand celebration of Lucifer's rebellion against Heaven for claiming Lilith, Adam's first wife, as his own.

Cue more backstory: Way back in Eden, Lilith was supposed to play happy submissive wifey to Adam, but she didn't agree that the dude was God's greatest creation and instead fell in love with Lucifer, who was still an angel at the time. And not just any angel, but the brightest star in

Heaven. No wonder our girl went for him instead of the human—wingspan, am I right?

sips more tea

Anywho, God didn't like that and kicked them out—Lilith from Eden, and Lucifer from Heaven. Lucifer asked Lilith to join him in Hell, as his queen and equal, and she happily agreed.

But, of course, that didn't last long, because God didn't like that either and snatched Lilith back, keeping her from Lucifer out of spite.

Which kickstarted the war between Heaven and Hell. Lucifer had quite a few former angels on his side who had taken the fall with him—he was real popular among his brethren—and together they made up such a force that, after a lot of devastating battles, Heaven was forced to propose a truce. Lucifer would get Lilith back, but in return he had to abide by Heaven's rules for the realms and vow to never set foot on Earth again.

The deal was struck, and Heaven and Hell have maintained an armistice for thousands of years.

Back to Zoe's story: Azazel hatches a plan to steal her dad's soul right from under Lucifer's nose at the Fall Festival by taking advantage of the crowds and the notorious chaos at the party, but Azazel's RSVP catches the unfortunate notice of Lucifer, who requests Zoe's presence, too.

Azazel therefore can't help but present Zoe to his grandfather...while still officially keeping up the farce about her being his pet. Because if Lucifer finds out that Azazel actually cares about Zoe, it would put her in danger.

Lucifer, sneaky fucker that he is, makes Zoe drink amrit, the demon booze that is most definitely not suitable for humans, and Zoe promptly goes on a drug-hallucination-induced blabbing spree and spills all the beans about the séance and the marriage contract, which humiliates Azazel in front of Lucifer's entire court.

Chaos erupts when Azmodea and Mammon trigger the glitter bombs they deployed as a distraction so Azazel et al. can go on the soul heist. Zoe gets separated from Azazel when a giant hellrat drags her into a tunnel, but she manages to escape...only to stumble right into the private quarters where Naamah, Azazel and Azmodea's mother, has been sequestered for millennia, very much not dead.

Through sheer dumb luck and a bit of skill, Zoe saves Naamah from an attack by insurgents who want to use Naamah to harm Lucifer, at which point she gets discovered by one of Lucifer's guards, who then drags her before Lucifer.

Lilith interrupts Lucifer's near apoplexy and subsequent murder of Zoe to gently remind him that Zoe actually helped Naamah and deserves a favor instead of a crushed throat, and the devil, being the good hubby that he is, listens to his wife.

Azazel arrives in that moment, and Lucifer, not about to miss the chance to humiliate his grandson yet again, turns the favor owed into an offer of annulling the marriage and sending Zoe back home to Earth, as if none of this ever happened—of course, that would mean Zoe wouldn't retain any memories of her time here, including Azazel.

Azazel rises to the occasion and publicly proclaims that he wants Zoe to stay—as his wife—revealing in front of Lucifer's court that he truly, deeply cares about Zoe.

Zoe, in turn, claims him as well, and rejects Lucifer's offer in favor of staying in Hell with Azazel.

Lucifer is ready to pop a few veins out of sheer rage, but he still owes Zoe, so he grants her two boons—fast healing and summoning powers.

Before they leave, however, he secretly binds Zoe to silence about Naamah, especially to Azazel, condemning Zoe to life with a secret so big it might just crush her.

Oh, yeah, and Azazel managed to successfully steal the soul of Zoe's dad. They release him at his other family's house, and Zoe and her father have a moment of complicated reconciliation.

Welp, that wraps it up, and this whole recap ran rather long, which should let you know how incapable I am of summarizing my own book. Alas, that ain't my talent.

If you read this far, congratulations, and I hope this *Previously on* helped jog your memory of the events of book 1, because now we dive straight into book 2…

CHAPTER 1

S artre once famously said, "Hell is other people."
Having lived in Hell for almost a year—albeit not as a damned soul—I could now decidedly say that he was onto something with that statement.

And not in the often misunderstood way his words were usually interpreted. That was to say, with a kind of misanthropic lens, seeing other people as inherently bad, and therefore it would be best to avoid them altogether.

Although, to be fair, as a socially awkward introvert, I could probably get on board with that idea.

Anyway. Sartre's original meaning of hell was more to the effect that we were all defined by the judgment of others, and our perception of how others saw us trapped us in a way that was torture all on its own. *That* was terrifyingly correct.

As I stood in Azazel's entrance hall, ready to play hostess alongside my demon husband, that judgment of others already pressed down on me before our honored guests even arrived. I took a deep breath that did nothing to ease the weight on my chest. My fingers fidgeted with the skirt of my elegant evening dress, a gorgeous thing of sapphire blue dappled with jewels that sparkled in the light of the chandeliers and torches.

In my previous life on Earth—I hadn't actually died, but I liked to think of my life cut into a *before* and an *after*, the dividing factor being that fateful night when Azazel had come to make good on our deal and brought me down here to Hell—I'd never worn anything so finely tailored, so exquisite, and probably worth more than I'd made in a year in my last job on Earth.

And yet, since coming to live here, I'd worn dresses like this more times than I could count, and never the same one twice. All given to me by Azazel, of course, gifts not only meant as a loving gesture by my devoted husband, but also to dress the part for the gatherings he held as a high-ranking demon. And there were *so many* of them. Whoo boy! These demons liked to meet up way more often than anyone had the right to throw parties. And of course, they all showed up in their finest attire.

The gowns I wore were an armor of sorts; I understood that much.

Unfortunately, the condescension leveled at me still managed to pierce it.

Azazel, dressed in a black tunic suit with stylized elements of fighting gear, subtly turned to me, his eyes of lightning not missing a thing. "You're absolutely stunning," he murmured.

I gave him a small smile, grateful for his attempt to soothe me, yet knowing it wouldn't help dissolve my anxiety. My mind had already played through all the things awaiting me in the next few hours.

His expression becoming solemn, he fully turned to me, framing my face with both hands. The light of the torches glinted off his sable hair as he leaned down a bit to bring himself to eye level with me. As always, his ethereal beauty struck me hard, his features so perfectly sculpted that looking at him both arrested my breath and hushed my thoughts with awe.

"Zoe," he said, his thumbs stroking over my cheeks. "Before Inachiel and his entourage arrive, there's something you need to know."

A thread of worry coiled in my stomach. Oh, God. What now?

"Inachiel," he said quietly, his voice deathly serious, "likes to sleep among a pile of stuffed animals."

I choked on my own laughter. "What the what?"

He faced the massive doors in front of us again, a smirk playing about his mouth. "Now you know."

"Right," I said through barely suppressed giggles. "But how do *you* know?"

"I have my sources."

I narrowed my eyes. "Have you been to his bedroom?"

Given that Azazel was a good two thousand five hundred years old, I had a veritable army of his exes to contend with, quite a few of whom I'd met during the past couple of months. And yes, I knew they'd all happened before my time, the past was the past, water under the bridge, no reason for me to be jealous, yada yada yada.

I just liked to know ahead of time if I would encounter one of them, because it was a special kind of feeling shitty when you ran into an ex of your man—demon, whatever— and they knew while you didn't, and then they *let* you know.

"No," Azazel said in answer to my question. "Never was my type."

"Then how do you know about his stuffies?"

9

A glint in his eyes. "Mephistopheles."

I flailed my arms. "And how would *he* possibly know that?"

"Hellcats are quite resourceful." He winked at me. "Which makes them excellent spies."

My eyes widened. "Are you telling me we could be spied on by sneaky felines hiding in the shadows at any time?" I glanced around the murky corners and gloomy ceiling of the entrance hall as if I'd spot a pair of glowing cat eyes right that moment.

"That is why," he drawled, "I have several hellcats of my own. The more there are, the lower the risk of someone else's cat sneaking in. They are quite territorial."

I pursed my lips, a new appreciation for Mephisto's presence sparking in my mind. I made a mental note to give him some extra love the next time I saw him. Over the course of the past year, the surly hellcat had gradually allowed me to pet him here and there, and let me tell ya, scratching a winged feline the size of a large bobcat behind his bat ears was quite the experience.

When he purred, the floor vibrated.

A trumpet sounded from outside, and with a start, I turned toward the giant double doors just as they opened with a deep groan.

I took a steadying breath, finding my nerves not as wired as they were before.

Bumping my shoulder softly against Azazel's arm, I sent him a message on the mental pathway we often used to communicate silently. *Thank you.*

With his masterfully delivered insight about Inachiel's sleeping habits, he'd effectively dismantled some of my anxiety. Knowing a no doubt embarrassing secret about one of the high-profile guests who would more than likely look down their noses at me—again—would make it easier to hold up my chin in the face of their patronizing attitudes.

Remember, Azazel replied silkily just as our guests began entering through the open doors. *Stuffies.*

I bit my lip to keep from snickering.

Not that I'd fault anyone for indulging in harmless coping mechanisms like wanting to cuddle with stuffed animals. Hell, my go-to comfort habit was to rewatch Disney movies and sing along, torturously out of tune, to the songs. But given the haughty, holier-than-thou way a lot of these demons treated those they considered inferior to them—and that included yours truly—it helped take them down a peg, even if only in my own mind, when I knew they were hiding things that would make them the laughingstock among their peers.

No one was perfect, least of all those snooty jerks.

"Inachiel," Azazel said as he stepped forward to greet the demon at the front of the group. "I bid you welcome to my home."

Inachiel shared the good looks of all his brethren, his face a vision of masculine beauty that drew the eye—sharp cheekbones, a strong jaw, and piercing eyes of emerald green. Long hair of warm brown that would be the envy of many a woman completed the look. Dressed in a decadently embroidered suit reminiscent of Jedi garments—if the Jedi ever indulged in colors other than muted earth tones, that was—he moved with the fluid grace of a large feline, all leashed power and unchallenged confidence.

Honestly, it wasn't fair. Every single demon I'd met looked like they'd stepped right out of a magazine listing the most stunning models of all time, dialed up by tens. I kept searching for physical flaws every time I encountered one of them, but I had yet to find any. They were impossibly, unearthly beautiful, the entire fucking lot of them.

That alone was enough to make a girl feel out of place.

Just yesterday, I'd discovered a pimple on my face. A pimple! I was almost twenty-six years old, and here I was, breaking out like a damn teenager.

That was particularly hard to contend with when surrounded by flawlessly beautiful demons who looked like they'd been photoshopped.

Azazel and Inachiel were just finishing up their greeting, which meant it was my turn now. Eek.

You'd think a year of playing high-society lady who welcomed all sorts of hoity-toity, gravely important guests would have given me the practice necessary to ace this crap.

Alas.

Enter my socially awkward clumsiness.

As Inachiel turned from Azazel to me, I repeated the phrase over and over in my head. *Welcome, it's a pleasure to meet you. Welcome, it's a pleasure to meet you. Welcome, it's a pleasure to—*

"And you must be Zoe," Inachiel said, inclining his head.

"It's welcome to pleasure you."

Oh, no.

CHAPTER 2

Inachiel blinked, his expression a study in perplexity. "So I've heard," he murmured after a moment.

I peered at the floor for a hole to swallow me. At this rate, I'd settle for a crack that I'd somehow wiggle into.

Just kill me now, I whispered into Azazel's mind.

That would put me in breach of our contract, sweetheart, was his purred answer.

I gave him a quick, disgruntled side-eye.

Just think of stuffies, he murmured.

Right. With a deep breath, I forced a smile on my face, beamed at Inachiel, and said, "Good to meet you. Please, come on in."

Gesturing toward the back of the hall, I stepped aside, bowing my head slightly. Seeing as Inachiel held the same rank as Azazel, a full-body bow wasn't necessary, not even for me, because as Azazel's wife, I officially ranked as high as he did. Hell was all about protocol, politics, and pomp—tempered by some truly gruesome displays of brutality—so following the rules of diplomacy, I had to be greeted and treated the same as Azazel, even though I was a lowly human without significant powers.

And therein lay the problem.

It was exactly that dichotomy between my theoretical high status and my actual being a nearly powerless human that tripped everyone up, including me. Not once, in all those months down here, had I been truly treated the way a demon of my status should.

Oh, they all pretended just fine, especially in front of Azazel. As soon as he turned his back, though, most of that pretense dropped to a level of just barely staying above outright insulting me.

Such *fun*.

These demons excelled at political power plays, at slicing into someone with words as precise and cutting as a surgical knife, at using the sweetest turn of phrase to deliver an insult just covert enough not to be considered a breach of protocol.

Me? I stumbled over my own words when I ordered a drink. Once, in my previous life, when I'd gone through a drive-through and picked up my food, the cashier had said, "Your receipt is in the bag," and my eloquent answer had been, "You too!"

Needless to say, I never went back to *that* fast-food joint again.

So, anyway, add that particular skill of putting my foot in my mouth to the thinly veiled condescension I had to endure at these meetings, and you had the perfect recipe for an excruciating experience. And here I thought I wouldn't be tortured in Hell just because I was married to a demon. Ha!

Joke was on me.

It was precisely the fact that I was *married* to Azazel that made it impossible for me to skip these damn parties.

Because as his wife—rare though that might be in Hell—I was head of the household alongside him and was required, by protocol, to welcome his guests and play hostess. If I didn't show at these gatherings, it would be tantamount to snubbing his visitors, and that affront would damage Azazel's reputation and standing among his peers.

And no way in Hell would I fuck things up for him down here.

So I gritted my teeth, plastered on a pleasant smile, and swam in those shark-infested waters while hoping I wouldn't cut myself and start bleeding.

Walking side by side with Azazel, I led our guests—a group of half a dozen—into one of the many, many rooms in this house that were solely meant to accommodate leisurely get-togethers. Had I ever wondered how nobility lived in previous centuries? I wondered no more.

Hell was a largely feudal system, and all those alliances and ties and complex relationships between demons and their territories demanded to be well maintained. Everyone's favorite way of doing that seemed to be to keep inviting each other to shoot the shit at their respective residences and indulge in gossip and often borderline orgy-like festivities.

Half of the time, I was tempted to loudly proclaim, "Let them eat cake!" But that would make them look at me even more weirdly than they already did, and my clumsy human self was tarnish enough for Azazel's reputation as it was.

Our honored guests settled onto the available lounging surfaces of the room, this one decorated in a color scheme that could best be described as *Let's make this look like a sunset*. Low lighting bathed the room in an intimate glow, and soft music filled the air, played live by a band in the corner. Plush couches and settees and chairs invited visitors to get comfortable, and little side tables held all sorts of hors d'oeuvres and refreshments. Demons didn't need food or drink to survive, as I'd learned, but they sure liked to consume it. And like everything else on offer in Azazel's home, it was of exquisite quality.

Given that there was no sun in Hell, no agriculture as far as I had seen, I'd wondered where it all came from...until I'd found out that, apparently, demons pilfered it all from Earth. Which had soured my stomach quite a bit, as I didn't like the idea of living off stolen food. Someone had grown all of this, and the ones down in the trenches, doing backbreaking work to plant and process, already barely made a living this way. It just didn't sit right that they'd continuously lose part of their harvest to the sticky fingers of some demons from down below who didn't even need this food to survive.

Except me, of course. I did need to eat and drink if I wanted to stay alive.

Azazel, bless his heart, had taken strides to ensure that at least the food *he* sourced for his estate would be properly compensated for. I hadn't asked him for it—he'd just mentioned it offhand one day—but I knew it was because he'd somehow realized my discomfort.

I loved him all the more for it.

Now I moved around the room, between groups of demons from Azazel's domain who were chatting with the visitors. These parties always attracted quite a few of Azazel's folks; for one thing, because it was good manners to have demons from his domain and household attend and mingle with the guests, and for another, because...well. There just wasn't much else to do for fun in Hell.

You'd either go to war against another demon, go to work to torture some sinners, visit Earth to collect some souls, take care of your estate if you were high-ranking, or you'd get shitfaced at one of these parties. Sometimes, a

TILL HEAVEN DO US PART

group would venture out for a dragon hunt. Thankfully, I didn't need to participate in *that* particular entertainment because I didn't have wings, which made me glad for the lack of feathers for a change.

Yeah, so these gatherings were really at the top of the list of fun activities for many demons. How had Azazel so succinctly put it, back when we were at Lucifer's Fall Festival? *Hell is a shithole and immortality holds endless ennui. We take pleasure where we can find it.*

I went from group to group in the room brimming with chatter, music, and the clinking of glasses, doing my best to pretend to be the social butterfly I really wasn't, wishing I had even an ounce of Taylor's extroversion. My best friend had always been at ease in large groups, energized by the atmosphere, charged by just being around others and interacting with them. She was such a natural at parties.

I felt a pang of longing in my chest. If only Tay were here, she'd hook an arm through mine and float through the crowd at my side, bridging the gap between my social anxiety and the demands of my position. She'd help me chat up the demons and make me feel less alone.

But alas, Tay was a whole dimension away, on Earth, in Australia, living her human life, unable to play emotional support human to her awkward friend.

Azmodea, my demon sister-in-law, was similarly extroverted as Taylor, and she'd sometimes help me out at these parties. Unfortunately, though, Azmodea couldn't attend every gathering, since she had her own domain and therefore her own schedule full of these things.

Same went for Mammon, her charming son.

So tonight it was just me, listening to the conversation of the two demon females from Inachiel's entourage, one of them a blonde with golden skin and sky-blue eyes, the other a brunette with a light brown tan, both of them wrapped in glittering dresses that accentuated their curves. They could have easily modeled for that famous lingerie line that liked to send their ladies down the catwalk with huge wings attached to their backs.

And, given these were full-blood demons, they'd even bring their own shiny black wings.

"So, Zoe," the blonde said. What was her name again? Argh, my damn brain. "What is it like being a human?"

I blinked. What the hell kind of question was that?

At my undoubtedly stupefied look, she elaborated. "You know, having no powers of your own?" Her voice was full of sincerity, her eyes holding just the right amount of pity. "You must feel so vulnerable. I cannot even imagine."

It took all my brittle strength to keep the smile plastered on my face. "Well," I said, clearing my throat, "it's not that bad. I do have some powers. I heal fast, and I can summon."

And to demonstrate, I materialized a glass of champagne and raised it in a salute before taking a sip.

"Ah, yes." Impossibly, the gleam of pity in the blonde's eyes grew, and she shared a look with her friend. "Like a half-blood, then."

Not even, I grumbled in my mind. Half-blood demons—the offspring of a demon and a human—could often control fire as well, a power I was sadly lacking. And the two I'd named were courtesy of Lucifer, in payment for a favor I'd done him.

It wasn't likely I'd ever grow into more power down here. What little I had gotten from my bond with Azazel was being impervious to fire, having an eidetic memory, and understanding every language ever spoken, scripts and all, including...Hellspeak.

When I'd first come down here, I hadn't even noticed

that demons spoke their own language, because I'd under-stood it immediately, as if it were a native language for me. It had taken me embarrassingly long to realize this, and that it was an effect of marrying Azazel. To be fair, some aspects of this power had trickled in over weeks and months. For example, I couldn't read the scripts of different languages at first. But a couple of weeks in, all those books in Azazel's library whose titles I hadn't been able to decipher before suddenly revealed themselves as legible.

This delayed timeline of magical gifts had given me hope that maybe I'd get more powers over time, but to my vast disappointment, the trickle of supernatural skills had stopped a few months ago.

Apparently, I was as magically jacked as I was going to get.

The brunette shook her head and clucked her tongue. "Remember that half-blood at Guthor's court?" she asked her friend. "What was her name?"

The blonde raised her brows. "Oh, you mean the one who fell into the dragon trench? At feeding time?"

"Yes." The brunette beamed, then sighed. "Gruesome death, that one."

The blonde nodded, the light of the candles making her hair appear like spun gold. "So fragile, those half-bloods."

They both faced me again, with those damn pitying eyes barely hiding the glee they truly felt. Probably imagining the many ways my own fragile self could die a gruesome death down here.

Point taken, thank you. I knew I'd never be as strong as a full-blood demon.

Stuffing my fizzling anxiety and simmering anger down lest it show on my face, I inhaled sharply. "Oh, if you'll excuse me, my fragile human condition is forcing me to get more food. You know, so I won't die of malnutrition. Terribly bad human habit, that need for sustenance. Cheerio!"

And with a little wave, I turned my back and wove my way through the settees and chairs, intent on finding Azazel for a quick reprieve from having to handle this shit alone. He usually tried to stay by my side as much as possible, knowing that I felt more comfortable with him there, but often enough, we had to split up to tend to different guests at the same time. He was currently sitting on a chaise lounge on the other side of the room, talking to a male demon from Inachiel's entourage.

Halfway before I made it to my salvation, someone flagged me down. I turned and froze. *Inachiel.* Barely restraining myself from grimacing, I beelined over to where he was draped across a divan, all casual elegance and leashed power.

"Inachiel," I said as I reached him, dipping my chin. "Are you enjoying the party?"

"I am, yes." His green eyes glittered like crushed emeralds under the sun, and he indicated the settee opposite his. "Do join me for a moment, will you? I haven't had the chance to talk to our unusual hostess yet."

CHAPTER 3

U h-*oh*. Inwardly, I cringed. What were the chances that this was going to be a pleasant chat for a change?

My brain helpfully supplied C-3PO's voice doing his statistical calculation of a rather depressing outcome, and I muttered, "Never tell me the odds."

"What was that?" Inachiel looked puzzled.

"Nothing." I gave him a shaky smile and perched my butt on the settee. I should really stop with the pop culture references. A lot of these demons didn't get them, which only made conversations with them more awkward.

"I must say," Inachiel began, plucking a grape from a cluster on a vine, "Azazel truly seems quite happy with you, despite the fact that you tricked him into a contract."

Ughhhh. That thing again. I would *never* live that down, would I? These demons would be harping on until the end of time about that ill-fated séance where I unwittingly locked Azazel into a marriage contract. And I still didn't know how I'd even done it!

I refrained from rolling my eyes. *Manners, Zoe. Manners.*

It was so hard not to let my irritation show, not to wipe that smug smirk off Inachiel's face with a well-deserved punch. More and more, I was getting these aggressive urges to settle any and all conflicts with violence. Seemed like living among demons was rubbing off on me—they all too often resorted to physical fighting to sort out differences. Brutal, yes, but also efficient. Much like among pack animals such as wolves, challenges and questions of hierarchy were decided with a quick tussle—flashing teeth and blood and all. But hey, afterward, things were settled.

Problem was, of course, that I wasn't in the position to challenge anyone. Aside from the fact that I couldn't go around beating up all those demons on friendly terms with Azazel because it would cause one diplomatic kerfuffle after the other, if I started a fight over some perceived slight, I'd lose. I simply wasn't physically or magically strong enough to take on a half-blood, let alone a demon of full power.

I held a rank equal to a third-generation demon of two thousand five hundred years, but I had nothing to show for it, no way to enforce my status on my own. It rankled.

And not just me. I could see it on Inachiel's face, behind his thin mask of pretend politeness. How it angered him that he had to treat me with the courtesy and respect reserved for someone who'd fought and bled for their rank, who'd earned this position over centuries of hard work.

His displeasure became clearer with his next words. "It was quite brave of him, was it not," he said, his tone all genteel benevolence despite the message, "to claim you officially even when presented with a gracious solution to his predicament. Granted, some might say it wasn't a brave move so much as it was a folly."

With a slow, consuming wave, heat flowed through my body, all the way up into my face. My nostrils flared.

"Not me, of course." Inachiel sent me a dazzling smile, a pretty ornament on a shit tree. "Others may deem his actions brazen; I say he's daring. How dauntlessly dashing to flaunt the rules we live by!" He made an honest-to-Hell chef's kiss gesture to underscore his point. "You should know I'm all in favor of foolish love. I find it quaint, a recklessly romantic ideal in a world that is often too harsh. You love him truly, don't you?"

I swallowed the bitter bite of sizzling anger and pricked pride and answered in the only way I could. "I do."

Inachiel sighed and laid a hand over his heart. "Ah, how precious. And with a true bond like yours, I'm sure you two can wither any adverse effects of his decision to claim you."

He plucked another grape and popped it into his mouth, his eyes twinkling as he waited for me to take the bait.

I didn't. Like Hell would I make his taunting any easier.

Leaning forward a bit, he lowered his voice to a confidential murmur. "Rest assured, my dear, that I do not participate in the gossip that many of the others like to trade in. Seeing as Azazel is a valued ally of mine, I would not want to pour fuel on the fire that is burning the edges of his reputation." With the hint of a sly smile, he ate another grape. "And I am sure that, in time, his decision to bond with a human and grace her with titles beyond her worth will stop costing him allies. I have all the confidence that he will recover from this perceived defect in character and repair his standing over the next few centuries."

Something hard lodged in my chest, pulling down with a weight that made me struggle for breath. A corrosive kind of hurt spread out from my heart.

"Your company really is enchanting," Inachiel said as he took a sip from his drink. "I have no idea where the others get their impression from."

My pulse pounded in my head.

Dark energy brushed up against my back a second before I heard Azazel's deep voice in my head. *Are you all right, love?*

Out loud, he said from where he'd come to stand behind my settee, "May I offer you some more amrit, Inachiel?"

"Thank you," our guest said with a genial smile. "That would be lovely."

"Certainly." Azazel waved a demon waiter down for the drink order, then he laid his hand on my shoulder, his thumb stroking up against the skin of my neck. *Zoe?*

I'm fine, I sent back along our mental pathway. I steeled the shields within my mind that would keep my thoughts and feelings private and tried not to let my mental voice show the strain on my emotions. Raising my hand to clasp his, I squeezed his fingers. *Just feeling the growing need to recharge my introvert batteries with a week of alone time.*

He chatted out loud with Inachiel, taking over the conversation, much to my relief, and after a moment he mentally responded, *Not much longer. This will wind down soon.*

If only there was a polite way to compliment guests out of the house. I'd once gone with Taylor to visit her relatives in the Midwest, and apparently, folks over there had this brilliant method of signaling when it was time for guests to leave by slapping their own thighs, saying, "Well!" really forcefully, and then standing up. Guests would then respond with a "We should head out," and the party would break up. Easy-peasy.

I'd tried that method down here once. Everybody had looked at me like I was a circus animal about to perform a trick.

Not an experience I wanted to repeat.

Fortunately, Azazel stuck to my side for the remainder of the party, which spared me more slights from our honored guests. They always did behave when he was right next to me. Fucking cowards.

Unfortunately, before *winding down*, the party first kicked up a notch. Several of the demons present decided it was time to get down to business in a very unbusinesslike way. I'm not sure what came first—the change in music from chill and relaxed to slow and sensual and throbbing with an erotic beat, or the free-spirited shedding of clothes and tangling of limbs.

In any case, though, I found myself sitting next to Azazel —currently talking with another one of Inachiel's demons— while the room around us fell more and more into a lustful frenzy. Left and right, demons peeled each other out of their clothes, and moans and sighs rose in the air, mingling with the suggestive rhythm of the music.

Like I said, there really wasn't much else to do in Hell other than fighting, fucking, or frying.

The change in mood started to affect me. My breath came a tad faster, my skin felt too tight and hot, and my pulse beat low in my core. I pressed my thighs together and shifted on the cushion.

Right in front of me, behind the divan on which the demon whom Azazel was talking to lounged, a couple was very busy testing the sturdiness of their chair. The female's hips rose up and down as she straddled her partner, who clutched her bare ass, his fingers digging into her cheeks.

I tried—and failed—to keep my eyes off them, my face flaming hot. It wasn't that I was a prude or that sex embarrassed me. If I'd had any such inhibition, living in Hell for a year sure would have disabused me of that notion.

No, the problem was that watching others—all of them

unfairly beautiful and attractive—go at it right in front of me kicked my own libido through the stratosphere and made me want to climb Azazel right then and there, audience be damned. I'd likely regret putting on a show for everyone later, but in those moments, when the scent of sex hung heavy in the air, when the erotic drums of the music mixed with the arousing sounds of flesh slapping on flesh, of moans and grunts and pleas for more, when all I could see was sweat-slicked skin and intimate caresses…the onslaught of impressions short-circuited my brain, transforming me into a quivering puddle of lust barely held together by my own skin.

Azazel's heated gaze met my own just as he gently plucked my hands off his waistband, where I'd begun to open his pants. I hadn't even been conscious of doing that. Damn orgy hijacking my brain.

Best save that for later, lustful little human, Azazel purred in my head while he kept up the casual conversation he held with the demon across from us, his skill of multitasking on enviable levels.

Luckily for me, my darling demon managed a lot better than I did to keep a cool head during this deluge of erotic impressions. He differed from his fellow demons in quite a few key aspects, not the least of which was that he did not like to indulge in intimacy in front of others. Something I normally agreed with, when my senses weren't momentarily overwhelmed by all the sounds, sights, and smells of this panoramic aphrodisiac all around us. Which was the reason I truly appreciated his level of control that kept me from making a spectacle of myself at these parties.

Much to his benefit—both of ours, really—the arousing effect of witnessing an orgy lasted well beyond the departure of our guests, and Azazel always took care to "help" me work off all the pent-up lust.

Needless to say, the end of these gatherings was my favorite part.

Later, I repeated mentally, pressing my lips together. *Right. Yes. Later.*

Azazel smirked and patiently removed my hand from where I'd just cupped his hard cock through the fabric of his pants—again. *Do I have to cuff you?*

His teasing murmur in my head only made the entire situation worse, because right now, the prospect of him restraining me poured oil on the fire burning me up from the inside. I squirmed in my seat.

Azazel's eyes flashed. *Later, then.* A silken sensual promise that made me shiver.

A torturously long time later, we finally watched Inachiel and his entourage leave through the massive double doors of the entrance hall. The deep metallic bang of the doors falling shut reverberated in my bones, the vibration stirring the barely banked throb of desire between my legs.

For a moment, everything was silent, the hush before a storm. The light of the torches danced over the walls, glinting off the black feathers of the numerous ripped-off wings hung up there as trophies. I hardly flinched anymore when I saw them.

Azazel spoke without turning to me, his voice holding a quiet threat. "Twenty-five."

"What?" I glanced at him, my pulse ticking fast.

He cast me a look from underneath his dark lashes, a glint in his eyes. "Twenty-four."

I jolted. "You mean—"

"You're wasting time you could use running," he said in a low rumble that caused goosebumps on my arms and tightened my nipples. "Twenty-three. When I catch you, I'll burn that dress off your body and take you right there, and I don't care if that's in the middle of a hallway. Twenty-two. So if you want to make it to our rooms before I fuck you, you'd better get those feet moving. Twenty-one."

I gasped. "That's not fair! You know I can't outrun you."

"That's why I'm giving you a generous head start. Twenty."

"Generous, my ass," I hissed, but I ditched my heels, wheeled around, and ran as if said ass was on fire. Because if that deviant demon caught me, it would be.

CHAPTER 4

My heart beat triple time as I dashed into the hallway that led deeper into Azazel's huge fortress, the thrill of being chased fanning the flames of my lust. Another time I'd run from him came to mind, right after I'd first discovered his intimidating wing collection. Back then, I'd tried to escape from him in earnest, primitive fear erasing all thought.

This time, I wanted to be caught.

Maybe not in a hallway, though, which was why I sprinted like an Olympian. If Olympians huffed and puffed like an old steam engine. Months of combat training had only increased my stamina so much, because apparently my body thought doing the bare minimum in physical improvement was enough.

I skidded around a corner just as I felt it—the faint press of dark energy and the prickling at the back of my neck indicating a primal supernatural predator had just begun his pursuit. I yelped and sprinted faster.

My heart was a frantic rabbit trapped in my chest, my breaths came short, and the walls of the hallway whizzed past. Excitement rushed through my blood. The instinctive fear that came from being chased by something stronger than me overrode the knowledge that I wasn't truly in danger of being eaten.

Well, at least not like *that*.

I snickered just as I ran up a flight of stairs. My legs burned something fierce, same as my lungs. I could sense his power coming closer, the pulse of his dark energy getting stronger. The fact that he hadn't caught me yet told me he was playing with me. Probably letting me think I could *alllll-most* make it to our rooms before—

A hush of darkness extinguished the torches on the wall, plunging everything into pitch-black. I stumbled on the stairs, my heart skipping a beat, my arms windmilling to break my fall.

I never made contact with the cool stone.

Instead, my palms slapped against something soft, downy, yet strong and solid underneath. The next second, two arms wrapped around my waist and pulled me back against a wall of heat. I squealed, both startled and giddy. The soft obstacle I'd smashed into lit up with tiny, iridescent flames that sizzled over my skin where I touched the feathers.

"Got you." Azazel's voice held a deep, dark satisfaction, his hot breath on my neck sending a shiver down my spine.

I squeal-giggled and tried to wiggle out of his hold, which, of course, only served to rub my body against his, making me feel his hard length pressing against my lower back.

His response was a terrifying growl. Not the kind that humans make to imitate a wolf or a tiger, no. This one was the real fucking deal, the rumbling, rattling sound of an apex predator, complete with the vibration that I felt in every part of my body that touched his.

The sheer, unadulterated ferocity of it liquefied my bones with innate terror—and made me clench my thighs against the renewed throb of lust in my core.

There was likely something very wrong with me for getting aroused by the kind of snarl that should have sent any being with half a brain running for its life. But all I wanted right now was for the demon at my back to strip the last bit of human pretense from me and take me in the most primal of ways...and then I wanted to know what that bone-melting growl felt like on the pulsing spot between my legs.

Zoe, Azazel said in my head, his mental voice barely above a snarl, too. *Are you projecting on purpose, or do you need another lesson in shielding?*

I stilled. *I'm...not sure?*

He slid one hand up my front, brushing over one breast and the tight peak of my nipple before grasping my throat in a light hold. I gasped, my mind filling with images of him taking me from behind while his large hand circled my neck, the grip possessive and primal and *thrilling.*

His fingers tightened their hold. *Do you want me to lose control?* A soft whisper in my mind, brimming with dark energy. *Because that's how you get me to lose control.*

Another shiver danced over my skin, fresh arousal pooling between my legs. I bit my lip and very consciously thought, *Yes.*

His entire being vibrated, down to the minuscule sparks of his energy tapping against my skin. "Don't say I didn't warn you," he murmured—and then he incinerated my dress.

The fabric went up in flames all around me, and fire rolled over my skin, caressing me with licks of heat. I inhaled sharply, more from being startled than from being hurt. I was fireproof, after all.

But the flames on my skin felt exquisite, like the most decadent stroke, like his tongue laving over my intimate flesh, only intensified by a thousand. All the while, he held me in place with his hand on my throat, his wings still caging me in.

When the last of the fabric fell off my body as ash, darkness once more claimed our surroundings, the only light the sparks flickering over his feathers. Not enough to illuminate the gloom for me. With a rustling sound, he moved his wings so they weren't in front of me anymore, letting the hushed black velvet of the stairway settle around me.

He slid his hand from my throat to the back of my neck and pushed. "On your knees."

Heart thumping in my chest, I slowly lowered myself until my knees met the stone step. His hand on my neck prodded me farther still, and I leaned forward and braced myself with my palms a few steps above the one I was kneeling on.

Desire was a pulse beneath my skin, every sense heightened in the darkness, through my position. I was acutely aware that I was naked and exposed on all fours on a flight of stairs, with a demon behind me who was about to have his wicked way with me. No sound but our breaths, charged with tension and promise, his power a beacon of heat behind me. Anticipation tightened my muscles.

His hand had moved to my hair, and now he tangled his fingers in the strands and pulled, just hard enough to sting deliciously. I followed the direction of his tug and tilted my head up and to the left, arching my spine. His energy brushed over me as he bent forward and claimed my mouth in a kiss that was a sensual assault.

Pleasure threaded through my blood, and my toes curled.

His heat caressing my back, he held me fast with an iron grip in my hair while he stole my breath with his kiss…and yet he didn't touch me anywhere else. The lack of contact made me half-feral, and I squirmed, trying to push back against him.

A wave of fire cascaded over my body, ending in licks of heat at my nipples and that aching spot between my legs.

I jerked and cried out. Too much. Not enough.

I needed more, needed him to touch me, to take me.

"Didn't you," I panted, "say something about losing control?"

His lips pressed against my neck, the soft kiss a stark sensory counterpoint to the stinging grip he still had on my hair. "You're not ready yet."

"I am *drenched*," I gritted out through my teeth as I wiggled my hips and thighs in a way that gave clear acoustic evidence of how wet I was.

A teasing touch of his energy fluttered over my intimate flesh. "Not there—here." He kissed my temple.

Ughhh. "Oh, come on," I whined.

His answer was a pinch of my nipples with his energy. The sting of it zinged straight down to my throbbing core, driving my arousal higher still. I felt like I was going to explode from unfulfilled need for touch, from this raw hunger for his brutal claiming.

More fire danced over my skin as he lowered his mouth to the curve where my neck met my shoulder. His breath a promise of more, he lingered for a moment without his lips touching me yet while his power followed in the wake of the flames, a thousand tiny taps over skin so sensitized that it made me gasp.

Then he bit me. His teeth grabbed my neck at the same time as he poured his energy like molten lava over my breasts, my inner thighs, my intimate folds longing for more touch. I sucked in a breath and shuddered, sinking further into the spiral of desire.

"When I say ready," he said in a harsh whisper against my neck, "I mean that I want you crazed with lust, not just begging for my cock, but *dying* for it. I want you helplessly writhing with need, every cell of your body craving my rough claim, that when I let loose, you'll not just take it, but you'll also worship every fucking second of it, no matter how hard. Because when I lose control, I'll ravage you."

A full-body shiver tightened my nipples impossibly further. "All right," I said breathlessly. "That just did it. I'm already there."

"I'll be the judge of that." He straightened behind me and let his free hand glide down my spine, trailing sparks in its wake.

I shifted to follow his touch, chasing the press of his fingers that was far too light. A slap on my butt made me freeze.

"Stay still."

Fiery heat feathered over the sting of his slap, simultaneously soothing and making it worse. I whimpered.

God, I was *so* ready.

He tugged sharply on my hair. "Either you shield your mind," he purred, "or you call out *my* name in your thoughts."

"One of these days," I shot back, "you should start seeing a therapist about this obsession of yours."

"Mouthy, are we?"

My even mouthier comeback got lost in a yelp as he swatted my butt again, this time with a quick double slap on each cheek. Incredibly, the pain veered right into more arousal, making my core throb with need.

And it only got worse when he slid a finger over my slick folds, his touch just enough to make me moan with pleasure, but not nearly enough to quench my thirst.

"Azazel, *please*." I closed my eyes, my nails scraping over the stone.

"Begging is a good start." He circled my clit, eliciting a strangled groan from me. "I always do like it when you plead so sweetly."

The next second, his mouth was on me, his tongue delving deep. I cried out, overwhelmed by the acute pleasure and the onslaught of his intimate touch. But what truly sent me over the edge was the growl.

Dark, bone-rattling, and feral, its vibration reverberated through my most sensitive flesh, all the way up to the top of my head, making me shake and tremble. The orgasm crashed through me with the force of a tidal wave. My thighs quivered, ready to give out.

He held my hips up with a tight grip as he worked me through the last tremors of my climax, his tongue and lips and teeth wreaking havoc on my nether regions.

My body felt wrung out and yet primed at the same time. As earth-shattering as that orgasm had been, it hadn't fully sated me. My inner muscles clenched around an aching nothing, and I uttered a sound of pure need, craving to be filled.

And I knew the fastest way to get him to oblige. "Please," I said, my voice husky and sex-drenched. "I need you."

He hummed as he kissed my lower back, his fingers languidly spreading my wetness over my folds, around my entrance, and I shuddered with want. "What, exactly?"

Always making me spell it out. And for him, I would. For him, I'd crawl.

Like I'd done once before.

"Your cock," I whispered. "I need you to fuck me. Hard."

His power darkened with pleasure. "Then hold on."

Easier said than done—there was nothing for me to grab on these damn smooth steps. And I had an inkling this ride was going to be the *I need a sturdy headboard for this* type.

A soft whoosh, and then I blinked at the dark shape of a large cushion that had materialized on the step between my hands.

"Bite into that," Azazel said. "You'll need it."

I'd have smacked him for his presumptuous arrogance if I didn't know he was likely right.

I had just grabbed the cushion when he thrust into me in one hard push. Crying out, I buried my face in the damn pillow and bit down on it. Delicious pleasure-pain sizzled out from where he stretched me, lighting up the nerve endings all throughout my body.

His fingers digging into my hips, he pumped into me in quick, ferocious movements, deep and hard. My eyes crossed at the sensation, my entire being zeroing in on the feel of his near-bruising thrusts.

Yes, please, was my last coherent thought before his relentless, aggressive pace left me no room to string any words together in my mind.

He fucked me with raw, savage force, his control truly shattered. With one hand, he grabbed my neck as he pounded into me, holding me in place with a possessive, primal grip, just like I'd fantasized he would. And, just like I'd envisioned, the sheer erotic demand of it, the unapologetically primitive claim of his grasp as he held me right there for his pleasure, thrilled me down to my soul.

With him, I could sink into the kind of sweet surrender of complete submission like I'd never dared with anyone else.

Because with him, I was safe.

It was a truth I felt deep in my bones, in every breath I drew, a profound awareness of the fact that I could show him my most vulnerable side, and he'd shelter and care for it, always.

He moved his hand from my hip to my thigh and shoved it forward so my knee came to rest on the next step, opening me further to his thrusts. The new angle let him push deeper, and my moans filled the air as he took full advantage of that and hammered into me with such force that I felt my insides liquefy.

I'd dared him to loosen himself from his leash, and he did. And I loved every fucking second of it.

I bit into the pillow so hard that my jaw ached, my fingers trying and failing to find purchase on the stairs. He kept pounding into me with merciless, almost violent thrusts, and his own sounds of pleasure kicked my arousal even higher. I loved hearing him like this. Raw. Untethered. Helpless to his own lust.

He was always so impeccably in control of himself, so careful to curate his image. He kept an iron grip on what parts of himself he showed the world.

But here, with me, he let me see everything.

His power vibrated over my skin, building to a crescendo of a sensual symphony. Targeted, hot licks of fire danced over my clit—and combined with the delicious ruthlessness of his unrelenting thrusts, it sent me careening over the edge.

I screamed into the cushion as pleasure exploded in me. He kept fucking me hard, impossibly more unfettered still as he went all in to chase his own climax. The unrestrained punch of power of his movements, the feel of him inside me, the way he just *took*…it all served to hurtle me into another orgasm even as the previous one hadn't subsided yet.

He came with a deep, throaty groan, and my inner muscles clenched hard around him as he emptied himself in me. A few more slowing thrusts, drawing out the pleasure for us both, and then he stilled, bent over me, one hand next to mine on the stone step. I could feel his quickened breathing where his chest touched my back, and it was incredibly satisfying in itself to know he'd exerted himself so much with me that he actually breathed faster. That was rarely the case.

His heat and power engulfed me like the most luxurious blanket as I half sprawled over the stairs, basically only held up by his one arm clamped around my hips. My panting echoed loudly in the dark.

Even had I wanted to say anything, I simply wasn't able to. Beyond my lungs still working hard to draw in enough air, my thoughts were scrambled, my mind floating somewhere in blissful, subspace-like nirvana.

So I only uttered a helpless sound as he withdrew and gathered me up in his arms. My head lolled against his shoulder, and I closed my eyes, the motion of his walking lulling me deeper into my afterglow trance.

I only came to again when he placed me down on our bed, infinitely gentle. When I opened my eyes, it was to the sight of his dark form hovering over me, his eyes glowing unearthly in the gloom. Lightning from outside the window intermittently illuminated the room, casting him in a blue-violet relief against shadows.

He was so fucking beautiful.

And he was all mine.

One side of his sinful mouth quirked up. "So possessive," he murmured.

"Yes," I whispered, basking in the knowledge that my claim was justified. "Yes, I am."

His eyes glimmered as he half settled his large body over mine, pressing down on me just enough to let me feel his weight—like he knew I loved. My legs went around his hips automatically, making room for him right where I wanted to feel him.

But he didn't enter me again just yet, simply stayed there with his still—again?—hard cock wedged against my mound. Given how overstimulated my clit was, the steady pressure instead of more movement actually felt great.

Propping himself up on his elbows on either side of me, he regarded me with the kind of focus that stripped all the layers of me away, bared me to him in a way that felt more raw and vulnerable than any kind of physical intimacy. I'd once shied away from this connection, when I'd just met him, when I didn't yet *know* him. He'd been little less than my enemy, and the last thing I'd wanted to do was let this aggravating demon peel away my protections with the intensity of a gaze that rattled me down to my foundations.

Funny, how much things could change. Now, when he gazed at me like this, I fell headfirst into that connection—because now, it was a two-way street. I saw him, too, all his layers and the very many parts of him he kept tightly locked up for anyone else.

And what I glimpsed there made me tremble. The depth of his devotion, the way he saw me as the greatest gift, infinitely precious. I'd never had anyone look at me like I hung the moon and the stars and powered the sun.

My heart flipped over, my chest aching. "Azazel," I whispered, my throat thick.

His black lashes lowered as his gaze dropped to my mouth, lightning in his eyes.

I swallowed, grasping for some levity to break the moment. It was too deep, too raw, threatening to shatter me. "I figured it out," I said.

"What?" His thumb stroked over my lower lip.

"Your kink. It's sex on stairs and ladders."

His eyes shot up to mine again, crinkling at the corners. "I didn't hear you complain."

I pressed my lips together. "Far be it from me to deny you your deviant pleasures."

"Hm." He leaned down and nibbled at my ear, causing a shiver of delight to roll over my body. "Lucky me."

I was still trembling from the sinful thing he was doing with my earlobe when he asked, "Who insulted you tonight?"

CHAPTER 5

M y mind was slow to catch up. "What?"

"Was it Inachiel?" He trailed kisses down my throat. "Or one of his entourage?"

"I—uh—no one. Did. Um. Anything." *Hi, I'm Zoe. Skillful liar extraordinaire.*

He lightly bit into my neck. Predictably, it scattered my thoughts. "Don't play. I saw you. Someone said something. Who was it?"

What the—how had this turned into an interrogation? And how the hell did I get out of this now?

"*Zoe.*" He gripped my chin between his thumb and index finger and caught my panicked gaze.

Eek. With a grimace, I closed my eyes just to escape his probing look, and I raised those mental shields as high as possible. I couldn't let him know. He'd already lost enough allies and trade partners.

"Tell me." His voice had dropped, now holding the kind of command it rarely did when he talked to me. This was the tone he used on his soldiers.

I opened my eyes just to narrow them at him. "Don't speak to me like that. I'm not one of your subordinates."

He blinked, the only sign of surprise in a face of hard angles and simmering anger. Other than Azmodea, no one else ever dared to rebuke him like this.

"You're right," he said, but his features didn't soften with his admission. "You're my wife. And I need to know if someone treats you with anything less than the respect you deserve."

"So you can what? Cut ties with them? Attack them?"

His expression darkened. "You're mine. To care for. To cherish." A rough edge slid into his voice. "To defend."

"Azazel—"

"I will not," he said through gritted teeth, "stand by while those snakes insult you."

"It wasn't even an insult. He just—"

Lightning flashed in his eyes. "Inachiel?"

My flinch gave it away. Dammit.

"What did he say?" A soft, soft question, but I still heard the fury hiding in its depth.

I shook my head. "It doesn't matter."

"It does to me."

And, Lordy, he really looked like it did. Such concern wrapped in anger tightening his features, giving his eyes even more of a demonic glow than usual. In another life, another time, I'd have appreciated that I had a sexy guy on my side determined to spill blood to defend my honor.

But this, here, was far too real, with damning consequences.

"Let's just drop this, okay?" I smoothed my hands over his shoulders, petting him in the small hope I could simply soothe this obsession away. "It didn't even affect me. Really, I'm fine."

A calculating gleam flared in his eyes, and then his expression shifted, as if rearranging itself in sync with a new strategy of his. "Did it ever occur to you," he asked quietly, "that when they dare to insult you to your face without me there, and I let that go unchecked, it reflects poorly on me?"

I blinked, stumped. Dammit. I had *not* considered that.

His look said he knew, and that was why he used it against me now. Because I might swallow my own pain and anger about how their slights made me feel, as long as I thought that, in doing so, I was protecting him. But if that wasn't the case, if my silence was actually causing him harm...

"When my allies"—he gave the word a sour taste—"disrespect my *wife*, and I continue to do business with them not even knowing what kind of toxic shit they've been throwing in her face, what message does that send? Would you like me to be ignorant, walking like a fool into a meeting with them without a clue about their insults to you, so they can smirk and snicker behind my back about how they can get away with treating you like trash?"

I numbly shook my head, my throat closing up.

"What do you think," he continued with surgical precision, "it does to my reputation when I walk around oblivious to how—and which ones of—my *friends* belittle you?"

God, this was so fucked up. *Damned if I do, damned if I don't.* Telling him of all the snide remarks would result in the kind of retaliation that would cost him allies and trade partners. Not telling him would make him look like a fool to his peers, or worse, like someone not strong enough to defend his own. And a show of strength in Hell was everything.

"We just can't win," I said in a voice as small as I felt. "No matter what, we just can't win in this."

His expression hardened "Oh, but I will."

I frowned and made a frustrated noise. "And how do plan to accomplish that? It's not like you can reach into their heads and change the way they see me."

"That won't be necessary."

I frowned some more. "I don't follow."

He cupped my face, his thumb tracing the line of my lower lip. "Lilith is human. Mostly."

At that, I raised my brows. "Statement of the obvious, but okay. What does that have to do with anything?"

"She's Lucifer's equal in rank and status." Something was brewing in those thunderstorm eyes of his. "Have you ever heard of anyone treating her with less respect than they would Lucifer?"

I shook my head, an inkling of where he was going with this uncoiling inside me, along with a vague fear I couldn't name.

"And why is that?" he asked quietly.

My answer was just as soft. "Because Lucifer would eviscerate them."

He nodded slowly and deliberately. "When he first brought Lilith to Hell and made her his equal, there were those who didn't take well to it. I wasn't born back then, but the whispers of it carried over the millennia since, the impact of his response indelibly etched into the minds of all demons, whether they witnessed it firsthand or not. Few of those who dared to even look wrong at Lilith are still alive. You walked right over them when we went to the Fall Festival."

My stomach cramped at the memory of those demons chained to the subfloor beneath the glass floor of Lucifer's entrance hall, being eaten alive by hellrats, but unable to actually die. "They've been there for all this time?"

His face was grim. "Thousands of years, for one slight against Lilith."

My God.

Azazel's eyes mapped my face, his energy vibrating darkly as he went on. "Mostly, though, Lucifer simply killed the ones who disrespected Lilith, after making a spectacle of their torture in front of his court. They say the blood on the floor of his throne room didn't dry for weeks and months because he kept spilling more in defense of her honor."

A shiver stole down my spine. Not just from the tale he was telling, but from the glint in his eye.

"In the end," he continued, "he'd cemented Lilith's rank and status so firmly that no one has dared to cast doubt on it ever since. She is afforded the same respect as he is, whether he is present or not."

I swallowed hard.

"So you see," he said, his voice lethally soft, "it can be done."

"Azazel," I whispered, and that vague fear I'd felt sharpened just a little. "What are you planning?"

His lashes half lowered, darkening his eyes. "It can be done."

That fear, it spread slithery roots across my heart. "You can't kill them all."

His knuckles gently stroked over my cheek. "I need you to tell me what Inachiel said."

I grabbed his hand. "Azazel, you cannot kill them all."

"No. But I don't need to. I just have to kill enough." His eyes met mine again, that brewing storm in them coalescing. "Power and fear. Those are the keys. Get enough of one, and the other will follow. They're not afraid of me yet. I don't rank high enough, and my power is at medium-high levels."

He interlaced his fingers with mine. "I intend to change that."

I was struck speechless, dread coiling in my gut. All I saw in my mind's eye was a path littered with mangled bodies, soil drenched in blood, a path leading up to…

"How high?" I whispered. "How high do you want to climb?"

"When I'm done," he replied, steely resolve in his voice, "only two people will outrank us."

Lucifer and Lilith.

He planned to seize enough power to rival the original rulers of Hell.

That slithery fear struck its roots into my heart.

I shook my head. "You don't need to do this. Not for me."

What he intended would not be accomplished without mass slaughter and seemingly endless war. The risks involved… I could lose him through this. That was a lot of fighting, the kind that required sharp blades and terrible demon power. He was courting death.

I frantically shook my head again. "Please don't do this. I'm not worth—"

"Yes, you are," he cut me off, his face harsh.

My breath lodged in my throat.

"What you have to understand," he went on, his energy rough silk over my senses, "is that I would tear all of Hell apart for you."

The room filled with water. Oh, wait, that was just my eyes.

He pressed his forehead against mine. "I would rend this sun-forsaken place from one end to the other to keep you happy. I have lived a long, long time, Zoe, and most of it was shit. Eternity is damnation in itself if you go through it missing half of your soul."

I couldn't breathe, my body melting into his in all the places our skin touched.

"So, yes," he continued, his voice raw, "you're worth it. And I will gladly bathe in the blood of all those who dare to make you feel less."

Okay, fuck, he really had a way with words.

I slung my arms around his neck and buried my face against his shoulder. My voice came out choked. "I don't want to lose you."

He pressed me close, his lips at my ear. "You won't."

He sounded so sure, as if he was simply acting out some prophecy that foretold his success. But when, in life, were things ever this certain?

Pulling back, he wiped the tears from my cheeks and kissed my nose. "Now tell me what Inachiel said."

And damn it all, I did. Because when he looked at me like that, when he made me feel like the only thing that mattered in Hell and beyond, I was ready to tell him everything.

Except, maybe, that secret I kept close to my heart, the one for which Lucifer had bound me to silence.

CHAPTER 6

Some days, I woke up to Azazel worshipping my body, which really was the best way to be plucked from sleep. Other days, I'd slowly come to in an empty bed, my darling demon having long gone to take care of his pressing business matters.

And then there were those days when I got startled awake by a thump on my mattress that felt like an earthquake. But it was the sight that greeted my eyes that was even worse.

I flailed awake, blinking into the light of the slowly brightening torches—they responded to my state of mind, apparently—and screamed bloody murder.

At the bloody murdered *thing* right next to me.

My hellhound, Vengeance, barked from somewhere to my left, agitated by my distress, and the hellcat on my bed let out a hiss in her direction.

You should calm your beast, Mephisto said into my mind.

I'd need to first fucking calm myself. Heart beating a million miles a minute, I scooted to the other side of the bed and pointed with a shaking hand at the scruffy, furry animal in front of Mephisto.

"What is—is that a dead hellrat?"

It is still fresh. Mephisto's voice was positively smug. *You should eat while it's warm.*

Oh my God. I buried my face in my hands, nausea churning in my stomach.

Not this again.

"You brought this for me?" I squeaked.

Obviously, he purred. The light of the torches played over his sable fur, and he extended and readjusted his bat-like wings. *You are the worst hunter I have ever seen, and your demon doesn't provide you with fresh kills.*

The breakfast I hadn't even eaten yet wanted to crawl its way back up my throat.

"You really don't need to—"

You are clearly in need of help, the infernal feline said, his yellow eyes glowing from within. *No claws, no fangs, no stealth whatsoever. I cannot watch you survive on scraps. It is pathetic.*

He nudged the dead hellrat toward me with one mighty paw. My stomach lurched.

Suppressing a gag, I instead managed to smile at Mephisto. I had to handle this delicately, or else his feline ego would get bruised and we'd all pay the price for the next few weeks.

"Thank you," I pressed out through my forced smile. "You are so very considerate. What would I do without you?"

Starve, was the cat's pragmatic answer.

My smile turned into a grimace.

Over the past months, Mephisto had taken a shine to me. He'd always hang out in my rooms, even though I didn't need him as a living fire extinguisher anymore. He said it was for vermin control. I suspected he liked my company.

My suspicion had proved to be correct when, after months of lurking in my presence and staring at me with an unnerving feline intensity, he'd started to curl up to sleep closer and closer to me. One day, he'd lain down right next to me, his furry flank in direct contact with my leg, his wings all neatly folded along his back. I'd sat paralyzed by the nearness of a lynx-sized feline with impressive fangs and claws for a good few minutes, watching his breathing turn to that of deep sleep. And then I'd surreptitiously brushed a fingertip over his shiny fur.

Just a little. Just to see if it was as soft as it looked.

He was a cat. I loved cats. I'd never met a feline I didn't want to pet, including the big ones at the zoo, even knowing I'd come out shredded to bits from that experience.

Because…if dangerous, why cute?

So, of course, I'd tried to pet Mephisto. I'd been fully prepared to lose a finger. It would have been worth it, because—Oh, Lord—he had the most amazing fur! So soft, so sleek, so silky.

Before I knew better, I'd had my whole hand pressed against him, stroking his pelt in a trance.

And instead of biting off my fingers, Mephisto had purred. The deep rumble of it had vibrated up my arm and made my hairs stand on end.

Ever since then, the surly hellcat had deigned to allow me to pet him every so often. Always making it clear it was the greatest gift in the history of gift giving. I'd asked Azazel, and according to him, no one else had ever been known to pet Mephisto. He'd deemed me worthy.

I felt like the Chosen One.

And then the dead vermin started showing up in my

rooms. The first one, I'd almost stepped on as I swung my legs out of bed. The next one had fallen from the ceiling and into my lap as I sat on the couch reading, giving me an inkling of what a heart attack felt like.

Infrequently, my own personal mighty hunter would present me with killed prey, sometimes even biting it open and pulling out the guts to give me "the best bits."

One of my proudest accomplishments in this life was not having puked right in Mephisto's face the first time he'd done that.

The hellcat seemed sophisticated in some aspects—he could speak and reason, after all—but then he'd pull a stunt like that and remind me that he was very much a primitive, predatory creature in a lot of other ways. His sense of logic wasn't always the best. And he stubbornly ignored my attempts to explain to him that I was a vegetarian.

I guessed in his eyes, I was a fellow cat, and as such, I needed a good amount of blood-dripping meat and juicy intestines. He'd somehow taken me under his wing—quite literally—and took his duty to care for me seriously.

The problem was, of course, the question of how to dispose of the dead animals without him seeing it and thinking I was snubbing his efforts.

"Thank you again," I said as I slid out of bed, petting one of Vengeance's three heads as she sniffed at me.

The hellhound's tail wagged like crazy, all three of her tongues lolling out, her large body practically vibrating with excitement. She knew what was up. Smart doggo.

Now almost twice the size of a lion, the hound had grown too big to sleep in our bed, so she usually plunked down right next to it, where I'd prepared a nest of blankets for her. She'd still spend most of her time with me, either dozing in our quarters while I relaxed or roaming the mansion at my side—deterring any critters who might consider me prey—or taking a walk outside with me. About twice a day, I'd bravely venture outside Azazel's mansion to let Vengeance run to her heart's content and do her business.

And on days when Mephisto graced me with one of his gifts, Vengeance would get one as well.

I threw on some clothes and then gingerly picked up the dead hellrat by its long, thick tail.

"I'll just take this with me while I walk Vengeance, yeah?" I gestured toward the door. "As a little snacky for the way."

Mephisto blinked those mysterious cat eyes at me. *Bon appétit.*

How he was able to speak all sorts of different languages but not understand how unappealing eating a rodent was to me, I'd never know.

"Thank you!" I called out over my shoulder as I made my way out of our quarters.

Vengeance followed on my heels, all excited doggie.

I waited until I'd shut the door leading from the mansion into a vast area enclosed by the black walls of the manor on one side, the humongous dark gray kennel building on the other, and open to the elements on the remaining two sides. Peering around in the ever-present gloom of Hell, I decided we were safe from prying cat eyes.

Vengeance danced in a circle around me, two of her ears adorably turned inside out again. One year in, and she hadn't really grown into her puppy ears. They simply were the floppiest bunch.

"Sit," I ordered.

She tripped over her own feet trying to come to a stop, parked her butt on the ground, and stared at me with the intense focus of a canine waiting for a treat.

"Wait," I drawled with a raised finger.

She whined.

Still holding the hellrat by its tail, I started to spin it, faster, faster, and then I yanked back my arm and hurled the spinning rodent missile away from me.

With a yelp, Vengeance took off after it.

I coughed as the dust from her kick start sprayed me in the face. A few yards out, Vengeance caught the flying snack right out of the air, and immediately, her heads started a growling fight about it. Even though she had *one* stomach, and the rat would end up there anyway, it was apparently of great importance to each of her three heads to get to chew a piece of it.

Shaking my head, I put both hands on my hips and watched her tussle with herself, which involved a few stumbles, tossing around guts and fur, and chomping sounds that made my skin crawl.

My gaze wandered to the purple lightning streaking across the dark sky, illuminating the desolate landscape in intermittent flashes. Barren, black earth stretched out in all directions, interspersed with craggy hills and odd-looking plants. Not a speck of green to be seen anywhere, though. Because where there was no sun, there wasn't any chlorophyll to give leaves their green color.

Instead, what grew down here was closer to fungi and some strange flowers that provided the only kind of color amid the rather depressing assortment of blacks, reds, and grays. What exactly those plants used to survive other than photosynthesis, I had no idea. Given the nature of Hell, it was probably a form of either parasitism or outright capturing and eating prey like a Venus flytrap.

They dotted the landscape with violets, whites, and oranges, some of them so bright they looked like beacons in

the dark. Which, considering their likely carnivorous character, was probably part of their strategy to attract prey.

I shivered despite the heat.

Far off, in the distance, fire erupted from dark, rough-
hewn shapes of what I assumed were volcanoes. Clouds
churned above, seemingly lit from within here and there as if
obscuring a firestorm. It was actually strangely beautiful, in
an apocalyptic kind of way.

And if this were one of many weather types down here,
I'd truly appreciate it for its doomsday beauty. The problem
was that it was the *only* kind of weather in Hell. It never
changed. Day after day, night after night, no matter where I
looked, it was gothic desolation that greeted me.

There wasn't even a difference between day and night.
No seasons, no change, *ever*.

My chest tightened as I scanned the bleak scenery. I
missed nature. *Real* nature, not this horrible prop for a
dystopian thriller. I missed the gentle warmth of sunlight on
my skin, a fresh breeze lifting my hair. The verdant green of
rolling meadows, the chirping of birds in summer trees.
What I wouldn't give to smell flowers in a park or feel the
bite in the air when winter approached. I never thought I'd
miss the cold, but my soul yearned to see even a little bit of
snow.

We didn't often get freezing temperatures in Portland,
where I grew up, but there were mountains close by, and if
we really wanted the winter experience, we just had to drive
to Mount Hood or Mount Saint Helens.

Now, though, all I had, all day, every day, was heat and
gloom and doom.

Sure, I got to see Earth's scenery on my visits, but there
was a huge catch attached to those trips—I couldn't feel,
smell, or touch anything. I saw colors and I heard sounds,

but that was it. The last time I'd smelled rain in the air was over a year ago, in my previous life. It had been that long since I'd felt the sun on my face.

I couldn't even remember what it was like to feel grass under my bare feet.

There were weird-looking grassy plants down here, like brown moss crawling over stones, but I didn't even want to imagine what kind of parasites might burrow into my feet if I stepped on that moss without shoes and socks.

Heaving a deep sigh, I rubbed my breastbone, where an insistent ache had settled.

An eternity of this.

It wasn't that I regretted choosing to stay with Azazel when Lucifer had presented me with the chance to return to Earth. What I had gained with Azazel in my life was worth all the things I'd given up. If I had the choice again, I'd make the same decision, without hesitation.

But at the same time, I keenly felt the consequences of that choice. I'd sacrificed a lot to be here with him, and some days it weighed more heavily on me than others.

A huge tongue slobbering all over my face yanked me out of my *woe is me* spiral. I squealed and tried to bat Vengeance away, to no avail. Now finished with her rat snacky, she was in high spirits and certainly let me know that. Her other two heads helped bathe the rest of my body in dog saliva until I was literally dripping. With their tongues the size of large dinner plates, it hadn't taken long.

"Stop!" I yelled.

Vengeance sat down and toppled over. Instead of getting back up, she stayed right there, presenting her belly to me.

I exhaled heavily, slobber inching its way down my neck, my back, and between my breasts, dripping from my fingers, nose, and hair.

55

"Good thing I haven't showered yet," I muttered and crouched to give Vengeance a few good belly rubs. "We need to work on your licking etiquette. Yes, we do. Don't we?"

Two of her heads grinned at me without an ounce of remorse. The third tried to catch her own tail.

"My lady," a voice called out from behind me.

I jolted, shot to my feet, and whirled around, flinging dog slobber in a huge semicircle around me.

Paimon, one of the full-blood demons in Azazel's service, stood just outside the side door leading back into the mansion, and when he beheld me covered in saliva, a pinched expression came over his handsome face.

I tried to right my hair a little, which ended up more like working the slobber into the strands like a hair mask. Dammit.

"Yes?" I managed.

"You, uh, have a visitor." He grimaced. "My lady."

A full year of living here, and I still wasn't used to being called that, especially not by demons who could crush me with a negligent wave of their hand. It made me highly uneasy, but I just had to suck it up. I'd tried to tell them not to call me that, until Azazel had set me straight—letting them address me informally was a breach of protocol and would reflect badly on me. It was the same damn thing again as with our honored guests. I held a high rank as Azazel's wife and was head of the household alongside him, and therefore all the demons in his employ ranked beneath me and needed to show respect by addressing me properly.

I was uncomfortable with that, they were uncomfortable with that, pretty much everyone was uncomfortable with that, and it annoyed me to no end.

This whole thing gave me a glimpse of what it must be like to marry into royalty as a commoner. I'd heard a few stories of regular women entering royal families, the pressure they found themselves under, the constant stress of trying to fit in and meet unreasonably high expectations born of dusty, centuries-old traditions.

Straight ticket to mental health issues, that one.

"I'll be right in," I said to Paimon. "Thank you."

He nodded. "Your company is waiting in the parlor."

And with that, he vanished back into the mansion before I could ask him who had come to see me or which of the gazillion parlors he actually meant.

I cringed, realizing that I'd have to greet my guest still covered in dog spit. Making them wait while I took a shower would be impolite. Meeting my visitor looking like I just got fished out of a slime vat would be embarrassing.

Sometimes, there really were no good choices.

Cursing my fate, I trudged into the mansion and went right for the parlor closest to the entrance hall, as that one would be the most likely destination to park a guest. Vengeance trotted happily after me, the slobbering fiend.

My predicament got about a thousand times worse when I opened the door to the parlor and beheld my visitor.

Loose black curls tumbled over her shoulders, framing a face of warm, earthen beauty. Her eyes a shade darker than her light brown skin, she regarded me with age-old poise and ancient patience. As always when I was in the presence of a Fallen, a demon from the beginning of time, I felt power pressing against my skin, the kind of humming vibration in the air of a being unfathomably old.

Even if she had once been human.

"Lilith," I breathed.

CHAPTER 7

Lucifer's equal in rank and authority inclined her head, the light glinting off the gold filigree chain adorning her hair. "Zoe."

I remembered to close my mouth so I wasn't gaping at her. This wasn't the first time she'd come to see me in the past few months. For whatever reason, she'd taken an interest in me after my fateful performance at the Fall Festival. I still cringed when remembering that.

The first time she'd visited, I'd almost gone into shock. There wasn't a more high-profile guest in the whole of Hell, except for Lucifer, and from what I heard, neither of them was in the habit of venturing out to meet others much. Most folks came to see *them*. That was just the way things were.

But Lilith chose to come here, without a large entourage —she often just had one or two demons with her as guards —without any fanfare. She never called in advance, never expected to be wined and dined, wasn't interested in any of the usual entertainment afforded honored guests.

She just came to see me.

During her first visit, I'd probably been the most

awkward version of myself ever. I'd been tongue-tied, uncomfortable, and anxious, I'd mangled half a dozen sentences—a new record?—and I even managed to fall out of a chair. I mean, who does that? While sitting down?

Anyway, I'd been sure that was the last I'd seen of her for a millennium after I'd basically acted like a motor-challenged robot trying to pass as human, but to my unending astonishment, she'd come back.

We would talk, or rather, she'd let *me* talk, about all sorts of things, but mainly about my life on Earth. She'd ask questions and prod me to tell her stories and anecdotes, and she'd listen intently, as if soaking it all up like a plant did with the first drops of rain after a drought.

I'd gotten a bit more comfortable around her, though I was still far from relaxed. Never would I forget that she and Lucifer were an item, that there was a reason she was with the dude who reveled in physical and mental torture. Nor would I ever fail to remember that she had sat there and done nothing to help me while Lucifer had humiliated me in front of his court.

My disgruntlement over her passive participation in that farce was tempered only by the fact that she had, indeed, intervened on my behalf in the end, stopping Lucifer from crushing my windpipe like an empty soda can. And it'd been her pointed reminder to her darling devil that I had saved Naamah's life and he owed me a favor, which had actually gotten me the boons of healing as fast as a demon and being able to summon things.

So, yeah, to say my feelings about Lilith were complicated was an understatement. She was puzzling me. As far as I could tell, her interest in me was genuine, and I didn't get the impression that she was fishing for information. Why would she? From everything I'd heard about Lucifer, he already knew most everything anyway. He'd known a whole fucking lot about me and my life on Earth, so he definitely had sources other than his dearly beloved.

And for some reason, I just didn't see Lilith playing spy for him.

Also, my human life really wasn't all that interesting in the grand scheme of things.

Still, I made sure to keep my trap shut about certain details, like the fact that we'd stolen my dad's soul out of Lucifer's personal sinner storage and now kept him as a ghost on Earth, protected by Azazel's demons so he wouldn't be dragged back to Hell. For all intents and purposes, when talking with Lilith, my dad's death wasn't even a blip on my radar, courtesy of the estrangement between us.

She didn't need to know that my dad and I had sort of reconciled after we'd dropped him off on Earth and that we now had a tentative relationship going, with me visiting him every couple of weeks.

"Your Grace," I now said, recalling my manners.

I made an awkward curtsy that probably looked more like a giraffe trying to lie down and forgetting how to do it halfway through.

The sole demon guard standing next to Lilith suppressed a laugh.

And that was when I remembered the slobbered state I was in. Oh, God. Of all the people to come visit me when I looked like this...

I grimaced and hopelessly tried to pat myself dry.

"Are you all right?" Lilith asked, her voice honeyed and melodious.

"I got slimed," I blurted out.

The hint of a smile ghosted over her lips. "So I see."

"My hellhound," I babbled, pointing at the perpetrator sitting innocently right next to me. "She likes to lick."

Dear Lord, someone should really stop me from talking. It didn't agree with me.

Lilith's gaze fell on Vengeance. She held out a hand. "May I?"

"Sure. Venny, go say hi."

The monster-sized doggo trotted over to Lilith and sniffed at her hand. Well, two of her heads did. The third tried to lick its own ear.

"She is magnificent." Lilith scratched the two heads with both hands, her expression warm and indulgent. "She reminds me of my Ruin."

"Oh, you've got a hellhound, too?" Pretty much every high-ranking demon had kennels full of hounds, but some actually kept a few special dogs more as pets than the others.

"Dragon," Lilith replied, patting Vengeance's flank.

My eyes widened. She had a pet dragon.

Because of course she did.

"Do you fly her?" The question was out before I could think better.

"I do, actually." A glint shone in her eyes. "It is the only way I can come close to having wings."

Yeah, being bipedal really sucked when living among feathered beings who could just take to the skies. Most of the time, the demons kept the wings magicked away out of sight, but they did come in handy for traveling, not just to and on Earth, but here in Hell, too. Flying a dragon was the next best thing to having wings of one's own when it came to going from one dominion to the other.

As far as I had seen, public transportation was sorely lacking down here.

"So, um, I apologize for my condition." I waved up and

down my body. "I would have taken a shower, but I didn't want to make you wait."

"No worries. Please feel free to clean yourself. I do not mind."

"Oh," I stammered. "Okay. If you're sure... I'll make it quick."

I bowed deeply and then hightailed it out of the room with Vengeance on my heels. After the quickest shower ever, I slipped into fresh clothes and raced back to the room, finding Lilith perched on a divan with her demon guard standing at attention behind her.

Every inch of her looked so regal. The way she held herself, her measured movements, as if she'd come into this world poured into the original mold of what an empress should look like.

And yet, for all the power she wielded, despite the hum of energy around her that spoke of a force that had long ceased to be merely human, she almost appeared...sad. It was in every breath she took, settled into her skin like a patina of melancholy.

I fidgeted with the hem of my shirt. "Would you like to watch a movie?"

Surprise flickered in her age-old eyes. "A movie?"

Jeez, I didn't even know if she'd ever seen one. From what I'd gathered, she hadn't really visited Earth in quite a long time, which might be part of why she was so fascinated by me. I guessed I was the first human she'd interacted with in thousands of years.

No pressure or anything.

"Uh...you know." I rubbed my nose. "Um, moving pictures? Like, on a screen?"

She tilted her head. "I'd like that."

I released the breath I'd been holding. "Okay, great. Please follow me."

Technology in Hell was...complicated. It wasn't that we didn't have electricity—we did, although in a rudimentary way and apparently generated by torturing sinners, which was the go-to for energy production down here. When I'd heard that, I'd puked up my guts, the thought of someone's suffering powering the gadgets I'd been using souring my stomach.

Azazel, bless his heart, had found alternative ways to source the energy necessary for producing electricity, among them letting hellhounds run in huge wheels—they genuinely loved to run for hours without being fazed at all—and setting up large wind turbines on nearby hills. It was enough to cover what little electricity I needed.

The real problem was even getting modern technology down here. Demons could carry whatever would fit through a hellgate, of course, and they did it often enough. But Lucifer apparently loathed a lot of human inventions of the last two centuries and had put in place an embargo on most modern tech stuff. Now, if a demon wanted a TV, for example, they'd have to apply for an import permit.

Yep, no joke, they had to petition the authorities to be allowed technological luxuries from abroad. It all felt very Soviet to me.

In fact, there was a thriving black market for smuggled tech from Earth. Some opportunistic and risk-happy demons had made a fortune trading in unsanctioned technology. I still giggled every time I imagined dark deals going down in back rooms over a PlayStation console.

Of course, if those demons got caught, they ended up decorating Lucifer's subfloor.

Which was why Azazel had pulled some strings in order

to officially procure a TV and DVD/Blu-ray player combo for me so I could watch old favorites and even stay up to date on newer releases. Every time I thought I couldn't love him more, he'd come up with a new reason for me to adore the fuck out of him.

I now led Lilith, consort to the dude who despised modern technology, trailed by her demon guard, to our home theater featuring a huge HD screen in front of a comfy couch and watched her eyes grow as wide as saucers as I turned it all on.

I'd never seen Lilith starstruck.

Her mouth hanging open, she slowly sank down on the couch, eyes riveted on the screen as the DVD began to play.

"I never knew this existed," she whispered.

Oh, honey. My chest tightened as I looked at her. "It's one of the better inventions we've come up with in the past century." I bit my lip, the remote dangling from my hand as I considered whether I should ask. "So, I take it you haven't been to Earth since this..." I gestured at the TV.

Her delicate brows drew together. "It has been so long...I don't quite remember when I last traveled to Earth." She shook her head. "Long before this, though. I'd have remembered this."

I hid my grimace and summoned a bunch of snacks onto the low table while Lilith ordered her guard to wait outside. *No movie for him, I guess.* Knowing that Vengeance was prone to snoring loudly enough to overlay the TV's volume, I sent her outside to keep the poor guard company, then I settled onto the couch as the movie started.

For the first-ever film that Lilith would watch, I'd opted for the 2005 version of Pride and Prejudice. For one thing, because of the Hand Flex. I mean, come on, it's the bomb.

More importantly, though, a period film from an era

before modern inventions radically changed the world might be the easiest for Lilith to digest, given that some of the pre-modern stuff in it could be a bit familiar to her.

I jumped in and explained a few things here and there, but mostly, I just let her enjoy it. Munching on my snacks, I furtively watched her watch the movie, and at the Hand Flex, she raised a brow and pursed her lips. Ha!

When the credits rolled over the screen, she sighed deeply.

"That was lovely," she said, a wistful note in her voice. "I take it Earth doesn't much look like this anymore?"

"Uh, no, not really. A lot has changed. Lots of technology everywhere. I mean, there are parts that are still quaint, but those are more remote." I hesitated, chewing my lip again, then I asked quietly, "Why haven't you been to Earth in all this time?"

Lilith was silent for so long that I started to fidget.

"I'm sorry," I said quickly and stood up. "You don't need to answer. I didn't mean to pry."

"He can't go."

Her soft reply made me stop gathering the snack bowls from the table. I glanced at her. Eyes distant, she stared at the black screen.

"The deal he made to keep me," she went on, "says he may never set foot on Earth again."

I stiffened as I realized she was talking about Lucifer. This was the first time ever that she'd mentioned him.

"And he hasn't," she continued. "In all the millennia, he has stayed in Hell to honor the agreement." Her lashes lowered over her luminous light brown eyes. "I'm free to go, and at first, I did. But over time…it didn't feel right, that I should enjoy something he deprived himself of for my sake. He never said anything. He'd never keep me from going. But

65

I could see it in his eyes. The longing. He would, you know." Her gaze met mine, a striking connection. "He would go in a heartbeat, if he were allowed."

Dumbfounded, I sank back onto the couch. This was the most she'd ever spoken to me in one go, and way more information about her and Lucifer than I'd ever thought I'd get.

Lilith lowered her gaze. "So I stopped going, after some time. It seemed almost frivolous. But it also…" She paused, her power humming softly in the air. "It becomes difficult, at some point, to visit a world you are no longer part of, will never be part of again. The disconnect grows sharper with the centuries, when you watch those you once belonged with build civilizations far beyond your imagining. When you realize you will forever be on the outside, looking in, not one of them anymore." Another pause, then, quietly: "It can be painful."

God, I felt that pain. I felt it as if it were my own… because one day, it just might be.

I'd walk the same path as she had, wouldn't I? With the difference that my beloved demon was allowed to go to Earth, but I could well imagine the disconnect she spoke of coming to haunt me in the future. It *already* felt strange to visit Earth when no one could see me, when I couldn't smell or touch or feel anything. Being a ghost really sucked.

"Staying in Hell," Lilith said, yanking me from my thoughts, "also meant I grew faster into the power needed to thrive down here."

At that, I sat up straighter. Little was known officially about Lilith's inherent power level. Her status and rank had long been established by Lucifer's brutal authority, his power basically covering for her human weakness. I could sense it, though, her innate energy that didn't feel much different from that of a Fallen—even though she wasn't truly a demon.

Rumor had it, she'd simply *become* something else.

Maybe some of Hell's power had seeped into her over thousands of years, like water trickling into cracks of barren earth.

"Still," she said in her molasses-smooth voice, "it took a long time. A long time of being something in between, neither here nor there. Not quite human anymore, but too human to truly fit in here."

Her warm, topaz-colored eyes met mine, and I twitched from the direct connection, the strength that lay within.

"You have been kind," she said softly. "I had almost forgotten what it is to be kind."

Yikes. What had her life here been like for her to forget something like that? My thoughts veered to Lucifer and the demons at his court, and I remembered the stories Azazel had told me of the cruelty rampant in that palace. Yeah, I guessed it would be hard to keep a core of kindness when surrounded by that bunch.

"I like you," Lilith continued, pulling my attention back to her. "You remind me of myself, when I first came here. And for that reason, I do not wish to see you struggle as I did. Maybe this will help ease your path."

"What?" I whispered.

She closed her eyes and brought her hand up to her chest, laying it over the silky fabric of her orange-hued dress. The hum of her energy swelled to a vibration that shook the room.

"What are you do—"

My question ended in a shriek when she plunged her hand right into her chest. I jumped up from the couch again, my hand covering my mouth.

Through fabric, skin, and muscle, she tore in one light-ning-fast strike. She barely jerked at the self-inflicted wound, her eyes still closed. With her hand buried up to her wrist in her chest, she stilled, her brow wrinkling in concentration. Blood drenched the edges of her dress around the tear, slowly spreading larger. Small wiggles of her arm indicated she was moving her hand or fingers inside herself.

My stomach wanted to crawl up my throat.

She made a sharp movement, grunted, and then a soft smile came over her face. When she opened her eyes to look at me, they glowed brightly from within while her power pulsed in the air. She withdrew her bloodied hand, her fingers curled into a fist as if holding something within.

I stared at the gaping hole in her chest. My heartbeat pounded in my ears, all the blood rushing from my head, making me dizzy. With my knees wobbling precariously, I grabbed the back of the couch for purchase. I could see right into her. Right to her organs...her heart, maybe? Or her lungs? It was all a bloody mess.

"Here," she said and rose from her seat.

"What?" I squeaked.

"It will hurt only a little. I will make it quick."

"Wait—"

But the next second, she'd already grasped my shoulder with one hand and rammed the other—the bloody one holding God knew what—straight into my chest.

The world went white with pain. All breath punched out of me, I jerked, held in place by Lilith's strong grip. A terrible tearing sensation shot out from my chest while I uselessly gasped for air, twitching and flailing. I tasted blood on my tongue.

Pain. So much pain.

I couldn't even see.

But the worst part was the very clear feeling of a foreign object right there within me, Lilith's hand rooting through flesh and blood until—

Something connected with my innermost self. A bright spark of power touching my very soul, that place I went to when I visualized my spirit form leaving my body to travel to Earth.

My entire being trembled. Quakes that rattled my bones shook my body as my spiritual core throbbed and pulsed, everything brightening in a flash of pure power.

I blinked to clear my vision, the shooting pain in my chest hazing my thoughts. When I could see again, I stared at Lilith leaning over me with a beatific smile on her face, sprinkles of blood dotting her nose and cheeks like gruesome freckles.

My lungs burned, my heart thumped furiously, each beat making me cringe with agony. I could *feel* my chest and my insides painfully knitting back together, thanks to my demon-fast healing.

I tried to speak and found my lungs unable to draw in enough air. All I got out was a helpless croak as I lay there on the couch like a broken doll.

"Do not worry," Lilith said, completely unbothered by the fact that she'd just played whack-a-mole with her chest and mine. "I simply gave you a gift." She laid one hand over her breastbone, over her own newly healed skin. Her body was a lot faster at putting itself together than mine. "A kernel of my power, from me to you. May it give you strength well before your years."

Again I tried to say something, but it came out as a wet gurgle. Something warm trickled out of the corner of my mouth, and I realized it was my own blood.

"It will all be fine," she said, stroking a strand of hair out of my face. She tilted her head. "I have not done this before, but I'm sure it will be fine."

My panic must have shown in my expression because she smiled in what I guessed should be a reassuring way. Of course, in my current mental state, that sailed right past my ability to process.

"You should sleep now so you can recover. Goodbye, Zoe."

And before I could croak and gurgle some more, she leaned in and kissed me on the forehead.

Everything went dark.

CHAPTER 8

When I came to, I was surrounded by heat and darkness, and the most delicious scent. Leather, bonfire, and heavy spice. I knew that scent intimately. I fell asleep each night with my nose pressed into a cushion that smelled like this.

Like him.

Azazel.

I wriggled and realized that it was dark because my face was pressed against a hard wall of muscle. As soon as I moved, everything shifted. Azazel loosened his hold on me enough so I could gasp for air and look around. I found myself in his lap, his wings out in full splendor, obscuring the room around us.

"Zoe."

Immediately, his hands framed my face and tilted my head up to meet his gaze. His eyes were wild, his expression stark with terror and a deep, dark kind of fury that made me tremble all over.

He kissed me before I could speak, claiming my mouth with equal parts raw need and tender relief. My hands found purchase on his shoulders as he peppered my face with additional kisses that felt like they were more for the benefit of reassuring him than me.

I gasped as he crushed me tightly to him, his wings trembling.

That was when I smelled the ash.

Peering out over his shoulder and the edge of his wing, I flinched when I saw the room.

Or what was left of it.

Ash particles floated in the air, and sparks of barely extinguished flames flickered in the corners, the walls blackened with soot. The couch I'd been lying on was now a pile of burned fabric, charred wood, and bent metal, and Azazel sat in the middle of it, holding me on his lap. The table was reduced to scorched rubble.

And there, across from us, warped and melted plastic stood in place of the former entertainment system.

"The TV!" I wheezed. "You melted the TV!"

Azazel slowly drew back until he could skewer me with a look so dark it made me cringe.

"I come home," he said, his voice a growl that skittered over my skin, "to find you here, alone, bloodied, and unconscious, with a hole torn in your top and a freshly healing wound in your chest. I am out of my mind with worry for you, not knowing what the *fuck* happened, unable to vent my rage on whoever hurt you, and when you wake up after *hours* of me holding your broken body, you *complain about the TV*?"

I grimaced. "Okay, it does sound bad when you put it like that."

His eyes flashed with lightning, his features harsh. "Who did this to you?" He laid a hand on my chest, right where I'd had a gaping hole not long ago, his gentle touch at odds with the promise of violence in his voice. "Whom do I need to kill?"

"Um." My face scrunched up as I tried to navigate this carefully. I grasped his hand with mine. "That might be a *bit* complicated."

"*Who*?" He bared his teeth.

"Lilith," I whispered.

The widening of his eyes was the only sign of how stumped he was at that revelation.

"Look, she just gave me a piece of her power," I hastened to add. "She wanted to help me, really. Granted, she did so in a gruesome, bloody way that was a lot more heart-to-heart than I would have liked, but she wasn't out to hurt me, okay?"

He blinked at me, his face a study in bewilderment. "She gave you a piece of her power?"

"That's what she said. A *kernel*, actually. Now, I have no idea what that really means. Like, will it strike tiny roots and grow? I have to tell you, I *am* worried that I'll have a little Lilith power tree spreading its branches inside me and—will it bear fruit? Will I have to prune it? Does it need fertilizer? I have so many questi—"

He laid his hand over my mouth to shut me up. I would've been mad at him for his high-handedness if it hadn't helped me out of my panic spiral.

His gaze intent, he moved his hand to my chest again, and his power rose in the air. Probing for mine, I realized. We still had that neat bond between us from when we'd gotten hitched, and I now felt the touch of his energy along the tie that bound us.

"She really did," he said after a moment, a note of wonder in his deep voice. "She gave you a piece of herself. I didn't know that was possible."

"Apparently, neither did she." I rubbed my nose.

His eyes flicked up to mine, his dark brows drawing together. "What?"

"Uh, yeah, funny story... So it seems she had no idea what she was doing."

Thunderstorms churned in his eyes.

"Or at least, she'd never done this before? That's what she said."

"So, Lilith decided it was a good idea to experiment on you? With something that has never been done? Not knowing if it might harm you?" He sounded like he was contemplating some experiments of his own. On Lilith.

I grimaced. "Her intentions were good, though?"

"You know what they say about good intentions, don't you?"

Ha!

I patted his hand. "Look, I get why you're mad—"

"Try *murderous*."

"But in the end, no harm, no foul! I'm okay. All healed up." I gestured at my chest. "I mean, I might have some nightmares about having a hand plunged into my rib cage—"

His eye twitched.

"But what if I get some cool new powers because of this? Really, you should thank her."

His lashes half lowered over stormy eyes. "Maybe I'll show my gratitude the same way she bestowed her kindness on you."

I rolled my eyes. "Oh, quit it."

The hint of a smile whispered over his face, and his gaze heated. That was the thing with Azazel—as icily commanding and used to instant obedience as he was with

74

most others, when I mouthed off to him? He secretly enjoyed it.

"So, about the TV," I said and graced him with a pointed look. "You need to learn some control. You can't keep incinerating entire rooms just because you lose your temper. Do I need to sign you up for an anger management cla—"

I never got to finish that sentence. My back met the cushiony ash of the couch's remains, and I squealed from the sudden movement while Azazel rose above me, a vision of sin and temptation with fire-licked wings and molten heat in his gaze.

"I need to learn control?" he asked softly, his voice all seduction between silken sheets.

"Badly," I whispered, my pulse already throbbing low in my core.

"The kind of control it takes to make you come a dozen times before I take my own pleasure?"

I bit my lip. "Yeah, you really need to practice that."

"Hm." That glint in his eye didn't bode well. Still leaning over me, he stroked a single finger over my chest, right over the healed wound. "Are you in pain?"

"No."

"Feel any discomfort?"

I shook my head. "Good as new."

His smile was positively wicked. "In that case…"

He sat back on his heels and summoned a…rope? I didn't even know we had any. Eyeing the ceiling, he threw one end of it up so it fell over one of the rafters up there and then caught it when it dangled down the other side.

"Um…" I said, rising up on my elbows and peering at the silken rope with a mix of anxiety and wayward anticipation. "Do I need to be worried?"

His mischievous smirk did all sorts of naughty things to my insides. "Maybe."

Eek.

The next moment, I found myself hoisted up to my feet, my arms stretched over my head, and my hands bound with the rope with my palms facing each other and the rope wrapped around both wrists. It pulled me up onto the balls of my feet, and I had to strain to balance. He'd tied it loose enough that I had some give, but not so much that I could wriggle free.

My heart beat a rapid tattoo against my ribs, incipient excitement flooding my veins—only heightened by the way Azazel regarded me like a hungry lion would a tasty snack dangled right in front of him.

He laid a single finger on my chest, on the edge of the hole torn in the fabric of my tight-fitting T-shirt. Something dark flickered over his expression as he gently rubbed over the new skin there. His gaze caught mine, and I was so distracted by the raw, unfiltered anguish in it that I almost missed the spark of heat as it flared over my skin.

Breaking eye contact with him, I looked down. He was moving his finger over my T-shirt, burning the fabric in its wake. But the flames didn't spread. He only seared away what his finger touched, flakes of ash falling down and baring my skin in strips as he slowly prowled around me. He never lifted his finger off me.

I panted. Heat and cool air teased my skin in alternating whispers of sensation, and I squirmed, the rope rubbing against my wrists.

Strips of my T-shirt fell to the floor as his rounds connected, and my upper body was now only covered in the last bits of T-shirt fabric over my shoulders, as well as my bra.

"It's incredibly wasteful to keep burning my clothes," I breathed.

"The T-shirt was ruined anyway."

Flames danced over the rest of the fabric on my shoulders, then died down. Now behind me, Azazel leaned in until I felt his heat against my back, but instead of the touch I anticipated, his warm breath coasted over my right shoulder, blowing the ash off my skin.

I shivered.

He repeated that on my left shoulder, and my nipples pebbled. I pressed my thighs together, trying to soothe the ache between my legs.

Sliding his finger along the straps of my bra, he burned them clean off me and proceeded to trace the lacy filigree of the bra cups. My chest heaved with my fast breaths, and I couldn't help following his maddeningly singular touch as he incinerated my bra one torturous caress at a time.

Each of my desperate little movements shifted my weight precariously as I balanced on the balls of my feet, making me hyperaware that my wrists were bound and I was helplessly dangling from the ceiling, at his complete and utter mercy.

It only kicked my arousal that much higher.

The last bits of ash from my bra flaked off my breasts, the ghostly whisper of touch as my skin was bared adding to the slow, sensual torture. Azazel, now in front of me, leaned in and gently blew on my breasts to remove any residue, and I uttered a soft moan.

Eyes of storms and lightning met mine, and then he placed a tender kiss on my lips. "All good?" he murmured against my mouth.

"No."

He tilted his head in question.

"I need you to touch me," I bit out.

I felt his smile in his insouciant kiss. "I have been touching you."

That one finger again, now running down from the middle of my chest, over my belly, until it traced the waistband of my jeans.

Even that small foray toward the epicenter of my lust was enough to make me moan again.

But instead of burning my pants right off like I'd hoped, he brought his hand up again, the same excruciatingly teasing way back as he'd gone down before. While he grasped my neck with his other hand and went in for a kiss that turned my brain to mush, he circled one of my nipples with that damned finger, his touch light and coaxing and driving me mad.

Uttering a vile curse against his lips, I strained and pushed my chest forward, right into his hand. *Touch me, dammit.*

His grip on my neck tightened, and he bit my lip and pinched my nipple—hard.

Sensation shot through my body, all the way down to my swollen core. I cried out, wanting less, wanting more, perfectly confused and delightfully needy.

He seemed to enjoy me that way.

I rubbed my thighs together, trying to get the firm material of my jeans to press against my aching flesh and give me some more pleasure.

Without so much as a warning, he laid his hand right over my mound, cupping me hard enough to make me go on tiptoes.

"Want that?" he asked, his voice stirring the flames inside me.

"Fuck yes!"

He rubbed firmly over my core, heat flaring from his

touch, making me gasp and squirm. His fingers met my slick flesh without any fabric between them and slipped inside me.

I jumped and moaned, straining against the rope holding my wrists. Oh, fuck—he'd burned my jeans and panties right out of his way.

The next second, all thoughts melted away in a firestorm of pleasure as he masterfully brought me to a climax with just a few targeted strokes. I threw my head back and rode his hand, surrendering to the explosion of pleasure inside me.

Leaving the rest of my jeans in place, which made for an interesting feeling with my heated core bared, he started trailing his mouth down my throat, over my collarbone, to my breasts. Cupping them with both hands, he leaned in and closed his mouth over the nipple he'd pinched.

A strangled moan escaped me, and I jerked at the intense sensation of his heat and tongue and the suction of his mouth. More delicious, aching pleasure throbbed between my legs, as if there were a direct line between my nipple and my core. The fire there was barely even banked, and now he merrily poured gasoline on it, the fiend.

He switched between my breasts, bestowing equal time and care on both, working my nipples and sensitive skin until I squirmed yet again with need. Holding me in place with one hand splayed over my back, he continued lavishing his attention on my breasts while his sinful fingers found my slick flesh once more.

I couldn't say for sure how many times he made me come like this, but I suspected it was close to what he'd promised earlier. Azazel was nothing if not thorough.

He slid his hands up my arms, his forehead pressed to mine. "Still good?"

I blinked against the haze of pleasure he'd inflicted on me, and checked in with myself. My arms felt the kind of strange that limbs did when suspended for longer than a minute, but not in a concerning way.

"Yep," I whispered.

His energy wrapped around me as he smiled. "Good girl."

And there I went, shivering with new arousal.

Before I could draw my next breath, he sank down in front of me, roughly pulling my ruined jeans and panties along. He helped me step out of my shoes and clothes, and then he lifted one of my legs to his shoulder and dove right in.

I jolted when his mouth met my sensitive, swollen skin. Wobbling, I almost lost my balance, trying to steady myself on my other leg. He grabbed my hips and held me in place for his oral enjoyment, making sure I couldn't twitch away from his ravenous mouth. Sensation pounded through me, twirling and coiling in twists of pleasure and helpless bliss.

Always, always, he ate me out like I was his own personal brand of drug and he couldn't get enough. The sounds I uttered would have made me blush scarlet if I heard them later on, but right here and now, I didn't give a fuck. I was too lost in the spiral of pleasure, too stripped down to a creature that existed on nothing but lust and wanton enjoyment of the moment.

He did that to me. Broke me down into my most primal parts, until nothing else mattered but his touch, the feel of him, the way he made *me* feel, and that connection between us.

I came again with a hoarse cry, and while my orgasm was still ebbing, he stood up, divested himself of his shirt, and opened his pants.

My toes curled in anticipation.

His heated gaze caught mine as he lifted me up, aligned us just right, and then thrust inside me. My moan this time mixed with the sound of his own, and my thoughts all scattered as I relished how he stretched me just to the edge of pain.

"Zoe," he whispered, his voice deliciously husky, his expression tight with pleasure.

Panting, I leaned forward and kissed him. Desperate. Needy. Seeking. "Let me touch you."

The rope holding my wrists went up in flames and then fell off as ash. Instantly, I framed his face with both hands, my arms tingling, and tunneled my fingers through his silky hair, pulling him to me for an urgent kiss.

As our lips met, I reveled in the knowledge that I was the only one allowed to touch him like this, that it was my privilege to caress him, to be this close. Thousands of years he'd lived, thousands of partners he'd undoubtedly had, but it was me he'd chosen in the end.

It was me he chose, every day anew.

Just like I chose him.

I love you, I whispered into his mind.

His power rose around us, trembling, pulsing, wrapping around me in a full-body caress as he held me tight, our bodies joined most intimately while he kissed me with a tenderness bordering on awe.

It broke me a little inside.

I'd burn the world for you, was his reply, dark conviction behind every word.

He rarely told me outright that he loved me. I found it wasn't necessary, when I could read it in the things he did say, when his actions spoke loudly enough that I never had to wonder.

"No need for that," I murmured in between kisses. "What I do need right now"—I rolled my hips and squeezed my inner muscles—"is for you to fuck me."

His fingers tightened on my ass, lust darkening his eyes. I knew how much he enjoyed it when I talked dirty, when I shed any veneer of decency and propriety and showed him my raw, unvarnished need.

Lifting me until he almost slipped out of me, he then slammed me back down, thrusting his hips forward at the same time. I moaned at the rough friction, the slide of his cock inside me.

Never enough. I would never get enough of this.

I held on to him for dear life as he moved my hips up and down to meet his thrusts without even straining a little, as if holding me up like this while standing was the easiest thing. My breaths had long turned to panted moans, and I wasn't even the one doing all the work.

He took me with deep, thorough strokes, measured in a way that told me he still held on to his control, hadn't reached that place yet where he truly let go and surrendered to his own fierce need.

With my fingers tangled in his hair, I buried my face in the crook of his neck, licked him—and then I bit down. Hard.

My back hit the wall, all breath knocked out of me, his body pressing mine against the smooth stone. His energy a storm of lust and pleasure and possessive need around me, he pounded into me, his tethers snapped and his control in shreds.

I relished every deliciously hard thrust that drove my own pleasure higher and higher. He ground against me with each shove, and the pressure on my clit sent me over the edge. My orgasm raged through me, and I honestly lost part of my soul in that firestorm of bliss.

Azazel came with a deep groan that sparked more aftershocks of pleasure inside me. With his face against my neck, he nipped at me in an echo of how I'd bitten him, and I shuddered with delight.

"Hold on," he muttered and stepped away from the wall, still grasping me tightly around my waist and ass.

The next moment, he sank down on a freshly summoned sofa with me still straddling him, his wings folding around me. I smiled against his neck. He knew how much I loved his wings, and he displayed them in front of me quite often, even though he still gave me some serious side-eye when I called them pretty. According to him, they were "magnificent harbingers of death," not *pretty*.

With Azazel casually stroking my back, I now shifted so I could run my fingers over the sleek black of his feathers while my heartbeat and breathing returned to normal.

"They really are *pretty*," I said with a grin, just to get a rise out of him.

He growled, and I felt the vibration of it where I lay sprawled across his chest.

"Pretty and…" I faltered as my eyes fell on a light spot among the shining sable of his feathers. "White?"

He sat up so fast I almost toppled off his lap. With a frown, he extended his wing so he could see the offending feather. When he spotted the single white plume amid the black, he gritted his teeth and shook his wing, his power sparking. The white feather turned black as if photoshopped.

"What the—" I pointed at the spot on his wing. "What did you just do? What was that?"

"Come back here," he said in lieu of an answer and

pulled me down to his chest again, tucking my head underneath his chin and refolding his wings around me.

"Oh, no, no, no." I flailed and fought against his hold. "You've got some 'splaining to do, mister. What was that?"

I managed to rise enough to glare at him, straight into a face of pretend nonchalance.

"What was what?"

Narrowing my eyes at him, I poked my finger into his wing, right where he'd just magicked away some incriminating evidence. "That was a white feather."

He extended the wing in question and regarded it with an earnest expression. "Looks all black to me."

"Oh, come on!" I huffed. Pursing my lips, I asked with mischievous amusement drenching my voice, "Is your angel side getting stronger?"

Given that his father, Azrael, had sired him before he'd fallen from grace, when he'd still been an angel, both Azazel and Azmodea were technically only half demon. Something Azazel liked to be disgruntled about, with me teasing him mercilessly.

Consequently, at my mention of his angel heritage, he shot me a pointed, dark look.

"Are your wings partially turning angel white?" I asked with a big grin, poking him even more.

A muscle flexed in his jaw, but then he sighed and made a displeased face. "They've always been that way."

With one shake of his wings, white sparked all over them, a rolling tide of change that painted his feathers in a mosaic of black and white. I gasped, my eyes roving over the new landscape of his wings.

Snow-white feathers now gleamed among the familiar glossy black, both colors evenly represented, though in clus-

84

ters that drew beautiful patterns of speckles and lines. A painting of contrasts, artfully combined.

I squealed my delight, both hands covering my mouth. "Oh my God!"

He cleared his throat.

I sent him a sheepish look. "Sorry. Let me rephrase that. Oh, magnificently speckled Azazel!"

My choked-down giggles erupted into laughter as he unceremoniously shoved me off his lap and dumped me next to him on the sofa. The twinkle in his eye betrayed the stern expression he wore.

I caught my breath and grinned at him. He was so cute, all pretend grumpy and peeved. "How come I've never seen this before?"

He shrugged one massive shoulder, the accompanying wing flexing slightly. "I always mask it."

"So, you can change the color?"

He inclined his head. "A simple illusion."

My gaze on the black-and-white-dotted wings, I frowned. "So what happened just now? Your illusion failed?" I met his eyes again. "It's never done that before, has it?"

He looked thoughtful. "No."

I sat up, unease worming its way into my amazement. "Are you…changing?"

He was silent for a long moment, his eyes on the wing where his illusion had faltered. "I think," he said slowly, quietly, "that *you* are changing me."

I blinked rapidly, drawing back. "Excuse me, what?"

When he looked at me, it was with unfiltered, raw openness, so much of him laid bare that it stole my breath. "I have been hiding my wings for two thousand five hundred years, Zoe. My mask never slipped. It's become second nature, an instinct I never questioned anymore. I haven't even seen my true wings in so long that I'd forgotten their pattern." He leaned forward, holding my gaze with an intensity that made me tremble. "And then you came along. And you pull up parts of me that I thought were long buried."

I swallowed, uncertainty weaving through my breath. "Is that good or bad?"

He studied me for a few heartbeats, a glint sparking in his eyes. "I could be cheesy right now."

I choked on a surprised laugh. "You? Cheesy? What would that sound like?"

A subtle smile warmed his features. "Like me telling you that you're making me whole."

My breath hitched. "Oh." I cleared my throat. "That, um, yes, that's very cheesy," I loftily said, rubbing my breastbone, where it felt like something was melting inside.

He grasped my hand and laid it on his chest instead, where his heart beat strong, steady. "All my life, I separated myself into two parts, one of which I've denied and suppressed. It seems you're bringing it back to the fore."

My eyes mapped his face, drinking in the sheer beauty of his features, the depth of his personality that lay beneath that beauty. "But it's not making you weaker, is it?" I asked quietly, voicing the thread of worry that had unfurled inside me.

"I've never felt stronger in my life." He lifted my hand and kissed my palm. "You bring out the light in me."

"Stop it," I whispered, my face blazing with heat. "You'll make me lactose-intolerant."

His deep chuckle coaxed a smile from me.

"So," I asked, walking my fingers up his stunningly speckled wings, "can you turn them all white?"

His power vibrated darkly. "Why would I want to look like one of those fools?"

"So you *can*." I grinned. "Will you show me? Please?" I gave him my best begging pout.

He seemed unaffected, the callous brute.

"I can't imagine what they look like all sparkly white," I said with a pleading note. "Can I see? Pretty please?"

He stared at me for a few pulsing heartbeats while I batted my lashes, and then he looked toward the ceiling with a long-suffering sigh.

"Hell is testing me," he muttered, but he shook his mighty wings once—and gleaming white washed over the feathers.

I had to blink hard against the blinding light, like silver glinting in the sun. When I beheld the whole splendor of his snowy white wings, I inhaled sharply. They were fucking *gorgeous*.

Immediately, I reached out to run my fingers over the white plumage, and silver sparks followed in my wake, like lightning tracing the filigree of the feathers.

With a gasp, I yanked my hand back. "Oh, no!"

Azazel looked alarmed. "What?"

I slapped the back of my hand against my forehead and dramatically turned away. "Devil take me! I'm having sinful thoughts about an *angel*!"

"Zoe." A deep, deep growl.

"Oh, my dirty soul! I'm plagued by filthy fantasies about defiling a messenger of the Lord!"

The last thing I heard was my own laughter and a snarled "I'm going to defile *you*" before I was dragged underneath a massive body and right back into another round of mind-melting sex.

CHAPTER 9

War had always been a distant concept for me.

Sure, I'd grown up with my country intermittently being engaged in military conflicts with other countries, but all of it took place in faraway regions—with the notable exception of the attack on the Twin Towers on September 11. My personal life never much changed because of these conflicts, though, other than hearing stuff on the news.

Now, living in Hell, among demons who seemed to thrive on violence, I came much closer to tasting the immediate impact of war than I'd ever liked.

I was having breakfast in our sitting room, alone—if you didn't count a salivating Vengeance hovering over my shoulder and eyeing the hash browns on my plate—as the door to the balcony in the adjoining bedroom opened and let in a gust of hot air. I looked up, a thread of worry unfurling in my chest. Not because I thought it could be an intruder— only Azazel knew the sigil combination to open that door, and Vengeance hadn't stalked forward in protective mode, which meant it wasn't some stranger coming to harm me.

No, what made my pulse spike was the overwhelming scent of blood that carried on the blast of outside air. And with my sense of smell as dull as any human's was, if *I* could make out the iron tang of blood...it had to be a whole fucking lot.

I was about to rise from my chair and rush over into the bedroom when Azazel strolled through the doorway. *Strolled*, quite casually, a lazy swagger in his step. I blinked at him in dumbfounded shock and had to look him over twice, because he surely couldn't be covered in blood from head to toe when he sauntered in here like he was on a relaxing Sunday walk through the park.

And yet, every inch of him seemed painted in crimson, a grisly image of violence. His boots left scarlet prints on the floor tiles, and drops of blood dripped from his arms and hands as he moved. Even his hair was drenched, the deep black overlaid with a red sheen.

I inhaled sharply and covered my mouth with both hands.

Azazel paused and looked down at the floor, frowning at the bloody trail he'd left. "Ah," he said, sounding a bit sheepish. "Good thing we don't have carpet here."

I made a squeaky sound and flailed my hands at him.

He seemed to really consider his bloody state for the first time. "Don't worry, it's not mine."

Winking at me, he walked over to a large armoire in the corner, opened it, and perused the assortment of weapons inside. He kept his favorites in there, the ones holding sentimental value or imbued with powers, and now he grabbed a big sword with a scabbard adorned with silver swirls.

He fastened it to his belt and then came over to steal a slice of toast out of the bread basket.

I'd recovered from my shock enough to blurt out, "What happened?"

He chewed, entirely unconcerned by my dismay. "I bathed in the blood of your enemies."

I stared at him. "When you said that the other day, I thought that was a metaphor."

He stole a forkful of hash browns. "I never joke when it comes to blood."

"*Azazel.*" It was a half whine, half growl.

One corner of his mouth quirked up. "Now that," he said and pointed at me with the fork in between big bites of my breakfast, "is dangerous, you saying my name like that. Makes me want to stay and do things with you that'll make you keep addressing me in that tone, but unfortunately, I don't have the time."

He shoveled more food into his mouth.

"What's going on?" I asked, a tremble in my voice.

"I made it clear to Inachiel that I don't appreciate the way he and his ilk talked to you."

Involuntarily, my gaze once more roved over the blood clinging to every part of him. "Is he still alive?" I whispered.

"Oh, yes." He waved that away with the fork. "Only part of it is his. Most of it is from his guards." He set down the fork, still chewing, and turned to go.

He'd cleared my plate, the ill-mannered brute.

"Wait!" I called out.

He paused in the doorway. "Do you really want a kiss goodbye?" He indicated the bloody mess he was.

"It's not that. I just—where are you going?" I knew he always had lots to take care of, being a high-ranking demon in charge of a territory, but this seemed…different somehow.

He sent me an insouciant smirk. "This war is not going to fight itself."

"War?" I choked out. "I thought you just had a fight with Inachiel? Isn't it settled now?"

Something glittered in his eyes, shadows pulsing around his shoulders. "It would have been settled," he said, his voice lethally soft, "had he apologized or simply taken the beating. But he said some things—about you—that warrant a stronger response from me."

"What did he say?" I wasn't sure I wanted to know, but the question was out of my mouth before I could stop it.

He blinked slowly, his black lashes lowering and rising over eyes of lightning. "Words I won't repeat in front of you, ever, so do not ask me again."

I swallowed hard.

"All you need to know is that I'll make him regret every single one of his words, and I won't rest until I have taken everything he built for himself and reduced him to sniveling snot."

My eyes widened. "Okay," I squeaked. It seemed like a huge overreaction, but I wasn't the one calling the shots here.

He sent me a last, lingering look full of heat and promise, and then he was off.

I turned back to the table to find two of Vengeance's heads fighting to lick my plate. The third was chewing something that could have been the last slice of toast.

My entire breakfast was gone.

Just as well. I wasn't sure I was up for eating anything anyway, what with the smell of blood hanging in the air and turning my stomach.

AZAZEL WAS OUT A LOT AFTER THAT, COMING HOME AT ODD hours, always a bit worn and with a hardness to him that only gentled at my touch. He wouldn't talk much about what was going on, but he also didn't seem worried. No, he was full of easy shrugs and confident smirks, completely sure he'd win.

Of course, given my brain, I worried enough for the both of us. Every time he left, my heart seized with fear.

Now, after I'd woken up once more alone in an empty bed, I opened the door leading out of our quarters and almost collided with a large demon standing right in front of the rooms.

"Oh," I said, stumbling back into Vengeance huffing behind me. "Didn't see you there. Sorry."

Getting a good look at my visitor, I realized it wasn't just one but two demons, one male and one female. I'd seen them before. These were among Azazel's most trusted soldiers. The fact that Vengeance was utterly relaxed behind me confirmed they didn't pose a threat.

At my mumbled apology, they both bowed deeply at the waist. "My lady."

Dammit, I *still* cringed at that.

I eyed them. They eyed me.

I shifted on my feet. "Uh, did you want anything?"

"No, my lady," the male demon said. His long brown hair was pulled back in a man bun, and he wore fighting leathers, like his female companion. He held his hand out to the side, indicating for me to go. "Please."

"O-kay." Giving them a bewildered look, I turned and walked down the hallway, Vengeance trudging at my side.

The demons followed on my heels.

I stopped dead in my tracks. They halted as well.

Pivoting on the balls of my feet, I speared them with a look. "What are you doing?"

"Guarding you, my lady," the female demon said.

I gestured at Vengeance. "I have a guard."

"Lord Azazel ordered additional protection for you."

"Oh." Crap. How bad was the situation when he felt I wasn't safe anymore with just Vengeance to defend me?

More worry wormed its way into my gut, and I started walking again, heading for the library.

EVER SINCE THAT DAY, I WAS FLANKED BY TWO FULL-BLOOD demon bodyguards whenever I left our rooms, all of them following me in unnerving silence and armed to the teeth. And they weren't the only ones decked out in weapons. Where previously, only the half-bloods walked around the house fully armed, now everyone carried.

Well, everyone except for the merihem, the little servant demon creatures scuttling around. I guessed they didn't have to worry about being cut down or caught in a skirmish. They seemed to occupy a rather weird position in demon society, a bit removed from all the bullshit the full- and half-bloods had to deal with.

Seeing all the demons armed and everybody being on high alert did a number on my nerves, and it got to the point where I stayed in our quarters for the most part in order to avoid the obvious signs of warfare out there. Fingers in my ears and head in the sand, that was me, right there.

Because what else was there for me to do other than shutting this out? There was nothing, literally nothing, I could contribute to this. I wasn't a warrior, I couldn't fight—what little training I had was probably just enough to buy me a few minutes in a real attack—and I certainly wasn't a war strategist.

I felt utterly useless, and it grated on me.

It wasn't that I had a deep, burning craving to go out and swing a sword around or whatever. But I found myself loathing the fact that I was sitting on my ass like a damned damsel while my beloved fought a war on my behalf.

There was an insistent voice in my head whispering that *I* should be the one spilling blood to gain respect. It should be *my* prowess proving my worth.

I had no idea where those sentiments came from.

I was, by nature, not a violent person. Confrontation made me uneasy, and I actively tried to avoid conflicts. My mother had once signed me up for self-defense lessons, and I'd spent most of the class apologizing for every rare hit I scored on my instructor.

So why I heard this niggling voice berating me for not joining in the fray, I had no clue. Because what would I do on a battlefield? Kill my opponent with my social awkwardness? *Death by schadenfreude it shall be!*

Yeah, all of that contributed to me not being in the best mood as I lounged on the couch in one of the sitting rooms in our quarters, reading a popular fantasy romance and living vicariously through the main female character, who—in direct contrast with me—actually knew how to wield a sword. A real one, and not just the euphemism for a beloved male appendage.

So when Azmodea breezed into the room, dressed as always in glittering finery that hugged her generous curves like a lover, I heaved a sigh of relief at the welcome distraction.

"Darling!" she cooed and gave me a kiss on each cheek, then held me at arm's length by the shoulders to get a good look at me. She clucked her tongue. "Ack, you look positively broody. Not enough orgasms? He's been neglecting you, huh? Want me to send someone over? I know just the guy."

"No!" I choked on my laugh. "No, thank you, there's no need."

"Right, right." She plopped down beside me and rolled her gray eyes, the same color as her brother's. "You two and your eccentric idea of exclusivity."

I gave her some good side-eye.

Ignoring my look, she flipped her copper-colored hair over her shoulder, summoned a platter of fresh fruit, and began to plop cherries into her mouth. "So, things with Inachiel are heating up. And not in an interesting way, if you catch my drift."

Did I ever.

My face must have shown some of the complicated feelings churning in my gut, because she tsked and said, "Now, don't feel bad about that, hon. Az has been eyeing Inachiel's dominion for some time now. Seizing his territory was the next step up the ladder anyway. My brother has always been driven, you know."

I nodded, remembering how Azazel had told me of the way he'd quickly risen in the ranks after his grandmother Daevi had taken him in, fueled by brutal determination to prove his worth and become powerful.

Azmodea shot me a look from underneath her dark lashes. "You just focused all that ambition for him. Catalyzed all of his pent up rage."

I grimaced. "I'm not sure that's a good thing."

"Oh, but it is." She pointed at me with an orange slice. "I haven't seen him this motivated in ages. He still has a bone to pick with quite a few folks, and there's something to be said for blood therapy."

I raised a brow. "I don't think killing counts as therapy."

"Eh." She waved that away. "We hardly ever kill each other. Maiming and dismembering, yes. Outright killing? Not so much."

"Really?"

She shrugged. "Archdemons usually turn a blind eye to any infighting within their dominion, because why not? Let them have at it. Keeps things interesting. But that only applies as long as there's no loss of life. No archdemon will take kindly to losing forces because of internal conflicts. If push comes to shove, all of us need to be able to show up for a fight against another archdemon."

I pursed my lips. "So that's why Daevi hasn't interfered?"

"Exactly right." She chewed on an apple slice. "She's aware of their fighting, make no mistake. But unless they start dropping bodies left and right, she won't step in. Like I said, a bit of quarreling is good. It makes sure none of us becomes complacent, and it's another form of entertainment."

I wrinkled my nose, and she laughed.

"You're so cute with your delicate human sensibilities. Just wait a few hundred years, and you'll learn to appreciate blood sport just like we do."

That…was kind of what I was afraid of.

"So, if a demon is really ambitious," I said, picking at a thread on the sofa, "and they work their way up to the top, doesn't that make them a threat to their archdemon at some point?"

Azmodea studied me with eyes that saw a tad too much. "Daevi won't harm him," she said after a moment, having guessed the intent of my question. "He'll likely be a seraph directly under her for some time until he makes a move. Not on her," she added when I raised my eyebrows.

She shook her head. "He's indebted to her for taking him in when he wanted to escape Lucifer's court. He'd never repay her for that by usurping her position as archdemon. No, if and when he's ready to move up, he'll take out another archdemon."

My eyes widened, my heartbeat picking up at the mere thought of that big a move. Archdemons were so incredibly powerful, many of them original fallen angels who'd ruled directly under Lucifer since the war between Heaven and Hell. From what I'd gathered, there wasn't often a change in their position. They'd fight each other for lands and souls, yes, but it was rare that an archdemon was toppled and another demon rose up to take their place.

The coil of anxiety in me made it hard to breathe. Dammit, I wasn't cut out for war and political games. I'd be absolutely fine just chilling with my nose in a book while the world out there did its thing. In my previous life, I'd always envisioned I'd someday end up the proverbial cat lady, unbothered by what went on outside my little circle of feline companionship.

And while I did have a cat now, albeit a surly, half-sophisticated hellcat with a penchant for spitting out fires, I also had a three-headed hellhound, a hot—if bloodthirsty—demon husband, and an assortment of more or less terrifying demons-in-law, not to mention I'd somehow found myself the center of a bloody territorial conflict.

One year in, and I still wasn't quite as used to all of this as I wanted to be.

"Say," Azmodea purred, squinting at me, "is there something different about you?"

I sat up straighter. Was this about the kernel of Lilith's power inside me? Was it actually noticeable?

I cleared my throat. "Why? Do you sense something... different about me?"

She narrowed her eyes and pinned me with a stare. "It's definitely not good sex because apparently you're not getting any with Az cavorting on the battlefield."

My face heated, and I resisted the urge to defend my— still definitely mind-blowing—sex life to my sister-in-law. "It's not that," I said weakly.

She leaned in and sniffed at me. Actually *sniffed*, like some predatory beast sampling my scent. "You're not pregnant, are you?"

"Good God, no." I reared back.

Having a baby was absolutely not on my radar, and I was more than glad about my IUD from my previous life that was still dutifully doing its job of keeping me kid- and care-free. I'd have to replace it at some point, though how I would do that when my body wouldn't be able to go to Earth, I had no idea. *Guess I'll cross that interdimensional bridge when I get there.*

Azmodea was just opening her mouth to say something when a knock sounded from the other room, at the door leading to the hallway.

"Come in," I yelled, not inclined to get up just now.

The door opened and in stepped a female demon I'd seen among Azazel's higher command structure. Dressed in fighting leathers, much like almost everyone I saw these days, she bowed deeply at the waist, her braided blond hair catching the light of the torches.

"My lady," she said as she straightened. Her gaze fell on Azmodea, and she bowed again. "Lady Azmodea." She focused on me once more, her eyes shrewd. "Lord Azazel has requested your presence. Please come with me."

CHAPTER 10

My eyebrows crept up. "My presence?" I echoed dully. "Where?"

"At the front. If you please?" She held her arm out to the side, indicating for me to come.

I exchanged a shocked glance with Azmodea. She shrugged, unperturbed by this development.

Clearing my throat, I said, "Okay. What's the code phrase?"

When things had heated up with the war, Azazel had suggested using a special word or sentence to check the trustworthiness of someone delivering a message or coming to escort me somewhere in his absence. I'd chuckled and called him paranoid, but to be honest, it wasn't that much of a stretch to think someone might infiltrate his security at some point. His people were good, but everyone had a breaking point.

So we'd settled on a code phrase. One I had come up with. Only Azazel and I knew it, and he'd only give it personally to whomever he sent with either a message or an order to take me somewhere. After which, we'd change the code phrase to something new.

A muscle ticked in the demon's jaw, and she shifted slightly on her feet. "Must I, my lady?" she asked quietly.

I narrowed my eyes. "I insist."

Clearly pained, she sent her gaze to the ceiling and said, "Hocus pocus, butt full of locusts."

Next to me, Azmodea doubled over with laughter.

I stifled some giggles of my own as I rose from the sofa. "Thank you—what's your name again? I'm sorry I forgot."

"Shemyaza, my lady."

"Thank you, Shemyaza. Let's go."

I turned to Azmodea, who got to her feet and gave me a kiss on each cheek again.

"Say hi to him from me." She put one hand on her hip. "Tell him that waging a war is not an excuse to skip our dinner dates."

"Will do."

Giving her a smile and a little wave, I then followed Shemyaza out into the hallway. My two demon bodyguards fell into step behind me, and Vengeance trotted right next to me.

Instead of going down to the ground level and leaving through the giant double doors of the entrance hall, Shemyaza led me to a large balcony jutting out from a big hallway, the small windows reinforced with bars and—what I now noticed after living in Hell for a while—powerful demon magic.

On the balcony, Shemyaza stopped and turned to me. "Ready, my lady?"

I eyed the ever-stormy, gloomy sky, and then I faced Vengeance.

"You'll need to stay," I said, scratching her middle head

under her maw. "We'll be flying, and you can't follow me, okay?"

Vengeance whined and pawed the floor, her massive claws raking the stone and leaving marks.

"I know," I cooed. "I know, girl. I'll be back soon. You just wait here."

One of her heads tried to slobber me, and I jerked back just in time.

"No licking!" I pointed at her with a finger. "We talked about the licking."

More whining accompanied three pairs of eyes looking at me with a dog's best pleading gaze.

I covered my eyes and turned around. "You guys never agree on anything," I groused and waved my hand toward the hellhound, "but in this, you're suddenly all aligned? Hell save me from a triple begging look."

Someone cleared their throat, and I peered around my fingers to see Shemyaza giving me a flat stare.

"Right," I said. "Yes, I'm coming. Sorry."

I stepped up to Shemyaza, self-consciousness gnawing at my composure. No one but Azazel had ever flown me anywhere. This was going to be awkward, but at least she was female. It'd feel a lot weirder to hop up into some guy demon's arms.

Clearing my throat, I gestured between her and me. "So how do we… Do I just—"

She sent me a look mostly used on children and idiots, and then she simply swooped me up without further ado, one arm around my back, the other supporting me under my knees. Instinctively, I looped my arms around her neck.

Ugh, okay, this was hella awkward. She'd just hefted me up like I weighed nothing, and she didn't even look strained.

Meanwhile, I'd struggle to pick up a pile of ten hardcovers and lug them around.

With a whoosh, her wings appeared, a shiny onyx threaded through with flames. I didn't often get the chance to see other demons' wings, and now I ogled hers like a feather perv. Pretty, but not as stunning as Azazel's.

But I guessed I was a bit biased in that regard.

Without a word of warning, Shemyaza took off, the kick start jostling me in her arms. Hot air rushed around us, tangling my loose hair, and flecks of the ever-present ash of Hell's landscape soon dusted my skin. I glanced down to see the sprawling mass of Azazel's fortress-like mansion zoom away, the distant lightning illuminating the walls and grounds around it for split seconds.

I'd never get my fill of this view, of taking in the world—even if it was the desolate scenery of Hell—from high above. The few times I'd flown anywhere in my previous life, I'd fought to get a window seat and then peered down for as long as no clouds obscured my view. It was endlessly fascinating to see everything reduced to miniature size, so small and yet so grand at the same time, to gaze out at the infinite expanse of sky and horizon. There was a feeling of freedom in that, and I'd never envied birds more than in those moments when I'd sat with my nose pressed to the cold pane of an airplane's window.

Of course, the feeling was quite a bit different when I wasn't perched safely in a seat with walls around me, but rather, exposed to the elements, with a death grip on the demon who literally held my life in her hands right now. In stark contrast to when Azazel flew my spirit form to a hell-gate to visit Earth, whenever he—or now, Shemyaza—carried my actual body anywhere, I'd truly die if they dropped me.

So the amazing view and awesome feeling of being up in the air was accompanied by a very visceral fear of tumbling to my death.

Wasn't it wonderful, living with anxiety?

We flew over the dark, craggy landscape, with the random wildfires of Hell and the glowing mushroom plants the only blips of light in the gloom. Distant howls of hounds rose every once in a while, making me shiver down to my soul.

I loved Vengeance, and I'd gotten quite comfortable with her, but hearing her or one of her fellow canines' chilling howls always reminded me just how different they all truly were from regular animals. That sound, like a thousand screams all wrapped into one, a lament of death and destruction, a symphony of bloodcurdling horror, it raised all the hairs on my body and made me choke back tears.

And then there were the screams of the sinners.

Quieter than the baying and howling of the hounds, but all the more striking for the true pain and suffering they bore, the wails shifted here and there on the wind, gone one moment and hitting me the next with a sharp gust.

No matter how much I braced myself, I was never prepared to hear it.

On and on we flew, the distance reminding me of that time we'd gone to Lucifer's palace for the Fall Festival. We were definitely flying out of Azazel's territory, then. Over the past months, we'd gone to some of his allies' gatherings at their estates, flying for an extended time to get there.

Finally, Shemyaza began a descent toward a smattering of lights ahead of us. As we got closer, I could make out the confines of a large courtyard, lit by torches, a crowd of what looked like dozens of demons within.

They cleared a circular space for us to land, and

Shemyaza touched down in the middle, my two bodyguards directly behind her. She set me down, and I stood on shaky legs, peering around at the demons while avoiding direct eye contact. My heart pounded something fierce, the impressions from the flight and the unnerving attention from pretty much all assembled demons jacking up my nerves. They were all clad in warriors' clothing, leather and metal, weapons clinking as they shifted.

And contrary to the demons I'd seen in Azazel's house, these didn't only dress the part but also showed the signs of recent battle—nicks and scrapes in their armor, and, of course, blood.

So much blood.

It was disorienting. Staggering. The sight, the smell, the…reality of it.

I'd only ever seen "warriors" on the screen, and while some of the shows and movies did an excellent job of portraying the unvarnished, horrific truth of war and bloodshed—looking at you, Battle of the Bastards from *Game of Thrones*—actually standing just a few feet from a crowd of real fighters who bore the evidence of genuine battle…it made me sway on my feet with the sensory impact of it.

"Greet your lady," Shemyaza called out from behind me.

One by one, all the demons who were on their feet bowed to me, some deep from the waist, some inclining their heads, indicating their different ranks with respect to mine. In terms of unnerving, I wasn't sure which was worse—the horribly real sights, sounds, and smells of war, or a crowd of battle-hardened, powerful demons bowing to me like I deserved it.

There was a commotion to my right, someone calling for Lord Azazel, and then the rows of demons parted. I noticed, for the first time, that many of the demons were kneeling, some bowing their heads, some looking up at me and the newcomers through blood-tangled hair and swollen eyes.

I swallowed hard, a coil pulling tight in my stomach.

When Azazel prowled down the opening in the crowd, I almost didn't recognize him. Like that one time in our quarters, he was splattered with the crimson proof of a brutal fight, but what made my breath hitch and my heart stumble in confusion was the look on his face.

His beauty had always been like a knife-edge, his features stunning in the way one would imagine the angels described in scriptures of old, with a sense of divine allure that was unearthly, glorious, and magnificent in a terrifying way, for it was so far beyond human imperfection. It was the kind of beauty that would bring people to their knees, weeping as they beheld that which seared their eyes with its light.

I'd seen him boiling with anger, his skin cracking to reveal part of his fiery nature beneath. I'd seen him burn with barely held-back fury as he looked upon Lucifer.

Now, though, a coldness lay upon him that was carved with an almost casual cruelty. He was every inch the victorious conqueror, all hard lines and cutting edges, his every step imbued with such confidence and self-assurance that it made the small, primitive parts of me want to shrink back in preemptive submission. Power writhed around him, drenching the air, glowing in his eyes, as he surveyed the kneeling demons with detached satisfaction.

His gaze found me, and I startled. Such steel in that look, no hint of the man who'd laughed with me, who'd caressed my body and kissed away my tears. He seemed like a stranger, one born of battle and blood and the rapture of raw violence.

It wasn't that I tended to forget that he was a demon. I'd

never mistake him for human, was always aware that he was something other, something far older and cut from a different cloth.

But I guessed I'd gotten kind of used to that subtler sense of his other nature, even to the point where I could glance at his collection of severed wings and not feel a frisson of fear anymore.

This right here, though, this moment, the way he held himself, the primal power radiating off him and the vicious gleam in his eyes, brought back the full awareness that he was so much more than my human mind could really come to terms with.

I couldn't have kept the tremors from taking over my limbs. They came from deep within me, from a place where the collective instincts of mankind all froze in terror of a being that our lore had immortalized in thousands of stories.

Azazel raised a hand and beckoned me closer. "Come here."

Swallowing past the tight knot in my throat, I walked over to him. Stepping to the side, he revealed a demon kneeling right next to him, and it was only when Azazel lifted the other demon's head by laying the tip of his sword under his chin that I recognized him as Inachiel.

A bloodied and beat-up Inachiel, his once beautiful face now carved with slashes and painted scarlet. His green eyes flickered to me for a second, then lowered quickly.

"Apologize." Azazel's voice was as soft as a whisper, yet it somehow carried all across the courtyard.

The muscles in Inachiel's throat moved as he swallowed hard. "I apologize, Lady Zoe, for all the slights and insults I have dealt you, directly and indirectly, and for treating you with ill-advised disrespect. I acknowledge your rank alongside Lord Azazel's, and I ask your forgiveness for the hurt I caused you."

I inhaled sharply. All right, as far as apologies went, that one was top-notch. I wasn't sure of the protocol here, but it was probably a good move to nod and say that I accepted his—

"Wings out," Azazel said with chilling calm.

I closed my mouth with an audible click, and the words on the tip of my tongue turned back around to choke me. He wouldn't. Would he?

Inachiel's jaw hardened, and he closed his eyes. No wings.

Azazel grabbed Inachiel by the throat, power pulsing in the air. Leaning down, he growled, "Out with them."

Inachiel strained, clearly resisting whatever magic was flowing from Azazel to force his wings out, but he only lasted a few seconds. With a grunt, he jerked, and his wings materialized behind his back.

Azazel casually sheathed his sword and then laid one hand on Inachiel's shoulder. With the other, he grasped the wing on that side hard around the edge where it grew out of the body, and the next moment, he tore it right off.

Inachiel screamed. Droplets of blood flew through the air, one of them hitting me right on my cheek. I reared back.

Memories of a scene just like this hurtled to the forefront of my mind—Lucifer ripping the wings off one of the demons who'd dared start an insurrection at his Fall Festival. And much like back then, when I'd been forced to witness the Devil casually dismembering someone, my stomach bubbled with acid at the sight.

Azazel handed the blood-dripping wing to one of his soldiers standing by and then moved on to the other shoulder. Inachiel panted, hunched over, his scarlet-drenched hair hanging around his face like a macabre curtain.

Despite the storm brewing in my gut, the revulsion closing my throat, I couldn't wrench my eyes away from the horror show in front of me.

Azazel grabbed Inachiel's remaining wing, his other hand applying counter pressure on the shoulder, and with smooth efficiency, he tore off that wing as well. Inachiel's scream curdled my stomach. Bile rose in my throat.

"Apology accepted," Azazel said and then signaled his attendant to take the second wing. Turning back to Inachiel, he continued, "I strip you of your rank and all of your titles. Your lands will be gifted to those loyal in my service, and your possessions will be seized, the souls in your pits added to those in my care. Your power will feed into mine." He stared at him for a moment, dark energy coiling and uncoiling around his shoulders, down his arms. Then he said, his voice devoid of all warmth, "You may join the principalities in the outer Burning Sands."

I flinched. *Principality*. The lowest rank among demons— and angels. Before, Inachiel had been a cherub, much like Azazel, enjoying the third-highest rank below the archdemons themselves.

While Inachiel trembled, still kneeling, Azazel turned to his attendant and took the wings from him. Carrying them draped over both of his hands, he approached me. I startled and took an involuntary step back, my wide eyes locked onto those blood-sprinkled feathers.

Azazel's voice echoed in my thoughts. *Take them. They are your due.*

My breath caught, my heart racing. I couldn't even formulate a mental response to his prompt, what with most of my energy going into keeping the bile contained to the back of my throat. I glanced at Azazel, standing there in front of me and holding out the freshly severed wings expectantly, and then my eyes darted to the crowd around us. They all stared at me, waiting.

This was part of the power play, I realized. Part of the message Azazel was sending with this whole bloody spectacle, the reason he'd called me here. He could have simply brought those wings back home to me, or maybe just hung them up on his collection wall without ever showing them to me. Not that I cared.

But everyone else did.

That was the crux of it. Hell was all about rules, reputation, and power. Quarrels and conflicts were best settled with political maneuvering or outright violence, and both benefited from the added dose of public humiliation to underscore a win.

Handing the severed wings of a once high-ranking demon to the human he'd mocked, which had lost him his wings, and doing so not just in the presence of said demon, but also in front of dozens of others, among them his defeated warriors…that was peak Hell humiliation, in all its merciless brutality.

So I understood just fine the role I was expected to play. I understood it, even if the thought of touching those wings made my skin crawl.

And because I didn't want to sabotage Azazel's efforts to cement my rank and position, I stepped forward on shaking legs, raised my arms, and accepted the still-blood-dripping wings.

Surprisingly not as heavy as I'd thought, they nevertheless made me stumble forward a step to keep my balance. Smooth plumage slid over my fingers, coated in warm wetness. The weight of muscles, bones, flesh and sinews, of blood and hundreds of feathers lay upon my arms, still warm, and so very, very real.

My gaze snagged on the torn-off ends of the wings—on the long string of what looked like a sinew dangling from the fleshy wound that was *still bleeding*.

That was it. That visual did me in.

With a heaving lurch, I emptied my nausea-stricken stomach right onto Inachiel's severed wings.

CHAPTER 11

" I mean," I said, picking at the cuticle of my thumb, "I
guess it could have been worse."

How? Mephisto spoke into my mind.

He was lounging on the chair opposite mine in one of the
living rooms in my quarters. After I'd decided to stay with
Azazel at last year's Fall Festival, my darling demon had
done some remodeling in the rooms that made up his and
my respective private spaces. The two bedrooms had been
combined into one, but he'd kept both bathrooms so I could
spread all my stuff out to my heart's content. The sitting
room right next to our bedroom was now the main living
room, often used to receive guests with whom we were on
the friendliest terms—like Azmodea and Mammon—but the
sprawling rooms of my old quarters were also still in use, as
even comfier lounging spaces.

Honestly, I often wasn't sure what to do with that much
space. *Pray tell, which one of our hundreds of salons shall I use
today?*

More often than not, I'd retreat to those old rooms of
mine when I was upset or needed to hide away for a bit.

Like now, after I'd come home from that disaster of a wing-chopping show. Shemyaza had flown me back here, Azazel remaining behind to take care of whatever needed taking care of after a successful seizure of another demon's territory. Maybe there were some more wings to rip off.

With a shudder, I remembered how many demons had been kneeling. They were obviously Inachiel's warriors, and they'd undoubtedly be punished right alongside him.

So now I sat here, trying to calm my stomach with a mug of chamomile tea, with only my enigmatic hellcat to talk to. Which wasn't going well.

"I don't know," I said and threw my hands up. "I guess I could have vomited right into Inachiel's face?"

Mephisto swished his tail. *Why are you upset?*

I speared him with a look. "Seriously? I just explained that I puked all over the freshly severed wings of the demon my husband had just subjugated on my behalf. You know, the wings I had been handed as a *gift*, to be accepted as a sign of higher status?"

Covering them in vomit sends a great message.

"Excuse me?"

Child. He gave me a condescending look out of those yellow eyes. *Have you no sense? How do you even survive without a minimum of strategic thinking?*

"Barely," I muttered.

I can see that. He licked his paw.

"Why do I even put up with you?"

I am the shining jewel among Hell's creatures, and you are blessed to breathe in my presence. He flicked one ear. *Also, my fur is soft and sleek, and petting me alleviates your anxiety.*

I sighed. "Right, so why is vomiting on those wings a good thing?"

Because it is an exceptional display of your disdain for the former owner of those wings. The only stronger demonstration of your view on his rank versus your own would have been if you'd urinated on them.

"Ew, Mephisto," I said with a grimace.

Covering the wings in a bodily fluid of yours shows ownership —your scent marking—but with that bodily fluid being vomit, you also display a certain amount of scorn. You're marking it as yours, yes, but in a way that degrades it.

"Okay, this just keeps getting worse."

I am simply saying that you acted in accordance with ancient laws of dominance.

"Just stop." I rubbed my closed eyes, my stomach still in knots.

Talking with Mephisto was *not* helping. If anything, I felt shittier than before.

God, I needed my best friend. Missing Taylor was a constant ping of pain in my chest, but in moments like this, it truly hurt on a soul level. I needed to talk to her, to call her up and just word-vomit—ha!—everything that happened and that made me feel like crap, and just telling her and having her listen with her expressive personality would make it all better. And she usually had the best advice, or at least the best commiserating things to say.

But my BFF was a whole dimension away, and I couldn't just zip over there and drop by for a visit. My birthday was coming up soon, and I was planning to have a celebratory visit to Earth on that day, which meant I wasn't able to go see Taylor earlier than that. The connection between my body—which had to stay in Hell—and my spirit form was tenuous, and apparently it might break if I remained on Earth too long or if I went there too frequently.

Now, what exactly *too long* and *too frequently* meant, not even Azazel could explain to me. As he'd told me more than once, there wasn't really a precedent for my situation. Well, there was Lilith, but seeing as she hadn't been to Earth in centuries, and there wasn't much information on how long she'd usually stayed, Azazel had nothing much to go on in order to gauge at what point the connection between my body and my spirit form might sever.

Demons could stay on Earth for a couple of days at most before they had to go back to Hell. They didn't have the issue with their bodies and spirits separating—apparently, their bodies *were* their spirits, the two forms inseparably linked, contrary to the metaphysical makeup of humans. But for demons, staying too long on Earth would mean they'd grow weaker and eventually lose their powers, turning them human for all intents and purposes. They drew their energy from Hell itself, and they had to go back to their home realm in order to stay healthy and powerful.

So going by that example, and paring it down a bit, Azazel guessed that staying longer than a day on Earth would likely be dangerous for me. And since demons had to remain in Hell for about two weeks after a one-week trip to Earth, he extrapolated that there should be about a month in between visits for me.

Yeah, there was a lot of guesswork involved, based on hunches and not really applicable examples.

All of which resulted in the consequence that I had limited means of communication with Taylor.

And while I did still have my phone and was able to keep it alive by charging it on one of the rickety outlets, there was no connection between Hell and Earth. So as much as I treasured my phone for the fact that it held a crap ton of photos and videos from my previous life, in addition to all my favorite music, it was quite useless for communication these days.

Which left me with the only other way to share my latest helltastic adventure with Taylor—writing her a letter. Like in the days of yore, before newfangled inventions like phones or internet. Or even just telegrams.

I swear, every time I sat down to write her a letter, I mentally transformed into one of those young women who'd been shipped from Europe to the colonies to marry some stranger, penning a report to her family an ocean away, hoping her epistle made it past the treacherous waters of the Atlantic. I was half tempted to ask Azazel for an oil lamp and a quill-and-ink set to complete the mood.

Alas, I wrote on regular paper, with a regular pen, albeit one that glided over the page with the perfect flow. It was a special kind of satisfaction to write with an excellent pen.

Giving Mephisto a last grumpy look, I got up and walked over to the shelf along the back wall. I pulled out the open box where I kept all my writing stuff and almost dropped it at the sight within. Stifling my startled sound with a hand over my mouth, I took a closer look at the box—at the small, fluffy, black ball of fur inside.

The ball of fur moved.

Two tiny yellow eyes blinked open and regarded me with sleepy curiosity.

"What!" I squeaked and flailed at the box. "What is this?"

I turned to Mephisto and gestured wildly at the thing inside.

Ah. He sniffed the air. *That is one of mine.*

"What do you mean, one of yours?"

The black ball of fur unfurled and stretched, its spine arching gracefully. Two small wings spread from its back, a sleek tail curling in the air.

"It's a kitten?" I didn't know my voice could go that high. Honestly.

Are you in the habit of asking redundant questions?

Ugh. That judgmental hellcat.

The kitten put its tiny paws on the edge of the box and leaned up to sniff in my direction. Its ears looked far too large for its head, resembling bat ears even more so than Mephisto's. Its little black nose twitched as it sampled my scent, and a moment later, it pawed at me.

"Ohmygod," I gushed in a high-pitched baby voice. "You are so cute! How are you so cute? Who gave you permission?"

She doesn't need permission, Mephisto said—as usual, totally oblivious to figures of speech or modern slang. *And she's not cute. She's a perfect killing machine in training.*

I whipped my head around to look at him. "So you're training her? Where did she come from?"

A beat of silence from my snippy feline friend. Then: *Given all the copulative activities you indulge in with your demon, I find it hard to believe that you would be ignorant as to where offspring comes from.*

"Oh my God." I facepalmed hard.

Invoking that deity won't help you here, Mephisto remarked.

I swear, he was doing that deadpan, unintentional humor on purpose.

The kitten had, in the meantime, climbed out of the box and up my arm, and with a few cute flaps of her wings, she now sat on my shoulder, and I was sent straight to cuteness heaven.

"You are so adorable," I tweeted. "Ow!"

Little Hellkitty was chomping on my hair.

"What's her name?" I asked Mephisto while I was trying to disentangle the tiny feline's claws from my locks.

She doesn't have one.

"What? Why not?"

We do not give the cubs names until they reach maturity. Why waste a good name on something that runs a high risk of dying?

"Excuse me?" I grabbed the kitten out of reflex, hugging her to me in order to protect her from all harm.

Little Hellkitty bit me for my effort.

Hell is a harsh place to grow up, Mephisto simply said. *Only a tiny percentage of our young make it.*

I whimpered and hugged Hellkitty closer. She clawed at me.

"This one will," I said, conviction in my voice. I lifted the kitten up and looked her in the eye. "You hear me? Nothing bad will happen to you here. I won't allow it."

You are not qualified to take over her training and protection, Mephisto purred. *Your hunting skills are lackluster, and you vomit at the sight of severed limbs.*

"That was one time," I hissed back.

The kitten escaped my hold—scratching up my arms in the process—and jumped to the floor. Going straight for one of the couches, she clawed up the side good and well, her little wings flexing while she did.

"I'm gonna need some scratching posts," I muttered as I went to retrieve my box of writing supplies and then sat down on the couch. "So where's the mom?"

Around somewhere, was Mephisto's nonchalant reply. *Taking care of the others.*

"So you guys split the child-rearing?"

Among most felines, it was usually the mother who took over the entire care of the young, with the male happily oblivious to his offspring. Lions were a notable example, but even among them, the females were the ones who really cared for the cubs, with the fathers just hanging around and maybe playing with the little ones at the most.

Mephisto flicked one ear. *It increases the likelihood of my genes being passed on.*

"Ah, yes, I can see how you'd put in the effort if it means your superior genetic material has a chance to dominate the world."

Exactly right. He gave me a smug look.

That hellcat really didn't understand sarcasm.

I was just getting my writing supplies out of the box to finally write that letter to Taylor when something dropped into my lap. I screamed and flailed.

This time, though, it wasn't some dead vermin brought as a gift. No, it was another ball of kitten fluff, fallen straight from one of the rafters under the ceiling. After a second of stillness—the kitten seemed just as surprised as I was by that sudden maneuver—it bolted away, making me yelp at the sting of its claws as it scrambled off my lap.

"What the—" I raised my arms and waved them around helplessly.

Mephisto's yellow eyes casually tracked to the ceiling. *She brought another.*

"She? The mother?" I craned my head and peered up as well, catching a glimpse of a black tail disappearing into the gloomy depths of the ceiling.

Obviously, Mephisto drawled.

"What's her name?"

Khailaw.

"So, you two have a little thing going on?" I waggled my brows and winked at him.

Are you having a facial seizure?

"Never mind," I muttered and returned my attention to

my letter writing. "Just so you know," I said as I set everything up, "I'm going to name those kittens. They can't run around nameless in anticipation of their untimely deaths. I won't have it."

Fine. He narrowed his glowing eyes. *But they will receive proper names when they are of age.*

"What do you mean, proper names?" I put both hands on my hips and glared at him. "Like the names I'll give them will be unsuitable?"

Did you or did you not name the cat you had on Earth when you were younger Mr. Fuzzypants?

I snickered, then caught myself and schooled my face into a serious expression again. "Look, his markings made it look like he had pants on, and his fur was very fuzzy, so..."

I rest my case. Your names for my offspring will not be permanent.

"Whatever," I murmured and bent to write Taylor all about my most recent predicament, which...I didn't feel quite as bad about anymore. I paused and glanced at Mephisto casually grooming himself on the chair, and then at the kittens currently chasing each other over the furniture.

A small smile stole onto my face, my chest infusing with warmth. Yeah, that oppressive weight and nausea I'd felt earlier had all but dissipated, thanks to one surly hellcat and his rambunctious progeny.

Once done with the letter, I called for Dariel, one of the full-blood demons in Azazel's employ. Insanely handsome like all of his demonic kind, he was more broad-shouldered than most others, though, and apparently one of the fastest fliers among his peers.

Which made him the perfect choice to deliver my letters.

Given the lack of any kind of automated messaging system between Hell and Earth, letters and such had to be hand-delivered by someone, and full-blood demons were the most suitable for that task. Their wings meant they could easily bridge great distances at a high speed, contrary to half-bloods, who had to use more regular types of transportation. Half-bloods were good for scouting, patrolling, and catching souls in the immediate vicinity of their sire's hellgate, or for missions that required a longer stay on Earth, as they weren't bound by the same time constraints as full-bloods.

Of course, the task of hand-delivering a letter between a human and her human friend was kind of demeaning for any full-blood demon. The entire thing took them hours, traveling from Azazel's domain to the one with a hellgate closest to Sydney, and then from there to Taylor's apartment. Elerion was the demon with a portal right near where Tay lived, but Azazel tried not to ask him for use of his hellgate too often, as Elerion was a bit of a sneaky fucker, and traveling through his domain came with strings attached. So most of the time, the demon chosen to bring my message to Tay had to go a longer way around, hours upon hours, all for one measly letter to a human on Earth.

Naturally, anytime I called upon one of them to deliver my letter, the demon I'd picked was bursting with enthusiasm. Not.

Dariel stood before me now, clearly trying hard not to let his annoyance show. He did a fairly good job of it, too. I could only spot one lonely glint of irritation in his eye.

"My lady." He took a nice and proper bow.

I held out the envelope containing my letter to Tay. "I hear Sydney is nice this time of year," I said in a poor attempt to cheer the guy up.

He grunted his noncommittal acknowledgment.

"Lots of cute magpies flying around," I ventured.

"They're not cute," Dariel replied and snatched the letter from my hand. "They're a menace to my wings."

I raised both brows.

"Try flying through a swarm of them protecting their nests," he grumbled, then bowed deeply and stalked off.

Australia, I thought, shaking my head. *The place where even cute birds are trying to kill you.*

THAT NIGHT, I SLEPT WITH TWO HELLKITTENS CURLED UP IN MY bed. One had draped itself over my head, and the other lay on my chest. It made it just a tad harder to breathe, but as per the universal cat laws, I was not allowed to move the kittens off me.

That they purred intermittently while sleeping was a mitigating factor.

Vengeance had taken the kittens' presence in stride, and her one and only attempt at eating one of them resulted in a scratched-up nose and bruised canine pride. Also, Mephisto's hiss in defense of his offspring was fearsome enough to make me shake in my boots, and even a hellhound four times his size beat a hasty retreat when faced with his feline ferocity.

Lesson learned, Vengeance now kept a healthy distance from the tiny minions of death, to the point where she let herself be chased off her nest of cushions and blankets by one of them. It was almost comical. I'd once seen a video of a Great Dane fearfully stalking away from a minuscule kitten the size of its foot, and that was pretty much the situation here.

I was deep in my dreams when something pulled me to the surface. I felt his energy before I opened my eyes, like a smooth blanket of dark power, electric heat coursing over my skin, sinking into my bones, connecting with the tie that bound us.

Humming with contentment, I turned toward the source of that heat, and strong arms came around me, pulling me into a cocoon of warmth and sizzling energy. I drowsily blinked against Azazel's chest, the room dipped in darkness.

"Did you move the kittens off me?" I asked, my voice still sleep-drenched.

"They were in the way."

I gasped. "You violated the universal cat law!"

"The what?" He pulled back a bit, and even in the darkness, I could almost see his raised brow.

"If a cat sits or lies on you, anywhere, you may not move it," I cited. "You may not get up and disturb it. You must stay in your position until the cat moves away on its own."

"That sounds like the kind of cat propaganda Mephistopheles casually dropped into human culture."

"Wait, he does that?"

"Who do you think gave the ancient Egyptians the idea of worshipping cats?"

I scrunched up my face. "I can absolutely see him doing that."

His hand stroked my back. "How are you feeling?"

"Tired but okay. Why?" With the last remnants of sleep drowsiness fogging my mind, it took me a second to really get his question. *Right.* I'd barfed all over the freshly severed wings he'd handed me.

Ah, yes. Fond memories.

My head now cleared of all sleepiness, I realized with crystal clarity that the last time I'd seen Azazel was in that damned courtyard—with his energy and demeanor a stark reminder of his otherness, in a way I'd never experienced before. The unearthly glow of power in his eyes, that hardness about him, the chilling calculation and detached cruelty of his actions. He'd felt so different, devoid of all warmth and familiarity, nothing left of the man who held my heart. A stranger had stood in his place, a stranger with cold eyes and terrifying power.

I knew—*knew*—it shouldn't rattle me.

And yet it did.

My breath left me on a shaky exhale, my muscles tensing despite my efforts to stay relaxed.

And as discerning as Azazel was, he immediately picked up on it. My shields didn't need to be down for him to read me like a book.

With his fingers under my chin, he gently tilted my head up. "What is this now?"

I shook my head. "It's silly."

His thumb stroked over my lower lip. "Not when it makes you cringe like that."

Heat rolled up my neck and into my cheeks. Ugh, but it really was silly. Of course he'd be different on the battlefield. Of course he had to have his armor in place, not just physically, but energetically and emotionally as well. I couldn't expect him to be the person out there that he was with me, not when surrounded by demons who'd pounce on any sign of weakness. And down here, in Hell, things like kindness and mercy were considered weak.

I *understood* that.

Now, if only that understanding would sink down into the place inside me where this perplexing coil of anxiety sat like a snake prepared to strike.

"Is this about Inachiel?"

I couldn't hide my flinch at the mention of his name. All I saw in my mind's eye was the blood spraying from his back, the defeated, broken look on his face…the ruthless brutality with which Azazel had ripped off his wings.

My stomach made a nice little flip at that memory.

"Zoe." Azazel's voice brought my attention back to the here and now.

Even in the darkness, I could make out the soft glow of his thunderstorm eyes.

"I told you once before," he said, "and I will tell you again. You do not have to fear me." Something echoed in his tone, something that felt an awful lot like his own kind of fear.

I sucked in a breath. "I don't." Heart thudding fast in my chest, I grasped his hand and squeezed it. Swallowing past the knot building in my throat, I went on, "I'm not afraid of you."

My words rang true even while part of them did not. I tried to make sense of it, tried to dig down to the root of it…

The pause that followed was heavy, and I had the impression he ventured to say something once or twice but then decided against it. Something pulled inside me, pulled me to him, as if bridging the physical gap between us might also dissolve whatever it was that had slipped into my connection with him.

He cupped my face with both hands, laid his forehead against mine. "You," he murmured, his breath brushing my lips, "are the one person I don't ever wish to look at me in fear. No harm will ever come to you from my hands, or my orders." He paused, and when he went on, it was in a rough whisper. "Do you want to know how you could slay me? Not with a Hell-forged blade, nor with angelfire. If you shied away from my touch with terror in your heart, *that* would destroy me."

My breath hitched, my chest hurting. I framed his face in a mirror of his hands on mine and whispered, "I'm not afraid of you. I'm really not."

Because whatever this was, *that* wasn't it. Right here, right now, he felt so familiar, like a part of me, the exhale to my inhale, the other half of my soul.

A beat of silence, then: "But you are afraid."

I opened my mouth to deny it, but nothing came out. That tightness in my chest, that thread of unease…yeah, it felt very much like fear. A nameless one, for I couldn't even grasp what it was about.

"Not of you," I said eventually in a small voice, because that was the only thing I was truly certain of.

He tunneled his fingers into my hair, his energy caressing me in soothing strokes over my body. "Never of me," he murmured, his tone making it a clear prompt for a promise.

"Never," I echoed, needing to reassure him of this unshakable truth between us.

He exhaled roughly and pulled me to him, and I slung my arms around his neck.

"You won't lose me." His breath warmed my skin as he spoke. "There is nothing to fear, all right?"

I nodded and burrowed my face into his neck. But while the worry about losing him in future fights was indeed ever present in the back of my mind, it wasn't the source of the new kind of fear that lay in brooding wait inside me.

When I thought about him being injured or worse in a fight, it was a sharp, heart-stopping kind of fear that arrested my breath. This felt different. This, whatever the source, was more subtle, yet none the less potent. It felt like I'd inhaled toxic fumes that corroded my lungs from the inside and turned my blood sour.

I pressed my nose into the crook of his neck and breathed him in, that familiar scent of leather and bonfire and dark spices. Maybe if I filled my lungs with his essence, it'd chase away that foreboding feeling of helpless fear of something yet unnameable.

CHAPTER 12

One day later, I received a Taylorgram.

The thing about Tay was that she did nothing by half measures. She always went all in with everything she did and often enough pushed boundaries of what was possible or proper, as long as it served her or piqued her interest. She seemingly had no fear. It was uncanny. Where I was plagued by constant worry about all the things, she lived her life in an enviable absence of concern. Her idea of a fun time was bungee jumping or skydiving. She'd tumble headfirst into the next challenge or adventure.

I, on the other hand, used to fret about having to make an official phone call and would rehearse what I'd say ahead of time. And then I still got it wrong, like that one time I wanted to order a pizza, repeating the right phrase over and over, only to end up saying, "I'm a pizza," as soon as the dude on the other end picked up.

One might wonder how Tay and I got to be friends in the first place, but it went the way most introverts find friends—an extrovert sees them, likes them, and adopts them. Way back in elementary school, Taylor had noticed me despite my awkward shyness and decided we should be best friends. And we had been ever since.

Even my going to live in Hell hadn't broken the bond we had, despite the fact that communication was so severely restricted. Being able to visit her once a month and spend hours chatting with her and catching up helped a lot, but even for the times in between, when I could only send letters, Tay had found a way to push those limits, quite precariously so.

I was sitting in the library, lost in a book—a paranormal romance featuring demons, a fact that made me snicker—when Hekesha, one of the half-bloods in Azazel's service, knocked and entered.

"You have a visitor." Instead of bowing deeply, she only inclined her head, and she didn't address me with my title—something I'd successfully convinced her to stop doing, seeing as she'd become more of a friend than a servant in the past few months.

I tensed and put down my book. It couldn't be Azmodea or Mammon, because those two always just waltzed in without announcing their presence, being family and all. So whoever it was had to be someone I'd have to be a bit more presentable and alert to greet.

I jumped up from the chair and fidgeted with my clothes and hair for a second. "All right, send them in."

Hekesha inclined her head again and waved the visitor inside.

I pressed my lips together when I beheld Belial's sour face. He was a giant of a demon, standing easily close to seven feet tall, with the shoulders and broad frame to match. And still, in spite of his size, he held himself with the same kind of predatory grace as all his brethren did. While his features were not as finely hewn as some of the other demons', he was still strikingly beautiful, in an arresting, more roughly masculine way, his face all harsh angles and strong lines, framed by unruly, dark curls.

"Shall I stay, my lady?" Hekesha asked, now using my title...for the benefit of our visitor. Appearances had to be upheld in front of others.

"No, no, it's fine." I rubbed my nose. "I've got this."

She cast a last look at the full-blood demon decidedly *not* in Azazel's employ and then left with another bow.

"Lady Zoe," Belial said and bowed his head, his deep voice just shy of a homicidal grumble.

I tried not to grimace while I bowed my head in turn. I really did. "Lord Belial."

Oh, God, this was so awkward. *Why, Tay, why?* Of all the demons to keep summoning to deliver her messages, she had to pick a high-ranking dude with murder in his dark eyes. It would have already been bad enough had she only commanded Belial to hand over a written message. He was a cherub, the same rank as Azazel, though from a different archdemonacy. He had vast lands and resources at his disposal and commanded thousands of lower-ranking demons.

Being *summoned* to deliver a letter from a human on Earth to another human in Hell was beyond humiliating for a demon of his rank.

And yet, Taylor kept calling him, with arcane methods she wouldn't explain to me, and was able to *order* him to do her bidding. She commanded a cherub demon from Hell with enough power in his pinkie finger to turn her into human dust.

Sometimes, I feared for my friend's sanity.

She could have simply waited for me to send another one

of *our* demons to pick up her response letter a few days after receiving mine. That was how we'd done it in the beginning, and it had gone well enough for a few months.

But then, one day, Belial had shown up here. Pissed as fuck, barely staying respectful, and clearly fighting against some invisible hold that forced him to act out Taylor's will.

And I really mean *act out.*

Because Tay being Tay, she'd found a way to make the whole situation worse just for shits and giggles.

Belial, commander of demon armies, crusher of souls, and scourge of the sinners, did not just simply have to hand me a letter. No, he had to recite Taylor's message verbatim, and not just that—but in her voice, her inflection, her intonation, as if playing back a recording.

The first time he'd done that, I'd almost had a heart attack. His rendition of Taylor's voice had been perfect. The combination of that and hearing my best friend talk, but seeing it coming from the mouth of a giant-sized, surly demon, had been enough to make my brain malfunction. Not to mention that the humongous demon had looked like he was one second away from going on a murder spree, in large part due to the fact that he'd been forced to act out this farce.

And here he stood again, glowering at me as if it was somehow *my* fault that my BFF was into kinky shit like turning powerful demons into her own personal voice actors.

"I have a message for you," he now said through gritted teeth.

"I gathered that," I mumbled with a grimace. "Look," I added and held up my hands, "you really don't need to do that voice thing for my benefit. Honestly, I don't care for it. Just give me the message in a normal manner. I won't tell on you, promise. Taylor will never know, and we'll be spared some extra embarrassment. Win-win!"

His eyes glowed so hot I involuntarily took a step back in fear of being cut through as with a laser. The muscles in his face seemed to rearrange themselves with the force it apparently took him to keep the bulk of his wrath at bay. "I am *compelled*," he ground out. "I must adhere to the letter of the summoner's command."

Ugh, Tay. I closed my eyes and rubbed the spot between my brows. "All right, let's hear it."

I settled back into the chair for the performance, because, knowing Tay, this was going to take more than a few minutes. That girl liked to talk.

"Z!" Belial began in Taylor's enthusiastic tone.

I'd need snacks for this. With a thought, I summoned my favorite chocolate that the kitchen staff kept on hand for me. As I bit into the sweet goodness of the nut-sprinkled bar, Belial began to act out Tay's message, which first covered her reaction to my lament about the wing-chopping-vomit incident, complete with a lot of commiserating and "Girl, same."

Tay had assured me that Belial was bound not to divulge or use any of the information revealed in these messages, but it was still hella awkward to have a third party be privy to the convos between me and my best friend. I mostly saved political details and more sensitive information for those times I saw Tay in person, so Belial mainly learned a whole lot about Taylor's dating life and the clubbing scene in Sydney, sprinkled with the latest celebrity gossip and her ranting and raving about shows and movies and books.

Tay was my lifeline to contemporary Earth life. Without her, I'd slide into complete obliviousness about what was going on, the most recent developments in pop culture, what was the hottest new thing in music or TV...

I'd already switched to popcorn halfway through Belial's magnificent rendition of Taylor's summary of the latest beef between a hugely popular singer and the wife of this other hugely popular singer, when the door to the library opened and in strolled Azazel.

My darling demon husband paused at the sight of Belial.

Belial paused at the sight of Azazel.

An awkward few seconds passed with both demons standing still and eyeing each other with the kind of suspicion that thickened the air.

Clearing my throat, I gestured at Belial. "I'm just having a message delivered. From Taylor."

Azazel's eyebrows crept up to his hairline.

"Um, maybe you could...wait outside?" I ventured. I could only imagine how embarrassing it must be for Belial to have to act out Tay's message like this while Azazel looked on.

Azazel fixedly stared at the other demon as he prowled over to me and took up position behind my chair.

"No, I don't think I will." He leaned against the wall with his arms crossed and a menacing smolder on his face.

"Azazel," I spoke quietly through gritted teeth.

His eyes flicked to me. "My love."

"Would you please give us some privacy?"

He managed the feat of appearing to settle in more comfortably against the wall. "Belial," he said, completely ignoring my request. "Please continue. Pretend I'm not here."

I could virtually see the amount of effort it took Belial to switch back to imitating the quirky voice of a human female in front of one of his peers.

"Okay," Taylor said from Belial's mouth. "So, remember how I told you about that guy I met at the bridge walk?"

I cringed and tried to sink lower in my chair. Secondhand embarrassment made my entire body flame with scorching heat.

"So we went out for drinks the other week," Belial-Taylor said, "and we really clicked, you know? I mean, he's super hot, like, the dude's a swimmer, so his body's ripped, right? Muscles, Z, muscles all over!" Belial did a fantastic job acting out Taylor's hand gestures. There were a lot of them. Tay was a handsy talker.

"And he's funny! Gotta love a man with a sense of humor. So, anyway, the chemistry was good, and we made out, and it was all great. We met up again and that's when we hooked up. And, girrrrrrl." Belial paused, gathered what appeared to be the last shreds of his dignity, and then gave a perfect imitation of Taylor's groan. "That was the best lay of my life. I had trouble walking the next day." Belial, commander of demon armies, giggled in Taylor's voice.

I closed my eyes for a second and breathed through the mental pain. *I will not look at Azazel,* I chanted in my mind. *I will not look at Azazel.* Feeling the sizzling heat of him behind me was enough.

"So, anyway," Belial continued, "we kept meeting up, it was still great, fantastic chemistry, he's affectionate with me, treats me well, no complaints, right? But then I casually mention something about 'now that we're together,' and he's all like, 'Whoa! What?' And I'm like, 'Dude, what do you think this is?' And he's like—get this—he's like, 'A situationship.' Excuse me, what? What the fuck is a *situationship*?"

If I could choose only one memory to keep that would make me laugh for the rest of my life, it would be the sight of Belial's face imitating Taylor's face as she made air quotes in a perfect mix of disgust and bewilderment.

"Like, Zoe, I swear, I can't even with this modern dating

shit. I mean, you know me; I don't mind a casual thing here or there, no-strings, easy sex. But that's like…you say that going in, you know? It's all about setting expectations. When I want something without commitment, I say that up front. But having to jump through hoops and doing weeks and months of casual fucking in an undefined 'situationship' where the dude still fucks around with other girls while I wait for him to make up his mind and sort his feelings and maybe one day agree that what we have should be a real, exclusive relationship…I'm gonna cut a bitch, you know?"

I'd covered my face with both hands, but through the slits between my fingers, I could clearly see how Belial had put his hands on his hips and gave me an Oscar-worthy imitation of Taylor's death glare.

"I mean, I'd never thought I'd say this, but—what happened to good, old-fashioned dating? Where have romantic manners gone? Oh my God, Z, am I getting old?" Belial slapped one hand on his chest. "I feel like that principal from The Simpsons, like, 'Is it me? Am I getting old? No, no, it's the kids these days.' Ugh." Belial rolled his eyes. "Anyway, so that's where I'm at right now. I told swimmer dude to take his *situationship* and shove it where the sun don't shine. Like, sure, he's a demon in the sack"—there was only the slightest twitch to Belial's eye when he said that—"but I already started catching feelings for him, you know? So I can't use him for casual sex. That'd only hurt me." Belial uttered a sad sigh, then perked up again. "Anywho, be glad you've got your stud demon husband who adores the fuck out of you. That shit is rare these days. Honestly, at this point, I'm this close"—Belial held his thumb and index finger half an inch apart—"to making my own demon marriage contract. Okay, that's it for now. See you on your birthday, babe!" Belial, crusher of souls, blew me a kiss.

A beat of oppressive silence, then Belial inclined his head. "I'll take my leave."

"Thank you, Lord Belial," I choked out.

"Yes," Azazel said from his position behind me, his voice devoid of any teasing. "Thank you. May I offer you an escort back to your territory?"

Belial flashed a smile that showed too many teeth. "No, thank you."

He turned on his heel and stormed out of the room.

When the door fell shut with a resounding thunk, a moment of silence wrapped around us, punctuated only by Vengeance's snoring. My trusty hellhound had slept through the entire performance.

"What in the nine circles of Hell," Azazel began in a lethally quiet voice from behind me, "did I just watch?"

I scrunched up my face. "A Taylorgram."

He was still outside my field of vision, but I could honest-to-Hell *hear* the puzzled expression he made. "Come again?"

I twisted around in my seat and finally looked at him. Peeking over the high back of the chair, I grimaced at the mix of utter bewilderment and discomposure on his face. "A Taylorgram," I repeated in a small voice. "Like, a message from Taylor, but not written down. She, uh, she summons Belial to 'record' her message and then perform it for me down here."

He stared at me, unblinking, for a few heartbeats, then he raised one hand, the other arm still crossed over his chest, and said, "There is so much wrong with what you just said that I don't even know where to start."

I was pretty sure if I grimaced any more, my face would get permanently stuck with my undoubtedly painful expression. "I know," I began, but he stopped me.

"She *summons* him?"

"Yeah."

"How?"

"I don't know." I chewed my lip. "She won't tell me."

"She's your best friend."

I threw my hands up. "Yeah, but she's super stubborn about this! I've asked her several times, and she just won't budge. And I told her to please stop making Belial act out her messages, but she won't listen."

He narrowed his eyes. "How would she even know how to summon a demon? Much less make him do her bidding?"

"I have no idea!" I wailed. "It wasn't me who told her. That's for sure. I mean, I can't even make *you* do my bidding, so it's not like I'm a great source of information on how to handle demons."

"Oh, you bend me to your will well enough," he purred, a gleam of heat in his eyes.

"Beside the point," I muttered while my cheeks blazed hot.

"True." All humor left his expression and tone. "Your friend is playing a dangerous game."

I closed my eyes and thunked my head against the chair's back. "Ugh, I *know*."

"She must have gotten the information from someone," he mused, his voice a dark murmur. "Even with all of humanity's many writings on the occult, it is rare to stumble upon real, authentic knowledge about our world and how to interact with us. We like to keep it that way."

There was a sinister sort of warning in that last sentence, and I gulped. "I have no idea where she got the information, let alone what it is she's actually doing. I mean, like I said, I haven't told her squat because I didn't even know about this."

He regarded me silently for a moment. "I'm wondering," he then said softly, "if it might be one of us."

"What do you mean? A demon?"

He inclined his head.

"But who? You're the only demon Taylor has met. I mean, other than—" I shut my mouth with an audible click, my eyes widening.

With a fluid motion speaking of leashed power, Azazel straightened from his leaning position against the wall. "Who?"

I shook my head. "He wouldn't."

Azazel's energy vibrated darkly around his impressive frame, and the shadow outline of wings appeared behind his back. "Let's find out."

amazon Gift Receipt

Scan the QR code to learn more about your gift or start a return.

Till Heaven Do Us Part (Infernal Covenant)
Order ID: 114-1830139-5397861   Ordered on December 3, 2024

CHAPTER 13

I was perched on a divan in our more private sitting room when my demonic nephew-by-marriage strolled in, a brilliant smile on his face. Smooth features of refined nobility, a warm brown tan accented by his dark eyes and black hair, Mammon was simply stunning to look at. I'd never seen him without a spark of humor in his eyes, or the ghost of a smirk on his lips. He was the type that drew all attention in a room by virtue of his magnetic character that shone through the allure of his physical beauty.

"Auntie!" he called out, opening his arms wide for a hug. "How lovely for you to call me over. What's the occasion? Are we celebrating your birthday early?"

Azazel, who'd been lurking out of view beside the door, now slammed it shut without taking his eyes off his nephew. Mammon flinched at the sound and whirled around.

"Dearest uncle," he said with a note of caution in his voice. "Lovely to see you, too. How's that wing collection going? I hear you've been adding to it."

"There's always room for more," Azazel drawled and prowled closer.

Mammon's smile seemed a bit brittle, and his eyes darted between me and his uncle.

I grimaced and cleared my throat. "We have a few questions for you."

"Uh-huh." His sense of self-preservation apparently on high alert, Mammon surreptitiously moved so that several pieces of furniture stood between him and Azazel. Not that it would help him much should Azazel decide to charge him.

"You remember my friend Taylor?" I asked. "You met her once, didn't you?"

"Once, yeah." He pursed his lips.

Sure. "So, she's been doing this thing where she summons a demon to deliver her messages to me."

He raised both brows. "Well, I hope she didn't sell her soul for *that.*"

"That's the thing," I said. "She didn't make a regular deal, as far as I know. Yet she somehow acquired the knowledge to summon and command a demon to do her bidding. You wouldn't happen to know anything about that, would you?"

"Me?" Mammon laid a hand over his heart and blinked at me in a picture-perfect image of innocence. "Why, I couldn't possibly—"

He didn't get to finish that sentence. Azazel had him slammed against the wall with his hand around his throat in the next second. The stone behind Mammon cracked and groaned with the force of the impact.

"Do not lie," Azazel snarled, his face inches from Mammon's.

Mammon made a choking sound and pawed at Azazel's hand.

"Azazel," I softly said.

He let him go and stepped back, and Mammon deflated and massaged his throat.

"Did you tell her how to summon Belial?" I asked quietly.

Mammon heaved a big sigh, still massaging his neck and now looking sheepish. "I...might have passed on some information she could use to her advantage."

"What, exactly, did you tell her?" Azazel's voice hummed with the same darkness that pooled around him.

Mammon shrugged. "How to summon and command a demon without making a deal."

"She's not a witch," Azazel said. "She has no latent powers to speak of. How would she be able to wield the magic necessary for this?"

I listened intently. This was the first I'd heard about there being a way to deal with demons without the standard soul-selling involved. Were witches actually a thing?

"There is another way," Mammon hedged. "It's...rather obscure."

Azazel flexed his fingers, and Mammon raised his hands in a placating gesture.

"All right, all right! I'll tell you. No more choking necessary." He perched on the armrest of a nearby chair. "A human, even one without vestigial powers, can summon a demon and bind them to their will...if the human knows the demon's true name."

True name? I glanced at Azazel, but he fixedly stared at Mammon.

"That's the first I've heard about this," Azazel muttered.

"Like I said, it's rather obscure. That knowledge is kind of buried, and—given the potential for abuse—for good reason." He shrugged.

"And you gave Belial's true name to Taylor?" Azazel's

voice dropped to a dangerous level. "And taught her how to use it to summon him, bind him to her will, and order him to deliver her messages to Hell, *to act them out like a recording to his unending embarrassment?*"

"Whoa!" Mammon held up both hands. "I didn't teach her that, not that last part." He wiggled his finger to indicate the recording thing. "I just told her to use it to make him deliver her letters, and *only* that. In fact, I warned her not to make him do anything else."

Ugh. Taylor and warnings. I facepalmed.

"Why?" Azazel bared his teeth.

"What do you mean, why?" Mammon frowned. "Obviously, she shouldn't be using Belial to deep-clean her apartment. I mean, that would take things a bit too far, don't you think?"

"Why would you give her Belial's name," Azazel growled, "and force him into a position where he is commanded to deliver messages?"

Mammon threw his hands up. "Because he has a stick up his ass and needs to be shaken up a bit!"

Azazel blinked at him, obviously stumped for a moment. "Let me get this straight," he then said, hollow disbelief ringing in his voice. "This is a *prank*?"

My mouth fell open. I stared at Mammon with my flabber well and properly gasted.

My demon nephew had the bad form to look smug. "It's a good one, isn't it?"

For a long, astounding moment, Azazel stood completely stunned speechless. Then, slowly, inexorably, his power rose, building pressure until it became difficult to breathe. His face got so hard that it appeared carved from marble, his energy whispering into the corners of the room.

Mammon gulped.

"Did it ever occur to you," Azazel spoke into the charged silence, his voice the softest of threats, "that by playing this elaborate *prank* on Belial, you've put Taylor in harm's way?"

Mammon blinked. "Um…"

"Do I need to spell it out for you?" A muscle feathered in Azazel's jaw.

Mammon squinted. "Maybe?"

Azazel visibly struggled to retain his composure. I couldn't blame him. "What do you think will happen," he ground out, "should Taylor lose control of her command over Belial?"

"Why would she lose control—"

"What do you think will happen?" Azazel thundered.

Mammon flinched. "Belial will be pissed?"

"He is *already* pissed." Azazel flashed his teeth, his canines elongating as they sometimes did with demons when they got really, really angry. "And once the leash Taylor has on him is severed, and he is no longer bound by whatever provision she has worked into her summoning of him not to hurt her, he will turn his considerable wrath on *her*, not you."

Mammon's face paled.

"Taylor has had him running to and fro," Azazel continued, "not realizing what the fuck she's dabbling in, and he's been forced to act as her mouthpiece for months, not just personally delivering messages to Zoe, but performing them like a live-action voice message. A demon of his rank and status, reduced to acting the fool for a human's whims. If word of this has already leaked to other demons and damaged Belial's standing, his wrath will be unimaginable. And the entirety of his rage will turn to find its target in Taylor the second she lets that leash slip her hand."

Mammon let out a shaky breath. "I...I didn't consider that."

"YOU NEVER DO!" Azazel roared, grabbing him by the collar and hurling him against the wall once more.

I half rose from the divan, my heart in my throat. "Azazel..."

Mammon grunted and tried to say something, but Azazel shook him and leaned in with his teeth bared.

"You *never* consider the implications of your actions," he snarled. "Just like when you thought you were doing Zoe a great service by teaching her how to use a sigil to escape her rooms, not considering *once*"—he shook him again, this time so hard the wall at Mammon's back gained another crack—"that she didn't have any powers to defend herself, and by letting her loose on her own, you made her the perfect prey for the inferni. They were *ripping her to shreds* when Zaquiel luckily found her."

Mammon's eyes widened and flicked to me. "Zoe, I'm sorry. I didn't think—"

"SHE COULD HAVE DIED!" Azazel's roar shook the room.

I jumped and fell back on the divan, a hand on my chest, right over my racing heart. Okay, wow, somebody had a lot of pent-up emotions about that incident. Not that I didn't sometimes have the occasional nightmare about being hunted and chewed on by those horrifying beasts, but I hadn't realized that Azazel had so much fury and fear bottled up about it. Because that was what it was—stark, naked fear that veered sharply into fury at the easiest target to blame for that incident.

But if Mammon hadn't given me that sigil to use, and if I hadn't been chased by the inferni and, as luck have it, run right into Zaquiel, Azazel would never have been forced to play me off as his pet in front of his guest. It was the scene that followed that had changed our pretend relationship to something more real, paving the way for the deeper connection that grew from there. If not for all of that, I might still be locked in my rooms, ignored by my demon husband in name only, withering away one boring day at a time.

So, in a roundabout way, I owed Mammon for almost getting me killed.

Which was why I rose from the divan and approached Azazel.

Laying a hand on his shoulder, not flinching at the bite of the near electrical charge of his power, I softly said, "My darling."

I almost never used endearments with him. The few times I had, it'd always gotten his attention.

Just like now. It snapped him out of the haze of fear turned fury, and his power immediately gentled, wrapping around my hand in a caress. Shoulders losing some of their tension, he released Mammon and stepped back, half turning to me. Looking up at him, I slid my hand down his arm and intertwined my fingers with his.

We wouldn't be here if it weren't for Mammon, I spoke into his mind. *I know it's scary to think I might have died, but I didn't, it's over, and you don't need to vent your fear on him. In a convoluted way, we actually have his lack of concern to thank for the love we found. Don't punish him for that.*

He fully turned to me, his free hand cupping my cheek. *I am not yet sure,* he said after a moment, his mental voice touching a chord deep inside me, *if the softness of your heart will be my ruin or my salvation.*

I don't know about salvation, I mentally replied, leaning into his caress, *but I'll settle for mitigating influence.*

The hint of a smile broke through the hardness of his features, his eyes warm as he held my gaze.

Mammon cleared his throat. "I don't mean to break up what is undoubtedly a deeply romantic moment between you two"—he wiggled his finger between us—"but I'd just like to know if I'm still in danger of being maimed or dismembered. Because if I'm going to lose a limb or two in the next few minutes, I'll have to reschedule my plans for tonight."

Lightning flashed in Azazel's eyes, and he slowly turned his head to glare at his nephew.

Mammon raised his hands. "Just asking."

"You," Azazel growled, pointing at Mammon with his finger, "will find a way to fix the fucking mess you created, or so help me Lucifer, I will add your wings to my collection."

Mammon grimaced and pressed his back against the wall as if to better protect his shoulders. "I will fix it. I swear."

Azazel's power rose in a snarling whisper and seemed to snap at Mammon with phantom teeth. "You'd better, or the wings will be just the start. If Zoe's friend comes to any harm through this, not even the blood we share will spare you from my wrath." He summoned a dagger and threw it with a flick of his fingers so it embedded in the wall an inch from Mammon's head. "Make sure Taylor is safe and will remain so. Should you fail, I will slice off the parts you are most fond of and feed them to you."

Mammon swallowed thickly. "Grandpa taught you well, I see."

"Out!" Azazel barked.

Mammon jolted and almost tripped over his own feet in his haste to get away.

When the door fell shut behind Mammon, Azazel blew out a heavy breath, his shoulders slumping.

"I'm sorry," he said quietly.

Startled, I turned to him. It was so rare to hear an apology from him—for anything—that it sounded almost foreign to my ears.

"Why?" I asked, grasping his hand again. "You didn't do anything wrong."

His stormy eyes met mine. "I know how much you care about Taylor. How much it would hurt you to see her harmed. And now Mammon has put her in danger."

My chest tightened, cold fear whispering through me. If anything happened to Taylor...it would break me. I'd already lost my home, my life on Earth, lost all contact to my mom—even though I could go see her, I wasn't able to interact with her at all—and Tay was the one living person still on Earth whom I could talk to. Sure, I had my dad, who hung around his family's home as a ghost, but Tay was the person closest to me from my old life.

She was so bright, so full of life and love. Just the thought of her being harmed in any way hurt me on a soul level.

"Mammon will fix it, right?" I asked in a small voice.

"I will see to it that he does." He pulled me to him and enveloped me in a hug. Kissing the top of my head, he said, "Regardless of the measures he'll take to remedy the situation, I'll post a guard for her to make sure she's protected."

"Thank you." I slung my arms around his waist and buried my head in his chest, breathing him in. After a few relaxing heartbeats, I said, "So, what's up with the true name thing?"

"Ah." He rested his chin on the crown of my head. "We have names that our parents give us and names that are branded onto our souls. We don't really use the latter, because it feels too personal."

"How so?"

"In human terms, it would be akin to walking around naked. There's a certain vulnerability in it."

"Is it like the stuff in faerie folklore, where knowing the name gives someone power over them?"

"I didn't think it was until just now. As far as I know, it doesn't work that way between demons, but maybe it once did, a long time ago. It could be something left over from before the Fall, a remnant of some divine quality that used to serve a purpose." He shrugged, his hand stroking my back. "I never gave it much thought. It just isn't an important factor in demon life. Unless, apparently"—his voice turned dark—"a human gets their hands on that information and is taught how to use it to manipulate the demon."

I shuddered at the thought of the serious trouble Taylor had gotten herself into. Next time I saw her, I'd make sure to shake some sense into her—metaphorically, since I couldn't touch her on my visits. I'd just really have to drive home the point that she needed to stop summoning Belial immediately. And maybe keep an exorcism kit on standby. Would wearing holy water as perfume do any good? Could she ward her apartment somehow?

Which brought my hippity-hoppity mind back to the other thing I wanted to ask Azazel about. "Now, about those humans with powers…"

I felt his chuckle where my head rested on his torso. "Picked up on that, did you?"

I peered up at him. "You need to elaborate on that. Are witches a real thing?"

He tugged on me to follow and then pulled me onto his lap as he sat on the divan. "To an extent. Humans aren't naturally born with powers. Those who find themselves with something 'extra,' with abilities that could be classified as magic—telekinesis, telepathy, being able to work energy —do so because of nonhuman heritage they know nothing about."

"Like having a demon somewhere down in their family line?"

Demons could mate with humans—as in, procreate—the half-bloods populating Hell being proof of that kind of inter-species breeding. It didn't happen all too often, though, from what I'd gathered, because demons were generally less fertile than humans, no matter their gender. And apparently, the biology between the demon and the human had to be just right to make it work.

But still, there had to be quite a few humans running around on Earth who were distantly related to a demon.

"That can be the reason," Azazel said, "though that rela-tion would be many times removed, and any powers highly diluted. A demon who sires a child with a human mostly makes sure to bring that offspring to Hell. It's bad form to leave them on Earth. Most demon families here take care to track their part-demon children over a few generations, and they take those who display a proper amount of power."

I thought of Caleb, the half-blood in Azazel's service, who'd been taken from Earth after he'd accidentally inciner-ated his home—with his mom in it. His father was appar-ently a real piece of shit, but Azazel had soon pulled Caleb from his sire's "care" and employed him directly here. Half-bloods generally didn't have a choice in where they were allowed to live, being completely at the mercy of their demon family...unless a higher-ranking demon stepped in, like Azazel had done with Caleb.

Playing with a lock of my hair, Azazel said, "There's

another reason a human might be born with vestigial powers."

There was that word again—vestigial. My years of reading on my phone's app, with the dictionary only a long press on a word away came in handy now. "So, powers that are left over from something…before?"

"Just so." He tugged at the lock. "What happens when a demon or angel dies?"

I blinked a few times. "Uh, no idea, but it sounds like you're about to tell me."

I honestly hadn't considered that question before. It was rather rare that a demon died, seeing as they didn't age or get sick, and as Azmodea had explained the other day, mortal combat was frowned upon among demons. That was, the real fighting kind of mortal combat. The video game, however, was very popular among the tech-loving demons.

"They are reincarnated as humans."

Azazel's casually dropped bomb made me sit up and stare at him. "What?"

"For demons and angels, to go to Heaven or Hell after their death would be ironic, wouldn't it?"

"Uh, yeah, sure. But I thought, maybe they just…go poof." I made a fitting explosive hand gesture.

Azazel shook his head, a slight smile on his lips. "Nothing ever just…*goes poof*. Energy doesn't vanish. It has to go somewhere. Even when we destroy a wraith, their soul is simply taken apart and then repurposed. For angels and demons, our soul is our body; we are metaphysically bound to our form. So when we die, our body and mind disintegrate and reform. No one knows exactly how it happens, but our spirit is then reborn in a human body, with no memories of the previous life, and only a tiny portion of the angel's or demon's powers carrying over. But that's enough to manifest as subtle 'magic' or supernatural abilities, like being able to move things or read thoughts. People with those powers often find themselves drawn to the occult and might dabble in the different magical arts known to humans."

"Wow. Okay. But they really don't remember anything from before? It's all just gone?"

He shrugged. "Over thousands of years, only a few reborn angels and demons have been found to have retained slivers of knowledge of their former lives. Sometimes something comes to light under hypnosis, sometimes it surfaces in dreams, sometimes it rises to the fore when the human's mind is fractured. But it's never a full picture. Just fragments. Enough for some of us to identify the demon if we knew them in life, but not enough to reforge any kind of connection. For all intents and purposes, that demon is gone, and all that is left is an echo of their former life in a human mind."

I played with the buttons on his shirt. "That is kind of sad. So some of you who have recently lost someone know there is a human out there who is a reborn friend or loved one, but you can't ever reach them. Reminds me of the folks who have family members with severe dementia."

"It's a bit like that, yes."

"So what happens when that reborn angel or demon dies? I mean, dies after living a human life."

"Same thing that happens to humans." He shrugged one shoulder. "Once reborn as a human, their soul is a blank slate. They can incur damnation based on their actions, or they can live a virtuous life and earn their place in Heaven."

I raised both brows. "Kind of coming full circle, huh? Wait—how awkward would it be if a reborn demon ended up in Hell as a damned soul and then gets tortured by their former demon buddies?"

"They wouldn't remember any of the demons, though," he said quietly.

I squinted. "But the demons might remember their old pal? That must be hella weird to have to roast a former friend on a spit."

He rubbed the bridge of his nose and closed his eyes. "I can honestly say that in two thousand five hundred years, I have never once thought about this."

"Have you ever recognized a human soul as a reborn angel or demon?"

He shook his head. "I hear that it's not often obvious. Some of them have an aura that is distinguishable from a regular human, but I've never seen it. And in some, the signs are apparently so subtle that they escape notice at first."

I chewed on my lip and then asked softly, "Is there someone you've lost who would have been reborn as a human?"

His eyes met mine, and the deep anguish in them stole my breath for a moment. "You know who."

I inhaled sharply. Oh, God, of course. His *mother*. Shit. He thought she'd died, still believed the lie fed to him for the past millennia, like Azmodea, and Mammon, and everyone else…well, everyone except Lucifer, Daevi, and a chosen few privy to the truth.

Including me.

For almost a whole year now, I'd been walking around with this huge fucking secret hanging over my head, poised to strike me down at any moment like the proverbial sword of Damocles, dangling from a flimsy thread.

The flimsy thread being my not-so-great ability to keep a secret to myself.

Gah, I was bad enough at not blabbing about tiny, inconsequential things, but a secret as big as this one? It chafed at me. At the oddest times, I had this strong urge to just blurt it all out, to just go, "Your mother's still alive!"

The only thing giving me the strength to resist that unholy urge was my bone-deep fear of what Lucifer would do to me if I broke my vow of silence on this matter. He'd said there would be consequences. And that I didn't want to find out what they were.

He was damned right about that one.

But even if I'd managed not to spill the beans to Azazel yet—a feat I was half astounded by and half proud of—there were more and more moments that brought me uncomfortably close to revealing what I knew.

Like just now, when I'd put my entire foot in my mouth by asking him if he'd ever lost anyone, even though I should have known damn well that his mother had died when he was a young boy.

Except, I knew the truth, and I'd spoken and acted out of knowing the truth, instead of remembering to keep up the facade of believing his mother dead just like he did.

Consequently, Azazel now looked at me with a mix of suspicion and...oh, God, *hurt*. Because to him, it looked like I'd *forgotten* that his mother was dead. When it was one of the most pivotal experiences that had shaped his life.

"I'm sorry," I breathed. "I—shit, I'm so sorry." I shook my head and closed my eyes, trying to escape the scorching heat of shame. "Sometimes, my brain malfunctions," I said in a small voice.

"It's all right," he muttered, but when I opened my eyes to glance at him again, I caught the flicker of grief in his eyes, the hurt in his expression, before he schooled his features.

Oh, no. Dammit, I didn't want him to think I'd forgotten the many times he'd personally told me about his mom being dead and gone. Like I was such a shitty wife that I didn't remember the most important details of my beloved's life history?

I breathed past the lump in my throat, past the hot coil of shame and remorse and the pounding need to tell him the truth. *I didn't forget that your mom is dead, because she's not actually dead, she's just locked up in a suite in Lucifer's palace because her mental state is fragile and she needs to be supervised so she won't hurt herself or others.*

I wanted to tell him so badly, to correct the impression he'd just gotten of me, to give him that crucial piece of knowledge about his own mother...to soothe some of the grief over losing her. It'd still hurt him to learn the truth, to find out he'd been lied to for thousands of years, and it might be difficult for him to know his mom had been struggling all these years, but he deserved to know the truth. And if Lucifer ever let him, he'd at least be able to see her. He'd know she was there, instead of thinking her irrevocably gone.

I thought of my own mom and how much it meant to me that I was still able to visit her, even if I couldn't talk to or touch her, even if I couldn't let her know that I was okay. Just seeing her, watching her go about her day...sometimes, that was enough.

Azazel had grieved for his mother for two thousand five hundred years, carrying a wound that had never quite healed. And here I was, with the knowledge to lift that grief, and yet I wasn't allowed to act on it.

And now he thought I'd simply forgotten about something that was one of his core wounds, and I just had to sit there and let him believe it. Let him think less of me, just because I was sworn to keep someone else's secret.

"There are some things I need to take care of," Azazel

said quietly, setting me on my feet and getting up from the divan.

My stomach felt like it was being eaten by acid. "Azazel..."

"I'll see you later." He kissed me on the top of my head, but it felt so horribly different from his kiss before. Hollow and distant.

I reached out to him, but he was already on his way to the door. And all I could do was watch him leave, knowing my blunder had just tarnished his image of me, knowing there was fuck all I could do about it.

Dammit, Lucifer. *Damn you and your fucking vow of silence.*

CHAPTER 14

The next day, I was snacking on a carrot cake—my favorite—in my old sitting room, when Azazel came back from wherever he'd gone earlier that day, doing whatever important stuff demons in charge of territories had to do.

I paused with the fork halfway to my mouth, my chest drawing tight at the sight of him. It wasn't that he'd avoided me since my blunder yesterday, but even though he'd come to my bed last night, every touch, every word, every glance had been underlaid with a current that felt off somehow. Like he'd pulled a part of himself back, and I was left grasping at the void.

My heart ached at the thought, my mind screaming at me to fix this. I breathed through the discomfort, pushing the urge to break my vow of silence down into the depths of my soul.

"Hi," I said instead, lowering my fork. And then I added softly, "I've missed you."

He came over, tipped up my chin, and gave me a kiss.

And there went that current of *wrongness*, whispering underneath his display of affection.

He glanced at my plate. "Early birthday cake?"

Seeing as my birthday was tomorrow, it wasn't a far-off guess.

"A gift," I said and picked up the card that had come with the cake.

Azazel took it and frowned at the message, which read, *Apologies for almost getting you killed. Xoxo, Mammon.*

"The nerve," he ground out and then crumpled the note in his hand.

"I know," I said, chewing. "The label on the box said it's from a bakery in L.A., but everyone knows it's only real carrot cake if it's made in the Carroté region of France. Otherwise, it's just a sweet salad."

The tiny twitch of his lips gave me life. If only I could fully joke myself back into his good graces.

He settled on the couch next to me and fixed me with a stare. "I've been thinking."

Oh, God. Oh, no. What now? There were only seconds between that ominous statement and his next sentence, but it was more than enough time for my brain to flip through a catalog of horrifying possibilities of what he'd been thinking about. Because, to be fair, that statement was right up there with the infamous "We need to talk." So, honestly, who could blame my anxiety-ridden mind for going full throttle into *the world is ending* territory?

"About that séance you did when you were thirteen," he continued, making my brain effectively stop with screeching tires in the middle of imagining Terrible Theory #132.

"Uh..." was all I got out while my mind scrambled to readjust. "We've been over this," I said after a moment.

And we really, really had been. Months ago, after I'd come to stay here, Azazel and I had talked about that séance where I'd somehow managed to bind him in a contract without even knowing what I was doing, and to his great frustration, I hadn't been able to shed any light on it. There was little I remembered from that summoning, my mind having blanked out a lot because it had all scared the bejesus out of me. At some point, Azazel had given up asking me more about it, his consternation at the lack of information evident.

"I don't have any new insights," I said. "I wish I did, but I'm afraid I still don't know any more than the last time we talked about it."

"The thing with Taylor and Belial got me wondering." His fingers drummed on the backrest of the couch while his eyes mapped my face. "It would make a whole lot of sense if you summoned me with my true name."

My mouth fell open. "Whoa. If I did, I wasn't aware of it."

He regarded me from underneath his lashes. "There was little you were aware of during that séance."

"Ouch," I murmured, but he was right, of course. I'd been reading from a book where only half the text was in any way intelligible. Tay and I hadn't taken it seriously, thinking we were just joking around and having a bit of fun on a Friday night, making up shit about getting hitched to a demon should we still be single at twenty-five, which, at the time, was the biggest concern my hormone-driven teenage brain could fathom.

I'd had no idea that the text I was reading from gave our made-up contract a very real framework.

"Do you remember anything from the text that could have sounded like a name?" Azazel asked me.

I frowned. "Well, no, but half the text was gibberish

anyway, or what I thought was gibberish. I mean, it could have been an obscure language, for all I know." I narrowed my eyes at him. "It would help me remember if I knew what the name *is*."

He held my gaze for a moment, tense seconds ticking by in silence, then he grabbed the plate and fork from me and took a bite of the cake.

Something in me deflated with a keen sense of disappointment...and a strange feeling of rejection. I swallowed and tried to push down the hurt. So he wouldn't tell me his true name. So what? No big deal. It wasn't the kind of information demons liked to hand out, and that was fine. It was fine.

And maybe if I told myself that a couple of times, it'd stop smarting.

"Given your lack of powers," Azazel said, having cleared my plate, "it stands to reason that it must have been the use of my true name that enabled you to bind me."

"Okay, but how did that information end up in the book?"

He put down the plate and met my eyes. "That's what I'd like to know."

I threw my hands up. "I told you—I don't know where that book came from. I found it in the attic. It was handwritten, so it must have been someone's personal journal or something."

And because I'd burned it in a fit of fear after that botched séance, we couldn't go hunting for it to find out more. I'd told Azazel as much when he'd first asked me.

"If it was lying around your house, did it belong to your parents or some other family member?"

I considered that for a moment. "I'm not sure. I'd have to

ask my mom, but—" I made a helpless gesture indicating the whole can't-talk-to-my-mom predicament.

"What about your father?"

"Huh. Right." I sucked at my teeth. "He *is* hanging around all ghostly and available to answer questions. Maybe we could ask him on my visit tomorrow."

Azazel nodded, his expression thoughtful.

I leaned back and regarded him for a moment. "But no matter who might have put the name in the book, the information would've first had to come from a demon, right? Someone who'd found out your true name?"

He inclined his head, his eyes still with a faraway look to them. "I know of only one demon who learned my true name."

"Well…why don't you ask them if they passed that info on to some unsuspecting human who then put it in a book that a hormonally challenged teenager found and used for desperate measures?"

"Because he died about a hundred years ago," he said quietly.

"Oh." *Go, Zoe, keep stepping in it! That'll endear you to him.* "Were you guys…close?"

He tilted his head in thought. "We weren't friends, more of the opposite, actually. We were always in competition, trying to one-up each other. That's why this would fit his character. He was just the type to use something like that against me, and he was sneaky enough at playing the long game that I can see him passing my true name on to a human with the intention of it resulting in a summoning at some point."

"That's a really convoluted way of getting back at someone."

He shrugged. "Demons have nothing but time and

endless ways to plot against each other. Over the centuries, it becomes almost trite to outright fight one another. Much more interesting to weave an intricate web of traps for your enemy to get caught in." A small smile softened his features. "We'd do this for hundreds of years. Back and forth, like a game of sorts. I'd always have to watch my step because I never knew what new intrigue Moloch had designed for me."

The way he said his name, the way he looked when he talked about him… "You liked him, didn't you?"

His intense gaze met mine. "He was a great adversary. Shrewd. Competent. Always thinking a dozen steps ahead. He challenged me and kept me on my toes. So, yes, in a way, I liked him."

I chewed my lip. "So…you never had a thing?"

A sly smile quirked his lips. "I didn't say that."

Oh. My face heated. Well, then. I cleared my throat and rubbed my nose. At least this was one former lover of his I wouldn't run into. "What happened in the end?"

"He perished in a skirmish with angels."

"I thought Heaven and Hell had a truce?"

"The truce is for the big war that was halted millennia ago. Doesn't mean there aren't smaller fights here and there. If they don't cause too many casualties, they are considered negligible exceptions to the rule. No one wants to elevate small conflicts to something that could endanger the truce, so the ones in charge turn a blind eye to minor brawls."

"Right." I picked at a loose thread on my jeans. "Well, for what it's worth, I'm sorry about your frenemy."

"Frenemy," he echoed, a note of warmth in his voice. "That's a good way to put it."

I tentatively reached out and grasped his hand, intertwining my fingers with his. "We'll ask my dad about the book tomorrow, okay? Maybe he knows something about where it came from."

"We'll see," he said and squeezed my hand.

B<small>IRTHDAYS WERE TRICKY FOR ME.</small>

And it wasn't just the last one that had made me apprehensive about celebrating another turn of the year for me, although having a real-life demon show up in my apartment and eventually drag me to Hell did top all of the negative birthday experiences I'd had before. Even if that whole getting-dragged-to-Hell thing ended up not being *that* bad, given that I'd found the love of my life that way—on the day of, it had literally seemed like my life was ending.

But I'd also had some really shitty birthdays in the past, among them the one where my new bike had gotten stolen, the one where I'd failed my driver's test—I still hold, to this day, that the stop sign hadn't been *that* noticeable—the one where I'd tripped and fallen down a flight of stairs and broken my arm, and the memorable one where, during stretching exercises in P.E. in tenth grade, I'd loudly farted in front of the whole class.

Of course, I rationally knew that birthdays were just like any other day in the year, meaning that shitty things could totally happen on that day and I didn't enjoy some sort of magical birthday glow that would protect me from harm.

But still...I didn't know of anyone else who had so much bad luck on their birthdays. Out of the twenty-five I'd been through, more than half of them featured something crappy or upsetting happening to me, and if I didn't count the ones I was too young to be conscious of, the ratio was even worse.

So, to say I was a bit nervous about today would be an understatement. I was watching this day like a teacher might a routinely misbehaving student during a school performance—with a healthy dose of suspicion and the sobering realization that getting rid of the troublemaker was not an option.

The day was starting out well enough, though.

I'd gone to sleep cuddling the hellkittens—one in each arm—only to be awoken sans kittens, but with Azazel's skilled mouth between my legs.

My mind shook off the last misty impressions of my dream—not surprisingly, it had been a fantasy of getting hot 'n' heavy with my demon darling—and I was writhing and arching into his touch before I knew it. I'd never considered morning sex to be especially great, but that was before I'd met Azazel, who knew all the right moves to get my body ready to go in no time.

Also, he made sure I didn't have to work one bit during those morning sessions, so it was totally a win-win. Waking up and receiving fantastic orgasms without having to move much? Yes, please.

His hands held my thighs spread apart for his pleasure as he lapped at me with almost religious devotion. Hitting point after point, his tongue, lips, and fingers wound me tighter and tighter, and I moaned and gripped his hair. He growled as I pulled hard, letting me feel his teeth on my most sensitive flesh.

It only made me shudder with more lust.

His tongue speared me, teasing me, then flicked upward and around my clit with enough pressure to make my hips shoot off the mattress. He calmly pressed me down again and held me in place as he dialed up his oral assault, leaving me trembling and gasping, hovering right there on the edge.

His energy rolled out and over me in a wave of hot sparks, circling around my nipples and then pinching hard enough that pleasure exploded in my core. My orgasm razed me from top to bottom, and I cried out, still gripping Azazel's hair.

He didn't let up. Instead, he kept thrusting his fingers in and out of me while sucking on my clit, and I came apart again, even harder.

The last waves of my climax hadn't ebbed yet when he flipped me over. My face was pressed into the mattress, and I didn't care to move. The corner of my pillow was right there, perfect for biting into. And bite it I did as he kicked my legs apart and entered me with one smooth thrust.

My husky moan got swallowed by the pillow, my fingers curling into the sheets at the delicious sensation of his cock stretching me just so. Hovering over me with his weight balanced on one arm, he grabbed my neck with his free hand to keep me in place for his thrusts.

Slow and deep and thorough at first, each rolling shove letting me know exactly how much I was his, until every cell in my body surrendered to his claim. *Yes*, my breath said. *Yours*. Yielding, soft, living for his touch, every part of me attuned to him, willing to give until there was no more, I craved his demand. *All yours*.

With a growl turned groan, he changed the pace, changed the dynamic. Pulling my hips up, he rode me harder, faster, making me grab on to the sheets at the exquisite friction and force of his thrusts. All the while, his power twined around me, a hundred little taps of arousing electricity, heat licking over my breasts, down to my clit. Where before, I'd been the one to give, now it was him.

All yours, his touch said. *Yours alone.*

The combination of his rough thrusts and the caress of his energy sent me over the edge once more, and I bit the pillow with enough force that I might have pulled a muscle in my jaw. My muffled scream turned into a drawn-out moan as he emptied himself in me and half collapsed on my back.

If I'd been a cat, I'd have purred at how sinfully good his weight felt on top of me.

"Happy birthday," he murmured in my ear.

I shivered the happiest little shiver.

That amazing start to the day was followed by equally bone-melting shower sex, after which I had to be carried back to bed, due to my legs surprisingly not working.

Azazel was attentive, thoughtfully taking care of me, bringing me breakfast in bed, and even dragging both hellkittens back for me to play and cuddle with.

But that underlying current was still off. His affection just a touch short. And the memory of how he'd looked at me right after he thought I'd forgotten his mom's death...ugh, it was burned into the backs of my eyes and overlaid his image every time I glanced at him.

I took a deep breath, determined not to let this thing between us ruin my birthday. It was going well so far, wasn't it? Okay, granted, I'd only been awake for, like, two hours, but maybe this time around nothing untoward would happen that resulted in either eternal embarrassment, physical harm, or enough stress to power an entire city if turned into electricity.

Having finished my late breakfast, I played with the hellkittens a little. I'd found out that they loved it when I hurled them into the air toward the other side of the room, where they'd unfurl their small wings and do a turn in midair, flying back into my arms to be tossed again.

They finally had enough and bolted away to harass their father, who took his offspring's playful attention with the growly patience of a saint.

"Okay, I'm ready," I said to Azazel, who'd been cleaning and sharpening his weapons assortment in the other room.

He laid the sword he was working on aside and frowned at my arms. "You're all scratched up."

I peered down at the red lines zigzagging over my skin. "Eh." I shrugged. "It's totally worth it. Plus, I heal fast now, remember?"

"Not fast enough," he murmured, then took my wrists in his hands and sent a pulse of his energy up my arms. The small cuts stopped stinging, the surface wounds closing until what little blood had been there dried and fell off.

"Thank you." I sent him a small smile.

He met my eyes with an answering smile, and for a brief moment, the connection between us was unmarred by any strife or lurking tension, a flicker of what we used to have. But then something shuttered in his gaze, subtle yet noticeable all the more for how my heart had just started to hope.

"Let's go," he said and released my wrists.

I pressed my lips together, fighting down the keening sense of loss in my chest. I had to fix this. I didn't know how yet, but I'd find a way. Normally, I'd talk with him openly and explain, but in this instance, explaining why I'd acted as if I'd forgotten such an integral part of his life would break my vow to Lucifer, incurring his wrath.

But letting Azazel believe me to be so thoughtless pained me down to my soul.

I really was stuck between the Devil and the deep blue

sea with this dilemma, or rather, between the Devil and almost equally torturous consequences.

Determined to look for a solution later, I lay down on one of the couches, closed my eyes, and began the mental descent into the core of my being, preparing to separate my spirit from my body in order to travel to Earth.

I'd gotten a lot better at it over the past few months, and what had taken minutes the first time I'd done this was now a matter of seconds. I didn't even need Azazel's help anymore to peel the last bit of my soul from my body. It was still tricky, like pulling dough off a surface without leaving parts of it stuck, but I managed it more smoothly by now.

My mind now in a dreamlike state, I opened my spirit eyes to see my body reclining on the sofa, my chest rising and falling slowly as my physical form lay there in a sort of coma. For all intents and purposes, I was in a deep sleep, with my mind going on a little trip outside my body. Kind of like astral projection.

"Good to go?" Azazel asked me.

I nodded, and we made our way outside to the balcony, where my ghostly form hopped into his arms as he unleashed his wings. Holding on to him, I relished the feel of his skin against my fingers, knowing that for the next couple of hours while we visited Earth, he'd be the only thing I'd be able to touch and feel.

For some arcane reason, my senses in my spirit form were limited to sights and sounds on Earth, except for Azazel, whom I could still feel and smell and taste, apparently because he was Hell-born. He'd tried to explain the reasoning to me, but my brain had decided it was useless information and hadn't even attempted to retain the details. My lack of some senses in my spirit form was what it was, and I was dealing with it.

NADINE MUTAS

We flew to an allied demon's territory with a hellgate to Portland, and soon enough, we were up in the air above Oregon's largest city, hurtling toward the small suburban town outside the city limits, where my mom lived. Since it was Saturday, my mom would be off work, and chances were good that we'd encounter her at her house.

After touching down in the yard, Azazel set me on my feet, and I turned to the humble single-level home where I'd spent my teenage years. It was always a bit incongruent how much things here had stayed the same, when my life had changed so completely since I'd lived here. The rose bushes still hugged the fence, the old bench still stood there in the corner, the paint chipping off, and the assortment of metal and glass lawn decorations filled every nook and cranny of the tiny yard like they'd done for years and years.

For a moment, just a moment, the memory of my days spent here shimmered to life strongly enough to drive away the here and now, and suddenly, I was a fifteen-year-old again, lying on a lounger and soaking up the sun on those seemingly endless summer days.

I blinked, and the vision vanished, plunging me back into my current reality—standing as a ghost in my mom's back-yard, on a visit from Hell, my demon husband next to me.

No amount of fantasy reading had prepared me for this life, honestly.

With a sigh I didn't really feel, seeing as my spirit form didn't actually breathe, I walked forward and right through the back door into the kitchen. The living room opened up behind it, and there was my mom, lying on the sofa and reading a book. Her dark brown hair, the same color as mine, was pulled back into a messy ponytail, and her skin looked paler than the last time I'd seen her a few weeks ago.

More lines marked her face, dark circles sitting underneath her eyes.

As always, when I saw her, happiness and hurt mingled in equal measures in my heart. She was so, so familiar, a thousand precious childhood memories wrapped up in her face, and yet, she might as well have been light-years away from me. I stood there, in the middle of the living room, watching her read, the quiet of the house enveloping us, and I felt like I was looking at her through an impenetrable glass wall, forever separated.

Some of these visits were good; some were a little bit harder.

Sometimes I'd be content to watch her for long minutes, even an hour, just sitting with her, or following her through the house as she cleaned or straightened things. If I was lucky, it felt like I was just there with her, silently joining her in her day-to-day activities, and the part of me starved for this connection to my mom would sigh in relief.

Other times, seeing her was like cutting open a barely scabbed-over wound. On those days, standing there, shadowing her around the house, was nothing but a stark reminder that she was forever lost to me, at least in the way she had been before. Watching her silently would cause me almost physical pain—or it felt that way in my spirit form, anyway—because a part of me expected her to turn around any second now, look at me, smile, tell me to go get the coffee started, and ask if I remembered to get the brownies from the store.

But she'd never again turn to me, recognize me, see me. She'd never talk to me again, and I'd never see my mom's eyes light up again when I walked through the door, never feel her strong hug and hear her mutter, "It's been ages."

I balled my ghostly hands into fists, phantom tears burning in my eyes.

This one, right here, was one of the harder visits.

Maybe it had been a stupid idea to come here on my birthday. The pressure was high to make it a good visit, but it wasn't something immediately in my control. I didn't consciously decide when I'd miss her so fucking much that it broke my heart.

Taking a deep breath that I didn't feel, I turned away from my mom. I had to cut this one short, or else I'd be a fucking mess all day. Maybe the next visit would be better, and I'd be happy to sit with her or follow her around like a silent puppy.

I walked back into the kitchen, and my gaze fell on Azazel, who stood over the table at the far wall, leafing through a stack of mail. I glanced back to check if my mom had noticed her letters basically moving through the air of their own accord, but she was completely focused on her book, facing the other direction on the sofa. Unless Azazel decided to make himself seen, he'd appear invisible, the same as me, and while he could touch and move things around as easily as if he were fully corporeal, the objects would seem to be moving as if by a ghostly hand. Which kind of was the case.

He frowned at a particular letter, already opened, but put it down as I neared.

"Isn't that sort of illegal," I asked with a teasing note, "reading someone's mail?"

"Human laws don't apply to me," was his deadpan answer, accompanied by a smirk.

"Anything of note in there?"

I tried to catch a glimpse of the letter he'd pondered, but

he'd put the stack of mail and leaflets to rights again, my mom's gardening magazine lying on top.

"Just some weird ads for pizza toppings that should be outlawed."

"Oh?"

"Pineapple on pizza was already bad enough. These new abominations people have come up with…" He shook his head. "Straight ticket to Hell."

I put my hands on my hips. "Hey. I like pineapple on pizza."

He closed his eyes with a heavy sigh. "This is it, then. Our irreconcilable difference. My divorce lawyer will contact you."

My lips twitched with the urge to grin. "I get the dog."

"She snores too loudly anyway."

"Pfft. That's what earplugs are for."

His smile was brief and beautiful, his features sobering as he regarded me for a heartbeat. "Ready to leave?"

I swallowed and nodded, lowering my eyes. "Yeah. Today's…"

"A hard one," he finished for me, always so attuned to my moods, having seen enough of the not-so-good visits to know what was up.

I nodded again, not trusting myself to speak. All that turmoil inside me might spill out and make me vomit feels all over my ghostly shoes.

"Let's go, then," Azazel said.

Grateful for not needing to explain myself, I followed him out into the yard, and he took me to the skies once more.

When we landed in the yard of my dad's house in Gresham, all the way on the other side of Portland, I slowly headed toward the back door of the two-story house after having checked if anyone was outside. I'd sent word to my father beforehand, letting him know I'd be coming for a visit on my birthday, and he'd said he would make sure to be home. He mostly hung out around the house, but sometimes, he'd accompany his family on an outing. I had yet to ask him if he parked his ghostly butt in the car with them or maybe rode along on the roof. Or the trunk?

Going places in spirit form was weird because the fact that I was incorporeal and could walk through walls and objects meant that it was purely based on an unconscious decision to even "walk" or "stand" on the floor anywhere. If I concentrated, I could likely make myself sink into the earth or something. Azazel guessed that my not having to focus on standing or walking on the floor had to do with certain presets of the human mind, meaning that when you lived your whole life experiencing the floor as solid, your ghost form automatically presumed that as standard and acted accordingly. That was why it took extra focus to walk through walls. I always had to turn off my acquired knowledge that walls were meant to be solid.

Inside the house of my dad's second family, I found him in the living room...playing cards with a female demon.

CHAPTER 15

I halted in my tracks at the sight. My dad and the demon both raised their heads and stared at me.

With a start, the demon got to her feet and bowed low, her brown braid sliding over her shoulder. "My lady," she said. "My lord."

"Cadriel," Azazel said from behind me in greeting. "Scott."

I blinked at my dad, who nodded at Azazel and then turned to me with a big smile. "Zoe! So good to see you. Happy birthday, sweetheart."

He stood and pulled me into a hug—given that we were both ghosts, we could actually touch and feel each other in a weird twist of metaphysical rules, the logistics of which my mind yet again refused to hold on to—while Azazel murmured to Cadriel, "A word, please."

Both demons left, and I released my dad and gestured at the cards laid out on the table.

"What is this?"

My dad glanced at the cards, then grinned and shrugged. "Well, these demons are always around, and it got kind of awkward to keep ignoring them, so I asked if they wanted to play. Cadriel is great at gin rummy."

I stared at him, open-mouthed. A year ago, my dad had been terrified of demons, an understandable reaction considering he'd been tortured in Hell for a few weeks before Azazel pulled him out. My infernal husband had also stationed a sort of demon bodyguard to watch over my dad, to make sure no other demon would drag him back to Hell. My dad's soul was still marked as a sinner and therefore ripe for the taking for any demon stumbling upon him. Having one of Azazel's subordinates shadow my dad ensured he wouldn't be snatched.

It also meant there'd always be someone to keep a close eye on any negative changes in my father's soul. Ghosts who lingered too long on Earth would eventually turn into wraiths, which were basically poltergeists who were unpredictable and aggressive...and tended to attack the people they'd known and loved in life.

It was a slow change, though, usually taking years or even decades. My dad hopefully still had a long time ahead of him before he deteriorated, at which point the demons tasked to watch him would put him down.

He knew and was more than okay with that. He'd once mentioned that it was his nightmare to maybe one day assault his own family when he became a wraith.

"So...you're chummy with demons now, huh?" I asked with a grin.

He shrugged again, looking sheepish. "Well, you know, it can get a bit lonely here. Watching the girls and Olivia is great and all, but other than during your visits, I don't really have anyone to talk to. The demons are always there, so I figured, why not make them company? And they're actually not bad. I mean, I only got to see the worst parts of them back when I...you know."

He never liked to directly mention his brief stay in Hell. Well, *brief* in the larger scheme, though to him it must have felt like eternity. My stomach still turned over at the thought of his suffering down there—part of which, apparently, had been mental and emotional torture with my image, making him experience the pain his actions had caused me. My feelings about his having a secret second family and basically leaving us for them when my mom found out were still quite messy, and I suspected that a part of me would never forgive him.

But that didn't mean I didn't love him or that I didn't cherish the fact that we'd reconnected and sorted out things as much as possible. Family was complicated, and having a human heart came with a complexity of emotions beyond our understanding.

"But when you get to know them," my dad continued, "they're actually okay guys. Good conversationalists. Even better card players." He grinned and waved at the cards on the table.

"How do you move them so easily?" I narrowed my eyes at him. "I'm still having trouble picking up a single large object and holding it, let alone handling several small objects like these cards."

It was true. I still failed half the time when I tried to move something in my spirit form. It was incredibly frustrating.

My dad gave me a rueful smile. "Practice." When I raised a brow, he elaborated. "You only come here for a few hours every couple of weeks. Meanwhile, I am stuck here on Earth as a ghost, and I've got nothing but time. Practicing my fine motor skills as a recently deceased was one of the things I did at first not to die of boredom." He paused and frowned. "Well, metaphorically speaking, since I'm already dead."

My smile was a tad sad. To be honest, I hadn't really considered what it was like for my dad "living" on Earth as a ghost. It hadn't occurred to me that, except for when I came to see him, he really didn't have much in the form of interaction with another sentient being. It shouldn't have been surprising that he'd turned to his demon "bodyguards" for company.

"I get it," I said softly. "There's probably a lot of down-time for you when Olivia and the girls aren't home, or when they sleep."

He nodded. "It's not that I mind it much. I'm happy I have this second chance at seeing the girls grow up, and being able to be around Olivia a bit longer, even if she doesn't know I'm here...it's worth it." He gave me a sly grin. "Sometimes, when they're not home, I manage to turn on the TV and watch some shows. But I can only do that when they're all out. Can you imagine their reactions if the TV turned on by itself?"

With a shudder, I remembered the one and only time I watched the Japanese original of *The Ring*. I'd covered all the TVs in the house for weeks after that, but it still wouldn't erase the memory of seeing that scary AF girl crawl out of the television in that movie.

"Yeah, no," I hurried to say. "Don't ever do that. No one wants to be scarred for life like that."

"It's probably confusing enough that their Netflix profiles show recently watched movies they never saw."

I just stared at him.

"Mostly, the girls accuse each other of messing with the profiles, so it's all good."

"Right," I said, drawing out the word. "Maybe you

should go to the neighbors' to watch on their device? Didn't you mention they were always up in your business, complaining about every little thing? Why don't you give them some ghostly payback?"

I couldn't believe I was actually egging on my departed dad to haunt some unsuspecting people. Hell was rubbing off on me.

My dad's face lit up. "That's a great idea! I could do some harmless pranks, like tie all their shoelaces together or replace all their pictures of Jesus with Ewan McGregor as Obi-Wan Kenobi."

I'd created a monster.

"Sure, yeah, you do that." I patted him on his ghostly shoulder.

Azazel came back into the house at that point, sans Cadriel.

I jerked my head at him. "Where's my dad's card-playing partner?"

"She's been tasked with another assignment." His eyes flicked to my dad. "I'll send a replacement once we're back in Hell, but until then, you'd best stay inside."

My dad nodded. Chances were lower that another demon would randomly spot him if he was inside the house.

I faced my dad again. "There's something I wanted to ask you."

He put his hands in his ghostly pockets. "Sure. Shoot."

"Remember when I told you about that séance I did that ended up binding Azazel and me together? I was actually going off a book I'd found in our attic. It was handwritten, bound in black leather, no title, a whole lot of gibberish inside with something intelligible here and there. Do you happen to know anything about this book?"

My dad's forehead was creased with deep lines. "Not that I recall... When did you say you found it?"

"I was thirteen."

"Hm..." He stared at the floor in thought. "We were still living in that house in Sunnyside, right?"

"Yep." Just a short year before our family fell apart and my parents divorced. "Do you remember if the book was maybe an heirloom or something on your side or Mom's?"

He shook his head, and my heart sank. There went our only lead to finding out more about that book and my summoning.

"I don't think I've seen it before," my dad continued, "and I don't remember your mom bringing along something like it when we married and moved in together."

Dammit. So much for that, then.

"But," my dad said, making me pause in my negative thinking spiral, "it could have been part of old Dorothy's stuff."

"Old Dorothy?"

"Don't you remember? She was the old lady we bought the house from."

Slivers of memory surfaced from the depths of my child-hood—the image of a woman, tousled gray hair, face lined with decades of a life fully lived.

"She was friends with your grandma Harriet," my dad went on. "And when she got too old to live alone and needed to sell her house, your grandma pounced on that information right away. We'd been looking at houses for a while, but the market was tough, and Dorothy's house was in a great neighborhood, with good schools, a quiet area, a big yard—everything we'd been looking for. And we got a deal, thanks to your grandma. She negotiated with Dorothy to not put it on the market but sell it directly to us, and we'd agree to take care of any furniture and household stuff left over from her move. She was grateful because she was already frail at the time, and she had no family to help her with the move and selling all her stuff. We said we'd do it for her, and that way she just had to pack what she wanted to take to the nursing home, and we took care of the rest." He smiled wistfully. "When we went to give her the money from the sale of her goods, she refused to take it, telling us to buy some nice new things for our home with it."

"So the book could have belonged to Dorothy?" I asked, bringing my dad's nostalgia back on track.

He shrugged. "Possibly, yes. You said you found it in the attic? Well, there was a lot of her stuff there that we didn't get to go through. After we'd cleared the main rooms of the house and had done all the necessary updates, we were just too exhausted at first to take on the things in the attic as well. So we said we'd do them later. Except...well, you know how it goes when you put things off." He gave me a self-conscious smile. "In the end, we never got around to tackling the attic. We just left it all up there, untouched. So, if you found the book in the attic, chances are good that it's one of Dorothy's old possessions."

My ghostly heart beat faster. "Is she still alive?"

"I don't know, honey. It's been—God, how long? Almost twenty years that we moved into that house? We didn't really keep in touch with her after, especially when your grandma Harriet died. For all I know, Dorothy could be long gone, too." He squinted at me. "Why are you asking, anyway?"

I shook my head. "We're just trying to find out more about that book. Maybe if Dorothy is still alive, we could ask her about it. Do you remember which nursing home she went to?"

"I don't recall the name, but it was on the corner of Southeast Sixtieth Avenue and Southeast Division Street. Redbrick building."

I clapped my slightly translucent hands together and did a little jump. "Thank you! We'll go over there right now."

I was already turning around when Azazel casually stopped me with an arm around my waist, still facing my dad.

"It would help us find her in the nursing home," Azazel said, "if we knew her last name."

Right, yeah, that'd be kind of important.

"Sure," my dad said. "It's Anderson. Dorothy Anderson."

"Thank you." Azazel inclined his head.

I waved at my dad on my way out the door. "Bye! See you in a couple of weeks. Good haunting!" I gave him two thumbs up.

"Haunting?" Azazel murmured as we stepped outside.

"Just a bit of fun. My dad's going to play some harmless pranks on his neighbors."

Azazel stopped me with a finger on my chest, his expression serious. "No. Indulging in haunting activities that harass the living might accelerate his transformation into a wraith. It's the first step toward losing the connection to his humanity."

I blinked rapidly at him. "He was just going to tie their shoelaces together."

"It's a slippery slope."

"So, harmless pranks are like a gateway drug for ghosts?" I made my voice lower, imitating a male narrator. "Are your deceased parents dabbling in haunts? It might seem innocent, but it's a slippery slope. First, it's swapping out pictures of Jesus with Ewan McGregor as Obi-Wan Kenobi—"

Azazel raised both brows.

"Then it's the full-on haunt with floating objects and nightly screeching. Notice the early warning signs and talk to your dearly departed about spiritual abuse."

Azazel covered his face with his hand.

But since I wasn't going to ignore his sage advice, I zoomed back into the house and yelled at my dad, "Change of plans—no haunting!"

He stared at me, dumbfounded.

I pointed at him with a finger. "Any haunting, no matter how small, will make you turn into a wraith faster. So don't do it. I know it's tempting, but you have to be strong. Got it?"

He nodded, his eyes wide.

And before I zipped back out the door, I gave in to the urge to replay key moments from my high school's anti-drug program. "Don't be cool," I said to him in a stern voice. "Stay in school."

My dad's parting grin warmed my heart as I rejoined Azazel on the porch. Ever since my dad and I had reconciled and started talking again, I'd remembered more and more how much of a connection we'd had before it all fell apart. I loved my mom with all my heart, and we'd always have this special bond, but I'd never joked with her like I'd done with my dad. He'd been my partner in silly crime, and he'd always appreciated my brand of humor, because it was pretty much his own, too.

I hadn't realized how much I'd missed cracking jokes around him and grinning about silly things until after we'd stitched our broken relationship back together.

I turned to Azazel, the reason all of this was even possible, and the smile I gave him wavered with emotion.

"Thank you," I said and laid my hand on his cheek.

"For what?"

I jerked my head toward the house with my dad in it. "Without you, I wouldn't be here talking to him. If I hadn't met you—"

"I kidnapped you and dragged you to Hell," he said with a glint of humor in his eyes.

"Particulars." I waved that away. "Besides, I went willingly."

"Because you didn't have a choice."

"Are you *trying* to twist this into a bad thing? Just shush and let me thank you."

His eyes danced with amusement, but he pressed his lips into a line and shut up.

"Anyway, if I hadn't gone to Hell with you, I'd have lost any chance at reconciliation when my dad died. And even in Hell…" I stroked my hands over his chest, tracing the lines and dips of his fighting leathers. "If you hadn't risked everything to pull my dad's soul out, I'd have lost him forever, too. I've thanked you before, but I just want you to know how much it means to me."

He studied my face intently, his eyes churning with storms and lightning. "Seeing you this happy is its own reward." Leaning in, he nipped at my lower lip, and my entire spirit form shivered in delight. "But that doesn't mean I'll forgo more physical rewards from you."

I grinned against his mouth. "Subtle, babe. Real subtle."

His kiss was scorching, curling my toes even in my incorporeal state, a promise of rewards to be demanded at a later point. I'd comply all too gladly.

Lifting me into his arms once more, he shot into the sky,

heading for the nursing home. It was a quick flight, and soon we touched down on the small stretch of lawn in front of the redbrick building. The big sign over the entrance read *Mt. Tabor Home for the Elderly*.

"Well, at least the nursing home is still here," I said as Azazel set me on my feet. "That's a good sign. With any luck, Dorothy is rocking a long life in there."

"Let's check it out."

He headed for the front entrance, and just before he grabbed the door handle, I felt a tingle in the air.

"Did you just make yourself visible?" I whisper-shouted.

Why are you whispering? he replied in my head. *And, yes. How else would I make an inquiry about Mrs. Anderson?*

But—you look like you just escaped the film set of a medieval war movie. I gestured at his apparel and the sword strapped to his back.

He paused with his hand on the door handle and glanced down at himself. *Good point.*

With a ripple, his appearance changed, his fighting leathers smoothing out into a modern shirt and pants combo, the sword at his back vanishing into thin air.

I pointed at him with my mouth hanging open. "That," I said out loud, having lost all mental finesse. "I didn't know you could do that."

Same concept as hiding my wings. He winked at me, opened the door wide, and walked in.

I followed through the closing door and caught up to him as he strolled up to the reception area.

The young woman behind the counter looked up from her PC and uttered a small gasp at the sight of Azazel. *I know the feeling,* I thought. And though he was already breathtaking under normal circumstances, he'd now dialed up his allure and demonically enhanced his attractiveness, the result of which was the receptionist gazing at him open-mouthed like he was the eighth Wonder of the World.

She nearly fell over herself in her haste to get to her feet, smooth down her clothes, and fluff up her hair. I noticed how she made sure to tug her blouse deeper to reveal more cleavage, and I narrowed my eyes.

I walked right through the reception desk to the other side and grabbed a pencil from the table behind the woman. Or tried to. Small objects were tricky to grasp.

Zoe, Azazel warned.

Out loud, he said, "Hello. I was wondering if I could see Dorothy Anderson."

"Oh." The receptionist started twirling her hair and batting her lashes at my husband as she came around the reception desk to stand right next to him. "Of course."

Oh, yay, that sounded like she was still alive!

While I internally celebrated that small victory, I finally managed to float the pencil off the table with my ghostly hand. Azazel shot me a warning look over the woman's shoulder.

"Mrs. Anderson, you say?" The receptionist pursed her lips much more than they needed to be pursed. "And you are…?"

"Off the market," I groused, focusing hard on floating the pencil closer to her.

Not even acknowledging my interjection, Azazel smiled at her—whoa, that was a megawatt smile—and leaned in a bit. "An old acquaintance."

"Oh." The receptionist giggled and twirled her hair faster. "Right. Well, I can show you to her, if you'd like."

She placed her hand on his arm, which was the moment I saw red. I stabbed the wandering hand with the pencil. I'd intended to stab hard, but my ghostly strength being what it was—a total bust—the pencil didn't even break the skin.

It was enough to smart, though, judging by the woman's cry and the way she pulled her hand back as if burned.

I met Azazel's accusing glare with a triumphant one.

Stop, he growled in my head.

Stop…and then what? I shot back. *Collaborate and listen? In the name of love? It's hammer time? You gotta be more specific; there's a lot of ways this can go.*

Stop antagonizing our source of information. He bared his teeth at me while the woman bent to pick up the pencil that had fallen to the floor, her expression bewildered and a little scared.

Stop flirting with her, I hissed back.

I'm manipulating her to help us achieve our objective fast and without hassle, and you're interfering.

I crossed my arms in front of my chest. *Manipulate this.*

Holding his gaze, I poked the woman in the side with my ghostly finger.

She uttered a shrill sound of surprise and whirled around, her wide eyes scanning the room.

Azazel rolled his eyes heavenward. *For Hell's sake, Zoe.*

To the woman, he said, "Stacy, was it?" He touched her elbow, pulling her attention back to him.

"Yes." She gave him a wobbly smile, her hand unconsciously going to the name tag on her blouse.

"Please show me to Mrs. Anderson."

"Of course. Yes. Right away." Fluffing up her hair once more, she sashayed in front of him, her hips working overtime to send her message.

"And here we can see the human female," I intoned, imitating David Attenborough's voice and accent as he narrated a nature documentary, "desperately trying to attract the attention of a male in order to mate."

Azazel, walking just a step behind the receptionist, pressed his lips together.

"Unbeknownst to her," I continued, infusing my narration with a sense of doom, "her flamboyant display has unfortunately made her the target of a supernatural predator."

Zoe, Azazel said, his mental voice sounding strained.

"As soon as the mighty ghost stalking her learns how," I went on, "she will find herself the victim of a wedgie."

Zoe, Azazel said, tension making his shoulders rigid, *if you don't stop, I will bring you back to Hell and come back here alone. I can't afford to laugh and ruin this mission.*

I smiled smugly.

"Oh, I have to warn you," Stacy said as she stopped in front of a door. "Mrs. Anderson's Alzheimer's is very progressed. I'm not sure how much you'll be able to talk to her. She might not recognize you at all."

My jealousy retreated long enough for me to digest her words. Here I'd been happy that Dorothy was still alive, only to find out now that she had severe dementia. Crap. We probably wouldn't get any information out of her.

"That's fine," Azazel said smoothly. "I'll see if she has a good day."

"Sure." Stacy bit her lower lip and stood up straighter, pushing out her chest. "If you need *anything*"—she purred that word—"don't hesitate to call me."

I rolled my eyes.

"Is that how women usually react to you?" I asked as she sashayed away again, leaving us alone in the hall.

His smirk was answer enough.

"Must have been quite the ego check when I verbally spit

in your face as you came to drag me to Hell last year," I drawled with a smirk of my own.

As I recall, he replied, his eyes hot on me, *that irrational resistance didn't last long.*

"Pfft."

And you did call me an achingly beautiful fallen angel with whom any hot-blooded woman—and many a man—would want to explore the very meaning of sin, he quoted my inner monologue from that night exactly one year ago, when he'd shown up in my living room.

And then he winked at me. Winked! The scoundrel.

"Those were private thoughts," I growled. "But if you're so good at remembering my innermost musings, you might recall that I also called you a creepy psycho."

He stepped closer, his eyes tender as he tipped up my chin with one finger. *You can shelve that jealousy now,* he said. *You know there's no need for it.*

I crossed my arms again and gave him my best narrow-eyed pout. "I'd like to see you keep your cool if some other male put his paws on me."

The twitch in his eye gave him away.

"Uh-huh." I sent him a smug smile and leaned closer. "You'd go ballistic, and don't you deny it."

We should go in, he said in response and turned toward the door.

I didn't even try to suppress my cackle.

He knocked and then pressed down the handle, slowly opening the door. With no one else around, he held it open for me to step in after him, and my gaze fell on the frail woman lying on the bed in the corner, staring at the TV on the opposite wall. A colorful quilt lay on the blanket covering her lower half, and the nightstand featured a framed picture of a much younger woman arm in arm with a handsome man, their faces smiling. Her late husband and her, maybe?

Dorothy Anderson didn't react to Azazel's presence, her milky eyes riveted on the TV screen, though it seemed she was staring far off. Deep lines carved her face, the hair on her head so thin and wispy it seemed like steam curling off the surface of a hot spring.

"Mrs. Anderson?" Azazel asked gently.

No reaction.

"Dorothy?"

At that, she blinked slowly, took a deep breath, and turned her head to look at him. Her hairless brows drew together.

"Who are you?" she asked, her voice cracking.

My heart broke a little at seeing her. More memories rose from the depths of my mind, revived by meeting her once again, this woman I'd seen a few times when I was barely old enough to go to school. What I remembered of her was a lot more vibrant than this version of her before me, bent and broken with age and a disease that ate away at her mind.

Azazel pulled up a chair and sat down next to the bed. "I'm married to the woman who used to live in your house."

Surprised that he'd stick to the truth so much, I glanced at him. He was intently focused on Dorothy, reaching out to gently grasp her wrinkled hand.

The moment he touched her, she gasped, her eyes going wide.

"What are you doing?" I hurried forward, my heart in my throat.

"That's not me," he said, something like shock on his face.

Dorothy's milky eyes moved rapidly, then stilled and fixated on him. The white film over them slipped away, their blue becoming clear and startlingly sharp. For a moment, she stared at him in utter silence, while the seconds ticked by with my quick breaths.

Her wrinkled face lighting up with a huge smile, she then said slowly, distinctly, "Azazel!"

CHAPTER 16

Azazel froze in the chair, becoming inhumanly still. My heart skipped a beat, and I held my breath —not that I needed to breathe in my spirit form, but…force of habit.

"Azazel," Dorothy repeated, her eyes glowing with warmth—and cunning. "You found me."

I'd never really seen Azazel this speechless. He just stared at this frail, elderly woman he didn't know, but who recognized him for who he was, impossibly so.

Dorothy leaned forward a bit, her shrewd eyes fixed on him. "Did I get you? Did it work?"

I blinked, dumbfounded, at the scene before me. What the *fuck* was going on?

"It can't be," Azazel murmured, still sitting so frozen in shock.

Dorothy's eyes tracked over his shoulder and settled on me. "Is that her? Is she the one who summoned you?"

Azazel sucked in a sharp breath.

I tensed, my eyes widening. "Can she see me?"

"I can hear you, too, sweetheart." Dorothy winked at me,

then looked back at Azazel. "How did she trap you? What did she do? Tell me." She patted his hand, her face eager.

Azazel's throat worked as he swallowed hard before he said, "She forced me to marry her."

"Excuse me!" I said at the same time as Dorothy cackled so hard she fell back against the propped-up pillow.

"I thought we'd been over this," I said to Azazel, gesturing wildly in the air. "I didn't know that I was *forcing* you to do anything. I just read from this book and added my own hormonal teenage drama spin so I wouldn't end up single at twenty-five."

Dorothy laughed so violently that I was scared she might suffocate or have a heart attack.

"Zoe," Azazel said, his gaze still on Dorothy, his voice solemn. "Meet Moloch."

My jaw hit the proverbial floor. "What?"

Moloch? As in, Azazel's erstwhile frenemy? The one who'd died a hundred years ago?

Dorothy wiped her eyes, her chest shaking with her fading laughter, and looked at me.

"Moloch," Azazel said, "this is my wife, Zoe."

"Pleasure to meet you, darling." Dorothy/Moloch grinned at me, then glanced at Azazel again. "I got you good, didn't I?"

A small smile bloomed on Azazel's face, his features softening. "Your best one yet."

Moloch nodded with the same expression a cat that got into the cabinet where all the treats were kept might have. "It took long enough. Thought I might not see it come to pass."

"How?" Azazel leaned forward, his elbows on his knees, his hands clasped.

Moloch shrugged. "Used to be, I'd get these seizures, and

then I *remembered*. That's when I wrote it all down. Of course, when I'd come to, my human mind refused to acknowledge what happened." His mouth twisted bitterly. "Refused to act on it. Oh, the things I could have done if I'd been able to summon you myself." Mischief sparked in his eyes as he looked at Azazel. "Alas, it wasn't to be. Had to be someone else." He glanced at me and winked. "You did good, kid. Making him marry..." He leaned back against the pillow and chuckled. "That is better than I could have imagined." Closing his eyes, he sagged a bit, his voice becoming weaker. "Didn't think I'd get to see it..."

Azazel reached out and grabbed his hand again.

A soft smile spread across Moloch's face, his eyes still closed. "I win."

"You win," Azazel repeated, his voice hoarse.

Moloch took a deep breath, his chest rattling, and when he opened his eyes again, the milky film on them was back, all cunning gone.

"Who are you?" Dorothy asked as she stared at Azazel, her voice burdened and cracked with age.

Azazel held her gaze for a long moment, then he softly said, "Someone from a different life."

Her brows drew together, but she nodded, her milky eyes sad. "I'm tired."

"Then sleep."

Nodding again, she closed her eyes. Her breathing deepened—then stopped.

I jerked forward, but Azazel held up a hand.

"Not me," he said quietly. "It's just her time."

I blinked, and in the space between my lashes lowering, I saw a fast blip of light go out from her body. Her soul, I realized.

"Where...?"

"She was slated for Heaven." He set her hand gently next to her body before he let it go. "She'll have been collected right away."

"Collected? By whom?"

"The Angel of Death."

I startled. "Your father?"

He nodded once, curtly, then rested his elbows on his knees again and let his head hang. I looked at Dorothy, lying so still in death, all life and warmth gone, and with it, the last traces of Azazel's old friend.

Sadness gripping my heart, I closed the distance to Azazel and hugged him as he sat there.

"I'm sorry," I whispered, tunneling my fingers through his hair.

How cruel life could get. How meandering. To lose someone you cared for, to mourn their passing, only to meet their reincarnation a hundred years later—moments before their final death.

I hugged him tighter, letting him know without words that I was there for him, that I understood his pain. A few heartbeats passed, and then his arms came around me, pulling me closer. His face buried in my middle, he held me as I held him, his shoulders trembling with his silent sobs.

My throat closing up, I petted his hair and curled over him.

And through the sadness and the pain I felt with him, I knew and understood and cherished the way he allowed himself to be this vulnerable with me, broken down and bleeding from the softest part of himself.

Because I knew, without a doubt, that he'd never let anyone else see him this way.

BY THE TIME WE CAME BACK TO HELL, IT WAS ALREADY LATE enough in the morning over in Sydney that I could continue straight with my second visit to Earth, for which Azazel flew me to yet another demon's territory with a gate near the city.

He'd been quiet ever since the nursing home, understandably so. I didn't prod him, knowing he needed time to process. I remembered my own numb shock after finding out my dad had died. I wished there was more I could do for Azazel, but for now, I'd respect his renewed grief, and I'd be there for him when he turned to me for comfort.

Taylor was home, as I'd asked her to be, already waiting with a birthday cake and a huge smile on her face. God, I missed her so much.

She jumped up from the couch at the sight of us materializing on her balcony, and her strawberry-blond hair bounced around her shoulders as she clapped her hands together and hopped excitedly.

"Zoe!" she squealed.

"Tay!" I answered with a big grin.

"You," Taylor said and snapped her fingers at Azazel, who lifted a brow at the imperious gesture. "Be a dear and hug her super tight, will you?"

He lifted the second brow and just stared at her in the most amazing silent mix of *What the fuck?* and *How dare you?*

Taylor rolled her eyes and blew out a breath. "I can't hug her, okay? But it's her birthday, and she deserves all the hugs, so come on."

Azazel's gaze swung to me, a glint of warmth in his eyes. "That she does."

TILL HEAVEN DO US PART

I grinned even more as he pulled me into his arms.

"Harder!" Taylor hollered. "Squeeze the ghostly life out of her. Give her the huggiest hug of all hugs."

"Your taste in friends is concerning," Azazel murmured in my ear as he pressed me closer.

"She friendopted me," I wheezed back. "I didn't have much choice."

"Happy birthday, Zoe!" Taylor shouted from right next to us. To Azazel she said, "You call that a hug? She isn't a delicate flower, dude. If she can still talk, you're not squeezing her tight enough."

"All right," Azazel said, releasing me. "I'm out. I'll be back in two hours to pick you up."

"Quitter," Taylor murmured at his back as he strolled outside and took off from the balcony.

I reeled from the tight hug he'd given me, swaying on my ghostly feet, and turned to Tay.

"Oh, I wish I could hug you myself, hon." She clasped her hands in front of her.

Taylor was a hugger. Obviously. In fact, Tay was everything physical, and she moved through the world with her every gesture an extension of her larger-than-life personality. I smiled and soaked up her energy, letting it pull me up as it always did.

"I know," I said and shrugged. "Alas, this spirit form is a bit physically challenged. Best I can do is poke you."

"No, no." Tay waved that away. "I'll find a dude for that, thank you."

I snort-laughed.

"Okay, so I got you this cake." She gestured at the birthday confection on the coffee table. "I know you can't eat it, but I thought it'd be nice to have one anyway."

"You just wanted an excuse to eat cake."

"Guilty as charged." She grinned and then pointed at it. "Look, though. Isn't it cute?"

I squinted at the cake topper, which looked suspiciously like... "Is that a basket? Surrounded by flames?"

"Yes! Get it?"

I stared at her.

She gave me an intense look. "Because you went to Hell in a handbasket?"

I covered my face with my hand. "Tay."

She erupted in laughter, and I cracked up right along with her.

"You're insane," I said between giggles.

"I prefer 'creatively ignorant of social rules.'" She pointed at me with the knife before she cut into the cake.

"Speaking of which..." I pinned her with a look. "You have *got* to stop summoning Belial for trivial shit like delivering your messages to me."

She narrowed her eyes at me but then nodded as she ate a piece of the cake. "Oh, I see," she said around chewing. "So you're saying I should use him for more important stuff..."

"No."

"I mean"—she gestured with the tiny fork—"there *is* this douchebag I dated a few months back who is in dire need of being taught a lesson not to cheat on his girlfriend. Belial could scare the shit out of him. And I mean that literally. How great would it be if that asshole actually shit his pants at the sight of a real-deal demon threatening to take his soul?" She snickered and took another bite of the cake.

"Tay!"

"What?"

"I mean it." I put my hands on my hips and glared at her. "Stop summoning him. He's pissed as fuck about this and just waiting for the chance to turn the tables and pay you back for humiliating him like that."

Taylor appeared unconcerned. Gah, sometimes I hated how dauntless she could be.

"He can't hurt me," she said with a shrug. "I commanded him not to harm me, and he can't act against that."

"For now. What if he finds a way around it? There's always a loophole. If he figures out how to evade that command…"

"There'll be *Hell* to pay," Taylor intoned in a deep voice and then chuckled at her own joke.

I facepalmed.

"Tay, please," I began again. "Stop with the summoning."

"Look," she said after taking another bite of the cake and chewing, "the way I see it, it's too late now anyway. The damage is already done, right? You said he's pissed as fuck. Well, even if I stop summoning now, he'll still be pissed as fuck. Demons live forever. I bet they have long memories. So what are the chances that he'll just forget about the whole thing if I stop calling on him now? How likely is it that he'll simmer down over time and won't come for me decades from now when he figures out how to get around the command?" She shot me an arch look. "You're the one who knows demons. Tell me—will he let this slide?"

I deflated. I couldn't lie to her. "No."

"See?" She gestured with the fork again. "Right now, I'm damned if I do and damned if I don't. And honestly, I'd rather get some fun out of it if I already have a target on my back. Squeeze it for what it's worth."

"Tay, you really shouldn't squeeze an already enraged demon."

"Oh, right, because he'll torture me a *little* less if I back off now?" She clucked her tongue and continued eating.

"No, Z. Nothing I can do right now will appease that demon into not getting back at me when he gets the chance. So why not take advantage while I can?"

"Because I don't want you to get hurt!"

Taylor set down her fork and met my gaze, her eyes gentle. "I know. I know you just want me to be safe and not take risks. But tell me, Z—have I ever lived my life that way?"

I swallowed hard. "No."

"If I went through life always staying in my comfort zone and never daring to do anything, I wouldn't have moved across the world to work and live in a foreign country."

"You can't honestly compare moving to Australia to summoning a demon."

She shrugged and grinned. "At least half of the wildlife here actively tries to kill you, so…"

"Tay!" I focused hard, grabbed a pillow from the couch, and threw it at her head.

"Just kidding, just kidding." She raised her arms to block the pillow missile and laughed.

"No, but seriously," she said after settling down again, "life isn't fun if you never take any risks. I only have this one life here, and it'll be just a few good decades." She gave me a pointed look. "Some of us don't have the privilege of living forever and having all the time in the world to do all the things."

"Tay…" My shoulders sagged.

She waved her hand in the air. "Now don't get morose. It's your birthday, so you don't get to mope. It is what it is. But I'm just telling you that I'm going to live this very human life of mine to the fullest, and if I want to summon a demon to scrub my toilet, I'll do that."

I choked on my nonexistent spit. "You didn't!"

She snickered. "No, I didn't. I just wanted to see your face."

I sank down on the chair opposite the couch and laid a hand over my chest, where the ghostly echo of my racing heart was pounding. "One of these days, you'll give me a stroke."

"Is that even possible?" She squinted at me. "Like, can your body in Hell be affected by what happens to your spirit form here?"

"I have no idea. And no"—I pointed at her—"I have no inclination to find out."

She grinned. "Coward."

"I prefer 'intensely focused on survival and comfort.'"

Her grin softened into a smile. "It's good to have you here."

"Yeah," I said with a smile of my own.

"So," she said and speared a piece of cake with her fork, "tell me about that last visit from Lilith. You mentioned that something happened?"

I'd only hinted at it in my letter, not wanting to give away too much in a written message that might be intercepted and read by prying eyes. So now I told her all about that encounter, and when I finished, she squinted at me again, her head tilted.

"You don't look different."

"No, you can't really see it." I glanced down myself. "Azmodea recently mentioned that she senses something different about me, so it must be detectable somehow." I shrugged. "Not that I feel it."

"You don't feel anything?"

I shook my head. "Whatever Lilith put inside me, it's subtle. I'm not even convinced it does anything. Which kind of sucks." I twisted my mouth into a frown. "I mean, if I go through having a hole punched into my chest and bleeding over everything, I'd at least want to get some cool powers out of it."

"Maybe it'll activate when you're threatened? Sort of like a dormant self-defense system?"

Tilting my head, I considered that. "Maybe. It *would* be nice not to be dependent on others defending me anymore. I'm so tired of having to have an escort wherever I go because I'm too weak to hold my own." I blew out a ghostly breath. "You don't know how exhausting it is to live among beings that consider you prey."

Tay raised a brow. "I'm a young, single woman living in a large city filled with men."

I laughed. "There's that. Now multiply that by a thousand, and you'll know what it's like not to be able to walk through your own home without a guard dog because there are beasts roaming the halls that will rip the flesh off your bones if they catch you alone."

She grimaced. "Okay, you win."

We continued to chat and laugh, and before I knew it, the time was up and Azazel came back to take me home.

"See you in a few weeks," Tay said with a smile that was just the tiniest bit sad.

I nodded, my heart heavy despite my answering smile. Even though I now actually saw her more often in person than when I'd still lived on Earth—given that for the last year or so before I'd gone to Hell, she'd already lived in Australia, and I couldn't just zip over there from the US—I wasn't able to video-chat with her in between, as we'd done before. So these brief hours every couple of weeks were the only time I could actually *talk* with my best friend, and I felt the strain of it every time I had to leave at the end of a visit.

But today was my birthday, and I'd promised myself that

I would try to stay upbeat. And, as Tay had so aptly put it, I wasn't allowed to mope.

"So," Tay said before I turned away, "are you guys throwing a party today? I mean, if you think about it, you have two reasons to celebrate—technically, today's your anniversary, isn't it?"

I stiffened. Oh, no.

Tay took in my expression at one glance, and her eyes widened just the slightest bit. *Dude*, she very clearly said without saying it, *you didn't forget your first wedding anniversary, did you?*

My eyes widened as well. *Crap, I totally did*, I said without saying it.

Tay inclined her head a little, her eyes flicking to Azazel standing behind me. Glancing back at me, she mouthed, *Blow job.*

I facepalmed and then glared at her. *Tay,* I said without saying it.

Azazel cleared his throat. "Are you two quite done?"

"Yes, absolutely, let's go." I turned on my heel and marched off to the balcony.

Tay's giggles followed me out.

I CAME HOME TO A SWEET LITTLE SURPRISE PARTY FEATURING Azmodea, Mammon—whom I gave a little side-eye for getting Taylor into that whole demon summoning mess— and Hekesha and Caleb, the two half-bloods in Azazel's service with whom I'd forged a casual friendship over the past few months.

It was quite telling, of course, that I'd felt more comfortable befriending them rather than other, full-blood demons. There was an instant kind of kinship in having fewer powers —or close to none, in my case—compared to the demons in Hell.

Plus, Caleb wasn't that old yet, having been born and grown up on Earth in the seventies and eighties, which meant he and I shared a lot of the more recent cultural Earth experiences. In demon terms, he was just a toddler.

Naturally, that made *me* an infant, but I wouldn't dwell on that.

Though I guessed I could always tease Azazel about being a cradle-robber.

Caleb had appeared a bit curt when I'd first met him, but he'd warmed up over the months, revealing more of his sometimes dorky personality. I'd never had a brother or a cousin, but I could almost imagine him in that role, the way we'd trade barbs and laugh at jokes together.

Azazel had watched our friendship with a good amount of suspicion at first, but after he'd growled at Caleb one too many times, making the poor dude virtually sink into the floor, I'd verbally ripped my darling husband a new one. Because while I did occasionally enjoy his jealousy for giving me warm tingles, I would not let it dictate whom I could or couldn't be friends with. Possessiveness was all good and well, as long as it didn't make me feel like I had to limit my contacts to appease my partner.

He now tolerated our meetings without complaint, though part of that could be due to the renewed threat he'd made to Caleb that he'd lose any part of his body that touched mine. Not that it would have been necessary—the young half-blood practically worshipped Azazel for saving him from his abusive father. No way in Hell would he ever disrespect Azazel by straying where he shouldn't.

Hekesha had been even more aloof than Caleb when I'd first met her a year ago, and I could have sworn she didn't like me much—until the moment she'd pushed me into that room with Azazel all those months ago, after he'd received the letter from Lucifer welcoming him to the Fall Festival. Azazel had trashed the room in his rage and had sat there for hours in the wreckage, frightening half his staff, who didn't know how to approach him in that state. Hekesha's solution was to get me —to make him happy, because according to her, I was good at that. That was the first time she'd shown me any indication that she kind of, sort of, maybe appreciated my presence here.

I'd since found out that Hekesha was the quiet, grumpy type who took some time to let people in, but once she did, she was fiercely loyal. She often joined me and Caleb when we met up, and the combination of Caleb's dorkiness and Hekesha's grumpy awkwardness made for a lot of situational fun. Our board game nights were a hoot.

"I didn't know we were having a party," I now said just after we'd stepped into our quarters and I'd had a little jump scare at two full-blood demons and two half-bloods yelling "Happy birthday!" at the top of their lungs.

Azazel leaned down from behind me and kissed me on the cheek. "I know you despise large gatherings," he murmured, referencing the annoying get-togethers I'd had to endure at his side for the past months. "But last year, you were sad to celebrate your birthday alone, and I recall you saying you wanted to have a party the next year."

Ah, yes, my morose birthday thoughts from a year ago, when I'd lit a sad, single candle on a sad, little cupcake all alone in my new apartment in a new city.

Well, I hadn't really been alone, after all. There *had* been a demon lurking in the shadows.

"You remembered," I said softly and turned to him, my chest tingling with warmth.

And he'd been thoughtful enough to invite only those I knew well and felt comfortable with.

"Of course." His eyes held mine as he cupped my face and stroked my cheeks with his thumbs.

Of course. Because he remembered every little thing I'd ever said, remembered all the pieces that made me who I was, from the trivial to the vital. He'd never forget a single thing about me, whether I'd said or done it in passing or revealed it to him in private.

Unlike me, who'd *forgotten* that his mother was "dead."

He didn't say it, and to be honest, I wasn't sure it was even a conscious subtext in this little interaction. He wasn't the type to deliver passive-aggressive jabs like this. In all our months together, he'd never shown himself to engage in that kind of relationship warfare. Whenever he had a bone to pick with me, he did so directly.

No, this humiliating slap across the face was all on my side, in my head. Because even when he didn't mean his words to poke at the stain of guilt inside me—and I honestly believed that wasn't his intention—I still felt it, because *I* couldn't let go of that moment. Because *I* knew that he still remembered my blank stare when I'd asked him if he'd ever had someone close to him die and he'd had to *remind* me about his mother.

No matter how well he tried to play it off, I still sensed it looming in the space between, and in moments like this, it solidified into something insurmountable and pervasive that tainted every word between us.

I swallowed and dropped my gaze from his, shame heating my face.

Shame and *anger*.

If I weren't so terrified of Lucifer, I'd have long stormed into his palace, punched him in the throat, and demanded that he release me from this fucking vow.

I didn't even know why he'd keep this from Azazel—just for shits and giggles? Given what I'd seen and heard about him, it would fit his character. Ugh.

Azmodea chose that moment to envelop me in a hug. "Happy birthday, darling," she cooed. "I got you this."

I peered at the gift box she'd shoved into my hands, then narrowed my eyes at her. "Is this safe to unwrap among company?"

"Oh, absolutely! It's *meant* for company."

My brain processed the underlying current in her words too late, and by the time healthy suspicion crept in, I'd already ripped off the wrapping paper—to reveal the most elaborate dildo-vibrator combo I'd ever seen.

"Azmodea!" I screeched and slapped my hands over the box in a futile attempt to shield the picture on it from the other guests' eyes. "What the fuck?"

She had the nerve to chuckle. "Oh, that sweet bashfulness. Never gets old. Anyway"—she waved her hand—"Az told me about that cute little thing you sometimes like to use—"

I rounded on Azazel. "*You told her?*"

If he could have incinerated someone with a single look, Azmodea would have been worse off than Anakin Skywalker on Mustafar. "I did *not*," he snarled and bared his teeth.

"Huh. Could have sworn it was you." She tapped a finger on her lips, completely unconcerned by the homicidal pulse of power emanating from Azazel. "Oh, no, wait, I think it was the cat."

"Mephisto?!" I squealed.

She snapped her fingers and pointed at me. "That's the one."

I'd kill him. I'd use his pelt as a bedside rug.

"Did you honestly just confuse me with a hellcat?" Azazel barked at his sister.

She threw up her hands. "Well, to be fair, you're both a bit surly—"

"Excuse me," Mammon cut in, "can we get back to the part where we talk about what kind of toys Zoe likes? I wasn't quite done taking notes." That perv had actually summoned an honest-to-Hell notepad and ballpoint pen, holding it at the ready.

Hekesha and Caleb appeared like they were doing their best to meld with the furniture and walls. Azazel, meanwhile, looked one second away from committing a murder.

Honestly, at this point, I'd cheer him on.

It was at that precise moment that a dead hellrat dropped from the ceiling to land at my feet with a wet plop, spraying my legs with blood.

Happy birthday, Mephisto purred from up high.

I would skin that cat alive.

CHAPTER 17

S urprisingly, the rest of the party went all right after that, and to my unending appreciation, both Caleb and Hekesha masterfully pretended they'd missed the entire humiliating start of the affair. At some point, I didn't even want to wring both Azmodea's and Mammon's necks anymore.

I kept reminding myself that everyone had those choice family members from Hell that randomly incited the urge to commit a violent crime. Mine just happened to be *literally* from Hell.

To be fair, Azmodea and Mammon were great most of the time, and I did love them. I was lucky to have at least those two to get along with, considering the rest of my in-laws were more firmly in the "infernal" category, especially my grandfather-in-law, Lucifer. I'd met some of Azazel's other relatives here and there, and the vibe I'd gotten made me glad they weren't involved in his life as much as his sister and nephew.

"Here," Azazel said as he sat down on the couch next to me while the others talked among themselves, the party having simmered down to the comfortable casually-hanging-out-together that I liked. He held out a simple black box with a bow on it, a bit bigger than a shoebox. When he saw my glance at Azmodea, he smirked. "It's safe to unwrap. Really."

"If you say so…"

I gingerly opened the lid and peeked inside. A stack of DVDs greeted me, the one on the very top being *Spaceballs*. Grabbing the stack, I flipped through it… *Naked Gun 1–3, Top Secret!, Hot Shots! 1* and *2, Robin Hood: Men in Tights, Airplane! 1* and *2, Monty Python's Life of Brian, Monty Python and the Holy Grail, UHF.*

I stared open-mouthed at the collection of movies, all of them the silly kind I loved so much.

"You got them all," I whispered. I'd mentioned these offhand here and there and how I'd loved watching them as a kid and teenager. I grinned as I looked at the back of *Top Secret*. "They just don't make 'em like this anymore."

Turning to him, I laid my hand on his cheek and leaned in for a kiss. "Thank you," I murmured against his lips.

"There's something else," he said, materializing another object in his hand.

I stared at the inconspicuous-looking, thick stack of paper he held out, the pages held together at the top by a simple black clip.

"What's this?"

"Something you've been waiting for."

Raising a brow, I flipped over the first page, which was blank—and then I gaped at the title.

"Is this…?"

"Sarah J. Maas's next book."

"But it's not even published yet!" I'd marked the date on my calendar, and we were still out a few months.

"It's an early, uncorrected proof."

"Ohmygod!" I clapped a hand over my mouth.

He cleared his throat and shot me a dark look.

"Sorry, sorry!" I grinned at him, giddy beyond reasoning. "Oh, my gloriously talented demon darling!"

Mammon leaned forward in his seat on the divan opposite us and clicked his ballpoint pen. "Is she always this creative in her exclamations?" he asked Azazel.

"Watch it," Azazel snarled.

"Oh, I am." Mammon scribbled something down on his notepad.

"This is incredible," I muttered, effectively pulling Azazel's lethal attention away from Mammon.

Azazel's gaze seemed to drink me in. "Happy anniversary."

I froze. *Shit*.

"This"—I swallowed hard—"this is an anniversary gift?"

He nodded and pushed a lock of hair behind my ear, his touch making tingles course over my skin.

Fuck me sideways.

I had nothing, zilch, nada, prepared as an anniversary gift for him, because my stupid, anxiety-ridden, all-over-the-place brain had completely skipped over the fact that, officially, our relationship had started on my birthday, with that fateful skit of a wedding in front of those three drunk women at the bar.

Crap on a shitstick.

Here he was, not only having remembered our anniversary like a perfect hubby should, but also presenting me with gifts that showed how well he knew me, how much he cared, and how much effort he had gone to in order to make me happy.

And here *I* was, with nothing to show for my love for him because I'd forgotten the entire thing.

Add this on top of the blunder from the other day—you know, the thing I had *not* actually forgotten, but couldn't tell him about—and I had to come across as the worst wife ever.

I met his gaze, his expression so warm and open, as it only ever was with me, and heat burned the back of my eyes.

What was I supposed to tell him? *Hey, honey, thank you for the most thoughtful gift that speaks to how much you love me, happy anniversary, oh by the way, I've got nothing for you in return because I* forgot *our anniversary, just like I forgot that your mom's dead, oops, sorry!*

What if he took this as a reflection of my love for him? As an indicator of how little I cared? If this was the first instance of me messing up, it might not be a big deal, but in combination with the other screwup…

Dammit, he didn't deserve to think the person he was passionately in love with and had pledged himself to seemed to be inconsiderate of things that mattered to him. He deserved better than to feel neglected like this.

His face blurred, tears now clouding my eyes. My chest burned, shame scorching me from the inside out.

"What's this?" he murmured, tilting my head up.

I pressed my trembling lips together and shook my head. *I'm the worst*, I wanted to say. "Just…happy tears," I choked out.

Through the shimmering veil of wetness blurring my vision, I saw his brows draw together. He opened his mouth to say something.

"Lord Azazel," someone interrupted from the other side of the room.

Still frowning, he held my gaze for a moment longer

before he glanced toward the demon standing just inside the open door—it was Cadriel, the female who'd been my father's guard until Azazel had sent her on another mission earlier today.

As soon as Azazel saw her, his features hardened, his energy giving off a dark pulse. Glancing back at me, he said, "Hold that thought. We're not finished here."

He rose from the couch and walked over to Cadriel, and I surreptitiously wiped my eyes, the conversations around me still going, the others thankfully unaware of my inner turmoil. My sight now less blurry, I watched Azazel listen intently to what Cadriel told him. They were too far away for me to hear what it was that she said in a hushed voice, but I could read expressions and body language just fine.

Cadriel held herself stiffly, her face serious, her eyes downcast. Azazel stood with tension in his shoulders, his features hard, his attention on her—until it suddenly shifted to me, his gaze hitting me like an electric current. Cadriel looked at me at the same time, her brows twitching closer together for a moment in what I thought appeared to be pity. Azazel's eyes, on the other hand, held something raw, a momentary glimpse at deep pain, before he schooled his features into neutral hardness again and broke our stare.

Looking back at Cadriel, he nodded and said something. Cadriel stepped back and bowed, then turned on her heel and left. For a moment, Azazel stood in place, his gaze on the floor, a whisper of dark power curling around him. Then he rolled his shoulders, the darkness dissipating, and came over to where I sat.

Me being me, I had to ask. "Bad news?"

He settled on the couch next to me, resting his arm on the back behind me, and nodded without meeting my eyes.

A sliver of dread snaked its way into my heart. "It's something to do with me, isn't it?"

He still wouldn't look at me. "No."

"Don't lie to me," I whispered, my throat feeling raw.

His gaze slammed into me, a second of unguarded, unmitigated pain, then he blinked and visibly corralled whatever lurked in his depths. "All right. I won't lie. But you won't get the truth, not tonight."

I blinked and drew back a bit. "What—"

"Zoe," he said, then took my hand in his and gave the back of it a tender kiss. "It's your birthday. I will not taint your joy."

That sliver of dread morphed into a full-blown wave of anxiety. "Tell me."

"Tomorrow." His face was hard, unyielding. "You might curse me for it now, but you'll be glad I stood firm." His thumb stroked over the back of my hand. "Now is not the time to worry. Enjoy your night."

I trembled from the inside out. When, in the history of mankind, had it ever worked being told not to dwell on impending bad news? As if I could simply erase the knowledge or switch off the part of my brain that excelled in imagining worst-case scenarios

"I can't not worry," I whispered. "Have you met my mind?" I gestured at my head. "I might frequently tell people 'No worries!' but it's a blatant lie, because I am, in fact, all worries, all the time. It's not like I can shut it off."

He tilted his head and regarded me with eyes of molten heat. "I know a way to shut it off."

I opened my mouth to say something, but Azazel beat me to it.

Without taking his gaze off me, he raised his voice over

the chatter of conversations and said, "All right, party's over, everyone out."

"You can't just throw them all out like that," I protested under my breath.

Hekesha and Caleb, though, had already jumped to their feet and were on their way out the door with hasty waves and muttered *Happy birthdays* and *Goodbyes*. Azmodea stood with her hands on her hips and a glare aimed at her brother.

"You have no manners," she snapped.

"What I have," he replied, glancing at her with a dark smirk on his face, "is a wife in need of physical attention, and you're keeping me from taking care of her."

"Azazel," I hissed.

"Well," Azmodea said, laying a hand over her heart and batting her lashes, "far be it from me to block your cock, brother. Enjoy!" And with a little wave of her fingers, she swished out of the room.

I covered my face with my hands. This family.

"You, too," growled Azazel, and I glanced up to see him level a death glare at his nephew, who was still lounging on the divan as if he'd just settled himself even more comfortably in his seat.

"Who, me?" Mammon raised both brows, his face all innocence. "I'm just a little fly on the wall. You won't even notice I'm here."

Azazel materialized a flyswatter—*we have those down here? What kind of flies need swatting here in Hell? Not sure I want to know*—leaned forward, and slapped Mammon over the head with it. "Get out."

"Fine, fine!" Mammon rose from his seat. "You're really no fun at all." Blowing me a kiss, he added, "Except for you. Just the look on your face..." He waved at his head and chuckled. "Too funny. Ah, always a pleasure poking at you.

Even if it's not the kind of poking I'd really like to do with you—"

His sentence ended in a squeal when Azazel shot up from the couch, and then Mammon took off, his laughter echoing in the next rooms over until the door falling shut cut him off.

I stared after him, feeling the heavy weight of Azazel's gaze on me as he settled back on the couch, my body already heating in all the places it knew his touch.

"That was very rude," I said, biting my lower lip.

"I agree."

I glanced at him and raised my brows in surprise.

"They all should have left an hour ago."

I tried and failed to suppress my grin. "You're impossible."

He tsked and leaned in, nipping at my earlobe. "Just being honest."

I shivered at the pleasure rolling out from his touch while the worry inside me hummed to new life. "Speaking of which…"

"Nope." He drew back enough so he could pin me with a stern look. "This"—he tapped my forehead—"is switched off for tonight."

He leaned in again and trailed hot kisses down my throat.

"But—"

Straightening, he gave me a smoldering look from underneath his dark lashes. "Do you want me to *actually* switch you off?"

I bristled, knowing he could do exactly that. The memory of that time he'd used his powers to knock me out when I'd panicked at the sight of his wing collection rose to the surface, and I narrowed my eyes at him.

"Don't you dare."

Something sparked in his gaze. "That's entirely up to you."

I sputtered. "You high-handed, overbearing—"

He softly flicked my nose, which effectively shut me up, though it only made my blood boil all the more.

Leaning closer until his breath mingled with my own, he silkily asked, "Am I making you mad?"

"Yes," I hissed. To think he'd threaten to magically put me under… The nerve. The audacity. The supercilious—

"Then fight me." The words seemed like a declaration of war, but the way he said them…was more like a gently murmured endearment, a verbal caress.

I softly sucked in air. "I know what you're doing."

"Oh yeah?"

"You're just trying to distract me. You don't want me worrying, so you're pretending to be all domineering to rile me up and get me to have angry sex with you so I won't have brain space left to think about what you won't tell me."

"You think I'm that manipulative?" he asked, but the spark of amusement in his eyes undermined the intent of his words.

"I know you are."

He nodded, not even disputing it. "Then you should also know," he said, his voice all silken seduction and dark charm, "that I don't *pretend* to be domineering."

Uh-oh. My stomach did a little flip at the way he looked at me, effortless power pulsing off him with every breath, the dominant energy he usually curbed a bit now on full display. He didn't often let me feel the extent of it, but it was always there, an undercurrent to his presence.

It swept over me now in a breathtaking wave, raising the hairs on my arms and neck—and making my lady parts tingle. It was almost embarrassing how instantly wet I got. Involuntarily, I shifted on the couch, and his gaze dropped to my hips, a knowing smirk flirting with his mouth.

"You look entirely too smug," I said.

His smile deepened, his eyes flashing. "On your knees," he purred.

CHAPTER 18

"What?"

His gaze flicked to the floor between his legs, then back up to me, and he raised a brow in challenge.

I really shouldn't get a pleasant full-body tingle at that nonchalantly dominant look and the way he just expected me to fall at his feet and—okay, yes, fine, it was fucking hot and I was all for it.

Biting my lip, I slid off the couch and knelt between his legs. The firm material of my jeans pressed against my already sensitive flesh, adding to the heat building in my core. I met his gaze, and the hunger in his eyes mirrored the need unfurling inside me.

Everything else fell away, the world reduced to the two of us and that brimming connection between our minds, hearts, and bodies.

At first, I might have demurred to his idea of distracting me from whatever loomed unspoken, my need to find out what was happening clawing at me from the inside, but in the end…I'd never say no to sex with him. I'd have to be comatose to turn that down. It was in the moments when we played, the energy between us shifting, pushing and pulling, that I felt most alive, that I lived and breathed this connection that went so far beyond anything I'd ever had with anyone else.

These were also the moments when all the things pressing down on me—the haunting knowledge of my shortcomings and all the ways I'd failed him—faded into the background. For a few blissful instants, there was nothing between us but heat and desire, primal need, and a deep, abiding bond that fed starved parts of my soul.

So of course I'd cave when presented with the chance to quiet the incessant chatter of my mind and focus on the one thing that was and always had been immediately compelling and unburdened by anything else in our lives—how perfectly we fit together in the most intimate of ways.

Whatever else we might struggle with, it never intruded into the pleasure we shared.

I looked up at him now from much the same position I'd been in during that meeting with Zaquiel, that pivotal moment that had changed so much between us. Back then, I'd been so overwhelmed with lust, my senses hijacked by the erotic impressions of the carnal party going on around us, that I'd had my hands on the buttons of Azazel's pants, ready to blow him right then and there, audience be damned.

He'd stopped me, much to my surprise, but I'd come to understand since then that his unwillingness to share even extended to public displays of intimacy. Where everyone else in Hell seemed to frequently engage in exhibitionist sex, Azazel kept this side of him—of us—private. It made me feel treasured in a strange but luscious way.

The lightning in his eyes as he regarded me now made

me wonder if he was as aware as I was of how our current position mirrored that moment when everything changed. His gaze stroked over my face with such sensual intent that I almost felt it as a physical touch. My nipples hardened, the material of my bra and tank top suddenly much too heavy, too abrasive.

"Not a day goes by," he said in a murmur, "that I don't think about you kneeling between my legs, with that look on your face, that fire in your eyes. I've been meaning to relive that moment ever since."

I licked my lips and shifted my weight, new arousal pulsing between my thighs. It wasn't like I hadn't given him plenty of oral in the past, but never in this exact position, never in this conscious reenactment of the first time I'd felt so inexorably drawn to him that it had nearly drowned me in sensation.

His gaze dropped to my mouth, and the power emanating from him sharpened. I drew in a breath, lifting my hands to run them over his thighs toward his groin, where the bulge in his pants spoke to his own state of arousal.

My mouth watered.

He gripped my chin, his thumb stroking over my lower lip. "Open my pants, love."

With pleasure.

Swiftly, I unfastened his pants, freeing his erection. More wetness drenched my panties at the sight of his cock. Thick and long, veins running up the underside, a bead of precum pooling at the slit on top, it made me squirm on my knees. I was so intimately familiar with how he felt inside me, my inner muscles already clenched in anticipation.

"Now wrap those lips of yours around my cock," he said,

the timbre of his voice making me shiver, "and show me how much you want me."

Holding his gaze, I grasped the base of his length, leaned in, and took him into my mouth. His energy pulsed violently as soon as my lips touched his skin, and my core throbbed with an answering beat of desire. Seeing—*feeling*—his reaction to me never failed to arouse me.

I swirled my tongue around the crown, sucked briefly, and then went down, taking him deep. I'd worked on my gag reflex over the past few months—a girl had to put in some effort to accommodate that kind of length—so when he hit the back of my throat now, my eyes watered only a little.

The guttural sound he made as I relaxed my throat and took him even deeper was the sweetest reward, making me clench my thighs against the building pressure inside me.

Up and down I bobbed, sucking on the way up, taking him deep on the way down. His hand fisted in my hair, the sting only adding to the pulse of lust between my legs.

I thought I couldn't be more turned on when he cupped my face with his other hand, slid his thumb to my lower lip to feel himself gliding in and out of my mouth, and said with a groan, "Good girl."

That made me melt into a puddle of arousal, my own need now so acute, so pounding, I couldn't take it anymore.

Slipping one hand between my thighs, I pressed my fingers against the throbbing center of my lust.

"Uh-uh." Grabbing me underneath my jaw, he pushed my head back, popping himself free of my mouth at the same time he used his power to yank my hand off my crotch. "You don't get to touch yourself. When you come, it will be with my cock in your pussy, understood?"

I whimpered. "Then fuck me already."

His expression was all sorts of devilish. "Not yet."

Ignoring my sound of utter frustration, he rose from the couch. I was already halfway to my feet as well when he laid a hand on my shoulder and pushed me back down to my knees. His power whispered over my wrists, and the next second, my arms were pulled behind my back, held there by invisible bonds.

"Because I don't trust you to keep your hands off yourself," he muttered, a glint in his eye.

I looked daggers at him for that while my core still throbbed something fierce, primed and ready and so close to climax.

He wrapped one hand around my head, fingers tangling in my hair. "Now open that pretty mouth."

My eyes widened just the slightest bit, but I obeyed and parted my lips. His gaze holding mine spellbound, he slid his cock inside my mouth, and I made a little sound of pleasure at tasting him again.

He watched with intense focus as I swallowed him whole, his dark lashes half hiding his stormy eyes, and the way his features tightened and pinched with lust when he thrust into my mouth made new wetness pool at my core.

"That's it," he murmured, deepening his shallow strokes until he tapped the back of my throat once more. "You're gonna take it all, aren't you?"

I hummed in assent, all my concentration on keeping my muscles relaxed so I wouldn't gag. This was very different from the previous position—with my arms held immobile behind my back and his hand on my nape keeping my head in place, I had no control over speed, angle, or depth. He was fully in charge, fucking my mouth as he pleased, and all I could do was take it.

It felt wonderfully wicked and delightfully dirty.

His thrusts became faster, rougher, though still only a

fraction of his normal speed and force. Dark energy curled around me, his power making the air shimmer as he kept his strength on the tightest of leashes. His cock filled my mouth, hot and hard and deliciously demanding, and my attention was riveted with rapt fascination on how he watched me, his face stripped of anything civilized, his expression one of pure primal need.

"I'm going to come down your throat," he said, his voice a touch rough, "and you're going to swallow every last drop."

I made a happy little sound around the thick length of him, sucking just a tad more—and he lost it. With three fast, powerful thrusts, he came, his hot cum splashing against the back of my throat. I worked hard to swallow it quickly without choking on it—not that easy when I couldn't angle my head or use my hands to control the distance—but I managed, my eyes still riveted on him, on his expression of sheer pleasure.

Goddamn, I might be able to come just from that look on his face.

When he pulled out, I chased the head of his cock and sucked off the last bit of his seed as if addicted to his taste. Which was likely true.

"Fucking Hell, Zoe," he said with a surprised chuckle.

I grinned up at him, feeling tingly and warm at the way his features had softened with his release and the satisfied smile he gave me.

He rubbed his thumb over my lips for a heartbeat, his eyes mapping my face, then he tugged upward at my hair with his other hand still at my nape. "Up," he murmured as he released his hold on my wrists.

I got to my feet, the over-sensitized, neglected spot between my legs throbbing with the movement. My entire body was strung tight and buzzing like a live wire, aching with unfulfilled need. With my arms now free, I immediately touched him, seeking the heat of his skin. He'd changed out of his fighting leathers and into a more casual outfit earlier, and I slid my hands under his shirt, needing to feel him.

"Off," I muttered.

His shirt went up in flames and then fell away as ash. I smiled at the impatience evident in that move, but the next second, he had his mouth on mine, claiming me with a rough, demanding kiss. My toes curled at how he stroked his tongue inside me, branding me, making me moan and melt against him.

"If you don't fuck me in the next five seconds," I panted as soon as he granted me air to speak, "I will spontaneously combust."

His hand slid to the front of my throat, holding me there with just enough pressure to make my knees weak and my belly flutter with excitement. With a roguish grin, he leaned in again and slowly, torturously nipped at my lower lip, then sucked on it.

I closed my eyes and let out a breathy moan. He was killing me.

Just when I thought I couldn't take it anymore, he turned me around and steered me toward one of the divans.

"Bend over," he said as his hand pressed against my upper back.

Heart thumping a mile a minute, I leaned over the padded backrest of the divan, its height sitting just a bit higher than my hips.

"More." He pushed me farther down until I set my hands on the divan's seat cushion to steady myself, my toes barely touching the floor on the other side.

I was now pretty much dangling over the backrest.

He stroked his hand up and down my spine and made a pleased sound before he reached between the backrest and my hips and opened my jeans with dexterous fingers. Feeling his touch so close to where I needed it tore a moan from my throat. I'd been in unfulfilled-sexual-need Hell for what felt like an eternity, that ache between my legs nearly unbearable.

Grabbing the waistband of my jeans and panties with both hands, he shoved them down roughly, baring me completely to his gaze. Cool air kissed my most sensitive skin, slick with my arousal.

"Beautiful." His velveteen praise stroked me a moment before his fingers did.

With a touch that was excruciatingly light, he caressed my entrance, gliding through my juices, his attention not nearly close enough to my clit for my liking. My inner muscles clenched around nothing. Heaven help me, I was *dying* to be filled.

"Azazel, *please*."

He hummed, palming my ass. "You've been good."

"Yessss."

"Did everything I asked." He squeezed my butt.

I nodded vigorously and bounced a little on my toes. "Yes, yes."

"Then it's time for your reward."

My enthusiastic agreement drowned in a drawn-out moan when he thrust inside me with one powerful push. Overwhelming sensation shot out from where his cock speared me in the best of ways. My nerves all fired up, stars exploding behind my eyes.

The move shoved my mound against the backrest, my clit rubbing over the padded fabric, and I came apart at the seams.

I cried out, splintering under a climax that seemed intent on undoing my very essence. Pleasure so acute it stole my breath rolled through me, unmaking every thread that held my being together.

"Fuck," I moaned, still in the throes of my sexual high as Azazel withdrew and thrust back in, setting off the fireworks again.

I loved it when he gave me half a dozen orgasms before he took me, but there was something to be said for the explosion that followed delayed gratification. I never climaxed as hard as I did when he tortured me by withholding my pleasure for what seemed like hours.

He pumped into me, harder, faster, every thrust shoving my mons onto the backrest again, and the combination of his cock pounding into me and the friction on my clit sent me over the edge yet again.

And again.

I was hoarse from screaming by the time he emptied himself inside me with a few last, near-bruising thrusts. His deep groan made me clench once more around him, my clit feeling delightfully battered.

Good grief, I'd probably be too sore to walk.

He withdrew, making me gasp at the loss of his cock, and then he pulled my jeans and panties all the way off and cleaned me quickly with a summoned cloth.

Attuned to my needs as always, he swooped me right up into his arms then, saving me from testing whether my legs still worked. Resting my head against his shoulder, I lazily petted his bare chest, the trimmed dark hair there tickling my fingers.

I was still high on endorphins when he laid me on our bed and divested me of my top and bra. Humming contentedly, I curled right into him the second he joined me on the mattress. He'd taken off his pants as well, and we lay there, skin on skin, our legs intertwined, my head on his chest where his steady heartbeat soothed me down to my soul.

That peace didn't last long.

"I almost forgot this," he spoke into the lightning-kissed darkness and moved his arm.

I drew back and blinked at the tiny box he held in his palm. With a flick of his fingers, he flipped it open. Nestled in the black satin inside was the most stunning ring I'd ever seen. Gleaming silver in the light of the flashes coming from outside the window, the band split into filigree tendrils coiling around a sparkling jewel in the middle. The gem seemed black at first glance but for a glimmer of light in its depths that turned the obsidian color into radiant iridescence.

"Last year," he said with a half smile, "you demanded a ring. I'm afraid I've been remiss, but better late than never."

I raised a trembling hand to my mouth, but he gently took hold of it and slid the ring onto my finger.

"Happy one year, and here's to many more." He turned my hand and placed a kiss on my palm.

My chest burned, my lungs seizing. I drew in a rattling breath. "I'm so sorry," I blurted out.

His brows pinched together. "For what?"

I shook my head, my throat thick. Several times, I tried to speak, opening my mouth only to close it again. When I managed to say something, it was barely a whisper. "I don't have anything for you."

He tilted his head, his look questioning.

"For our anniversary." My lower lip quivered. Embarrassment seared me from the inside out. "I don't have a gift for you."

He stared at me intently for a moment.

My pulse pounded so loud I almost didn't hear him when he asked, "So?"

I scoffed. "So?" Flailing, I sat up. "You got me these amazing things, and I'm over here with nothing!"

He shook his head. "It's not a competition."

"No, but..." I rubbed a hand over my face. "You're so thoughtful and attentive and just all around perfect—"

"Me?" He raised both brows. "Perfect?"

"Yes. You think of all the things. You remember everything. You're loving and considerate. You always know just what to say, and you do all the right things—"

His hand covering my mouth cut my speech short. "Careful," he whispered harshly, making a show of looking over his shoulder. "If anyone hears you, my reputation will be ruined."

"That!" I said emphatically after removing his hand from my mouth. "That's exactly what I mean. You're funny on top of everything else, and you deserve better than—" I broke off and bit my lip.

His gaze homed in on me with laser-like focus. "Nu-uh. Go on. What were you saying?"

I wilted under his intense stare. "You deserve better than a wife who forgets your anniversary," I mumbled, lowering my eyes, cringing at the sting of shame accompanying my words.

I didn't know what I'd expected, but it wasn't to hear him laugh. Glancing up at him through a film of tears over my eyes, I noticed the genuine amusement lighting his face.

"It's not funny," I said, my voice cracking.

Sobering, he leveled a serious look at me. "All right. Then let me make this clear. I don't give a fuck if you remember anniversaries or birthdays."

I flinched.

"I am thousands of years old," he went on, his voice a calm rumble in the dark. "I've seen centuries go by in the blink of an eye. For an immortal, celebrating annual dates doesn't have the same importance as it does for humans. I remember and commemorate them for you, because I know you'll appreciate it, and I love the unadulterated joy on your face when I give you a gift. But I don't require the same in return. I won't measure your love by whether or not you have a present for me on a certain date. You think I deserve better than you?"

I sniffed, the tears spilling over.

He wiped them from my cheeks. "You light up my life. You're the best thing that's happened to me in a tragically long time. When I'm around you, I'm the best version of myself I've ever been. You make me *better*." He cupped my face with both hands, his fingers gently digging in. "You don't need to give me gifts, not when your presence in my life is the greatest one I've ever received."

"Stop," I sobbed.

"No. You'll hear me out, because I know where this comes from." He pointed a finger at my head and made a little circle. "I know all your previous relationships were short—"

"And whose fault was that?" I croaked.

"Shush." He gave me a *look*. "You've never been serious with anyone. Always kept them at arm's length. But this here is different. With me, you're all in, and it scares you. Because deep down, a part of you thinks you're not lovable. That you're not enough."

All blood rushed from my head. He was cracking me open one word at a time.

"And part of that is due to what happened with your father. The way he abandoned you left scars, the kind that

228

are subtle but sink deep. The kind that makes you doubt, in your heart of hearts, that anyone could ever truly love you for who you are. You never let anyone close enough to make it all rise to the surface. Until me." His eyes glowed in the gloom of our shared bedroom. "But now that you're faced with the kind of deep connection that challenges the shit your father's neglect ingrained in you, you can't believe it's real. So you keep looking for things that confirm what you think is true—that you're not lovable enough for someone to choose you before anything else."

I stared at him, dumbstruck, while distant thunder rumbled outside the window. "How?" I rasped. "How do you know all that?"

"I'm a demon," was his simple answer. "We excel at seeing into people's souls and picking apart minds to find hidden trauma." His shoulder lifted in a fluid shrug. "All the better to torture the damned."

I swallowed hard. "I never realized..." Shaking my head, I continued in a small voice, "Never realized that about me."

"It's not a conscious thing," he said gently. "That's why I told you. Because I need you to understand, to believe"—he took my hand and laid it over his heart—"that this is real. That I am the one who will always choose you. That I am fucking lucky to have you."

Fresh tears burned in my eyes. "Even when I'm an anxious mess who never does anything special for you?"

The way he stared at me sent a chill down my spine.

"I would like to shake you right now," he said with quiet menace.

I gulped.

He grasped me under my jaw, his large hand a hot brand on my skin. "You," he growled, "never did anything special for me?" He narrowed his eyes, the irises swirling with inhuman silver. "You *crawled* for me, in front of Lucifer's entire court." His grip tightened. "You stayed when you had every reason to turn away. You *chose* me, over the comfort and familiarity of your old life. You gave up everything to be with me, even knowing what life in Hell is like. You think I care about anything else?"

I blinked rapidly, my throat tight and my chest aching.

Wiping the fresh tears from my face again, he laid his forehead against mine. "When you see me showering you with gifts and feel like you are lacking for not doing the same, you've got it all backwards. It's the fucking least I can do for you for what you did for me. I'd lay the world at your feet if I could. It's no less than you deserve."

The pressure inside me broke free on a sob. I buried my head in his chest, my shoulders shaking as I wept. His arms closed around me, enveloping me in warmth and reassurance and the kind of love I could never have dreamed of.

He held me like this for the longest time, while my tears slowly dried and my breathing calmed.

Kissing the top of my head, he eventually murmured, "Sleep now."

And I tried. I really did.

With the mental and physical exhaustion from the events of the evening, I should have slipped right into a comatose sleep. Alas, the rawness of my emotional state somehow allowed the nagging worry I'd all but banished to return with force, making my heart pound and my skin itch.

That moment when Cadriel had spoken to him played over and over in my head, the memory of the anguish in his eyes as he'd glanced at me... The reassurance of his declaration from earlier notwithstanding, whatever had put that look on his face had to be devastating.

"Zoe." His sleep-drenched voice pulled me from my anxious thoughts. "*Sleep.*"

It wasn't a mental command, though, just a grumpy admonishment, so I disentangled myself from him and sat up.

"I can't," I said, chewing on my lip. "I need to know what Cadriel said."

He rolled onto his back with a deep sigh.

"Please tell me," I whispered.

For a moment, he lay there unmoving, his eyes closed, and I almost thought he'd gone back to sleep, but then he rose from the bed in one swift movement, coming to his feet with inhuman grace. Grabbing his pants, he pulled them on, then he summoned a pile of clothes and held them out to me.

"You'll want to be dressed for this."

CHAPTER 19

He'd sat me down in the living room of my old quarters, both of us fully clothed.

I waited for him to start talking, but he just paced back and forth for a minute, his energy vibrating darkly. Scanning the room, his gaze fell on the hellhound snoring on her doggie bed in the corner.

He snapped his fingers. "Vengeance."

All three of her heads whipped up, two of six ears adorably turned inside out.

Pointing at me, he said, "Go soothe."

I frowned. "Azazel…"

Vengeance trotted over to me and started licking my face. With all three of her big tongues.

"Not the licking!" I squealed and did my best to clamber away from her. "Sit!"

She plonked her butt down and gave me her adoring puppy eyes, panting happily.

I carefully sat down again. "Stay," I warned her. "No licking."

Her tail went thump-thump, but she obeyed and kept her slobber away from me.

"Good girl," I crooned and scratched her three heads. I focused back on Azazel, who'd taken a seat on the chair opposite me. "Okay, you were saying?"

With his elbows resting on his knees, he rubbed a hand over his face, then let it fall, only to wring both hands while he grimaced. Staring at the floor, he opened his mouth, closed it again, and cleared his throat. He was about to say something when he apparently decided against it and jumped to his feet instead. Marching into the adjoining room, he muttered something like, "Not enough," under his breath.

My heart was in my throat, fear skittering down my spine on icy feet. I'd never seen him this flustered.

A few seconds later, he returned, carrying one of the hellkittens in his arm. Without further ado, he deposited the furball in my lap, where it blinked up at me out of sleepy eyes.

"Um," I said while stroking the purring fluff of happiness, "not that I'd ever object to holding a kitten, but…"

"You'll need it." He sat down opposite me again, his frame brimming with nervous energy.

My heart sank. "You brought me an emotional support kitten?"

He nodded, his expression grim.

I made an involuntary sound of distress and hugged the kitten close. It bit me and kept purring. "What is it?" I asked, dreading the reveal of whatever the fuck was going on. Tight bands constricting my chest, I added in a whisper, "Are you breaking up with me?"

"What?" Stopping short, he glared at me. "After all of

233

that"—he gestured to our bedroom next door—"you'd still think I'd leave you?"

I grimaced. "Sorry."

Exhaling roughly, he shook his head, then rubbed a hand over his face again. "Zoe," he began, "what Cadriel told me —" He broke off, clenched his jaw, then shot to his feet once more. "You need more kittens," he murmured, turning to the adjoining room again.

"Azazel, wait."

He paused, tension knotting his shoulders.

"Just tell me," I whispered. "You're scaring me."

Heaving a sigh, he then gave a single terse nod and sank down on the chair. His elbows on his thighs once more, he clasped his hands between his knees, took a deep breath, and then said, "Your mother has a brain tumor."

I heard the words, and yet I didn't *hear* them. They were nonsensical. Just syllables strung together with no meaning.

Noticing my lack of a reaction, he swallowed and repeated, "Cancer, Zoe. Your mother has cancer."

Something twitched in my face. A muscle, maybe? "What?" I asked numbly.

"When I brought you to see her today," he explained, "I noticed several letters in her mail. Medical bills. For tests and procedures. I also sensed…something off about her. Sickness."

From deep within me, a trembling started, spreading outward.

"Demons can often tell," he added quietly. "I didn't have time to check it out more thoroughly, so I ordered Cadriel to look into it. When she came to talk to me, she gave me the report on her findings." He paused, his nostrils flaring. "Your mother has been diagnosed with glioblastoma multiforme. It's an aggressive and fast-growing tumor in the brain, and it's 90 to 95 percent fatal even with treatment."

"I don't understand." My voice was so, so hollow.

"Zoe," he said, his own voice rough, "your mother will die within the next year."

I shook my head. "No."

He exhaled a ragged breath. "She has surgery scheduled to remove as much of the tumor as possible, and after that, she'll undergo radiotherapy. But even with that...the cancer will come back. It almost always does. Treatment means she'll have a few months more than without, but she won't live to see next year."

My mind still struggled to make sense of his words. The full impact of this revelation loomed just out of reach of my consciousness, threatening to shatter my foundations.

The compassion on Azazel's face pierced through some of the fog hazing my thoughts. "I'm sorry, Zoe."

I sucked in a broken breath, fine tendrils of incredulous pain stabbing and weaving through my chest. "Heal her," I pressed out through shards of fear maiming my throat. "You can heal her."

"I can't," he said with pain in his eyes.

"Why not?"

"Outside of a deal for a soul, we are not allowed to interfere that way."

My heart pounded so fast, so overwhelmingly loud, it seemed to shake the room. It drowned out all thought aside from—"Then make a deal with her."

He stilled, everything about him becoming eerily silent. Even his power quieted.

I rose from the couch, the kitten jumping off my lap as I got to my feet, my hands shaking. "Make a deal to heal her."

"Zoe."

"That's what you do, isn't it?" My voice trembled. "It's what demons do. You can do that."

A muscle ticked in his jaw. "You don't know what you're asking."

"*I'm asking you to save her life!*" I yelled, the pain and fear spreading through me veering sharply into anger.

"No," he ground out and stood up. "You're demanding that I damn her soul."

My thoughts all stumbled over one another, panic gripping me tightly. I shoved my hands through my hair, pacing back and forth. "We could keep her soul on Earth. Like my dad. We wouldn't have to torture her."

"Zoe…"

"We did it for my dad!"

"It's not the same," he snapped. "Your father was already damned. Your mother isn't."

I stopped my pacing to stare at him.

"She's slated for Heaven." His eyes glittered hard. "Your father's fate was sealed. Hers isn't. Unless she makes a choice that damns her soul, she'll ascend when she dies."

And she'll be forever lost to me. I wouldn't ever see her again once she entered Heaven. My lungs seized, and I couldn't breathe. I wasn't ready. It was too soon. I couldn't let her go.

I didn't see Azazel coming over to me, my vision hazed, my mind racing. I only felt his hands on my back, pulling me into his arms.

"I'm sorry, love," he murmured, his breath warming the top of my head.

"I want to see her." I gripped his shirt. "Take me back."

His muscles tensed, his energy sharpening. "I don't think that's a good—"

"Take me back," I choked out, tears stinging my eyes.

His fingers twitched where he held me, the grinding of his teeth evident in his voice as he said, "You've already been to Earth today. Several hours. It's too soon to go back."

"I don't care. I need to see her."

"Another visit to Earth right now might risk severing the connection between your body and spirit," he ground out. "You can go see her in a few weeks."

I pushed against him and stepped back until I could pin him with a glare. "Do not," I said, despair and fear and fury vibrating in my voice in equal measures, "deny me this. You said she has a brain tumor. An aggressive one. What if"—my voice cracked—"she won't be there in a few weeks? What if I wait until next month, and she's gone?"

Real pain shone in his eyes as he looked down at me.

"Please," I whispered. "I need to see her now. Don't take this from me."

"Zoe..." He rubbed both hands over his face and then speared his fingers through his hair, turning away.

I balled my hand into a fist and bit into it to keep the sob from breaking free. My breathing was choppy, my fingers cold and tingly.

With a heavy sigh, he faced me again, his throat muscles working as he swallowed. "All right. I'll take you. But it will be quick." His gaze slammed into me, the silver swirling in his eyes glowing brightly. "It's dangerous enough as it is for you to go back so soon. I won't risk your life by allowing you to stay long."

Jaw trembling, I nodded. "I understand."

ONCE MORE, AZAZEL TOUCHED DOWN IN MY MOM'S BACKYARD with my spirit form in his arms. Night had fallen, bathing the yard in velvet darkness but for the faint light coming from a room on the side of the house. My mom's bedroom, I knew.

She was still up.

The echo of my heart pounded through my ghost form as Azazel set me on my feet. Grabbing his hand, I turned to the house and hurried inside. At the back entrance, he let go of my hand in favor of opening the door and slipping inside.

"You can walk through walls," he said quietly. "I can't."

Right.

With a nod, I turned around again, crossed the kitchen, and went into the hallway, toward the sliver of light falling through the cracked door to my mom's bedroom. There, I halted, my pulse racing.

Clenching and unclenching my hands several times, I gathered my nerves. Then I focused on making myself visible. The telltale tingle spread over me, letting me know it'd worked.

Zoe, Azazel hissed in my head, then grabbed my arm and pulled me back from the cracked door before I could walk through it. *What the fuck are you doing?*

I faced him with defiance lifting my chin. *Letting my mom see me.*

For the first time since I'd gone to Hell with him. One whole painful year of keeping myself invisible, hidden from her gaze, unable to tell her that I hadn't, in fact, died a horrible death as a victim of some violent crime. The fact that I'd had to let my mom suffer from never having closure, watching her vacillate between believing she might still find me one day and the devastating acceptance of the possibility

I'd truly been murdered, it had broken some essential, soft part of my soul.

You can't let her see you, Azazel said along our mental pathway, his expression incredulous.

Why? I shot back. *Because it would break her mind? She's dying. If ever there was a moment to show myself to her, it's now.*

I could see that he wanted to argue, so I added, *This is my only chance to talk to her. To let her know that I'm okay.* My mental voice became brittle. *I don't want her to go thinking I suffered some horrible fate. She needs to know that I'm fine.*

He clenched his jaw, the planes of his face hardening. *And what if revealing yourself to her will damage her mind to the extent you won't be able to talk to her? I don't want your last memory of your mother to be of a woman lost in the broken labyrinth of her own mind.* Old, old pain glimmered in his eyes. *I know what that's like.*

I grabbed his hand, kissed his knuckles, and then pressed our entwined hands against my chest. *I appreciate your protectiveness,* I said softly. *But this is my choice to make, not yours. I'm willing to take the risk.*

For a long moment, he held my gaze, then he gave an imperceptible nod and released my hand. I sent him a shaky but grateful smile and turned toward the door. Nerves making my spirit form jittery, I reached out a hand, focused, and pushed the door open.

My mom was reclining on her bed, a book open on her lap, the light of the bedside lamp painting her in soft warmth. At the movement of the door, she lifted her head—and her gaze fell on me.

For the first time in over a year, I found myself staring into my mom's eyes, seeing her *see* me, recognition sparking in the instant connection.

Her features slackened. Her eyes widened. She raised a trembling hand to her mouth.

"Mom," I whispered, my throat too thick to get out more than a rasp.

She closed her eyes tightly, her face scrunching up. With a jerky movement, she raised her hands and pressed the heels against her temples, rubbing vigorously.

"Mom?" I ventured, my voice trembling.

She shook her head and massaged harder.

She thinks she's having a hallucination, Azazel spoke into my mind.

Are you reading her thoughts right now?

Yes. He laid his hand on my shoulder and squeezed. *She's been having headaches, issues with concentration, fatigue… Right now, she believes seeing you here is another symptom of her brain tumor.*

My chest pinched with pain. "Mom," I tried again. "Please look at me. I'm real."

She drew in a shuddering breath but kept her eyes closed.

"I'm not a hallucination," I said hoarsely. "This is not a symptom of your tumor. Your mind is not playing tricks on you. I'm really here. Please look at me."

Haltingly, she lifted her head and raised her eyes to me once more.

My smile was brittle. "It's really me. I know this is hard to believe, but…" I wanted to say it, but, for the life of me, I couldn't get the words out. No matter how I tried to phrase it, it all sounded so outlandish, so far-fetched and beyond anything a reasonable person might be able to accept.

It had been different with Taylor. She'd been in on the whole thing from the start. She'd been there when I'd first summoned Azazel, she'd understood that something had happened that defied our world's rational explanations, and when I'd called her that night a year ago, on the run from Azazel, it'd been easy enough to tell her the rest.

Same thing with my dad. I'd had no trouble telling him the entire story after we'd brought him up from Hell because...well, he'd have no problem believing it, considering his recent firsthand experience with being tortured in Hell as a damned soul. Once someone had seen and been through what he had...yeah, they'd easily accept the unlikely tale of how I came to be living in Hell happily married to a demon.

But as I stood there in front of my mom, who wasn't even particularly religious, I struggled to find the words to explain my current existence to her.

I glanced at Azazel, my heart heavy. *How do I make her understand? What do I even say?*

Something like resignation shone in his eyes. *This is why I told you to keep yourself hidden.*

You're not helping. I balled my hands into fists.

He sighed. *Just say it. Keep it simple. And then go from there.*

Turning back to my mom, I said, "Okay, so you have to suspend your disbelief for a while because what I'm about to tell you may sound outrageous, but I swear it's the truth."

She stared at me, unblinking.

I grimaced. "All right. Um. Last year, when I disappeared, it wasn't that I was trafficked or someone snatched me and killed me. Well, someone did snatch me, but, like, not in *that* sense. And in the end, I kind of went willingly. Ish. I mean, it was either that or be tortured as a damned soul, so I took my chances. You see, I'd unwittingly entered into this insane contract with a demon when I was thirteen and did this séance with Taylor, the result of which was that, if I was still single on my twenty-fifth birthday, I'd have to marry that demon and follow him to Hell, but it sounds worse than it turned out to be because he's actually a total dreamboat and I love him and he treats me like a princess—"

Dreamboat? Azazel's voice in my head sounded suspiciously like he was holding back laughter.

I cleared my throat, my cheeks warming. "Yeah, um, anyway, so that's what happened. I didn't just fall off the face of the earth." I paused and chewed my lip. "I mean, I kind of did, what with Hell and Earth being different dimensions…"

"Zoe," my mom whispered.

I stilled and looked at her.

Eyes glistening with unshed tears, she stared at me with one hand pressed against her mouth. "It's really you."

My own eyes burned with the ghostly echo of tears. "It's my rambling, isn't it? Tay said the same thing the first time I visited her. That's how she knew she wasn't dreaming. Said she could never come up with that much weird stuff in a dream."

"You always talked like that," my mom said, her voice husky and trembling.

"*Talk,*" I corrected her gently. "I still talk like that. I'm not dead."

She shook her head. "How…?"

"I'm still alive. Just…living in Hell. And this"—I gestured down my spirit body—"is just sort of an astral projection. My real body is in Hell. It's bound to that dimension now, so I can't physically leave and come here. Hence the ghost form."

My mom slowly shook her head, her eyes tracking up and down my body. With trembling hands, she set her book aside and threw the covers off, swinging her legs over the side of the mattress.

"No hugs," I pressed out, my heart breaking a little.

She halted in the process of getting up and looked at me questioningly.

"Big disadvantage of this form," I whispered. "I can touch and move things if I focus really hard, but it's not enough to make myself solid enough for a hug. I'm sorry."

Her face fell, and she sat back down on the bed. "I thought you'd..." She swallowed hard, her eyes filling with fresh tears. "The police said you'd just run away. But I knew you'd never do that. I thought you'd—you'd—"

"I know." I took an involuntary step toward her, my hands twitching with the need to touch her. Knowing I couldn't was a spike of pain through my heart. When I spoke again, my voice came out husky. "I saw you."

Her delicate brows drew together.

"I've been coming here," I rasped. "Every few weeks, as much as I could. Just to see you. To be near you. Even if I couldn't show myself..."

"Why not?"

"I'm not really supposed to let anyone see me. Apparently, there's the risk that a human mind wouldn't be able to process seeing something beyond their rational understanding. It could drive people mad." I chewed my lip. "So many times, I wanted to show myself, to tell you that I'm fine. It was so hard not to."

She shook her head the slightest bit. "But you're showing yourself now. Why?"

My eyes burned with phantom tears. "I know about the tumor, Mom."

She sucked in a breath, her face paling.

"I know that you—that you might not have long. And if you're already..." I couldn't say it, the words turning to ash on my tongue. "I couldn't just let you go without telling you that I'm okay. Because I know how much pain you've been in. How much you've worried. And mourned." My voice broke, and I shook my head in jerky movements. "So please don't grieve me anymore. I'm doing fine. I'm happy."

"Zoe…" The tears spilled over and rolled down my mom's face, and her shoulders shook with her small sobs.

"I know it sounds weird, and unbelievable," I said, trying to get my voice back under control, to not fall apart right in front of her, "but I've been doing great. When I went to Hell last year, I never imagined that I'd find happiness there, but I did. Azazel has been wonderful. He's the best thing that could have happened to me."

"Azazel?" my mom asked, trying out the syllables while she wiped her tears.

I nodded. "That's his name. He's actually right here."

Looking over my shoulder, I grabbed his hand. His gaze slammed into mine, surprise and hesitation glinting in his eyes.

What are you doing? he asked in my mind.

I want her to meet you. I tugged on his hand. *Please?*

With a sigh, he relented. My ghostly skin prickled where I held his hand, signaling that he'd made himself visible.

Though my mom's gasp would have told me that as well.

I glanced back at her and couldn't suppress my smile at the expression of complete and utter shock on her face, tinged with a healthy amount of awe and adoration. He sure had that effect on people, especially women.

"This is Azazel," I said. "Azazel, meet my mom."

"It's an honor to meet you, ma'am."

I craned my head to stare at him, blinking at him in astonishment. *Did you just "ma'am" my mom? Who is this deferential dude next to me? And what did you do to my demon?*

His gaze slid to me with a perfect side-eye. *Like I'd greet your mother with anything less than the proper respect.*

Just when I thought I couldn't love him more...

My mom cleared her throat. "You're a—demon?"

"I am."

"You don't..." She frowned. "You don't look like one."

"Mom," I ground out.

But Azazel just smiled with saintlike patience. "Human traditions tend to imagine us in ways that are much more telling as to their own biases than the truth of our existence. Few accounts throughout history are correct in their description of what we are like."

My mom pursed her lips. "I see." Her eyes flicked between him and me. "And you two are...together."

I nodded. "Married."

She blew out a breath. "Okay."

I raised my brows. "You're taking this awfully well."

Her laugh was a touch fragile. "Honey, I am dying." At my flinch, her expression softened, and she continued, "I've been staring death in the face ever since my diagnosis a few weeks ago. Facing the immediacy of your own mortality...it changes you. Makes you ponder what will come after, makes you more open to all sorts of theories." She shrugged. "At this point, I'm just rolling with the punches."

My heart thumped against my ribs as I considered how to phrase my desperate thoughts. "You don't have to be," I finally said.

"What?"

I swallowed hard. "Dying. You don't have to be dying."

Azazel's energy sharpened.

"What do you mean?" my mom asked.

"Azazel can heal you."

Zoe. A thundering reprimand in my mind.

Ignoring him, I forged on ahead. "You can make a deal with him, and he'll heal you."

My mom's gaze swung to Azazel. "And what do you get in return?"

He clenched his jaw. "Your soul."

Her eyes widened.

"But you wouldn't have to go to Hell," I blurted, desperation making me jittery. "When you die, you could just stay on Earth as a ghost, and I could visit you. It'll all be okay. He heals you, you live a long and happy life, I come to see you, and we can actually talk now, and then when you die, you stay as a ghost and I keep coming to visit you and—"

"Except," Azazel interrupted me, his voice deathly quiet and with a serious note that made my heart skip a beat, "that if I heal your mother of the tumor now, she still won't live a long and happy life."

"What?" I croaked.

His stare was mercilessly cold. "Whenever a human makes a deal with a demon to save their life, it's only a short reprieve. Say someone is fatally sick. The demon heals the person's illness, and they think they've beaten Death. They go on living, healthy and strong, only to die in a car crash a few months later. Fate"—his eyes glittered hard—"has a way of catching up."

I inhaled sharply. "You guys *Final Destination* the people you make a deal with?"

"It's not us," he said through gritted teeth. "Demons aren't the ones orchestrating that. We are happy to collect the souls, make no mistake, but this is not our power at work. Call it destiny or God's grand plan, but without fail, if we save a human's life in a deal, the person dies shortly after by some other means."

"You didn't mention that earlier when we talked about it."

"We didn't talk about it; you yelled at me and wouldn't listen. There was no way to explain the logistics to you at that moment."

I was speechless, a heaviness settling in my stomach.

Azazel faced my mom again. "If you make a deal with me, your soul will be damned. And while it's true that I could refuse to collect your soul after you die, you would be barred from ever ascending to Heaven unless you entered Hell first and suffered the torture necessary to redeem your soul."

My mom stared at him with wide eyes.

"If you have any loved ones," he continued, "who have passed before you or will pass after you and whom you would like to see again someday, then making a deal with me means forsaking that. Your parents, your grandparents, your sister—they will be forever lost to you. If your soul is damned but never redeemed through torture in Hell, you will never be eligible to enter Heaven, and thus you will never see anyone who might wait for you there."

"Azazel," I hissed.

He glanced at me, no give in his expression. "Your mother deserves to know the full extent of the deal and its consequences." To her, he said, "And while staying on Earth as a ghost so Zoe could visit you might sound all right at first, you need to consider that she'd be the only one you could truly interact with. As a ghost, you won't feel, smell, or taste anything. Your senses are reduced to sight and sound. Since you live here alone, with no immediate family, you'd have no real anchor after your death. You'd have no purpose, no focus except to wait for Zoe to visit you."

I sucked in a trembling breath. Every word of his was

like a nail driven into my flesh, accumulating spikes of pain that spread through my entire being.

Unaware—or uncaring—of my inner turmoil, he went on, his attention still on my mom. "There will be weeks in between Zoe's visits because she can't leave Hell too often or for too long, and you'll have no one to talk to, no one to lean on, no one to give your afterlife meaning. There will be nothing for you to do except linger among the living as a shadow of yourself, removed from a world you once knew but won't ever be a part of again."

I wanted to keep him from talking, if only to stop the anguish seeping into my mom's expression, but my throat seemed sewn shut, the serrated hurt spreading through me, shredding all the words on the tip of my tongue.

Mercilessly, Azazel continued laying out all the reasons my mom should decide against the deal. "Not having an anchor will also speed up your soul's deterioration into a wraith, which is when a ghost degenerates into something dark, vile, and unpredictably violent. It's known as a poltergeist, and it will be your fate, whether accelerated due to not being anchored, or slowly over years and decades. Once turned into a wraith, your soul can only be smashed into parts, to be redistributed and reborn. You won't enter Heaven then either. Shards of your essence will reincarnate without any trace of the soul you once were."

I trembled all over, unable to voice a single one of my clamoring thoughts, nor any of the pain lancing through me.

My mom stared at him for a few heartbeats, her mouth hanging open, something like horrified agony twisting her expression. Then she swallowed and asked quietly, "If I don't make a deal, and the tumor takes my life, where would I go?"

"Heaven," was Azazel's gentle answer.

She inhaled with a quiver, closing her eyes and rubbing her forehead. "Will Zoe go to Heaven at some point?"

Azazel was silent for a moment. "No."

My mom's tear-filled gaze met mine, but her whispered question was aimed at Azazel. "Will I be at peace in Heaven?"

His reply was just as soft. "Yes. It's where all souls are supposed to be."

She sniffed, the tears wetting her cheeks. "My sweet, sweet baby girl," she began, her voice breaking.

I didn't want to hear it. I couldn't. I knew before she said the words; I felt it deep in my soul. The finality. The goodbye that would shatter me.

"I love you so much," my mom said hoarsely, her heartbreak written on her face. "You are the best thing I ever did in my life. I am so, so proud of you." Stifling a sob, she went on. "You don't know how much it means to me to know that you're okay. That you're alive and well. Happy."

Deep inside me, something cracked and twisted and bled.

"For the past year," she continued, "I have mourned you. I grieved for you, every day, and it nearly broke me. There were times—" She paused, inhaled sharply, and closed her eyes for a moment. "There were some dark times. When I didn't think I'd have the strength to go on." The muscles in her throat worked as she gulped, not meeting my eyes. "I would love to spend more time with you. To make up for what we lost." She raised her gaze to mine, her lips quivering. "But not like this. Not at the expense of my soul." She shook her head, her voice dropping to a pained whisper. "I don't want to be a ghost, sweetheart. I don't want to linger where I don't belong. I just—" She paused again as if to gather her strength to keep speaking. "I just want peace."

"Mom." My voice broke.

"I will always love you, honey. Please know that." She pressed her lips together, her cheeks glistening with her tears in the soft light of the lamp. "But you have to let me go."

My knees gave out from under me, and I sank to the floor with a sob, my eyes burning without being able to shed any tears. So violent were the sobs shaking me that I didn't hear what else my mom said.

Didn't hear her goodbye.

I dimly felt Azazel scoop me up into his arms and carry me outside, where he launched into the sky.

We didn't speak on the way home. I cried—without tears —for most of the way, until the devastating pain wrecking me morphed into something hot and acidic and nearly as violent as the sobs that had shaken me before.

A storm brewed inside me, and it erupted as soon as we came home and I reconnected with my body lying on the bed, all my pent-up emotions suddenly highlighted and ready to explode.

I got up and immediately rounded on Azazel. "How could you?"

He paused and looked at me. "How could I what?"

"You talked her out of a deal," I spat at him, the acid souring my blood.

Understanding flickered in his eyes. Infuriatingly, he didn't snap back at me, instead saying in a voice that was far too gentle, too kind, "No. I simply gave her all the information to make an informed choice."

"*Bullshit*." I balled my hands into fists. "You made it sound so horrible that she had no other choice but to turn it down. You *wanted* her to say no, and you made it happen." My voice wavered, the hurt that lay at the core of my rage rushing to the surface and making my words choppy. Hot tears spilled over, thanks to the curse of being an angry-crier. "You stabbed me in the back. You were supposed to be on my side, to support me. You know how much she means to me, but instead of helping me save her, you manipulated her into refusing the deal."

With a sigh, he stepped up to me and took my face in his hands. Not matching my biting tone, he calmly said, "I know where this comes from. You're hurt, and you're lashing out. I understand that. You're in pain, you're emotional and not thinking clearly, but with time, you'll see why what I did was necessary."

Oh, no, he didn't.

"Do not," I snarled, jerking back and pointing a finger at him, "pull the *you're hysterical* card on me."

"I didn't say *hysterical*." He pinned me with a look. "But you're having strong emotions that cloud your judgment. You feel deeply. You love even more deeply. It's one of the things that drew me to you. And when you love someone, you'd move Heaven and Earth for them. Your love, Zoe, is a force of nature. But right now, you're being selfish."

I reared back as if he'd slapped me.

Still with that infinite patience and gentleness, he forged ahead. "Your desire to keep your mom around by any means necessary isn't born out of consideration of your mom's needs—only yours."

I gasped, his words smarting like a physical blow—all the more so for the bitter glimmer of truth I tasted in them.

"I know you think that you want to save her," he said, his soft voice and expression such a stark counterpoint to the raging storm of pain and anger inside me. "I know you love her with all your heart. But loving her should mean putting her needs above your own. Withholding vital information from her so she'll enter a contract with me at the expense of her salvation, all so you can have her in your life longer… that's putting your own needs first. And in the end, that's not love. It's fear. Fear of losing her. Right now, you're hurting, and you're acting out of a deep-seated need for comfort and security, and it makes you act irrationally. But that's not you. You're better than that. I know you are."

His face blurred, burning hot tears drowning my vision. My heart drummed in my chest, a toxic cocktail of emotions scorching me from the inside out. Fury mixed with shame, which morphed into despair, spiked with a bone-deep fear that came from the smallest part of me, from a young girl trying to hold on to the one person who'd been her steady anchor, her safe haven when her world had fallen apart after her father had left her.

My mom had always been there. She'd held me through the many times I'd cried, when I'd felt abandoned and unloved after my father had chosen his other family, his other daughters, over me. My mom and I had grown so close during those years after the divorce, sharing the pain and the struggle of having to go on alone. Her love had never wavered, never waned, her presence in my life a rock and a fortress.

And now she'd be gone. *Forever.*

"I can't lose her," I said with a sob. "I just—I can't."

"I know." His voice was closer, the heat of his energy brushing against my skin.

Despite the aggravatingly logical way in which he'd explained his reasoning, despite the fact that a part of me grudgingly recognized the painful truth of his words, his compassionate understanding enraged me all the more. I was so high-strung, so raw and reeling from the anguish and the helplessness, I couldn't seem to simmer down, to accept his kindness and support.

All I could do was snap and snarl like a cornered, injured animal.

"No, you don't," I ground out. "I'll lose her forever. I won't ever see her again."

Tipping up my face with a finger under my chin, he met my tear-streaked gaze, soft pain shadowing his features. "I know exactly what it's like to lose one's mother far too soon. What it feels like to grapple with the understanding that I'll never see her again."

"But you could!" I snapped. "She's right here!"

Everything, *everything*, about him became inhumanly still, all the air in the room hushing in terrible silence.

Then, a single harsh whisper: "*What?*"

CHAPTER 20

O h, *shit.*

I sucked in a breath and then closed my mouth with an audible click, as if I could inhale back the words I'd just spoken and hold my fucking tongue. All of the whip-sharp anger and hurt I'd felt a moment before evaporated in the blink of an eye as the realization of the monumental fuckup I'd just committed settled over me like some chill-inducing mantle.

Azazel's searing focus on me made me tremble and back away a step.

He followed me with terrible predatory grace. "What did you say?"

"Nothing," I squeaked.

He grabbed my chin and bared his teeth as he leaned in, every inch the otherworldly being that he was. "Don't lie."

My heart sank to somewhere beneath my feet.

"What do you mean," he said with lethal softness, "my mother is right here?"

I withstood that drilling gaze and the force of his power

pressing against my skin for exactly five seconds. Then I broke.

"Your mother is still alive," I whispered, closing my eyes so I wouldn't see his reaction. "She's in Lucifer's palace, cloistered away in a secret suite"—my voice became almost inaudible—"where she has been all this time."

The silence that followed was deafening. The quiet actually rang in my ears; the pressure was that intense.

His hand fell away from my chin.

The push of his energy against my skin faded.

When I opened my eyes, it was to see him stare at me with the most shell-shocked expression I'd ever seen on him.

"How do you know this?" he asked hoarsely.

I wrung my hands. "When we were at the Fall Festival—"

"Last year?" he snapped.

I flinched.

"You've known about this *for an entire year?*"

"I wanted to tell you!" I rushed to throw in, my heart hammering up into my throat. "Believe me, it killed me that I couldn't say anything!"

"And why couldn't you—" He bit off the rest of his question, his eyes widening a little. "The vow. The one you had to make to Lucifer about the—" He broke off again, glaring at me.

"About the *treasure* I found," I completed, my shoulders slumping and curving forward. "Yes."

"Treasure," he echoed, his voice hollow. "My mother."

I nodded, every breath struggling against a leaden weight sitting on my chest.

He rubbed a hand over his face and turned away, as if looking at me right now was too much for him. Hurt and nausea and sizzling anxiety boiled in my stomach.

"Tell me everything," he ground out, facing me again, his hands balled into fists.

I had to swallow several times to be able to speak. "When we got separated in Lucifer's palace, I got trapped in this cavern with hellrats on my tail, and there was no way out, but Mephisto was suddenly there, and he told me to use your sigil to create a doorway, so that's what I did, and then I stepped out into this suite, and that's where she was." I took a deep breath and continued. "She noticed me, and she said I smelled like her son, and that's when I realized who she was. I told her I was bonded to you." My voice cracked a little with my next words. "She asked about you."

Few times I'd seen Azazel's composure shatter like this, when all the masks and the iron control over his appearance and features splintered to reveal the rawest, most brittle and vulnerable core of him. It was a sequence of involuntary, minuscule twitches of his facial muscles, a slight blink of his dark lashes over eyes that nearly glowed with the intensity of the pain and stark longing in them.

All of who he was, all of who he'd fought to become with gritted teeth and blood on his hands, all the hardness and calculation he'd had to cultivate to claw his way up against cruelty and adversity, it slipped and fell, gave way to reveal a glimpse at the young boy he'd once been, yearning for the love of a mother who'd been ripped from him.

"She did?" was his husky question, barely intelligible because his voice was so rough.

I nodded, my eyes prickling with incipient tears. "She asked how you are. And she wanted to know…if you remember her." I fought hard not to let my voice break again. "If you remember more than just the bad things."

A tremor went through him, his eyes glistening.

"I reassured her that you do," I continued while he

visibly struggled to regain his composure. "She—she didn't even know how long she'd been in there. And she got angry when she thought of how everyone assumed that your father's abandoning her had broken her mind. She said it wasn't that." I paused as the details of that moment floated back to me from the depths I'd stuffed them into. "She said that it's always been her. That something's not right with her, inside her mind, and she can't get it out."

Naamah's anguished face as she'd yanked on her hair and sunk to her knees was indelibly etched into my memory —just as my powerlessness in the face of her pain felt like a stain on my soul. I'd wanted to help her so badly, but I was barely equipped to deal with my own anxiety, much less with what looked like some deep psychological issues in someone else.

"I think she had a mini breakdown," I went on, "and then she just sort of withdrew into herself, humming a song and tracing the pattern on the rug. She healed my injuries from the hellrat fight, right before the door burst open and one of the insurgents stormed inside and threw a dagger at her. He incapacitated her and then went for me, but I managed to stab him with my dagger and knock him out. I pulled the blade out of Naamah's chest and tried to get her to wake up. Another demon entered and hauled me up, ready to take me with him, and that's when one of Lucifer's guards showed up and incapacitated him. Naamah woke up and strolled into another room, and the guard dragged both insurgents to the throne room and barked at me to follow." I swallowed hard. "And that's how I met your mother."

He exhaled a rough breath, his power a wild hum in the room.

"Lucifer was livid that I'd been in Naamah's quarters, and he was about to crush my throat when Lilith intervened and said that he owed me a favor because I'd saved his daughter's life. He grudgingly conceded her point and granted me a boon to repay his debt, which is where you entered the throne room, and...well, you know the rest." I worried my lower lip. "When we were on the way out, Lucifer spoke directly into my mind and demanded that I swear an oath not to reveal anything about Naamah, *especially* to you. That's why I couldn't tell you. It's been tearing me apart for a year to know this and not be able to say anything." I wrung my hands together again. "And that's why, by the way, it seemed like I'd 'forgotten' that your mother was dead when we had that conversation the other day. I did *not* forget. I just knew the truth, and I slipped up in *pretending* that she's dead."

There. It was finally out! But instead of a weight being lifted off my chest, instead of feeling like I'd righted a wrong and redeemed myself in his eyes, the magnitude of the disaster I'd brought upon me by spilling the secret pushed down onto me like the pressure of an impending thunderstorm.

Fuck, fuck, fuckity fuck.

Azazel sank down onto the edge of the bed, his face a mix of grim resignation and profound agony. "He'll be coming for you."

The breath stalled in my lungs. "Do you think he knows?" I asked, my voice trembling.

He uttered a humorless laugh and looked to the side. "Of course he knows. He'll have felt it the second the words left your lips. That's how it works here. When we make a vow or a deal, it's magically binding." His gaze slammed into me, making me flinch. "That's why there would have been consequences for me had I refused to marry you."

I dimly remembered that he'd alluded to losing his powers if he hadn't fulfilled the contract.

"What will he do to me?" My voice was barely more than a squeak, ice-cold fear seizing every cell of my body.

Flames rolled out from Azazel in a sudden explosion that rocked me to my core. The entire room went up in a blaze, the bed, the chairs, the rugs, the armoire. Instinctively, I shied away and shielded my face with my arms...though the inferno didn't touch me.

I blinked down at myself. I stood in a perfect circle of unscorched floor while all around me a firestorm ravaged our room, Azazel's shadowy silhouette somewhere in the middle of it.

His rage, when he let it loose, was a force to be reckoned with.

Even had the fire touched me, though, I wouldn't have been harmed, thanks to the fireproof powers I'd gotten from Azazel when I'd bonded with him. Still, it was a boon not to lose my clothes to his fiery rage.

"Azazel!" I called out over the noise of the furniture crackling and breaking under the flames.

The amount of smoke in the room should have made me cough and severely threatened the health of my lungs, but apparently the whole fireproof thing extended to being unaffected by the fumes of a blaze, because I could breathe just fine.

"Stop," I pleaded with him, the din of the fire almost drowning out my words.

Overhead, the sprinkler system he'd installed—so Mephisto wouldn't have to spit out fires anymore—came on with a gargling sound and sprayed the entire room. I gasped when the water hit me, sizzling on my overheated skin. The sprinklers doused the flames, the fire hissing where it was drowned, and within moments, the blaze was extinguished.

Drenched from head to toe, I stood in the middle of the room, water dripping down my nose, from my fingers. All around me, the remains of the furnishings lay charred and smoking. My gaze fell on Azazel, kneeling across from me, his head bowed, his power a tangible force around him. Behind his back, his wings rose in the air—with half a dozen white feathers peeking through the cracks in his illusion.

I twitched forward to go to him when a giant stream of viscous liquid hit me full frontal from above. I froze in midstep, trembling as the warm saliva sluiced down my body, and raised my gaze to the ceiling—where two luminous yellow eyes stared down at me from the shadows.

You're welcome, purred Mephisto.

"The fire was already *out,*" I said through gritted teeth, trying not to get cat spit into my mouth.

His pink tongue flashed as he nonchalantly licked his paw. *Are you sure? I thought I saw a flicker there.*

Ugh. That cat.

Ignoring the fickle feline, I closed the distance to Azazel and sank to my knees in front of him. The sable hair hanging in his face half obscured his expression from my gaze, but the tense set of his shoulders and the bite to his energy told me enough. The fury simmering in him was not as easily doused as the fiery representation of it.

"Hey," I whispered as I reached out a hand and tentatively touched his cheek.

A tremor went through his massive body. He grabbed my hand, squeezed it tight, and softly kissed the knuckles of my fingers. The juxtaposition of the sharpness of his power making the air shimmer and the gentleness with which he caressed my hand was staggering. He'd lay waste to the world, but me? Me, he'd only ever touch with reverence and love.

Earlier, he'd told me that I felt deeply, as if that were unique to me. As if he didn't also have the capacity to feel with such force that it manifested in elemental power. I'd once teased him that he had some anger issues to work through, and maybe he did, but...could anyone blame him that the depth of his emotions most violently revealed itself when it came to fury? When that was, by all accounts, the only permissible emotion to show in Hell—when you had to mask and mold all other feelings such that they'd be channeled into rage...so you could actually release them?

When he spoke, he proved my guess that there was a whole lot more folded into the fiery fury he'd just displayed.

"What will he do to you?" The words were a whispered snarl. "What won't he do to you? Whatever the fuck he pleases! Even if he didn't already have supreme authority over all of Hell, the broken vow gives him the right to exact whatever punishment he deems fit, and there is nothing, *nothing*"—he spit the word out between clenched teeth— "that I can do to stop him. I have no recourse. I have no justification to appeal. I can't even ask Daevi to intervene because the laws of Hell put him firmly in the right." His tortured gaze lifted to mine, and the anguish there broke my heart. "When he comes for you, I will have to watch him take you away, powerless to stop him. Anything I could do to step in would make it all worse. He knows how much you mean to me, and he must have been itching for an excuse to legally get his hands on you, so he can hurt me through you."

I inhaled a trembling breath. "You—you think he'll take me with him?"

The cynical, resigned set of his features broke my heart

impossibly more. "Whatever he'll have in store for you won't be quickly done. He's known for dragging things out."

I uttered a sound of dismay, shivering despite the ever-present heat of Hell.

Azazel remained kneeling, his gaze unfocused for a moment, then he rose to his feet and shook his wings once. Gleaming black rolled over all of his feathers, swallowing the scattered white until nothing remained but shining onyx. Perfectly acceptable demon wings. The kind that wouldn't draw undue attention or cast their owner in an unfavorable light.

He turned to the balcony door, then paused. Glancing around the destroyed room, he sighed. "You can't sleep here."

He walked over to the adjoining sitting room of my old quarters, and I followed him on his heels. With a wave of his hand, he telekinetically cleared a space against the wall and then summoned an entire bed. Like it was nothing.

"The merihem will clean the other room," he said as he turned to me. "For now, you can sleep here. Don't wait up for me."

He was already striding into the trashed bedroom again as I jolted out of my stupor and ran after him.

"Where are you going?"

He halted inside the open balcony door, the dark sky behind him intermittently illuminated by purple lightning. "I have to tell Azmodea."

"What?"

Muscles feathered along his jaw, each of his words enunciated clearly and with a biting note to it. "I have to go tell my sister that our mother, whom we have mourned for so long, is alive, and that our grandfather has kept this from us for thousands of years."

I grimaced. Right, he wasn't the only one who was directly affected by this. Azmodea had lost her mother just the same, and I knew for a fact that she still grieved her dearly. She'd once mentioned to me that she couldn't even remember her face because there were no images of her—photographs weren't invented back then, and apparently, there were no paintings of her either. Wistfully, Azmodea had recalled how her mother used to sing to her, that she'd had a lovely voice...even if she couldn't remember what that voice sounded like, the centuries having erased that memory.

Azmodea would be distraught. As glittery and nonchalant as she usually appeared, I'd learned that this version of her was just as much a calculated mask and armor as Azazel's cool control. Everyone had to curate their image down here, keeping their softer, more vulnerable parts safely contained behind the face they showed the world. Hers was that of a carefree, frivolous, flamboyant tease, and she played the role so well that few noticed the depths she hid behind that facade.

I opened my mouth to ask him—what, exactly? To tell Azmodea that I was sorry? That I didn't mean to keep this enormous secret from both of them? That I felt their pain?

I resisted the urge to do just that, instead forcing myself to bite my tongue. Telling them that would make this about me. About appeasing my own guilty conscience.

I rationally knew that it wasn't my fault, that I hadn't *chosen* to withhold this vital piece of information from them. I'd been coerced to do so by Lucifer. But the emotional part of me didn't understand that. The fucking guilt remained, uncaring of the circumstances, and I felt awful, just unbelievably miserable, about my lie of omission to them both. Which was why I had this insane need to apologize and beg their forgiveness, as if that would make it right.

But it wouldn't help either of them. It would be purely to soothe my own conscience, something that *I* needed, not them.

And the last thing I wanted right now was to appear *selfish*. Again.

So instead I softly said, "I'm here for you."

He held my gaze for a heartbeat, then he nodded and walked out.

Leaving me alone with the weight of the secret I'd carried, the anticipatory grief for my own mother, and the paralyzing fear of Lucifer's revenge.

CHAPTER 21

I couldn't sleep.

My body was as antsy as if I'd had ten cups of coffee, my mind was working overtime going through all of the possible torture scenarios Lucifer could come up with for me, and my heart…better not go there.

I'd tried to lie down on the newly summoned bed in the corner of the sitting room, with Vengeance watching over me with a worried expression on two of her heads—the third was trying to catch its own tongue—and the hellkittens joining me in a cuddle puddle. But try as I might, I didn't get a lick of sleep.

Every unknown noise startled me to the point I sat upright in bed, and the kittens soon left my side due to my tossing and turning. My heart racing, I'd glance around the dark room, expecting Lucifer to waltz right in and snatch me away.

I was sure he'd have no trouble getting in here. There probably wouldn't even be a servant to announce his arrival —I could just imagine his reaction if anyone tried to keep him from going straight for what he wanted.

In the minutes in between scary noises and almost heart attacks, my thoughts looped back to either my mom's impending death and my desperation to hold on to her, or to Azazel and Azmodea finding out their long-lost mother was still alive, though still firmly out of their reach.

Thus I vacillated between fear so acute it stole my breath and gave me heart palpitations, and the squeezing, stabbing kind of hurt and anguish that made me whimper and cry until my face felt so swollen it might rival a boxer's after a bloody match.

Azazel didn't come to bed that night, which only poured fuel onto the fire of my anxious thoughts and churning emotions. That he'd leave me here alone, with the uncertainty of Lucifer's maybe/maybe-not impending arrival to snatch me away hanging over me like the proverbial sword of Damocles...it didn't sit right.

Was he mad at me? Oh, God, he probably was. I'd kept this huge secret from him, even if against my will, and for an entire year, I'd lived with him, talked with him about a thousand different things, slept next to him, shared so many intimate moments, while all that time, I'd kept quiet about something that impacted his life a whole fucking lot.

Even if he rationally understood that I didn't have a choice, some part of him must feel betrayed.

I knew I would.

Feelings weren't rational, and it would only make sense for him to be hurt by my deception.

Which, of course, hurt me in turn.

God, by now, I had so many layers of hurt wrapped around me that I wouldn't even know where to begin to peel myself out of it all.

Underneath the pain I felt, knowing that he was no doubt angry with me, festered a different kind of sense of betrayal

—because he wasn't here for me. No matter all the sharp and broken things between us right now, I'd have thought he might have at least wanted to be here for whenever Lucifer came to claim me. Should Lucifer take me away, who knew how long I'd be gone? Going by how immortals measured time and the appropriate length of punishments, I could be looking at months, maybe even years, of paying for my transgression in Lucifer's palace.

And with Azazel gone, I wouldn't even get to say goodbye.

When the morning rolled around—noticeable as such only by my own time keeping, because the sky never changed—I decided I couldn't lie in bed any longer, unsuccessfully chasing the oblivion of sleep. With a sigh, I got up and went to clean myself up. The lack of rest made my hands shake, and I fought dizziness as I showered and then dressed.

My breakfast came and went, with me barely able to eat anything, and I eyed the coffee with a healthy amount of suspicion. I was tired AF, but if I drank that cup, it would likely not make me more awake and better equipped to take on the day, but instead make me smell colors and give me two heartbeats for the price of one.

I was already anxious and jittery enough. No need to make my nervous system even jumpier.

For a moment, a really low and shameful moment, I considered ordering a bottle of amrit. If I got drunk on that —and stayed drunk on it—I'd be successfully rid of any anxiety until Lucifer decided to come and collect me. Riding out the time until my punishment in a bubble of bliss seemed so fucking tempting.

That was the moment I knew I had to get out of my rooms and find myself something to do. Azazel still hadn't come back, and when I inquired about him with one of the servants, they told me he'd gone to work. An estate like his didn't run itself, I knew that, but it still smarted that he hadn't even stopped by to check in with me.

So I called Vengeance and took her for a walk.

She had to go potty anyway, and I figured it made no sense for me to stay put in my quarters. If—no, *when*—Lucifer came for me, he'd find me either way.

I threw some giant balls for her outside, which was mainly possible because I'd had a catapult built that would launch those balls the size of small boulders high into the air to crash down hundreds of yards away. Vengeance loved it. She was wicked fast and always caught the ball before it even touched the ground, and then she'd trot back over to me and deposit the ball into the catapult's bucket.

It was uncanny with her, but when she was on the spot and the situation was serious—like needing to catch that ball —she never failed. She was all predatory canine power and prowess, impressively so. But as soon as the pressure was off, she was Ms. Clumsy. Like when she trotted back to me with the ball in one or more of her maws, she'd trip over her own feet more times than not. I knew that should I really be in danger at some point, Vengeance would be one hell of a bodyguard, and woe be those who meant me harm.

All other times? She was delightfully goofy.

And for a few minutes, it actually took my mind off my sorrows.

Of course, that only lasted until I was done playing with her, and we walked back into the mansion. I sat down in the giant hall with the many pillars and a huge fountain in the middle—an ostentatious display of Azazel's wealth and power, since water was so valuable down here—and while Vengeance drank with the grace of a toddler smashing their face into a birthday cake, I perched there on the rim of the fountain and sank into my maudlin thoughts and feelings.

Some more-outgoing people sometimes assumed that introverts were aloof, islands unto themselves, somehow removed from the need for casual physical touch. They couldn't be more wrong. We did need it, just from those few we knew well and felt comfortable with.

Right now, I was in dire need of a hug. I'd spent the last twelve-plus hours in a constant state of fear, grief, despair, and distress, with nobody to vent to and no one to offer me comfort. At this moment, I'd kill to be able to see my bestie and talk to her, but that was out of the question, of course. Another visit to Earth so soon after the last one was a risk not even I was willing to take, as much as I disagreed with Azazel's stern stance on the time frame between visits. And even if I were able to go see Taylor right now, the hug of comfort from her was impossible anyway.

So I sat there, kicking my feet, feeling like shit, because the more I thought about it, the more I realized that Azazel had been right about what he'd said after we'd come back from my mom's.

He'd been right, and it hurt like hell.

No one liked to have a mirror held up and see their own faults reflected back at them, especially if those shortcomings were ugly as fuck. Last night, he'd shown me exactly how ugly I could be, and though I'd hated seeing him point out that side of me...I'd needed to hear it.

Because he was right. I hadn't been thinking of my mom, of what was best for her. I hadn't considered her needs or wants. Just my own. I'd been ready to demand that she damn her soul, just so I could have her for a while longer.

Thinking of that now, it made my skin crawl.

That was not the kind of person I wanted to be. And it was not the kind of person *my mom* had raised me to be.

That thought really drove it all home.

So while I grudgingly, and with no small amount of shame, accepted that Azazel had been warranted in calling me out, which doused the anger I'd felt right after we came back, I still wasn't too fond of how he'd basically called me emotional. It might have been true, *yes*, but that wasn't the smartest thing to point out to the overemotional person at that moment. Just like telling someone who was agitated to calm down never really helped them to actually calm down.

Of course, in the grand scheme of things, this was an inconsequential detail to stay mad about.

What wasn't, though, was the fact that he'd walked away and left me here by myself.

He'd been MIA since he stormed out last night on his way to inform his sister of the whole fucking mess, and I'd had to struggle through the nauseating mix of my emotions alone. To be fair, he had his own deep feelings to sort out as well, but…we could have worked through this shit together.

Not to mention that Lucifer could have shown up at any point in the past twelve hours, and Azazel wouldn't even have been here to say goodbye or maybe plead with him or *something*.

Instead, he'd left me all alone, with the looming possibility that the supreme overlord of Hell might waltz in here any minute and drag me with him to face certain torture.

Deep inside me, the part of me once before traumatized by abandonment and neglect bled anew.

I hung my head, feeling so damn lonely.

"Zoe," a voice said, pulling me from my painful musings.

I raised my gaze to see Hekesha standing a few feet away, dressed, as always, in her fighting gear, her dark hair braided, not a strand out of place. Her brown eyes studied me with a note of worry.

"Are you all right?"

Sudden tears burned in my eyes, and I sniffed, my chest constricting. "No."

"Oh," was all Hekesha got out before I launched myself at her.

She twitched back as if ready to fend off an attack but didn't strike me as I slung my arms around her and squeezed tight.

"Hold me," I choked out between sobs.

"Uh…"

My words were garbled because I was crying so hard at this point. "I feel so much. So sad…I can't…I just need…a friend…hug."

Stiff as a board, Hekesha stood there as I clung to her like a particularly sopping-wet scarf, and after a moment, she tentatively laid one arm around my shoulders and patted my back in awkward taps.

"There, there," she said, though she made it sound like a question, as if she were trying out a new language and wasn't sure of the vocabulary.

I sobbed harder.

Eventually, over the course of several sloppy, tear-filled minutes, I told her about the stress with Azazel—leaving out the details about Naamah, because while the vow was already broken, I wasn't sure whether or not revealing her existence to even more people might not make everything worse—and about my mom.

"And so I'll lose her forever," I croaked, "and I'll never see her again, and it just rips me apart, you know?"

Pat, pat. "I don't."

Sniffling, I drew back and looked at her.

She shrugged. "My mother tried to kill me when she found out I was half demon."

"Oh." *Yikes*. But also, that explained a lot.

I cleared my throat. "I'm sorry. That must have been…" *Hard* didn't quite cut it. I settled on "Devastating."

She shrugged again, looking away to the side.

And now I felt shitty. Here I was, with a great childhood with loving parents, and sure, I'd had a bit of trauma with my dad leaving us, and now my mom dying, but…considering what Hekesha and Caleb had lived through, complaining about my sorrows felt like a privileged pity party.

"Thank you," I mumbled.

"For what?"

"Giving me a reality check." I tugged at a stray thread on my top. "I'm lucky to have had a mom like mine, and I should be grateful for the time we had together."

Hekesha regarded me for a minute. "Your feelings are still valid," she said eventually. "Just because others have had it worse doesn't mean your grief is unwarranted. Life is not a trauma competition. There isn't a threshold of bad experiences you have to meet to be allowed deep feelings about what happens to you."

I stared at her, my eyes watering yet again. "You're a good friend, you know that?"

A flush darkened the warm tan of her face, and she cleared her throat and glanced away. "Your hound is trying to eat her own paw."

"That's okay."

And we both turned to watch Vengeance chew on her left hind paw with one of her maws and then startle when she kicked herself in the mouth, looking around with wild eyes as if searching for the perpetrator who'd just slapped her across her snout.

AFTER ANOTHER NIGHT WITHOUT AZAZEL COMING TO BED—AS per the servants, he'd been working nonstop, which was quite possible, seeing as demons didn't strictly *need* sleep and could go indefinitely without rest—I decided to go searching for him, decorum be damned. I'd march right into whatever meeting or task he was completing and demand that he talk to me. I could understand if he was mad at me, but it wasn't right to leave me here stewing and not knowing what was going on with him, sitting on pins and needles and expecting Lucifer to kidnap me at any second and having to deal with all this crap alone.

I was already dressed and fuming and ready to stalk out the door when said door opened and in walked my darling demon.

I halted in midstep, all my pent-up frustration going poof at the sight of him.

His face was set in hard lines, his shoulders tense, while resignation lay upon his frame like a transparent cloak, weighing him down. A dark, slightly bitter note vibrated in his energy, tendrils of shadow curling behind his back and over his arms as if the essence of his wings wanted to leak out past his control.

When his eyes met mine, the silver in them was so pronounced they fairly glowed.

"Zoe," he said quietly, then crossed the distance to me,

framed my face with both hands, and kissed me with the kind of reverence afforded to unexpected blessings.

I almost melted on the spot, the part of me starved for reassurance blooming under his obvious display of affection. Still, I was trying hard to hold on to all my misgivings about his long absence. Nope, no, I wouldn't be pacified with a kiss.

I pulled back, retreated a step, and then slapped my hand on his chest, baring my teeth. "You left me."

Something like contriteness shone in his eyes. "Yes."

"You left me," I repeated, pointing at him with a finger, "knowing full well that Lucifer could show up at any time and take me away, and yet you walked out and stayed away for two nights and one day, and I had to sit here, alone"—my voice broke and tears burned my eyes, because, dammit, I was an angry-crier—"and I was so afraid, and I needed you to be here, but you weren't!"

He took a deep breath. "I am sorry for that."

I balled my hands into fists. "Where were you? Why didn't you come back sooner?" *Why did you leave me all alone?* I wanted to add, but I didn't trust myself not to break into sobs at the hurt behind that question.

He clenched his jaw, anguish flickering over his features. "Sometimes," he said quietly, his voice threaded with pain, "there are no good choices."

"What do you mean?"

He flexed and curled his fingers, almost absentmindedly. "I stayed away so I wouldn't fuck things up."

"What?"

Looking to the side, he rubbed a hand over his face. "I didn't trust myself to be here when Lucifer came to take you away. If I had stayed, and I had witnessed him coming to collect you..." His expression was the darkest I'd ever seen on him. "Zoe, I wouldn't have been able to stand by. I *would* have tried to stop him. Not by pleading with him. Not by asking nicely. No. Whatever leash holds my fury at bay would have snapped, and I'd have *assaulted* Lucifer, the King of Hell."

He paused to let that sink in. I shivered at the savage glow in his eyes, and at the picture he'd painted.

"I'd have damned myself," he continued, "as well as you. An unprovoked, unwarranted attack like that would have made everything worse. Whatever he might have planned for you, he'd have heaved more punishment on top for my transgression. Not to mention that he'd be justified in retaliating against me directly. I could have ended up in his dungeon, or maybe chained beneath the glass floor of his entrance hall, for who knows how long." Quietly, he added, "And where would that leave you?"

I gulped, my stomach a pit of nausea.

"I am well aware," he said, stepping closer and cupping my face again, "that I am your sole anchor down here, your only protection. That if I were gone, and you'd be left to fend for yourself, whatever status and power you had gained through me would be stripped away, and you'd be fair game for anyone."

I trembled in his hold.

"I won't let that happen." Deep, deep conviction vibrated in his voice. "I will *always* be your shield. I will do whatever it takes to keep you safe, and in this instance, that meant staying away in order to protect you. Because I know, without a sliver of a doubt, that despite my best intentions, I would not have kept my composure had I been forced to watch Lucifer take you away." His thumbs stroked over my cheeks. "But don't you think for a minute that it was easy for me to stay away. That it didn't hurt me to leave you here, knowing you were scared, that you needed me. It tore me apart."

I laid my hands on his, my heart aching. "You should have told me that before you left. I still wouldn't have liked it, but at least I would have understood your motivations."

He was silent for a moment, then he nodded. "You're right."

I raised a brow. "Conceding my point so easily?" For a being of several thousand years, he sure showed quite some adaptability here.

"I am not used to this." At my frown, he added, "Relationships. Communication at eye level. Compromise. I've never had to consider making someone privy to my thoughts and feelings on a regular basis. I've been used to deciding things for myself, without consulting others. This" —one of his hands slid down and caressed my neck in a gentle hold—"is new for me."

A swarm of butterflies took flight in my belly.

"You're my partner," he said softly. "I should have let you know what I was thinking."

I nodded, biting my lip. "Okay." I lowered my eyes, then asked softly, "Are you mad at me?"

"For keeping this from me?"

I played with the collar of his tunic. "Yeah."

There was a considering pause, then: "I was a bit, yes. At first. But there was no malicious intent on your part. You didn't *want* to keep it secret from me. I know that."

"Knowing and feeling are two different things, though."

"True, but I choose what to hold on to and what to let go of. This is something that couldn't be helped, there was no other course of action, and it's clear you regret it as much as I do. Which means I won't dwell on it."

My fingers dug into his shirt. "So we're good?"

"We are."

And then he pulled me to him and into the hug I'd sorely needed from the male I loved. I melted into his embrace, inhaling his scent, letting the heat of his body sink into my chilled bones.

"Why hasn't he come?" I whispered after a long moment, and I knew I didn't have to elaborate on whom I meant. "I broke the vow. Shouldn't he be champing at the bit to punish me?"

He was silent for a few aching heartbeats, then he stepped away and pulled me with him to sit down on one of the sofas.

Facing me with an arm slung over the backrest, he said, "I will not ask him to see my mother."

"What?" I sat up straighter. "But…why?"

He hadn't seen her in so long, and I knew how much she meant to him. I'd thought for sure he'd be on Lucifer's case immediately, demanding to visit his mother. I definitely would be, if I were in his position.

"Azmodea and I agreed that it's best if we don't change the status quo." At my surely puzzled expression, he softly added, "The fact that he hasn't come for you right away could mean two things. Either he wants to draw out your punishment by making you wait, thereby playing on your increasing anxiety the longer he delays coming to collect you."

I gulped. Yeah, that sounded like a Lucifer thing.

"Or," Azazel went on, a focused gleam in his eyes, "he will not come for you as long as the status quo doesn't change."

I blinked at him in confusion.

"If there is a reason," he said, "that he has kept my mother hidden from us for so long—be it to be petty and

277

cruel to us, or out of some other, unrelated motive—he might have a vested interest in keeping it that way. So as long as he doesn't come here or summon you to him to dole out punishment, both Azmodea and I will refrain from asking him about our mother. We won't mention it. We will not make waves or poke at him in any way." His eyes burned into me. "And maybe if we act as if you never said a word about our mother, as if you never broke your vow, it will keep him from coming for you."

I was stunned speechless for a good long moment. That they would do this…for me? Refuse to demand to see their mother, relinquish their right to visit her, on the off chance that it would spare me punishment? Something sour settled in my stomach, and I hugged myself.

"But what if that's not the reason he hasn't come yet?" I asked, worrying my lower lip with my teeth. "What if you guys make this sacrifice for me, only for him to show up after some time to punish me anyway?"

"Then we will have no reason anymore not to ask him to see our mother." His face turned hard. "And while he might not want to let us see her, we'll have Daevi's backing should we go and demand to visit her. We went and talked to her the other night, and we confronted her about keeping this from us all this time. She knew, and she didn't tell us. She has quite a lot of guilt built up from that, and she seeks to make amends. As Naamah's mother, she has a say in this. Should Azmodea and I decide we want to see Naamah, Daevi will make Lucifer grant us access."

My eyes stung. "So you're just holding back on seeing your mom again to keep me from being hurt."

He held my gaze with unwavering strength. "Your safety is my first priority."

"And what about Azmodea?"

I was sure that keeping me unharmed was important to her, but...*that* important? More important than seeing her long-lost mom?

"Azmodea agrees with me that this is the best course of action."

Then why did it make me feel so shitty?

I opened my mouth to say more, but Azazel cut me off.

"This is not up for debate."

"But—"

"I will never," he said through gritted teeth, grasping the back of my neck in a gentle grip, "consider handing you over to Lucifer for punishment. Not even to see my mother. I've done well without seeing her for thousands of years. This doesn't change anything."

But it does, I wanted to say. This was different than before. Not seeing her because he'd assumed her dead was one thing. In a way, it was easier because he'd believed she was gone, so there really was no chance of ever seeing her again. But now that he knew she was alive and right here, in Hell...

I didn't believe for one moment that it would be just as easy for him to ignore this now. Knowledge like this had a way of creeping up on someone, always lurking just there, never going away. He'd remember every time he'd think of Lucifer, or his palace, or Daevi, or his mom. So many different factors in his life that could trigger the reminder that, oh, yeah, his mother was alive—but he couldn't see her.

He tipped my chin up with one finger, his eyes shrewd. He likely saw right into my doubts and fears and objections, and his next words proved me right. "Promise me you won't bring it up again. Don't try to change my mind."

I swallowed, met his gaze steadily, and nodded.

His power pulsed around him. "Say it."

"I promise I won't try to discuss this with you again."

I felt the binding of the small vow I'd just made lay itself around me, and Azazel released a deep breath and squeezed the nape of my neck. Even for promises, this kind of magic seemed to work, which was probably why he'd insisted on me speaking the words.

But the thing about words was...they had to be precise for the meaning intended. What I'd just sworn to was not to mention the whole thing to Azazel again, and he thought that meant the issue was settled. He thought it would mean the status quo would be cemented.

But I'd only sworn not to speak to him about it.

I had not said one word about not *doing* something about it.

CHAPTER 22

I waited more than a week.

Partly to make sure Lucifer really wouldn't just show up with some delay, but also to give Azazel a chance to simmer down and settle back into his routine. All the better for him not to suspect anything.

I passed those days in a constant bubble of fear, determination, more fear, heartache, grief, and the deep-seated knowledge that I had to do this, because if I didn't, I'd one day break under the strain of guilt and anguish.

As I waited in one of our elaborate rooms for welcoming guests, my foot tapping the black marble of the floor, I checked and double-checked my outfit. Totally unnecessarily so, seeing as I wore pretty much what I did on the regular—jeans and a black tank top. I'd considered dressing up in one of those beautiful gowns of my collection that filled an entire room in my quarters, but in the end, I'd gone with the kind of apparel I felt most comfortable in. That, in itself, was a different type of armor.

Besides, any pretty dress I'd wear would just get ruined.

Deep breath in, deep breath out. I could do this.

The double doors leading to the hallway flew open, and Mammon strolled in, his arms raised in greeting. "Dearest aunt," he crooned.

I gave him a warm smile and met his hug.

His hands on my shoulders, he held me at arm's length and peered down at me, a twinkle in his eye. "To what do I owe the pleasure of your call?" He quickly scanned the room, narrowing his eyes. "It's not another ambush in cahoots with my uncle, is it?" Absentmindedly, he rubbed his throat.

"No," I said truthfully. "Azazel isn't here."

"Oh, good. Not that I don't enjoy his grumpy company, but I'd like to evenly space out the times where I annoy him to the point of assault."

"It is a kind of ambush, though."

His clever gaze zeroed in on me. "What?"

"This meeting." I shifted on my feet. "The reason I called you…"

I trailed off, my palms suddenly clammy, and the words I'd practiced seemed to sink back into the dark depths of terror within me.

Mammon tilted his head. "Yes?" he drawled. When I just stared at him in mute paralysis, he sighed. "For Hell's sake, you're making me antsy with that heavy silence and the impending doom of whatever you want to say. Out with it!"

"I need you to take me to Lucifer."

The volume of my own heartbeat almost drowned out my words. Something flipped in my stomach as I spoke them.

Mammon laughed, not even missing a beat. It was entirely, impossibly, unfair how handsome he became when he laughed like that. It was like his whole face lit up with the kind of magnetic charm that would have a roomful of people turn his way and draw closer.

He wiped his eyes. "Oh, that's a good one, kid."

"It's not a joke."

"Uh-huh."

"I mean it." I put my hands on my hips and glared at him, the bottled-up fear in me veering sharply into indignation.

"Totally cute, that look." He wiggled a finger in my direction. "Tell me, does that one usually work on Azazel?"

"I'm serious. I need you to fly me to Lucifer's palace so I can walk right up to him and get this whole punishment thing out of the way, and then Azazel and Azmodea will have no reason anymore to forgo their right to see their mother."

Mammon crossed his arms, raised one hand to his chin, and stared at me for a few seconds. "That," he said and waved at me. "Is that what lunacy looks like? I've never seen it in the flesh quite like this."

"Listen, I'd walk there myself if I could, but it's fucking far, and I don't know the way, and I don't particularly want to end up as fodder for whatever lurks out there in this hellscape. So I need a demon to fly me there."

He laid a hand on his chest. "And you picked *me*? I feel like the Chosen One." His radiant expression turned sour. "By which I mean, *chosen* to have my wings ripped off by my violently inclined uncle. For starters."

When I made as if to speak, he cut me off. "You do realize that besides surrendering yourself to Lucifer being the stupidest idea in the history of idiocy, if I were to fly *you*, Azazel's cherished wife and prized jewel of his realm, to be adoringly delivered into the torture-loving claws of Lucifer, Azazel would kill me? As in, actually *murder* me?"

"No, he won't." I crossed my arms. "He might posture a lot and threaten you with all sorts of bodily harm, but in the end, he wouldn't actually kill you. I know him. Family's important to him—well, at least the part you belong to." I gestured at him. "You're part of his inner circle, his only nephew, and he'd never hurt Azmodea by murdering you. In all honesty, besides Azmodea, you're the *only* demon who could get away with delivering me to Lucifer at my request and not be killed by Azazel. If I chose anyone else—one of the demons from this estate, which means I could actually order them to do my bidding—they would most certainly meet their untimely death when Azazel found out. So, really, you'd be saving someone's life with this!"

Mammon massaged his temples. "The audacity."

"That's rich coming from you, considering you're the reason my best friend has made it onto a powerful demon's shit list and will have to evade his wrath for the rest of her life."

He flinched. "I didn't intend—"

"You can shove your real intentions up your ass," I hissed.

Stumped, he blinked at me.

"Yeah, I'm not playing, Mammon. Do you want my forgiveness for putting Taylor in harm's way? My oldest and best friend in the whole wide world? The person I love like a sister?"

He had the good grace to look chastised.

"You owe me." I poked him in the chest with a finger. "Big-time. You will take me to Lucifer, and when Azazel finds out that it was you and he rips off your wings, maybe that'll make you truly regret the dangerous game you played with my best friend's safety."

"Damn, girl," he whispered. "You really picked up a few things from living in Hell."

"I learned from the best." I bared my teeth at him.

"I can see that." He tilted his head. "You know, Spicy Zoe is even hotter than Regular Zoe."

"Oh, shut it."

"No, I mean it. I'm both frightened *and* aroused."

"Perv." I rolled my eyes. "Now let's go." Before I lost my nerve, after all.

Mammon fell into step with me as I marched toward the exit leading to another huge balcony/landing platform jutting out from Azazel's fortress-like mansion.

"Will you yell at me some more?" he asked, an eager note in his voice.

"Mammon." I gave him the biggest side-eye as we came to a stop on the platform.

"Do you yell at Azazel in bed?"

"I swear," I said through gritted teeth, "if you make this flight awkward, I will punch you in the throat."

He shivered and made a delighted sound.

I buried my face in my hands. "Ugh."

GETTING PAST THE PATROLS ALONG THE BORDER TO LUCIFER'S territory was only possible because Mammon played the family card.

Well, that, and the fact that apparently the guards recognized me as the awkward human who'd made a fool of herself at the Fall Festival and had somehow ended up as a person of interest to Lucifer *and* Lilith. I'd have felt like some kind of celebrity if it didn't also make me cringe.

But Mammon's presence as a member of Lucifer's extended family truly helped to smooth the way, which was another reason that I'd chosen him to take me there. I was sure that some other, lower-ranking demon from Azazel's domain would not have gotten as far as Lucifer's palace.

Just as we'd done at the Fall Festival, we touched down in the wide-open courtyard of pristine white stone—still immaculately clean, which meant that servants surely stood by to swipe off any flecks of ash touching the floor—and to my surprise, we weren't the only ones here. Other demons seemed to be coming and going at a steady pace, observed by guards and ushered to and fro by staff.

Of course, I thought. Even outside the Fall Festival, Lucifer's palace must be the center of political and economic business here in Hell. It made sense that it was a place bustling with activity. Azazel's territory saw regular visitors for all sorts of purposes, and he wasn't even among the highest-ranking demons, his domain not one of the linchpins of Hell. How much more commotion must there be in the heart of the dominion of the supreme ruler of Hell?

As soon as we landed, a member of staff approached us, recognizable by the black-and-gold livery she wore. Her uniform featured more embroidery than that of the guards, filigree threads of gold woven into the black fabric of her tunic. Her dark red hair was pulled into a severe bun, emphasizing the stern look she gave us.

Ignoring me completely, she bowed her head at Mammon. "What is the purpose of your visit, my lord?"

He gave her a genial smile, and her features visibly softened. "I am here to escort Lady Zoe to His Grace for an urgent matter."

After a few seconds, she wrenched her gaze away from Mammon's face to finally give me her attention. Her eyes narrowed. "I know you," she murmured.

Oh boy.

"You're that human. The one from the Fall Festival."

Mammon leaned forward. "Lord Azazel's *wife*." He cleared his throat. "Lady of his estate."

Her brows shot up, and she straightened. With some redness darkening her cheeks, she took a stilted bow and said, "Apologies, my lady. What is the nature of the matter for which you wish to see His Grace?"

"Um." I glanced at Mammon, who shook his head ever so slightly. Focusing back on the guard, I said, "That is between His Grace and me."

Out of the corner of my eye, I saw Mammon give me a furtive thumbs-up.

The female demon studied me intently, then nodded and stepped back. "Follow me, please."

I was pretty sure that it was, yet again, the fact that Lucifer had taken a public interest in me at the Fall Festival that spurred the staff member to grant us entrance to his palace. I could very well imagine anyone else having to make an appointment or plead for an audience. There had to be hundreds of demons vying for Lucifer's attention at any given time, trying to talk to him in order to curry favor or solve some issue. Access to him surely had to be tightly controlled, or else he'd be swamped by supplicants and sycophants. I had no doubt there was some system in place to prescreen visitors based on Lucifer's priorities and interests, and his staff would know to filter arrivals accordingly.

That I was waved through and would apparently be ushered directly to him was a sign of how much of an impression I'd left. I suppressed a grimace at that thought.

I'd really rather not be of any special interest to Lucifer, but at least it made it possible to quickly get an audience with him so I could settle this score.

Mammon and I followed the staff member as she walked us through the giant water garden—I kept hearing Mephisto's disgusted description of the wastefulness of it—and then the entrance hall with the infamous glass floor, underneath which the many, many demons who'd wronged Lucifer in some way over the millennia were chained.

The first time I'd come through here, Azazel's warning not to look down had come a second too late, and by then the damage had already been done. I'd struggled to keep my gaze off the floor after that, the horror I'd glimpsed forever etched into my mind.

This time, I was prepared. Lifting my chin, I deliberately looked far ahead and made sure my gaze never strayed too low.

I heard the screams, though.

Even muffled through the thick glass, there was no ignoring the shrieks of pain, the wailing, the pleas for help. This time, there weren't as many other demons walking through the hall as at the Fall Festival, and the lack of more background noise made the sounds more audible.

I dimly wondered how much it would break someone's mind to be chained down there, year after year, century after century, to watch countless others walking right over you, hearing you, seeing you, yet unable to help.

All while hellrats gnawed the flesh off your bones.

Demons had fast healing and could even regenerate limbs, which made them a never-ending, open buffet for the rats scurrying around in the subfloor. The demons' flesh, muscles, and organs would regrow, only to be chewed off again.

I shivered, and nausea fizzed in my stomach.

"You okay?" Mammon asked quietly, slowing a little to put more space between our staff escort and us.

"Yeah." I cleared my throat. "Better than last time."

"I'd like to say it gets easier, but I'm afraid this is probably as good as it gets."

I cast him a quick glance. "You're still affected?"

I wouldn't have thought that. Mammon always seemed so cheerfully aloof, and right now, he even looked nonchalantly bored.

"Always," he murmured even more quietly, not breaking the mask he wore like a second skin. "Not the best attribute to have in a place like Hell."

I raised a brow.

"It's considered a weakness," he stated, and centuries of lived experience among bloodthirsty, coldly cruel beings echoed in his toneless whisper.

I shook my head slightly. "Compassion and empathy should never be a weakness."

He looped my arm through his and patted my hand. "Oh, my sweet spring baby."

I snorted a laugh at his butchery of the famous line from George R.R. Martin's *A Game of Thrones*. "That's not how the quote goes, Mammon."

"I know." His smile was beatific. "Just wanted to hear you laugh."

I squeezed his arm, grateful for his distracting me, and we continued following the staff member the long way through the hall of horrors. The intimidation of this part of Lucifer's palace didn't just come from the demons chained underneath the glass floor, but also from the hundreds—thousands?—of wings pinned to the walls. Azazel's collection was impressive. Lucifer's put his to shame.

It was yet another visible reminder of how many times Lucifer had triumphed over those who'd sought to cross him, an unfathomable display of his power and cruelty.

It made it all the harder to put one foot in front of the other, considering I intended to offer myself up to him for punishment.

Doubts crept in.

Was I really going to do this? Did I really *need* to do this? Lucifer hadn't come for me yet. I could just sit this one out. Not too late to turn back. My visit hadn't been announced, nor did Lucifer know I was coming, so I could just make a beeline for the exit again, and Mammon would all too gladly fly me home.

Azazel probably hadn't found me missing yet. I'd be back before he knew it, no harm done, nothing amiss. He didn't want me to do anything about this, and I could just take him at his word and accept his—and Azmodea's— waiver of their right to see their mom to keep me from being hurt.

Something pulled tight and twisted in my insides, and my breath faltered. A heavy weight settled on my chest, choking me.

No. No, I had to do this.

I wouldn't be able to live with myself, knowing I was the reason Azazel would never see his mom again. And considering I was now immortal, that was a hell of a long time to not be able to look at myself in the mirror.

Taking a bracing breath, I pulled my shoulders back, lifted my chin, and walked on.

We exited the hall into the large lobby with two staircases curving up the sides, the giant double doors to the throne room—currently closed—in the opposite wall. The staff member made a beeline for another demon in staff uniform to our right and conferred with him for a few seconds. The male demon jerked his head to the average-sized door behind him.

Our escort signaled us to follow as she marched on through the door the other demon had indicated. We walked through side corridors that, while a fraction of the size of the halls we'd come through, were still decked out in luxurious decorations, tastefully arranged to not overwhelm the senses, but nonetheless screaming, "I'm rich, bitch."

Even after living in Azazel's mansion for a year, which didn't lack in opulent furnishings and featured more wealth than I'd ever seen in person in my entire life, I hadn't gotten used to being surrounded by so many ostentatiously expensive things. It still made me feel like a dog who'd rolled around in mud and now tracked it all into a freshly cleaned house.

Finally, we seemed to arrive at our destination. Our staff escort walked out into what appeared to be a courtyard—of giant proportions, of course—where a small crowd of demons lingered, their attention focused on something in the center of the square that was currently hidden from our view. The gloom of Hell's sky stretched overhead, purple lightning adding to the scant illumination of braziers set up around the courtyard's perimeter.

"Your Grace," the staff member called out and sank to one knee, bowing her head.

Mammon tugged on my hand as he kneeled as well, and for a second, I was frozen in indecision. Last time, Azazel had advised me to go down on *both* knees, a subtle indication of my difference in rank as opposed to the other demons who knelt on only one knee.

But that was back when I'd been playing the part as Azazel's "pet." Things had changed since then. My rank was now officially equal to Azazel's, and it would only be proper to kneel on one knee like the others.

Then again…I was here after breaking an oath I'd sworn to him, coming from a position of debt. Wouldn't it be more appropriate to kneel on both knees? Or should I prostrate myself completely before him? Would that appease him somehow?

"Zoe," Mammon hissed under his breath.

I'd hesitated too long. Demons were already turning around to look at us, the crowd parting in the middle, revealing a tall figure with gleaming blond hair—

I made a sound of distress and scrambled to get down to my knees, but my foot slipped on the smooth stone. Arms windmilling, I tumbled down in a graceless heap, slipped again on my knees, and landed on my front, barely keeping my face from kissing the ground as I slapped my hands down to at least break part of my fall.

One year of martial arts training with Azazel, and I still managed to have the elegance and dexterity of a fish flopping around on land.

My breath puffed against the cool stone. All right, then. Prostrating myself, it was. I was just going to stay right here, make it seem deliberate.

The low chuckles coming from the group of demons proved they'd seen my clumsy scrambling for what it was.

"What do we have here?" Lucifer's voice floated over to me, still melodious and charming despite the shitty character of its owner.

I kept my gaze glued to the floor.

"Your Grace," the staff member began. "Lady Zoe, wife of Azazel, here to call on you in an urgent matter. Do you wish to grant her an audience?"

Silence.

Heart pounding, I dared to lift my eyes to peek through the strands of my hair hanging down over my forehead to check out the situation.

Lucifer, first fallen angel, former brightest star of Heaven, stood over the mangled body of some unlucky demon. The King of Hell's finely tailored clothes might have been of some dark gray color at some point—it was a bit hard to tell with the splatter of blood painting them scarlet. A few flecks of red dotted his face of pale, angelic beauty, his turquoise-colored eyes glowed, and his usual crown of black metal sat atop his golden hair.

"*Lady* Zoe," he purred, smiling with all the sharpness of a shark. "My, my. Do I wish to grant you an audience?"

He leaned down, reached toward the mutilated demon at his feet, and tore something from the body. The demon's scream rent the air. Lucifer's bloodied hand came away holding an entire arm, sinews dangling from the point where it'd been ripped off. He nonchalantly flipped it in the air, then hurled it far up with a mighty swing.

The arm flew up toward the gloomy sky, and then a shadow darkened the courtyard. A humongous beast streamed overhead, snatched the arm out of the air, and swallowed it.

A dragon. He'd just fed a fucking dragon that apparently lurked in standby mode to dispose of the limbs Lucifer ripped off some unfortunate demon who'd pissed him off somehow.

Lucifer turned back to me, and his smile chilled the marrow in my bones. "Why, do I ever, my dear."

CHAPTER 23

Lucifer's eyes flicked to the staff member. "Dismissed."

The female demon got to her feet, bowed low, and left the courtyard.

"And what is it," my devilish grandfather-in-law drawled, "that brings you here, *Lady* Zoe?"

I glanced up—still prone on the ground because he hadn't given me permission to rise yet—at the group of demons that still lingered around Lucifer. "Um… Can we, maybe, talk in private?"

Lucifer just stared at me.

Okay, right, great. I cleared my throat. "I'm sure it has come to your attention that I recently broke a vow I made to you."

A shadow passed over his expression, his features growing tense. "So it has."

"Well, I am here…" My heart pounded so loudly I was sure every single demon in the courtyard could hear it. And the dragon, too, probably. The ebbing nausea in my stomach

294

fizzed to new life as fear grasped my soul in a spine-chilling hold.

"To plead with me for leniency?" Lucifer asked in a mocking tone.

"No, Your Grace." I fought back my nerves. "I'm here to face the consequences of breaking that vow."

A quick glance up at Lucifer let me know he regarded me curiously, his head tilted. "Let me get this right—you are *asking* me to punish you?"

Breath stuck in my lungs, I swallowed past a parched throat. "Yes."

Snide laughter from the demons assembled.

"I think that might be a first," Lucifer purred.

More laughter echoed in the courtyard.

"Outside of the bedroom, that is," he added with a chuckle.

Ew. I hid my grimace. I did *not* want to imagine Lucifer engaging in any sort of sexual activity, thank you very much.

"You don't strike me as a glutton for punishment."

Leading statement, I reminded myself. He hadn't asked a question. I didn't need to answer.

Out of the periphery of my sight, I saw him step closer. "Why?"

"Your Grace?"

"Why are you here eagerly asking for me to dole out punishment? I have not summoned you."

I hesitated. For some reason, I didn't feel like it would be the right choice to tell him about my hope that this would take the leverage away in the case of Azazel not seeing his mom. In fact, I felt with utmost certainty that mentioning Naamah in any way, shape, or form right now might put me on *very* dangerous ground with him.

Rationally, he knew this was about her. I knew this was about her.

But that was an abstract kind of knowing. Actually speaking about her was a whole different thing, and she'd proved to be a subject to which he responded with a high degree of volatility and irrationality.

And the last thing I wanted right now was to make Lucifer volatile and irrational.

More than he usually was, anyway.

So I just shrugged and said, "I can't stand the pressure anymore. I just want to get this over with."

"In that case, maybe I should let you stew in that anxiety a bit more." Spoken in the tone used on cherished pets or loved ones.

Ugh. Of course he'd go for that. Azazel's first theory about why Lucifer hadn't immediately come for me might not be that far off after all.

All right, time to switch tactics a bit. "Would you like me to beg?" I asked meekly.

"That would be lovely."

I suppressed the whole-body shiver that wanted to take over my muscles. Pushing down the disgust rising up from my middle, I kept my voice submissive and said, "Please punish me."

Oh, God. I had the urgent need to rinse my mouth out with soap and contemplate my life choices that somehow led me to the point in time where I lay flat on the ground in front of the Devil and begged him to punish me.

"I could watch this all day," Lucifer said with a chuckle. "Unfortunately, I have a tight schedule and more important matters to deal with than to witness you mop the floor with your entire body, so *shoo*."

With a gasp of disbelief, I raised my gaze to him again. He made actual shooing gestures with his hands, the asshole.

"Chop-chop, out with you."

"B-but—the punishment!"

"Will be all the sweeter when you are even more eager for it at a later point. Or maybe I'll wait *years* to come and get you, when you've all but forgotten that you still owe me. Just imagine the shock when I remind you."

Oh, that motherfucker.

No. I would not leave here unpunished.

And there was another thing I never thought I'd say.

I lifted my upper body from the floor so that I sat on my legs and glared at him. "Sad," I said in a voice as cold as it was bored. "So sad. I was so scared to come here, thinking about all the ways you might exact your revenge. Your reputation precedes you, of course. But it looks like you lost your edge. You're not even up for punishing a measly little human anymore? I heal fast now, thanks to your boon. That's a lot of torture to be had." I waved up and down the length of my body.

"What are you doing?" Mammon hissed through clenched teeth.

The part of my brain responsible for self-preservation was currently screaming the same question at me.

"But instead you use excuses to send me away," I continued, pressing on despite the goosebumps spreading across my arms. If there was anything I excelled at, it was being contrarian and poking at someone I absolutely shouldn't poke. "You say you'll punish me later. What a great pretext for not stepping up to the plate right now." I leaned forward a bit. "Cop-out."

Mammon sucked in a breath that sounded like a machine seconds before it collapsed.

Silence reigned in the courtyard. The demons around Lucifer raised their brows and exchanged looks, some of them uneasy, some eager. They'd obviously read my speech for what it was—a gauntlet thrown, a deliberate challenge.

And if I'd judged Lucifer even the tiniest bit right, it was one he couldn't ignore. A silly, easy-to-figure-out manipulation, but…it would still make him look weak if he sent me away now. That was the nature of the power plays in Hell, when might was right, and one could allow no doubt about one's strength and ability.

Did he have the ultimate authority and could simply choose to ignore my taunting, trusting that his reputation and power were firm enough that he wouldn't have to answer a challenge like this? Sure, maybe.

But some little, tiny doubt might stick. Someone would talk, the talk would spread, and it might even coalesce with other little doubts here and there, other instances where his reputation suffered some scratches.

Like the fact that he'd tried to set me and Azazel up at the Fall Festival, assuming I'd pick the option to renounce Azazel and return to Earth—thereby hurting and humiliating Azazel—only to watch me stand there in front of his whole court and publicly choose Azazel and a life in Hell.

Lucifer had obviously been stumped. He'd been so sure I'd turn my back on Azazel, and if I thought too long about it, I'd want to scratch Lucifer's eyes out, because his certainty that I wouldn't choose Azazel pointed at a deeper conviction that Azazel couldn't possibly have someone who truly loved him and would choose him over everything else.

Yeah, that one got my hackles up something fierce.

In any case, though, the fact that his little attempt at

humiliation of Azazel hadn't panned out back at the Fall Festival, but instead left Lucifer in a less-than-favorable light, must have already chipped away at his reputation.

Add in my taunting of him now, in front of witnesses, and he *had* to act.

He couldn't let me get away with defying him twice.

The shadows in the courtyard deepened, the sky darkening without the shape of a dragon to blot out the light. Holy shit. The amount of power this spoke to, the fact that Hell *itself* responded to Lucifer's moods... The goosebumps on my arms spread all over my body while my breath seemed to freeze in my lungs.

"Have a care," Lucifer said in a voice of deceptive calm, an unholy glimmer in the depth of his eyes, "how you speak to your king."

He crooked a finger, and an invisible force pushed me back onto my front. I jerked up my hands to break the fall.

"If you so dearly desire to be hurt," he said, stepping closer, "let us start with this."

Another wave of his hand, and his power pulled me up to kneeling again. Now directly in front of me, he grabbed me by the throat, tilted back my head, and used his other hand to force my mouth open with disturbing calm.

"Maybe ripping out your tongue will teach you not to speak out of turn."

Panic snaked through me. For all my posturing and all my bravado and the determination to accept my punishment, I couldn't help being abso-fucking-lutely terrified at the very real threat of violence that was staring me in the face right now. Every single primal instinct in me rebelled, seized hold of my muscles, my thoughts, my emotions.

I jerked in his grasp and tried to close my mouth, grabbing his wrists as if I could dislodge his hands from me. As if I could actually fight him off.

Fear clouded my mind, my vision, as I struggled powerlessly in his grip, had to watch as he pried my mouth open again and went to reach inside—only to stop short. A shadow whispered over his expression, and he pulled back his hand, waited a beat, and then reached forward again, clearly intending to grasp my tongue to rip it out.

His hand froze before he made contact.

Features tense, he stood there for the span of a few rapid heartbeats, his dark blond brows pulling together, a magnificently puzzled look on his angelic face.

He seemed as utterly confused as I was.

A quiet snarl on his lips, he let go of me, stepped back, and then raised his arm as if to backhand me. I flinched in anticipation...but the strike never came. Peering at him through the corners of my eyes, my head still turned sideways, I saw him standing there, still as a statue, all his muscles bunched in what appeared to be some terrible inner battle he was embroiled in. His arm, yet raised to slap me, trembled ever so slightly, like he was trying his hardest to complete the blow, but some unseen force kept him unmovable.

I hardly dared to breathe. What the hell was going on?

The snarl took over his face, the sound of it rolling through the courtyard. Lowering his arm, he bared his teeth and barked, "Leave!"

Not missing a beat, the demons around him scattered. Some extended their wings and took off into the air, launching far away beyond the high walls of the courtyard. The others ran for the doors like cockroaches skittering out of sight when the lights turned on. Even the unlucky demon who'd been tortured by Lucifer managed to scuttle away on his remaining limbs.

Beside me, Mammon grasped my hand and tugged hard enough to almost make me lose my balance and plant my ass on the floor.

"Not you," Lucifer growled, his eyes on me.

I gulped and freed my hand from Mammon's hold. "Go," I whispered to him.

He hesitated, real fear shining in his wide eyes. "Zoe..."

"Go!" I said with more insistence. "You don't need to tell him where I am. I left him a note."

Mammon's face took on an *Are you fucking kidding?* expression.

I grimaced. Yeah, maybe not the best way to break the news to Azazel that I'd voluntarily handed myself over to Lucifer for punishment, but I didn't want Mammon to be the one to deliver that particular message, or else he'd lose his wings right there on the spot.

I gave Mammon another urgent look, and he finally had the wherewithal to run for the hills like the others.

Leaving me alone with a supremely pissed-off Lucifer.

I swallowed hard as I turned back to him. His face a storm of rage, he curled his lip and lifted his hand, making a fist. A whisper of his power coursed over me, coiled around my throat, but it was a mere shadow of the invisible stranglehold he was capable of. I still vividly remembered what it had felt like when he'd tried to magically crush my windpipe back at the Fall Festival.

Overhead, lightning rent the air, dozens of flashes streaking through the darkness, followed by thunder that rocked the ground. Lucifer's expression was equal parts frustration and bewilderment as he lowered his hand and stepped closer again.

Reaching out slowly, he touched his fingers to my face. I cringed away, but he grabbed my chin and held me in place as he brought his other hand up to poke at my skin.

What the hell, dude?

Fast like a snake, he pulled back one arm and made as if to strike me once more—and again, he halted in midair, like someone had pushed a pause button on him. Gritting his teeth, he lowered his arm slowly and then touched his hand to my forehead.

"What sorcery is this?" he hissed.

"What?" I whispered, completely puzzled.

"You have done something to yourself. Some kind of magic…" He grabbed my throat—gently—and turned my head from side to side, then up until my eyes met his. Leaning down until he was inches from me, he studied me intently, his gaze boring into mine. "Some power that makes me incapable of touching you with the intent to hurt."

I shivered in his hold, a chill stealing through my bones.

His gaze still drilled into me as if he was trying to read my soul through my eyes. An infinitesimal jolt went through him, and he whispered, more to himself than to me, "Could it be—"

He laid his hand on my chest, right between my breasts, but the touch didn't feel sexual at all, just…searching. A pulse of his power shot out from his hand, through me—and connected to a spark that had recently fused with my soul.

With a hiss, he snatched his hand back. "How is this possible?"

I bit back a whimper. "Your Grace?"

"How?" His fingers twitched against my throat, as if he had the urge to choke me. "How do you carry a kernel of her essence inside you?"

My eyes widened. *Lilith's power.* Was that it? The reason

he couldn't bring himself to hurt me—because he sensed a piece of her inside me, and it automatically stopped him from causing me harm?

Holy fuck. If that was true, Lilith had somehow preventively saved my ass.

"Speak!" he snapped.

"S-she gave it to me."

"Gave it to you." He stared at me with a blank face.

I nodded and licked my lips. "Punched a hole in her own chest, pulled out...a piece of her power or soul or whatever, then punched a hole in my chest and put that thing in there, and it was a whole bloody mess, worse than those scenes in the Alien movies, you know, when the little alien babies burst out of people's chests—well, I mean, they're not really babies, that's too cute a description, they're these small monster thingies—"

He closed my mouth with apparently just enough gentleness not to trigger the Do Not Hurt the Bearer of the Spark response and pinched the bridge of his nose.

So I knelt there, keeping my blabber mouth submissively shut while the supreme overlord of Hell processed the fact that he couldn't hurt the impertinent little human like he'd planned.

"Magoth!" he called out.

A sound echoed in the air, and it took me a second to realize it was the flapping of mighty wings, right before the courtyard darkened and a giant beast landed behind Lucifer with far more grace than a monster of its size should be capable of.

My eyes widened, my muscles jerked in primal fear, and I barely kept myself from wetting my pants as I stared at the thing of myths and tales of terror looming just feet from me.

The dragon was as big as a private jet. Covered in thick

black scales, horns protruding from its head and along its spine, it crouched on its hind legs and the middle joint of its massive wings—which didn't grow out of its back, but were actually its front legs, like those of a bat. Yellow-green eyes of high intelligence tracked my every move, while saliva dripped from its maw that displayed a set of teeth that would have humbled a T-rex.

"Magoth," Lucifer said without taking his eyes off me, "be a good girl and—" His sentence ended in a choked sound.

Heart racing, I stared at him.

He looked like he was straining to say something but couldn't get the words out. Taking a deep breath, he closed his eyes, cracked a kink in his neck, then resumed glaring at me.

"Magoth," he began again, "go ahead and—"

Again, he choked on whatever words he'd intended to say next.

"Damn it all to Heaven," he growled, then turned away and kicked a brazier.

The metal container tipped over and spilled the burning coals all over the floor. I winced.

Still turned away, Lucifer stood with his hands on his hips and scowled at the coals like they'd committed a personal offense against him.

"Can't even *order* someone to hurt you," he muttered.

I pressed my lips together to keep a wholly inappropriate grin off my face. Wouldn't be smart to antagonize him even more. Then again...what would he do? Tickle me in retaliation?

He faced me again, a calculating glint in his eyes. "I might not be able to harm you physically, but that is certainly not the only way to punish someone."

A thread of worry wormed its way into the pit of my stomach.

"What do you say," he purred, "we explore whether the magic she gifted you protects you from other forms of penance?"

Uh-oh.

CHAPTER 24

Lucifer took me deep into the bowels of his palace.

With every staircase we descended, an invisible fist closed tighter around my heart. Still, I wasn't quite as intimidated as when I'd initially walked in here. The realization that he couldn't really hurt me had taken off a lot of the pressure and foreboding.

As I followed him down through winding, ever-narrowing corridors and flights of stairs, black walls barely lit by crackling torches here and there, I pondered this new development.

Would I even have to do what he said? How would he possibly enforce any of his orders to me if he couldn't lay a hand on me, nor order one of his lackeys to do so? Maybe I could simply refuse to obey if he commanded me to do something egregiously vile?

Of course, I'd try to comply with his orders as much as possible, seeing as I *wanted* this punishment to be fulfilled so I could return home. But this unexpected turn of events might have just given me the opportunity to evade the worst kind of nonphysical torture.

I really needed to give Lilith a big hug the next time I saw her.

I also wondered whether the protective aspect of the spark inside me was intentional, or maybe just an unplanned side effect of her inherent power. Had she deliberately calibrated her magic like this, to ward off aggression by Lucifer? Or did whatever bond she shared with him simply have this effect; did the fact that he genuinely cared for her make him incapable of harming her, and that automatically extended to the kernel of her essence in me?

Questions upon questions.

From all I'd seen and heard of him, there seemed to be two people he truly loved with unwavering affection— Lilith, and his daughter Naamah—which appeared at odds with the rest of his personality.

Somehow, I'd become connected to both of them, and I had yet to find out whether that was a boon or a bane.

Farther and farther down we went.

One might think that the deeper levels of the palace should be the coolest, as they were the farthest from the oven-like air on the surface, but somehow, the reverse was true. Every time we stepped down a staircase, it seemed the temperature rose by a few degrees. It was like we were drawing closer to the boiling mouth of a volcano.

Sweat dripping down my spine, my temples, I panted and held on to the smooth black stone wall as I paused for a moment. "I think," I gasped, "I just saw two hobbits pass by. How much farther to Mount Doom?"

Lucifer halted and turned around, his look pinning me to the spot. "Are you already delirious? We haven't even started the torture yet."

"How come none of you demons are *Lord of the Rings*

fans?" I muttered under my breath. "Seriously bad look for you guys."

Out loud, I asked, "Where exactly are we going?"

I had a hunch, of course. Descending this far down in his palace...it was either the dungeons or the Pit—where he kept his personal stash of damned souls to torture. The place from which Azazel and Azmodea had stolen my dad's soul at the Fall Festival.

"You should know," Lucifer purred.

A tingle of ice crept down my spine. I checked and rechecked my mental shields. They were all in place, my thoughts safely hidden from him. "Your Grace?"

"I'd have thought you would have recognized the way by now."

I didn't like that glint in his eyes. Not one bit.

I straightened. "I've never seen this part of your palace, Your Grace."

And that wasn't even a lie—while Azazel and Azmodea had executed the rescue mission for my dad's soul, I'd been knocked out, sleeping off the effects of amrit. I'd only come to after they'd successfully retrieved him and were already on their way up again. So, *technically*, I had been down here once before, yes, but I'd never *seen* these corridors.

Words were important. Like most demons, Lucifer could scent a lie.

"Someone," he said with silken danger in his voice, "stole a soul from here at the last Fall Festival."

My nostrils flared and my eyes widened. That was the extent of my outward-facing reaction, because I grabbed hold of my physical response with an iron fist and beat the wild panic wanting to rise in me into submission. I couldn't reveal how fucking scared I was. It would be tantamount to a confession.

"Who would do such a thing?" I whispered, losing the fight against the weighted silence pressing down on me. I babbled when I got nervous. I couldn't help it. "Surely no one would dare anger you in this way."

The light of the torches cast his face in a changing relief of shadows, the only constant the disturbingly bright glow of his turquoise eyes as he glared at me.

"H-how do you even know if a soul is missing? Do you do a roll call in the morning, like they do at school? Like, do they have to recite a pledge?"

A hint of confusion on his face.

"You know, the pledge?" I stammered. Cue my babbling. "'I pledge allegiance to the flames of the United States of Hell, and to the inferno for which they stand, one nation, under Lucifer, indivisible, with torture and suffering for all.'"

I'd even laid a hand over my heart for full effect.

He rolled his eyes heavenward.

I wrung my hands, my heart threatening to beat out of my throat. "Do you guys have an anthem? I mean, it could come in handy as a way to foster team spirit. Like, your demons could all sing it together before they start the tortur—"

My sentence ended in a choked gasp when he grabbed my throat—just enough to make me shut up, but not enough to hurt or trigger the Lilith Protection Charm.

Leaning in close, his power pressing against my skin, he asked in a harsh whisper, "Did you think I did not know?"

I made an embarrassing whimpering sound.

"Not a single soul has ever gone missing from my Pit," he continued. "Until the last Fall Festival. Incidentally, the first one in ages that my dear grandson deigns to attend. With his new wife, disguised as his pet. Whom, as it turns out, he loves. Truly. What a coincidence, then, that the soul that went missing is that of his beloved wife's late father."

If my eyes widened any more, they might just pop out of my head.

Shitfuckingshitfuckdammit.

He knew.

My heart pounded so hard, so loud, it drowned out all rational thought. Pure, unfettered fear pulsed through my veins.

He *knew*.

Something writhed underneath his face, as if some giant beast was pulling at the leash that kept it chained inside him, rearing to burst out. Here and there, his skin seemed to split, revealing a glimpse of fire-touched lightning beneath.

"Do you take me for a fool?" he whispered, almost gently.

"No," I choked out.

He studied me silently for a long, aching moment, still holding me by my throat. "Remember that when you think to defy me." Letting me go, he stepped back and resumed walking down the corridor, his hands in his pockets, as if out for a leisurely stroll. "And yes," he threw back over his shoulder, "I know exactly where you keep him."

I deflated with an exhale that hurt all the way out. Pulse still painfully fast, I slid down the wall and collapsed in a heap on the floor, all my earlier bravado and false sense of security gone in an instant.

He knew.

Why hadn't he come for us? For my dad? Why had he let this slide until now?

Of course, it now gave him the perfect leverage over me to make sure I did not step even one toe out of line. Had I contemplated just minutes ago that I could simply refuse to obey certain commands of his if I didn't feel like it? Yeah, scratch that.

I'd lick the floor if he told me to.

With the fate of my father's soul on the line, I'd do whatever Lucifer asked of me. I still vividly remembered what it had felt like to know my dad was being tortured down here, with me unable to help him. I'd endure whatever Lucifer had in store for me to make sure that didn't happen again.

I'd been desperate to get my dad's soul out of Hell even when I hadn't yet reconciled with him. It would be even more important to keep him out of here now that I'd made up with him and had been talking to him regularly for a year. We weren't as close as we'd been before his betrayal had torn our family apart, but I deeply loved him, despite everything, and he'd become a vital part of my life again.

I wouldn't risk losing that.

"Keep up!" barked Lucifer from somewhere up ahead.

I flinched and jumped to my feet. "Yes, Your Grace," I panted as I jogged after him.

I'D IMAGINED THE PIT AS, WELL, AN ACTUAL *PIT*. LIKE A HUGE ditch or trench or something along those lines, where the sinners writhed in one giant tangle of limbs while demons poked them with pitchforks from the ledges.

Yeah, I know. Super cliché. But hey, considering that the rest of Hell pretty much resembled many of the most stereotypical descriptions of the underworld found throughout Christianity, it wasn't an unreasonable assumption.

The reality was a bit less gruesome, for which I was quite thankful.

No canyon-sized ditch with masses of damned souls crammed inside. Instead, each soul had their individual room, accessible from a maze of hallways. The soul could be restrained in some form or free to move, but they were clearly bound to the room, and the space itself appeared to operate in a sort of illusion-powered virtual reality.

The demon in charge of the torture could make the room seem endless, change it to resemble any other space, drawing on the soul's memories to craft the illusion in a meaningful way in order to torture the ever-loving fuck out of the soul.

Because physical torture was only one aspect of the punishment in Hell.

As I'd learned when we'd rescued my dad's soul, often-times emotional and psychological torture were even more effective, especially when the soul already felt guilt over what they'd done in life. Making someone live through their worst mistakes, repeating the situation over and over, each time making them think they might be able to change the course of what happened or maybe make amends to those they'd harmed, only to have them fail, again and again, helplessly reliving their shame…it was a very potent kind of pain.

The demon in charge would delve deep into the soul's memories, into the mind of the sinner, analyze the person's individual vulnerabilities, the things they'd done in life to incur their damnation, and then come up with the best way to squeeze the most pain—whether physical or emotional—from the soul.

Some of this I'd learned from Azazel, some now from

Lucifer as he led me through the maze of hallways before stopping at a dark metal door.

"Your assignment today," he said, leaning with one shoulder against the black stone wall next to the closed door, "will be to watch a session of torture."

I flinched. There was a reason I'd never enjoyed horror flicks such as the *Saw* movies. It wasn't that the sight of blood made me queasy—as a woman, I'd had my fair share of bloody incidents. I'd been using a menstrual cup for years, and sometimes it would slip when I took it out, and the bathroom subsequently looked like someone had been butchered there.

So, no, blood I could deal with.

It was the severed limbs I couldn't handle. The sheer brutality of the butchering in horror movies. Almost worse than that, though, was the psychological aspect of those films where a group of people were systematically broken down, mentally and emotionally stripped of every last bit of civilized humanity, until they turned on each other and became little more than cornered animals who'd gnaw off their own limbs—or someone else's—to get out alive.

I couldn't stand to see someone get hurt. It hurt me, too, on a visceral level.

"Okay," I squeaked, because what else was there to say? If this was Lucifer's choice of how to punish me without laying a hand on me, then I'd just suck it up and endure.

Lucifer studied me for a moment. "The soul in here"—he jerked his head at the door—"is that of a young mother."

I swallowed hard, my stomach turning over.

"Ah, no," he said and tsked. "No compassion necessary for this one, I assure you. Not even your bleeding human heart could find a shred of sympathy for this wretched excuse for a soul."

I doubted that.

"This woman had a little daughter. Only got to be three years old, because dear Mom here let the girl starve."

What?

His gaze seemed to be lit by some inner flame. "Locked her in her room, in her crib, and starved her over the course of several weeks. Brought her a banana every now and then as her only food. This *mother* sat in front of her computer for hours every day, playing games online with her friends, while her little daughter lay in the next room, in the dark— because Mom had also closed the shutters, you know, making it all pitch-black to better discourage the girl from crying—too weak to climb out of the crib, so hungry she tried to eat her own diaper."

My eyes burned and my vision clouded over. My God. That callous cruelty...

"Dear old Dad was a truck driver and wasn't home much during the week," Lucifer continued. "When he came home on the weekends, he was too afraid of his dominant wife to push back and help the girl. So he just retreated to his own room and played games as well, ignoring the starvation of his daughter." A cold, cold smile graced his face. "It's not his time yet, but I've got a room for him down here as well once his mortal life is over."

My breath hitched.

"The mom"—he patted the door—"came to me right quick. Not long after her daughter was found alive but not much more than skin and bones, the mother was admitted with aggressive cancer that killed her only shortly after her daughter breathed her last. She'd been sick for some time but had ignored it." He tilted his head in an eerily animal- istic manner. "She never stood trial for her crimes before a human court." He flashed a smile that showed some fang. "But she's here now, and she will stay a long, long while."

I shuddered. "Good," I rasped.

He raised a brow, a hint of his feral smile still lingering. With a glance at the door, he said, "Cases like hers are my favorite. Humans such as this woman do not feel empathy. They lack the emotional understanding for what they have done. Lock them away and let them stew for a hundred years, and still they will not grasp the gravity of their sins. You can torture them physically, make them live through what they did to their victims, but they won't *understand*. Not truly." He shook his head. "What we do, with someone like this, is flip the switch for them."

I blinked at him.

There was that feral smile again. "We give them a *conscience*. We make them feel. Their lack of empathy allowed them to walk through life with comfortable aloofness. They were a step removed from the emotional reality of their cruelty. When we drag them to that place where they feel *everything*, every last drop of pain and suffering they caused, it's the emotional equivalent of being hit by lightning. Of all the damned souls"—he leaned forward, his gaze intense—"their screams are the loudest. *No one* suffers more than they do."

He straightened and threw open the door. "So, in you go. Enjoy the show."

I stared at the black entrance to the room. It was like a mouth of darkness waiting to swallow me.

"Someone will be by to pick you up later," Lucifer said and unceremoniously pushed me into the torture chamber.

The door fell shut behind me with a clang that reverberated in my bones. I jolted and suppressed a whimper.

The darkness was stygian, all-encompassing, with a

weighted presence of doom. After a few seconds, though, my eyes adjusted, and gradually, shapes rose out of the gloom, forming the shadowy outlines of furniture. Up ahead, a sliver in the form of a rectangle cast the tiniest amount of light in the room, and I realized it was a window —blocked out by heavy shutters.

My breath was the only sound in the room as I turned, ever so slowly, and looked around. Behind me, another small sliver of light close to the floor indicated where the door was. When I turned back, I saw it.

The crib.

My heart stuttered. I wanted to close my eyes, avert my gaze, but I couldn't. I stared, my pulse racing, at the shape inside the crib that I could just make out.

No. I don't want to see this. No, please.

Frantically, I tried to turn around, back to the door, out of here, anywhere else—only to run into a large body.

I screamed.

The telltale energy of a demon brushed up against my senses seconds before whomever I had run into grabbed me by the shoulders and turned me back around.

"Watch," the demon said. "We're about to start."

He forced my gaze back to the crib, and I realized with a start that it was actually several times too large for a regular baby bed. And that the shape inside it…was that of an adult, a woman.

In the dark of the room, I could just about see her gaunt face, the signs of starvation hollowing her cheeks, stretching her skin. She lay as if sleeping—until she opened her eyes.

"This is when," the demon said from behind me, still holding me by the shoulders, "we flip the switch."

A pulse of his power vibrated through the room, and the woman flinched as if struck by an electric current. For a moment, she was still, her breath coming faster and faster, her bony chest rising and falling in rapid movements as her eyes scanned the room.

Then she screamed.

And screamed.

And screamed.

The sound tore through me, slicing into me like a scalpel, over and over, until I wanted to sink to my knees and curl into a ball.

But the demon held me upright, making me bear witness.

The woman writhed on the bed, sobbing, wailing, crying out a name that I assumed was her daughter's, as the full weight of what she'd done crashed upon her like the unstoppable wave of a tsunami.

Inside me, the rising nausea that wanted to spill from my stomach battled it out against a grim sense of satisfaction at seeing the woman's well-deserved agony. Something fierce and righteous bared its teeth in the depths of my being.

Still, the nausea won out.

With a giant heave, I lurched out of the demon's grip and puked the meager contents of my stomach out onto the floor.

The woman kept screeching.

I kept puking.

Even after my stomach was entirely empty, I couldn't stop retching. The taste of suffering in the room was too visceral. Like some corrosive poison absorbed through the air, the woman's pain seeped into my pores, deep inside, tainting everything it met until I wanted to turn myself inside out and scrape it all off with a sharp blade.

Kneeling on the floor, I trembled all over, my throat aching, hot tears wetting my cheeks.

"Please," the woman sobbed. "Please, make it stop! Make it stop, make it stop, make it…"

I almost joined her in her chant.

The demon, however, stood steadfastly behind me, his dark presence the unyielding specter of an unlikely instrument of postmortem justice. He watched, unaffected, as the woman kept pleading for mercy she'd never shown her daughter in life.

I had no idea how long a "session" of torture usually lasted in Hell, but it felt like hours to me. Days? Time eluded me as I sat there on the floor, rocking back and forth on my heels with my eyes closed and my hands clapped over my ears, which did little to block out the auditory signals of someone dying a thousand deaths of agony.

I only knew that by the time large hands hauled me up and dragged me outside the room, I was raw and numb at once. Inside me, a storm of violent emotions brewed, while on the outside, I shuffled through the corridors barely aware of my surroundings. If the demon escorting me hadn't kept dragging me along, I'd have just sunk to the ground somewhere and not moved again.

At some point, my demon escort pushed me through a door and into a room that I'd have found cozy under any other circumstances. A huge fireplace spilled light onto a carpeted floor, and small lamps between tall bookcases lit the rest of the room with a warm ambience. Massive armchairs were grouped throughout the space, looking for all the world like they'd give me the equivalent of a sedentary hug if I sat in them.

"Your Grace," my demon escort said from his position next to me. "The human, as you requested."

"*Lady Zoe*," Lucifer corrected him without glancing up from where he lounged on one of those damn comfy-looking armchairs, cleaning a blade. "She outranks you, Parachmon."

"Forgive me, Your Grace." The demon bowed low, then murmured to me, "Apologies, my lady."

I just stared at him. My lack of a reaction wasn't because I was mad at him. I just couldn't muster up the energy to do anything else but stare.

"How did you like the session?" Lucifer asked.

I swung my gaze back to the Devil. "It was riveting," I said, my voice hollow.

He wiped the gleaming blade with a small cloth and smiled.

"Your Grace," I said tonelessly. "May I go home now?"

"Home?" His eyes the color of Caribbean seas flicked up to meet my own. "Do you think we're done?"

A flicker of panic flared inside me. "We're not?"

He laughed softly before he addressed my demon escort. "Take her to her room."

My room? As in, I'd *stay* here? Of course, I'd known it was possible that he'd keep me for longer, but to actually face that reality made me break out in a cold sweat.

"Wait," I rasped as the demon grasped my elbow. "Your Grace, h-how long will I be here?"

"For however long it takes."

"Takes to what?"

He leaned back in the armchair, his eyes glowing coldly. A chill spread in the room, banking the flames of the fire. "For fury not to overtake me anymore whenever I look upon your face."

When the demon dragged me from the room, my breath frosted in the air.

CHAPTER 25

The room I was taken to was simple, a far cry from the luxury and splendor of the other spaces I'd seen, but I was honestly surprised I wasn't thrown into a dungeon cell. Instead, I was given accommodations that were better than some of the motels I'd stayed in on Earth. The sparsely furnished room—a no-nonsense bed and an armoire—even had a bathroom. With a shower.

I trembled when I saw it. Yeah, I'd definitely use that one right away, even if I doubted that it would help me get rid of this horrible feeling clinging to me like some sticky residue.

When I came out of the shower after what felt like hours, towel wrapped around me, I discovered a tray of food on the bed along with a set of fresh clothes. I dressed but ignored the food, opting instead to set it aside.

No way could I stomach anything of sustenance after what I'd witnessed.

I slipped into the bed and hunkered down beneath the cover, with only the top half of my face peeking out. The lamps on the walls dimmed to a glimmer.

Despite the ever-present heat of Hell, I shivered.

When I closed my eyes, all I saw was the woman in the crib. Her screams echoed in my mind. The memory of her pleading, of her pain, ebbed and flowed, drowning me again and again. And underneath all that, the horrible, gut-wrenching, heartbreaking suffering of her daughter made my chest burn and my limbs shake with rage and despair.

I buried myself beneath the covers, missing Azazel with a fierceness that bordered on pain. I longed for his warmth, the safety of his arms, for the way he'd kiss my forehead and pull me close when I had a bad dream or a bout of anxiety. The way he'd listen to me tell him what bothered me, and how his calm presence and poignant, empathetic comments would soothe my sorrows. I wanted, *needed*, to share this excruciating experience here with him like I'd shared every-thing else the past year, and yet I couldn't, by my own choosing. Because I'd gone and done this against his implicit wishes, and now I was separated from him for who knew how long, and I had to carry this all on my own.

I was so lost in pain and fury and heartache that I almost didn't hear the flapping of wings.

But I most certainly heard the smacking sounds that came next.

Heart drumming against my rib cage, I sat upright in the bed and scanned the darkened room.

There, hunched over the tray I'd put close to the door, was a shadowy shape. A shape that moved in a distinctly *feline* way as it apparently ate my rejected food.

A hellcat. I squinted into the gloom, a frisson of fear stealing into my blood. Mephisto was friendly because he was compelled not to harm those who lived in Azazel's house, but I couldn't say that the same applied to any other hellcat outside of my darling demon's mansion.

Was this one going to ignore me, or would it try to extend

its dinner by snacking on me next?

Should I talk to it? Or would that only unnecessarily draw its attention to me?

I opted for silently sinking down beneath the cover and pretending I didn't exist.

When the bed shook with the impact of a large feline jumping on it, I let out a shriek. A paw slapped me over the head.

Quit that, a familiar voice spoke into my mind.

I uttered another shriek, this time of relief. "Mephisto?"

When I poked my head out from under the cover, I got another paw to the face, claws retracted.

I said, quit that. Your screaming hurts my ears.

"Mephisto!" I cried, then threw the cover off and hugged him.

My relief was so acute it made my breath choppy. Heart overflowing with the sheer happiness of having a familiar, friendly being here with me, I dove forward and squeezed the hellcat to me. He was large enough that it felt like hugging a human, in a way.

Unhand me at once, Mephisto said, but his voice was lacking any kind of snarl or bite. *This is unseemly.*

"I'm just so happy to see you!" I did not let him go.

But you can't really see me. He pushed against me with a paw. *It's dark and your human eyes are ridiculously weak.*

"God, I never thought I'd be ecstatic to hear your blunt remarks and lack of understanding of human sayings." I finally let him go. "But—how did you find me?"

I'm a cat.

I rolled my eyes. "Come on, you can't use that as an explanation for everything. Seriously, how do you keep showing up in the most unlikely places just when I need you?"

I could barely make out how he blinked at me in the dark. *Pure coincidence.*

"Uh-huh. Sure. I don't buy it."

I'm not selling anything.

Ugh.

You seem upset. The low glimmer of the lamps reflected in his luminous eyes. *Are you in need of a fresh kill? Shall I hunt for you?*

"No!" I gentled my voice. "No, thank you. I'm not hungry."

You did not touch your human food.

Was he actually concerned for me? My little heart melted. "I'm fine. Don't worry. My stomach is just a bit woozy right now." I paused and sat back against the headboard, biting my lip. Anxiety fizzed through me. "Does...does Azazel know I'm here?"

Yes.

Aaaaaand my stress level just went through the roof. "How—how is he?"

In a rage.

Oh, God. I buried my face in my hands. "He's not coming after me, is he?"

In the note I'd left him, I'd asked him not to, but there was no telling if he'd listen to me. I wouldn't put it past him to try to get me out, be it through official channels or by subterfuge. Which would undoubtedly make everything worse.

"Can you please tell him not to come? When you go back?"

I am not a messenger bat.

"I know. I'm sorry. It's just—wait, there are messenger bats down here?"

Not anymore.

"What? What happened?"

They were found to be an unreliable means of communication.

"Unreliable? Like, they couldn't be bothered to actually deliver the message and just did what they liked?"

No. They kept getting eaten on the way to their destination.

I rubbed my face with both hands.

"Okay," I said after a moment, "just, when you go back, and, if you're so inclined, could you please remind him what's at stake and that coming after me in any way, shape, or form will only complicate things further? Please?"

All right. He blinked at me. *I shall tell him to cease any moronic notions of riding to your rescue because it might well result in your death or his own, unless he intends to prove why his genetic material deserves to be removed from the evolutionary chain.*

"Mephisto!" I gaped at him. "You did not just say that."

Is your hearing impaired? He leaned in and sniffed at my ears, his whiskers tickling me. *You will not survive long if that is the case. How will you hunt? Evade your enemies?*

I squealed at the tickling sensation of his whiskers, then slid down on the bed until I lay curled in a ball, the cover pulled up to my neck. "I need to find some sleep," I whispered.

Who knew what else Lucifer had in store for me tomorrow? More torture sessions? Some other way of hurting me?

"Will you stay?" I asked my surly hellcat.

The prospect of going to sleep here alone was freaking me out.

Mephisto walked over me, his paws pressing down on my side, and I grunted. I thought he was leaving, but then I felt the touch of his paws on my back—followed by the fine prick of his claws.

"Ow." I half turned my head to look over my shoulder,

not that it did me any good in the semidarkness. "Are you kneading my back?"

He purred.

Prick, prick went his claws on my back, sharp enough to puncture through the cover and my clothes. I cringed but didn't have the heart to tell him to knock it off. Universal cat law: thou shalt not interrupt a cat when it kneads you, no matter how much it smarts.

Prick, prick, purr. Prick, prick, purr.

Ouch. I'd had cats turn my thighs into needle cushions before, but this was a whole other level. I just hoped he didn't draw blood.

After a few moments, something happened. The initial pain subsided, replaced by a slowly growing sense of relaxation. I'd experienced that before—when I'd tried a yoga session that ended in lying on an acupressure mat.

Inspired by the ancient practice of some yogis to recline on a bed of nails, an acupressure mat featured dozens of small spikes—mostly plastic with modern mats—that were sharp enough to harmlessly poke the skin and muscles of the person lying down on it. It was supposed to stimulate blood flow and relax the muscles, thereby reducing anxiety, improving sleep, and increasing energy.

Having a hellcat knead my back wasn't that different. Within minutes, I floated in a sea of peaceful relaxation, my worries pleasantly far beneath the surface.

"Thank you," I murmured into the dark.

You're welcome, Mephisto replied, and his purr followed me into sleep.

THE LAST THING I EVER WANTED TO SEE WHEN I OPENED MY EYES in the morning was the Devil staring down at me... Yet that was exactly what happened.

I woke with a start and a shriek because *someone* splashed cold water on me. *Cold* water! This was Hell! There was not supposed to be anything cold down here!

I bolted upright in bed, only to stare right into Lucifer's cheerful face.

"Good morning," he drawled. "Time to get to work."

I wiped the water from my face. "Work?"

"Fill this up." He held out the bucket with which he'd just splashed me. "You're going to clean."

With a note of wariness, I accepted the bucket and refilled it with water from my bathroom. "What, exactly, am I supposed to clean, Your Grace?"

He summoned a bottle with some liquid and squirted it into the water, then handed me a cloth. "Just the floor, dear."

That didn't sound too bad. My gaze fell on the floor of my room.

"Not here," he said with a smirk.

A tight knot formed in my stomach, which chose that moment to growl. I'd puked up everything I'd had to eat yesterday, and I hadn't touched the food brought to my room before I'd gone to sleep.

"Hungry?" Lucifer asked.

Why did everything with him feel like a trick question? If I said no, I'd be gone for who knew how long, cleaning floors on an empty stomach. But if I said yes, there was a chance he'd shrug and send me to work hungry anyway. Or maybe he'd give me some moldy scraps to eat.

He studied me with mirth lighting his eyes. "So much thinking for such a simple question," he said with a soft chuckle. "I can just see the gears turning." He wiggled a finger in front of my forehead. "Let me help you before you hurt yourself."

And with a flick of his hand, he summoned a tray with food onto the bed. I half expected it to be something disgusting, but the aroma of French toast, scrambled eggs, and syrup-soaked pancakes rose in the air and proved my worries wrong. My legs almost buckled at the delicious scents. God, I was *so* hungry.

"Eat," he said and leaned against the wall, arms crossed.

"Now?" With him just standing there, watching me?

He tilted his head. "Unless you'd like to go without food?"

"Why even give me any?" I muttered as I sat down on the bed and dug in. "Shouldn't you want me weak?"

He clucked his tongue. "Starvation makes humans delirious. Why would I put you in a state where you cannot even appreciate the intricacies of your punishments anymore?"

So he wanted me lucid enough to truly suffer. Lovely.

"Then I guess you won't make me drink amrit again?" I asked around a mouthful of pancake.

His smirk was unholy. "That option is not off the table yet."

The pancake turned to ash on my tongue. Oh, no. I all too vividly remembered the humiliation I'd suffered in front of his court after Lucifer had forced me to drink amrit. And more to the point—the humiliation *Azazel* had suffered when my drunk babbling revealed that he'd been trapped in a marriage contract by a human teenager.

There was no telling what else I might do or say under the influence of amrit. If Lucifer truly wanted to break me, all he needed to do was make me chug that stuff and let me run my mouth.

A shiver stole through me.

"Ever so delightful," Lucifer murmured, his face alight with vicious joy, "when the threat of something already does half the work."

My fingers tightened around the knife I was holding.

His attention zeroed in on that small movement. "By all means, do try."

And lose my life in the process? Or maybe end up chained and snacked on by hellrats?

I took a deep breath to calm the raging sea of fury inside me and then used the knife to cut off a piece of pancake.

"It might be hard to infer from my actions and words," I said, "but I am not stupid."

"Says the girl who willingly walked into the lion's den to be punished instead of sitting this one out."

I sent him a sharp look. "Why did you wait? Why not come for me right away?"

Even when I'd marched up to him, he'd been curiously reluctant to punish me until I'd pushed him over the brink.

An easy shrug of his shoulder. "Maybe I wanted to let that wonderful anxiety of yours simmer a bit longer."

He'd said as much the other day, but for some reason I couldn't explain, that didn't ring entirely true. He'd been surrounded by his courtiers—or whatever they were—and down here in Hell, even the most powerful being had to play by certain rules or expectations. Lucifer's words and actions in front of an audience would always be calculated to an extent, more so than if he were alone.

I thought of Azazel's theory that Lucifer might have a pressing reason to uphold the status quo. Someone as aware of underlying motives as he was might see the intricate web of leverage and subtle reasoning behind each of our actions and decide that pulling on one thread—punishing me—could well upset the entire balance.

"Why didn't you tell them?" I asked quietly.

Why keep it a secret that Naamah was still alive? If his aim was to hurt Azazel, wouldn't it make more sense to let him know his mother wasn't dead, but forbid him from seeing her? Wouldn't that hurt a whole fucking lot more?

Telling Azazel and Azmodea that their mother had died had actually given them a sort of closure. Knowing a loved one was gone gave someone the chance to move on, no matter how vicious grief could be. At least one didn't cling to the desperate hope of seeing them again.

How much crueler would it have been to dangle the fact that their mother was still alive but nevertheless forever out of their reach in front of them, for thousands of years? Maybe even use it as leverage—as in, "Behave, and you'll get to visit her."

"It doesn't seem like you," I whispered.

A silver sheen rolled over his eyes, and a visual echo of mighty wings flickered behind his back. For a split second, I saw him as he must have been before he'd fallen from Heaven—startlingly white-silver wings, gleaming armor, his power brimming with the force of the first elements of all that existed, divine light limning his form. The Morningstar, in all his glory.

"Let's go," he said, his voice seeming detached, rolling with thunder. "Time to put you to work."

I left my half-eaten breakfast, grabbed the cloth, bucket, and detergent, and hurried after him as he strode out into the hallway. It took all of my concentration not to spill any of the water inside the bucket, and so it didn't dawn on me where we were going until we stepped out into the giant hall.

I stopped dead in my tracks, my gaze glued to the floor

under my feet—the glass floor of the Hall of Horrors, under which scores of demons lay chained and suffering.

Oh, no.

Lucifer faced me and waved at the hall with one hand. "This is where you'll clean the floor today."

My hands trembled so hard that the water sloshed in the bucket. "All of it?"

"Why, yes. I expect it to be spick-and-span."

I glanced at the demons walking through the hall, some of the many visitors of the palace. They looked on with unveiled curiosity as Lucifer, King of Hell, First of the Fallen, stood with a lowly human and personally instructed her what to do.

"Will the hall be closed while I clean the floor?"

Lucifer smirked. "No."

So there'd be demons walking in and out, tracking fresh dirt over the areas that I'd just cleaned...making sure I'd never get finished with this task.

"Come find me," Lucifer said, leaning down to me, "when you're done."

So...never.

He patted me on the shoulder and strolled away.

Closing my eyes on a sigh, I set the bucket down and collected myself. I could do this. I'd just keep my gaze unfocused and not look too closely at what lay underneath that floor. Easy-peasy.

And he couldn't truly leave me here until the floor was clean. That was hyperbole, right?

Wrong.

I scrubbed that floor for hours upon hours, with no end in sight. I only stopped every once in a while to drag the bucket over to a fountain near the entrance to refill the water and pour in more detergent, not even taking potty breaks. I didn't know if there was a toilet anywhere nearby, anyway. I was only glad I hadn't had any coffee, or else this whole thing could have been so much worse.

At first, ignoring the demons writhing just inches from me, only separated from my mopping hands by glass, worked rather well. I kept my gaze in that state of half focus necessary to see one of those hidden images in the Magic Eye books, and it allowed me to avoid taking in any details of the horrific scene underneath me. Who knew nearly wrecking my eyesight squinting at those books when I'd been a child would come in handy someday?

Still, I knew the demons were there, of course.

And as the hours dragged on, as my physical and mental strength waned, it became harder and harder not to *see* them.

Some were still fully clothed, looking rather fresh. Probably recent additions to this horror show. Others lay there in tatters, their clothing torn and ripped, chewed through by the rats to better get to the meat.

The eyes were a favorite of the rodents.

The first time I vomited while I cleaned that floor was when I couldn't keep my gaze from straying to the sight of a rat plucking the eyes out of a demon's face. He screamed through the entire process, throwing his head from side to side in an effort to dislodge the rat, unable to use his hands due to the restraints, but the beast had sunk its claws into his skin and rode him like some grotesque caricature of rodeo.

All while chewing off his eyes.

The breakfast from this morning splattered onto the floor

before me, effectively obscuring the view of the eye feast.

Tears streamed down my face, my throat burned, and my stomach wanted to heave some more as I cowered there on all fours. Derisive laughter echoed in the hall, the demons passing me snickering and making snide comments.

With a sob, I wiped my cheeks with the backs of my hands, took a rattling breath, and then went on to clean the mess I'd just made.

The next time I puked was when I had to witness a group of rats tearing into one and the same demon. One of the rats was eating its way through the demon's guts, as in the rat was *inside* the belly, and the way the abdomen's skin rose and fell with the movements of the rodent sent the rest of my breakfast careening out of my mouth.

As I blinked through tears at the new mess on the freshly cleaned stretch of floor, I realized why Lucifer had insisted that I ate this morning.

He knew. He knew that having to watch the demons on the subfloor would make me nauseous, so he'd made sure I had something in my stomach to puke out.

He truly didn't need to lay a hand on me to torture me.

On and on it went. I scrubbed the floor, demons walked over it—some taking extra care to specifically stomp their boots where I'd just cleaned—I rescrubbed those areas, my gaze unwillingly strayed to the live-action butchering going on in the subfloor, my stomach rebelled yet again, I vomited and sobbed, rinse and repeat.

In the end, I only dry-heaved, nothing left in my stomach to really make a mess. The only thing I stained the floor with then was snot and tears.

My arms burned, my muscles so weak I could barely move the cloth over the floor anymore. I didn't even have any strength left to wring it out. I'd gone hours—days? I couldn't tell—without anything to eat or drink. Not that I'd be able to keep anything down, but the exhaustion, dehydration, and starvation were getting to me.

When I moved, I swayed. The room seemed unstable. I couldn't think straight anymore.

I knew I was definitely hallucinating when I heard a friendly voice ask, "Zoe?"

I tried to look up, but it only made me lose my balance, and I toppled over myself and planted my nose on the glass floor. Directly underneath me was the half-eaten face of a demon. She screamed. I sobbed.

"Zoe?" asked the voice again, the one I'd surely made up in the desperate attempt to interrupt my torment.

A strong hand grasped my arm and pulled me upright, and then fingers under my chin lifted my head…to meet the gaze of Lilith.

Her warm brown eyes studied me, her elegant brows drawing together. "What are you doing here?"

"I'm hallucinating you," I rasped, my throat raw from all the puking and sobbing.

She examined me more closely and then took in the bucket, the cloth, the way I crouched on the floor. Her expression darkened, and it was like a storm front casting its shadow over a spring valley. "What is the meaning of this?"

"P-punishment," I whispered.

A second longer she looked at me with something like anger brewing in the depths of her honeyed eyes, then her features smoothed out and she raised her chin as if in understanding. "The vow."

I nodded.

"He called you in?"

"I came on my own."

Her brow furrowed again. "Why?"

Maybe it was the exhaustion, but I told her the truth. "Azazel wouldn't see his mother because he didn't want to give Lucifer any incentive to punish me. But if I face the consequences of breaking the vow and endure my punishment, then Azazel won't have a reason anymore not to visit his mother."

She sighed and rubbed her forehead, the most human gesture I'd ever seen her make. "Come," she said and rose to her feet.

Still on my knees, I peered up at her, not at all sure if I could actually stand up. And remain standing.

Lilith frowned down at me. "How long have you been here?"

I swallowed past my parched throat. "It's hard to tell time. Hours? Days?"

With a wave of her hand, she summoned a bottle of water and handed it to me. Remembering to pace myself, I took small sips until my mouth didn't feel like the desert anymore and some of the haze in my mind cleared.

Lilith eyed me, something dark simmering underneath her outwardly calm exterior. "Can you walk?"

"I'm not sure," I answered truthfully.

She made a gesture over her shoulder, and the next second, a female demon stepped up.

"Carry her," Lilith said.

The demon bent, grabbed me around the waist, and hefted me over her shoulder like a sack of rice.

"*Respectfully*," Lilith added with a hiss.

"Apologies, Your Grace."

The demon maneuvered me until she carried me with one arm under my knees and the other around my upper back. I hung there limply and grimaced at the utter indignity of it all, but I'd very likely crumple in a heap if set on my feet right now. It was either be carried out or stay here to scrub the floor some more.

Lilith turned on her heel and marched in front of us, her golden dress glittering in the lights of lamps and chandeliers as we passed through corridors and halls. She was as resplendent as ever, her black locks cascading down her back in a shining waterfall of onyx silk. Damn, I really wanted to know her hair routine. Did she use oil? I had to ask her.

Beside the demon carrying me—her blond hair complementing her fair skin—there were two others who apparently made up Lilith's retinue for the day. A male with a bronze tan, dark, curly hair, and assessing eyes, and a female with light skin and ginger hair, who kept sneaking curious glances at me.

Lilith approached a set of double doors and threw them open, striding inside with all the brewing tension of an impending storm.

"Leave," she barked.

I peered around her back and saw a group of three demons seated on armchairs around Lucifer, apparently interrupted in some weighty-looking conversation. At Lilith's command, they shot to their feet without hesitation, bowed low, and hastened out with murmured greetings.

Lucifer rose from his seat, genuine warmth lighting his eyes as he beheld Lilith. "My heart and soul," he said, clearly not the least bit bothered by how she'd just chased off those demons with no regard for whether they'd been talking about something important with him.

"I found your *guest*," Lilith said without preamble and waved at me. "When were you going to tell me that you're torturing someone who holds my favor?"

Lucifer's eyes flicked to me, the warmth in them frosting over. "Enough favor to bestow a piece of yourself unto her."

His gaze slid back to Lilith. "When were you going to tell me about *that*?"

I felt like a proverbial ping-pong ball between them both. Even though I'd lived through a divorce of my parents, I'd never experienced someone using me as an excuse to fight. This was a novel feeling.

"She needed power," Lilith said. "I gave her a head start."

"And made it so I can't hurt her."

Lilith tilted her head and frowned. "That is no magic of mine."

Lucifer studied her for a moment, then he sighed and shrugged. When he spoke again, his voice had gentled. "It's because I won't hurt you. Not even the smallest spark of your essence, entrenched in someone else. My soul rebels against the very thought."

I blinked at Lucifer in shock. He could be like this?

Lilith exhaled roughly. "Her punishment ends now."

His eyes glinted hard. "I wasn't finished."

"She is." She waved at me again as if to underscore her point by indicating my sorry state of being.

"Breaking a vow requires penance." Lucifer crossed his arms. "Her debt is yet unpaid."

Lilith huffed. "Breaking *that* vow was inevitable, and you know it. She did not fail so much as she ran afoul of an impossible ask. She's suffered enough."

"Because of her," Lucifer said with a growl rumbling in his voice, "a secret kept for millennia has been revealed."

"A secret that was never yours to keep."

I pursed my lips, and I could swear I heard one of the demons from Lilith's retinue inhale sharply. If we were in a Jerry Springer episode, the audience would be howling by now.

"It was time," Lilith said more gently and stepped up to Lucifer. "I know you meant well, but it was never right to keep her from them."

Meant well? Lucifer? Was she talking about a different person than the one I knew?

"As for Zoe"—Lilith laid her hand on his face, and his features softened, his attention rapt on her—"I am claiming her. If the vow she broke requires more penance, she will make amends with me."

He held her gaze for the span of several heartbeats, then he said, "As you wish."

A small smile on her lips, she laid her forehead against his and murmured, "My love."

When she drew back, Lucifer grasped her hand. "Nessar's teeth need cleaning. You should make her do it. Her hands are small enough."

"No." Lilith clucked her tongue. "I will not make her brush your dragon's teeth."

"She heals fast. Her fingers will regrow."

Excuse me, *what*?

"Shush, Lu." Lilith squeezed his hand, then let go. "I will find her something to do that will not harm her."

"Pity," Lucifer murmured, his cold gaze on me.

I narrowed my eyes at him.

Lilith turned to me. "Come. I will take care of you."

She walked out into the hallway, her retinue following her, the demon carrying me included. Before the door closed, I glanced back over the demon's shoulder. Lucifer stood watching us leave, and the entirely contrary part of me that wasn't the least bit concerned about self-preservation made me lift my hand and give him a cutesy little finger wave as I winked at him.

CHAPTER 26

A delicious meal, a hot shower, and a full night's sleep in a luxurious bed later, I woke rested and recovered in the room Lilith had assigned to me. In stark contrast to the chamber Lucifer had put me in, this one was finely appointed, the walls hewn from glittering light-gray marble, hung with decorative tapestries, the floor covered in comfy rugs. The room was large enough to feature a bed of impressive size and a sitting area.

I dug into the breakfast that some merihem had delivered, knowing I wouldn't have cause again to puke it all out later. Lilith had made it clear she wouldn't have me do anything that would come close to what Lucifer had put me through.

Thank fuck and all my lucky stars.

I'd somehow managed to procure protection from the only person who could slap Lucifer's fingers and make him say thank you for it.

I was just finishing off the plate when a knock sounded at the door.

"Come in," I called out.

Lilith smiled at me as she walked in. "I take it you're well rested?"

"Yes, Your Grace." I put down my fork and wiped my mouth with a napkin, then stood and bowed deeply. "Thank you. I cannot tell you how much I appreciate your help."

I hadn't had a chance to properly express my gratitude last night, what with how exhausted and wrecked I'd been. I'd pretty much only been able to scarf down food, clean myself up, and then fall into bed.

Lilith clucked her tongue. "None of that now. You are my guest. I am happy to provide you with comfort."

"Thank you," I said and then grimaced. It was like when I was at a restaurant and kept thanking the waiter for every little thing they did because I wanted to be polite. Waiter set the table? Thank you. Waiter brought the bottle of water? Thank you. Waiter poured the water? Thank you. Waiter set the water bottle down? Thank you.

Dining with me was a cringe fest of nervous politeness.

"Now," Lilith said, "please come with me."

I followed her out into the hallway, where the same demons from yesterday made up her retinue again. As we walked, Lilith made introductions. The blonde who'd carried me was Enaia, the dude with the curly hair was called Thamuz, and the ginger-haired one was Destatur. They'd been serving as Lilith's entourage and inner circle for millennia, apparently.

While Enaia peered at me with open disdain, Destatur gave me a warm smile. Thamuz seemed kind of aloof and uninterested in pretty much anything.

Lilith stopped at an ornate door and faced me.

"I'm sure you must be eager to return home," she said. "Before I can give you leave to go, however, there are still amends to be made for breaking the vow. It is not quite an arbitrary decision—there are rules for how this works. Once begun, a penance must be completed."

I gulped. "Okay."

She nodded gravely, and with a push of her hand, she opened the door and waved me inside. Warily, I stepped over the threshold and into...a massive library. My mouth hanging open, I craned my neck up to take in the high book-shelves that covered every wall of the ballroom-sized hall. An old, intricately carved desk stood in the center of the room, with several other seating areas off to the sides. Books littered the desk and other tables next to the armchairs and sofas.

"Your task," Lilith said from behind me, "is to sort these books back into their proper place, by alphabetical order within sections based on subjects." Her hand came to rest on my shoulder. "We are so messy, you see." She gave it a slight squeeze. "We never seem to have the time to put back the books we pull out. It's just so tiresome. No one wants to do it. Quite the right task for a penance, don't you think?"

I looked back at her over my shoulder. A sly smile sat on her lips, a glint of mischief in her eyes.

"Oh, yes." I nodded with all the fake earnestness I could muster. "Very punishing indeed."

"Tedious work."

"Absolutely onerous. I will have nightmares about this."

Lilith pressed her lips together as if to keep in a grin. "Then it is settled. A fitting punishment for breaking the vow. It will suffice."

"Yes, Your Grace."

She gave me a curt nod. "I will come back in a few hours, and we'll have lunch together."

"Okay."

With that, she left, and I allowed myself a grin as the

door closed behind her and her retinue. As far as pleasurable punishments went, this one was high up on my list, and of course, Lilith knew it. The only other one that would top having to do the "tedious" work of a librarian would be having to take care of a roomful of kittens. Oh, the horror!

She'd cleverly phrased it in a way that would still make it work as a penance. I didn't know exactly how the magic around vows, oaths, and such functioned, but I guessed there was some leeway as to how the requirement for making amends might be satisfied.

And because I didn't want to trigger anything within the framework of this "penance," I cracked my knuckles and really did get down to business. There were scores of books scattered across the available surfaces in the room, and depending on how intricate their shelving would be, it could well take me hours to put them in their right places.

Of course, I also checked out some of the books and leafed through them, which was the part that made the whole thing enjoyable. So many of them were old tomes from centuries ago but were so well preserved that there had to be some magic keeping them from falling into decay. And not all of them were books in the modern sense of the word —quite a few were parchment scrolls or a stack of leaves tied together with string.

Thanks to my Azazel-gifted ability to understand any language that ever existed, I was able to actually read the different scripts and peruse the contents of the tomes. Poetry, fairy tales, collections on mythology, historical accounts, treatises...all from various countries and empires and cultures throughout the ages. A veritable wealth of human knowledge, creativity, and ingenuity.

Right in the heart of the home of Lucifer, who—by all accounts—seemed to despise humanity.

Curious.

I'd started by clearing the side tables and the armchairs, working my way across the seating areas until I eventually tackled the piles of books on the desk. The surface was barely even visible; so many tomes littered the table. The more I cleared it, the more I noticed the elaborate wood carving underneath a glass topper. The image depicted a version of the Fall from Grace, with clouds billowing in the heavens and an angel hurtling down toward roaring flames. The carving details of the feathers on the wings were incredible, and the flames looked stunningly real. The kind of talent and skill it took to make a wood carving look so lifelike…

I picked up the last book on a pile to my right and stopped short.

Underneath the volume lay some pages.

But not pages that had come loose from a book.

They were *letters*.

My eyes had tracked over the content of the sheet on top before I could decide whether or not I should snoop. And then the names I'd picked up made the decision for me.

With trembling fingers, I leafed through the letters.

They were, all of them, addressed to Gabriel.

No last name, no title, no other honorific, just Gabriel.

And the content of the letter made it clear the addressee was the first of his name. As in, the *archangel* Gabriel.

All the pages were essentially drafts of one and the same letter, with some of the earlier versions being struck through, with variations in tone and depth of description, telling the tale of someone taking great care to phrase this letter in the right way.

There was no name signed to the bottom because none of the letters were truly finished, but even still, I had a good hunch about who the author must be.

My heart in my throat, I held the pages in shaking hands and kept staring at the fine scrawl of Lucifer's handwriting. I recognized it from the note he'd sent Azazel last year when he'd acknowledged Azazel's RSVP to the Fall Festival. The language he'd used back then was Hellspeak, the script elegant yet archaic, like a mix between Hebrew and Arabic. Aramaic, maybe?

Without realizing it at the moment when I'd read the note about the Fall Festival, I had already been able to read and understand Hellspeak, and now I grasped, almost intrinsically, that this language was a twin of sorts, using the same script with only a few variations, the structure and grammar and vocabulary very close to Hellspeak.

Looking at whom it was addressed to, I figured it was likely the language native to Heaven. Heavenspeak? Angel-tongue? Who knew?

The letter in its various forms addressed the archangel with much more respect than I'd have imagined Lucifer capable of when dealing with his erstwhile heavenly brothers, but then again, given the nature of the request he was making, it made sense that he'd try to be conciliatory, maybe even nervous about hitting the right note.

He was trying to ask Gabriel to pardon Naamah and let her ascend to Heaven.

And it was obvious from the way he phrased the petition that this was an unusual ask; he even referred to the unprecedented nature of a Hell-born demon being admitted to Heaven. Fallen angels had been pardoned in the past, yes. But a demon who'd never been to Heaven in the first place? I'd never heard of it, and the letter acknowledged that this would be the first instance of that happening.

Still, some of the drafts showed how Lucifer had apparently struggled with wrangling his disdain under control when addressing Gabriel. There were slips of snide comments, word choices here and there that revealed his underlying contempt for the archangel and Heaven as a whole. Either those passages were struck out, or the letter draft abruptly ended there, indicating Lucifer had scrapped the draft at that point, possibly due to his slip of the tongue, or hand for that matter.

I perused all the pages, trying to find the most complete version. But there was no telling which was the most recent one, and I didn't know whether this whole endeavor was an abandoned project that was centuries old, or whether it had indeed been finished and all those drafts had resulted in one completed letter that was actually sent.

I squinted at the desk. The letters had been covered by books, so someone—Lucifer? Lilith?—had sat here and either deliberately or accidentally laid stuff on top of them. Maybe it had been Lucifer after taking a break from letter drafting. Maybe he'd been frustrated because he hadn't been able to find the right words, and he'd paused the project for a while.

Worrying my lip, I considered the facts. Chances were that Lucifer hadn't finished the drafting yet. Because if he had, why keep all those earlier drafts here? He'd have likely either destroyed them or put them away somewhere since they'd served their purpose. That the drafts were still here on the desk could mean that this was an ongoing project he planned to revisit at a later point. I knew from experience of drafting cover letters for jobs and internships that I liked to keep earlier drafts on hand to check back on how I'd phrased something and to play around with words and sentences and structure.

And if this was truly an unfinished project...the implications were staggering. He wanted to get Naamah into Heaven? Petitioning for her to be an angel? Why?

The entire idea was mind-boggling. Wasn't she his favorite daughter? Even with her mind broken, confined to her chambers, she still seemed to hold a special place in Lucifer's esteem. If she ascended to Heaven...Lucifer would never see her again. He was forbidden from setting foot on Earth, as per the deal he'd made with Heaven to keep Lilith. If Naamah went to Heaven, it'd be like she died—she'd be forever gone from Lucifer's life.

Noise in the hallway outside jerked me out of my musings. With a start and a gasp, I restacked the letters and carefully laid the book on top of them again. I didn't remember what order the drafts had been in, but I could only hope that Lucifer didn't remember either. I sure as fuck didn't want him to find out that I knew about this. This might snowball into another vow of silence right quick, and I'd had my fill of them, thank you very much.

The door swung open, and I tried my best to look casual. Which resulted in me putting my hand on my hip, then deciding it might look better if I leaned on the desk, then thinking, "No, that looks staged!" and then removing my hand from the desk, only to accidentally knock off a pile of books in the process, bending down to pick them up, hitting the back of my head on the underside of the desk while getting up, jerking my head down from the pain and consequently punching myself in the face with my knee, staggering upright and stubbing my toes—peeking out of open shoes—on the leg of the desk, and hopping on one foot while holding the other and uttering an ungodly howl, only to stumble and fall over the desk chair.

And this is how Lilith found me with at least three work-related injuries, sprawled out on the floor and groaning in pain.

"Zoe!" she called out and rushed to my side. "What happened?"

"The books got feisty," I murmured.

She studied me from head to toe. "I guess I was wrong when I thought this assignment wouldn't harm you."

"I'm resourceful," I said and grunted as I heaved myself up off the floor with her help.

Lilith patted my back. "Well, it is a good thing you heal fast."

"Yeah."

Surreptitiously, I threw a glance at the desk. The book still covered the letter drafts, and it looked like that area of the desk hadn't been disturbed.

Lilith followed my gaze.

I held my breath.

"Don't worry about the rest," she said. "It is enough. The work you did will satisfy the requirement of penance."

I exhaled a sigh of relief, and Lilith smiled, obviously thinking I'd been concerned about my workload instead of anyone finding out I'd discovered yet another sensitive piece of information to do with Lucifer and Naamah.

I really should stop falling into these situations.

Yeah, I'd add that to my to-do list right after *Stop being socially awkward.*

"Let us eat together." Lilith linked her arm through mine and led me out of the library.

We dined in a cozy room decked out in colorful fabrics that flowed from the ceiling and across the walls, giving the entire thing the feel of being inside a tent. Seat cushions were arranged around a low table that featured a mouthwatering feast. Lilith gracefully sat with her legs folded to the side, and her retinue settled down around her. I followed their lead and parked my butt on a comfy cushion across the table from Lilith.

"Please," she said and waved at the selection of food that looked like it had a little bit of the best of every cuisine on Earth. "Enjoy."

She watched me as I perused the food and then went straight for a platter of falafel, added a bit of what I assumed was yogurt sauce, and grabbed a piece of fluffy bread, then piled some delicious-smelling biryani on the plate as well and topped everything off with a good helping of vegetable curry.

"So you like rice," Lilith said as she started filling her own plate.

I nodded with a mouthful of biryani. "So versatile. The perfect grain." I made a thumbs-up gesture.

"Is it your favorite food?"

I squinted as I considered it. "No, I think that distinction goes to pizza."

"Pizza?" Lilith inclined her head a little to look at Destatur, the ginger-haired female in her retinue.

Leaning closer to Lilith, Destatur explained in a soft voice, "A round dish made of dough and topped with tomato sauce and other foods, baked in an oven."

"Ah." Lilith raised her brows and nodded.

I paused with the spoon halfway to my mouth. "You've never had pizza?"

"I'm afraid not."

"Oh." I laid my hand over my heart. "You should get one someday! I've never been to Italy, but I hear they've got the best ones, so you should get one from a traditional pizzeria in, like, Naples. That's sort of where it all originated."

"Destatur," Lilith murmured.

"On it." Destatur summoned a notepad and pen and scribbled something down.

It was kind of cute how Lilith wanted to take notes on human culture. But also…how sad was it that she was so out of touch with modern life on Earth?

We spent the rest of lunch chitchatting about everything and nothing. Lilith was, as always, very interested in hearing about my experience of living on Earth, and I, in turn, carefully asked her about her life down here.

At one point, the conversation had gotten so comfortable that when Lilith casually mentioned Lucifer, I couldn't hold my tongue fast enough to keep in the question that had been burning a hole in my mind ever since I'd gotten to know Lilith.

"What do you see in him?"

CHAPTER 27

Lilith drew up short, her brow furrowing. "I beg your pardon?"

Enaia, Thamuz, and Destatur all became very, very still.

Crap.

My pulse racing, I scrambled around for words. Too late to take it back now. I'd have to plow forward. "It's just...I mean..." I flailed and grimaced. "You—you seem like a nice person. You're kind, and gentle, you appear to have a full range of human emotions—"

Lilith raised a brow.

Shit, shit, shit.

"What I mean to say is, you have a good heart. You're compassionate and considerate. And Lucifer is..."

"None of those things?"

If I grimaced any longer, my face would probably get stuck that way. "Yeah?"

"He's different with me." She picked a grape from a plate and ate it.

I didn't dare say anything into the silence that followed while she chewed, sensing that I should wait.

"He wasn't always like that," Lilith eventually said quietly.

I barely even breathed, just stared at her in wary fascination while a thread of something dark and chilling inside me wormed its way to the surface.

"When we first met..." Her voice trailed off, her gaze becoming unfocused. "It's been so long. There are many things I don't remember, but I do recall those first years. He was different then. I was, too. So much younger, with untamed wildness in our hearts. Eternity..." She sighed. "Eternity has a way of grinding you down. Even more so in a place like this." The brilliant brown of her eyes met my gaze. "When we settled here, and he had to establish his rule, enforce his position—and mine—it took a lot out of him. There were parts of him he had to harden, others he had to break. Hell is an unkind place for those with soft hearts. He did what he had to do to survive...to make sure *I* survived."

I flinched, and that subtle thread of ice-cold darkness spread inside me, reminding me of something I couldn't quite name yet.

Her eyes downcast, she exhaled softly. "Though it is true that who he has become, by choice and necessity, is so different now from who he used to be that the earliest version of me, from the beginning of our courtship, might not even recognize him today. For the longest time, I hadn't realized how much he'd changed, how much *I'd* changed. It feels like I've been in a stupor for many, many years, grown numb to petty cruelties and malignity. What is the saying among humans?" She tilted her head, her face thoughtful. "About a frog in boiling water?"

I cleared my throat. "When you throw a frog into a pot with boiling water, it will jump out. But when you put it into a pot with tepid water and gradually increase the heat until boiling, the frog will not realize the danger and will be cooked alive."

Her smile was sad. "Yes. It is like that."

Damn. I shivered despite myself, that unnamed fear within me growing claws and teeth.

"But I am numb no more. Thanks to you."

I looked at her with wide eyes. "What?"

"When I saw you at the Fall Festival...something changed. It was as if I woke up from a long dream. I hadn't realized how calcified parts of me had become until seeing you made me remember how I used to be."

I stared at her in disbelief. *I* had somehow helped Lilith reconnect with her humanity? "Is it the clumsiness? I have a hard time imagining you were ever clumsy. You are grace personified."

Lilith laughed softly. "It is just this." She nodded at me. "Your spirit. Your spontaneity."

Spontaneity? More like missing a verbal filter.

"Your heart." She gave me a warm smile. "All of it helped me remember and find a way back to parts of myself I'd forgotten about."

I shifted around on my cushion, feeling a bit self-conscious. I didn't truly believe that I'd done anything to cause such a massive mind shift in Lilith. More likely, she'd already been on the verge of a big change anyhow, and I'd just happened to trigger it maybe.

"I used to..." Lilith frowned, her eyes darkening. "I used to be much more present. I'd speak up more. I became complacent to suffering, much as he has developed a taste for it. Not with me." A wistful smile flickered over her face,

"Never with me. But toward others..." She shrugged. "There are few who are now privileged to witness what remains of his capacity to love, who get to see a side of him he has all but excised from his persona."

Heart in my throat, I waited a beat, then ventured, "Like Naamah?"

Lilith nodded. "Just so."

Remembering those letter drafts, I wanted to fish for some more information, but I had to be careful about it. "He really cares about her, doesn't he? It almost seems obsessive... He gets extremely tense whenever she's brought up."

Lilith shook her head. "He feels guilty."

I raised both brows. "Why?"

She uttered a mournful sigh. "Because he cannot heal her." At my stare, she elaborated. "All his power, all his might...useless in the face of what ails her. Can you imagine? Being second only to God, the ability to alter reality itself at your fingertips, yet you cannot give your daughter peace. Living makes her suffer, yet you cannot let her die."

I felt a pinch in my heart. "He really can't help her? I thought demons could heal all manner of wounds and diseases."

"Of the body. Repairing a broken mind is not in his power."

Not in *his* power... Pieces clicked together in my head. Was this why he wanted to get her pardoned and have her ascend to Heaven? Because it was the only way to heal her mind? I wet my lips and dared to push forward a little. "So there's no one else who could heal her?"

Lilith was quiet for a moment, her features hardening. "Could? Yes. Would? Doubtful."

Oooh, the plot thickens. Did that mean Lucifer had already sent the letter about Naamah, and Heaven had declined?

"Who is it?" I asked cautiously, trying to angle for just a little more confirmation.

Lilith shook her head. "It is of no matter. A question unanswered, for it will never be asked. Some divides are too vast to bridge."

Interesting. This sounded very much like Lucifer had never finished and sent the letter. I wondered if it was due to him struggling to find the right words—or whether it came down to him overcoming his ego and hatred of Heaven. That letter...it was tantamount to prostrating himself before his former brethren. A request that would reveal a vulnerability and which would put him deep into debt with Heaven.

Leverage.

Ah, didn't it all come down to that? Favors and debts, knowing someone's secrets and weaknesses, knowledge as power, and holding a deed done for someone's benefit forever over their head.

And not only would granting Naamah a pardon and allowing her into Heaven mean that Lucifer owed them, but it would also mean Heaven could wield Naamah's continued well-being like a weapon against Lucifer. I'd spent enough time down here, and among highly political and ruthless beings, to know that even angels wouldn't shy away from basically holding Lucifer's favorite daughter hostage—not in the sense of a modern victim of terrorism, but more like an old-world political hostage.

In ancient times, a country, empire, or other power might receive children from nobles of another dominion with whom they'd either been at war or just signed a treaty. These children would live at court and receive a good education and basically were part of the nobility there, and their continued health and well-being were security measures in order to ensure that the other party kept to the terms of the treaty or didn't show new aggression toward the kingdom or empire that took care of their children.

Sending Naamah to Heaven would be very much like this.

Plus, they already had a deal with Lucifer about Lilith, which made up the basis for the truce between Heaven and Hell and forbade Lucifer from coming to Earth. If Lucifer asked for a pardon for Naamah and she got accepted into Heaven, it would throw everything out of balance.

And maybe this was another reason he hadn't sent the letter yet? This was about a lot more than just her mental health.

A knock on the door interrupted my musing.

"Come in," Lilith called out.

"Apologies, Your Grace," a demon said, poking her head inside. "If I may have a word with you?"

"Can this wait?"

"I'm afraid not. It's an urgent matter, but it will only take a minute of your time."

Lilith sighed and faced me. "There is always someone or something requiring my attention. Excuse me, I will be back in a moment."

"Of course. No problem." I inclined my head.

When the door closed behind Lilith, I stared awkwardly at the three demons remaining in the room with me.

Destatur's gaze lay heavily on me. "Did you enjoy the meal?"

My brain couldn't decide between "It was great" and "It was awesome," so naturally, what came out was, "It was gruesome!"

With a grimace, I corrected, "I mean, yes. I enjoyed it."

A small smile played about Destatur's lips. Leaning

forward over the still-packed table, she said with a note of urgency in her voice, "I've been meaning to tell you—thank you for being our lady's friend."

I blinked and drew back, stumped.

"Your company is good for her," Destatur continued. "I've been at her side for a long time now, and I can't remember seeing her this…awake and happy. Spending time with you has invigorated her. What she told you earlier is true. You've started uncovering parts of her that have been buried for too long."

I didn't even know what to say to that. I shifted on my cushion again, utterly uncomfortable by this unexpected—and, in my opinion, unearned—praise.

"Every time you talk about Earth," Destatur went on, "our lady lights up. It gives her new life." She paused, then glanced at the door and back at me. "And I think you should suggest that she visit Earth with you."

"Me?" My eyes nearly popped out of my head.

"Yes, you." Destatur gave a firm nod. "I think it would be good for her. She hasn't been to visit in a long time, and I believe she would benefit from the experience." When I opened my mouth to protest, she shook her head. "In the past, we used to ask her if she wanted to go every now and then. She refused every time, but she seemed conflicted. I don't think she stays here because she doesn't truly want to go, more likely she has been too stuck in her rut to make the change. Through your friendship with her, you have the potential to give her the nudge she needs to visit Earth again. She favors you and values your opinion and insight. You are exactly the guide she needs to return to Earth after so much time away."

"I—I don't know…"

"You have a unique understanding of what it's like to

live as a human on Earth. Your first-hand knowledge means you can explain and guide her on her visit much better than we could. If anyone can convince her that it's a good idea to go to Earth, it's you."

I bit my lip, glancing at the door.

"Please," Destatur said and reached over the table to grasp my hand. "My lady needs this. You heard her earlier. She's been drowning down here. This will be good for her, and you're the right person to make her see it."

Worry and doubt crowded my mind, my heart. Something niggled at me beneath my thoughts.

"She has shown you so much kindness," Destatur said softly. "Will you not do this one thing for her?"

Goddammit. That did it. I exhaled roughly. "Okay."

The smile on Destatur's face lit up her eyes. "Thank you. You truly have a gracious heart."

As if on cue, the door opened and Lilith came back inside.

"Now," she said, settling back on the cushion, "let's have some dessert. Which one is your favorite?"

I peered at the selection of cakes and pastries and then picked up a slice of carrot cake. "This here," I said with a smile.

Her expression intrigued, Lilith took a slice for herself and ate a bite. The next second, her eyes rolled back, and she uttered a moan of pure food satisfaction. "I've never had this before," she murmured. "It's divine."

I grinned at her, then threw a glance at Destatur. She gave me a subtle nod.

Clearing my throat, I launched my proposition. "Um, Your Grace. I was thinking...I would love to show you Earth. Not just through movies or my stories, but with a...visit."

Lilith stopped eating and looked at me, her graceful brows drawing closer together.

"I know you haven't been there in a while," I hastened to say. "And I remember what you said about why. But I think...I think this would be good for you. Maybe...maybe the change that my presence here has started in you will be supported by visiting Earth—with me."

"I am not sure that is a good idea." Lilith looked troubled, but there was also a spark of something in her eyes. The glimmer of a fire banked for too long, belying her words.

"I will be there with you," I said. "I can show you Earth as I know it, as I've experienced it. It's one thing to watch a movie and see all the new things humans have come up with over the past centuries, but it's another to stand between the skyscrapers of a big city and see how light and shadow play between buildings of steel and glass that people from thousands of years ago could only have dreamed of. To hear the noises of the city and see the people rushing by. There's no better way to experience the vibrancy of humanity, to feel the richness of modern life."

That glimmer in her eyes grew. Tentatively, she said, "One of our portals here opens to New York City." Quietly, but with a note of eagerness in her voice, she added, "I have thought about visiting there."

"New York!" I exclaimed. "That's perfect. I've actually been there."

It had been the summer after I'd graduated high school, when my aunt had invited me to stay with her for a few weeks. She worked and lived in Philadelphia, which was only one and a half hours away from NYC, so of course I'd gone there several times while my aunt was working during the day.

Growing up, I'd seen so many movies and TV shows set in New York that it felt like I *knew* this city before ever having been there. Actually setting foot in it was a tad like coming home, in a weird way. Even though I'd chosen not to move there for my studies or job—I'd wanted to be closer to my mom's—the city would always hold a special place in my heart.

And thinking of my mom…

"We can go visit New York together," I said to Lilith, "and I can show you around there for a bit, but I can't make it a full day. I want to go see my mom, too, because—" I broke off and swallowed the sudden sharp spike of anticipatory grief that shot up from the depths of my soul where I'd stuffed it for the time being because the past few days and weeks had been so chaotic and overwhelming that I'd had no resources to deal with all it entailed. "She's dying, and I need to visit her while I still can," I finished, my voice husky.

"Oh," Lilith said, her eyes darkening. "I am so sorry, Zoe. I didn't know."

I shrugged and blinked fast, trying to clear my eyes of the moisture pooling there.

"There is no rush." Lilith reached over the table and squeezed my hand. "We can wait to go until you have made the most of the time you have left with her."

The burning in my eyes and throat increased. "No." I shook my head. "It's fine. Just sitting with her for an hour or two will be enough for a visit."

Anything more than that, and it would grind me down until I couldn't breathe through the impending grief hovering above me. Anything longer would feel like holding a wake for her while she was still alive, and the thought made me want to sob.

I'd had people I cared about taken from me suddenly,

without warning—like my grandfather, who'd died of a heart attack—and the shock of it, the abrupt onset of grief after the initial numbness would easily knock me over for a while. Back then, I'd thought that losing someone suddenly was surely worse than when you'd been warned about their death, that when your loved one slowly died of a disease, for example, you'd be more prepared for the inevitable end.

But when my grandmother had died from cancer a few years later, I'd learned the truth—that neither option was the easier one. As I'd watched my nana suffer through chemo, only to be told—much like my mom now—that her cancer had come back and was now inoperable and too far progressed, I'd understood that knowing someone was going to die was its own method of torture. The knowledge that time was scarce, that every minute spent in the other's company was suddenly immensely valuable, and at the same time, your human mind and heart couldn't live minutes and days as if savoring every last breath...it could break something fragile in you.

It was incredibly hard to be with a loved one whose death was imminent and not already mourn their passing while they were still alive. A constant struggle to keep up good cheer to make the most of the remaining time, to make a few last happy memories and not more sad ones—because when it was all over, you wouldn't want to look back and know that your last moments with them had already been tainted by grief.

But it was an impossible fight. Our brains just didn't work that way. Same thing with the mantra "live every moment as if it were your last." Nobody could live that way. It was exhausting. We were not made for it, and yet we kept striving for that impossible, constant enjoyment.

So, inevitably, when you spent time with a dying loved

one, anticipatory grief would intrude, and then you'd feel shitty for letting it.

Back then, with my grandmother, I didn't have a name for the pain that came before a loved one's passing. Later, I'd read about someone explaining about anticipatory grief, and that it was like mourning them twice, and that was just so apt.

So I shook my head now, giving Lilith a sad smile, and said, "Seeing my mom for a little bit is enough to keep her in my heart."

Lilith inclined her head. "All right."

"The visit will have to wait until sometime next week, though. It's only been about two and a half weeks since I was last on Earth, and I need to make sure that the connection between my mind and body won't be jeopardized."

"Of course." She nodded.

"Let's set a date," Destatur said. "We'll need to make some preparations ahead of time so that everything can run smoothly for your first visit back to Earth after such a long time, Your Grace. We'll make sure your trip will be enjoyable and safe."

Lilith nodded again, and we settled on a day and time I'd come to the palace again to escort her to Earth.

I was really going to do this. Play tour guide to Lilith, the first human woman, Lucifer's most beloved.

Life truly took the weirdest turns.

We finished our lunch, and then it was time for me to go home. It felt strange, almost like I'd had a nice sleepover with a friend, rather than having been voluntarily psychologically tortured and then saved.

Weird turns indeed.

"I know the start of your stay here was an awful one," Lilith said as she led me through a hallway, "but I do hope you enjoyed the end. I appreciated your presence here." She came to a stop in front of a nondescript, unremarkable door and turned to me. "And I dare hope you'll choose to come visit me again, under more auspicious beginnings."

"Of course. And I'll be back next week for our trip to Earth."

Lilith inclined her head. "May it be the first of many more."

That was probably the closest an ancient being like Lilith could come to saying, "I'm so excited!"

I gave her a genuine smile. "I can't wait."

"Your escort home is waiting for you just through here." She gestured at the door. "I shall see you next week."

"Thank you."

When I made as if to bow—*remember your protocol, Zoe!*—she stopped me with a hand on my shoulder and instead leaned in and kissed me on each cheek.

"Friends don't bow," she said as she drew back.

I stood frozen and sans response, because I was too hung up on the fact that I'd managed not to make this awkward. This type of greeting/goodbye was fraught with clumsy pitfalls for me. I still remembered in excruciating detail that one time back in high school when the new French exchange student had greeted everyone with kisses on the cheeks, and when it was my turn, I'd suffered from a momentary lapse in coordination and hadn't known which cheek to present/go for first.

That was the one and only time I'd ever kissed a girl on the mouth. Accidentally, to boot.

It wasn't that she wasn't pretty, but doing an unplanned, full lip-lock with a girl I didn't know in front of my entire class as the inadvertent first foray into non-heterosexual exploration really wasn't the best look for a sixteen-year-old.

Needless to say, the French girl had avoided me for the rest of the year.

Yeah, making friends was not my forte.

I *was made* friends by those with more social grace than me. See Lilith, Exhibit D (A–C were Taylor, Caleb, and Hekesha, respectively. Yes, even grumpy Hekesha had shown more initiative with befriending me than I had shown her. Oh, and Azmodea and Mammon didn't count—they were family).

"Okay," I now said with a wobbly smile. "Friends."

With a nod, Lilith opened the door, and I wondered about whoever it was that would fly me back home. I wasn't particularly looking forward to being carried in an unavoidably close hold by a strange demon for a longer stretch of time, and the flight home wasn't exactly short. Eh, the important thing was to get home.

The door led onto a large balcony without a railing, which made it a convenient platform to land on or take flight from. I had a brief second of relief that I wouldn't have to walk through the Hall of Horrors toward the main entrance and exit of the palace again—before I recognized the figure silhouetted against the churning, lightning-streaked sky beyond, and pure joy erased all other thought or feeling.

"Azazel," I gasped.

CHAPTER 28

"I took the liberty of letting him know to pick you up," Lilith said from behind me. "I thought you'd like that."

"Yes," I whispered.

Azazel executed a deep bow, his fire-licked wings spreading low in a display of deference. "Your Grace."

"Safe travels," Lilith said and then the door closed behind me.

I ran.

Azazel had barely straightened again when I launched myself into his arms. He caught me without missing a beat, and I wrapped my legs around his waist as I clung to him as if he were the only piece of driftwood in a stormy sea. I pressed my nose against his neck and inhaled deeply, needing the reassurance of his scent. For the first time in days, my soul relaxed.

Hell could burn and darkness could rage all around me, but with him, I was safe.

"I missed you," I choked out, my face still buried in the curve where his neck met his shoulder.

He didn't respond, except to clutch me closer, as if afraid I might slip away. His fingers dug into my thighs where he held me, and his ragged breath warmed my head where he pressed a hard kiss to my hair. Unlike me, he hadn't relaxed, his muscles still awfully tense. I could feel how tightly knotted his shoulders and back were, and the agitated buzz of his energy tapped over my skin in a near-painful way.

I wanted to tell him that everything was okay now, that he had me back, in one piece, but just as I opened my mouth to speak, he launched into the sky with me in his arms. The abrupt takeoff tore the air from my lungs, the words from my tongue. He hurtled across the sky with such speed and force that I had no hope of talking to him.

At least not out loud.

Hey, I said into his mind. *It's—*

Not a word. His mental voice was barely more than a growl.

My heart lurched. *But—*

I cannot speak with you right now. Such repressed fire behind those words, it seared me along the mental pathway of our connection.

Why? I asked despite the warning.

Because, came his snarled reply, *I am much too furious with you for a normal conversation at this moment, but I cannot adequately yell at you when I'm holding you in my arms.*

Oh. My stomach made a nosedive for the ground. The ground far, far below us.

He was furious with me. I cringed in his hold. Of course he was. Mephisto had mentioned how enraged he'd been when he found out I'd surrendered myself to Lucifer. And apparently, that rage hadn't abated one bit in the time since.

Not that I could blame him. I'd be fucking pissed in his place, too.

But I still stood by my actions. Knowing that Azazel was mad at me didn't make me regret what I'd done. I'd known that it would anger him, and I'd gone through with it anyway because it was more important to me to remove the leverage Lucifer had on him than to avoid incurring Azazel's displeasure.

Of course, that didn't make it any easier to bear the force of his simmering rage as he flew me back in weighted silence. I held on to him, feeling relieved to be back in his arms and, at the same time, apprehensive about the storm I knew would be waiting for me once we were home.

By the time we landed on the balcony outside our bedroom, I was a mess of nerves.

He set me down with more gentleness than the sharp whip of his energy would suggest and unlocked the door with his sigil combination. His eyes blazed fire as he held the door for me, and I got the first real look at his face. Back at the palace, he'd been silhouetted against lightning, and I'd run to him so fast I hadn't really taken him in.

Now I did.

He looked ragged, more than I'd ever thought was possible for an ethereally beautiful being like him. As if he hadn't eaten in days, hadn't slept, even though as a demon, he didn't actually need either to survive and stay healthy. Demons drew their sustenance from Hell itself, but judging by his appearance, you wouldn't know it.

The lines of his face were sharper, almost haggard, his expression somewhere between desperate fury and ravaged pain.

Between the two of us, he was the one who looked like he'd been tortured.

"I'm sorry," I whispered as I stepped inside, my heart aching.

He closed the door with a quiet snick that was still somehow loud enough to make me startle.

"For what, exactly?" he said with the kind of calm that harbored a caged inferno.

I swallowed hard.

"For going behind my back?" Lightning in his eyes, the stirrings of a growl in his voice. "For doing what I specifically asked you not to do?"

"Actually," I began, lifting my index finger, "you never asked me not to go to Lu—"

"Because I didn't think you'd be reckless enough to do that!" he thundered, the leash on his anger finally severed.

I flinched, my pulse drumming in my ears. Okay, yeah, maybe being nitpicky about how he hadn't worded his request for noninterference on my part to exclude my mission of self-sacrifice wasn't the best idea right now.

His wings were still out, and flames rolled over the feathers, his power manifesting as dark smoke around him. "You left," he snarled, sparks popping over the exposed skin of his arms, neck, and face. "You left without a word."

"I wrote a note," I ventured.

"A note!" His bellow shook the room. The furniture—all replaced after his last outbreak of rage—rattled as if struck by an earthquake.

I pointed a finger at him, some anger of my own stirring. "Don't you dare incinerate the room again!"

Several muscles in his face twitched. With a flick of his hand, he summoned a fire extinguisher and handed it to me.

Well, all right, then.

I got it ready and cocked it at him. "I left you a note," I said through gritted teeth, "because I knew you'd prevent me from going if I told you in person, and I was worried you'd kill whoever would deliver the message for me."

His fingers jerked, as if he imagined decapitating anyone unlucky enough to have to tell him that his wife just waltzed herself into Lucifer's palace to be tortured.

"Tell me I'm wrong," I prompted.

"Oh, you are wrong on so many levels that I don't even know where to begin," he bit out.

I hid my flinch this time, glaring at him instead. "Like what?"

"Like thinking you can pull this stunt and I'd just shrug and go along with it."

"I didn't think—"

"You clearly didn't! At all!"

Darkness exploded from him, bathing everything in gloom except the flames dancing over his feathers and the sparks and gashes of fire on his skin.

He bared his teeth at me. "I told you that I would forsake the right to see my mother specifically so you wouldn't be punished by Lucifer, and what do you do? You walk right up to him and *ask* to be punished!"

"I did it for you!" I yelled right back. As conflict-avoidant as I was, once embroiled in a fight, I'd give as good as I got. He wanted a shouting match? He'd get it. "I'm the one who started this whole mess, and I didn't want to be the reason you couldn't go see your mom! So I went ahead and took away Lucifer's leverage!"

"How magnanimous of you," he snarled, his every word like thunder rocking the room. "And did you stop to consider, in your noble crusade to fall on your sword for my sake, that my having to sit idly by while you're being tortured hurt me more than not being able to visit my mother?"

Tiny spikes of regret poked at my heart. Still, I didn't back down. "He would have come for me anyway! Sooner or later, Lucifer would have called in the punishment. What difference does it make that I pushed for it to happen earlier? At least that way, it was on my terms!"

"On your terms." His face carved from stone, he glared at me, his nostrils flaring. "Yours alone. Is this not a partnership?" He gestured between me and him. "Did you not recently rebuke me because I acted without including you in my thought process?"

I gulped, my throat suddenly thick. He had a point, dammit, and I didn't like it.

"You went behind my back," he snapped. "You hatched out this plot, knowing I didn't want you to interfere, and then you left and presented me with a fait accompli. You didn't discuss it with me. You didn't respect my opinion. You just did what *you* thought was best, regardless of how it affected me, consequences be damned!"

My chest drew tight, my stomach turning.

"Does that sound like a partnership to you?" he barked.

I didn't answer his question because it hurt too much to admit he was right. In a small voice, I said instead, "I just wanted to do this for you. Because I know how much your mother means to you."

He turned away and rubbed a hand over his face, his wings trembling. When he faced me again, his expression was equal parts pained and furious. "You still don't get it. You still don't believe—" He broke off and took a deep breath as if to rein in the mighty beast that was his anger. "When will you see? What will it take?"

Shivering from the nauseous cocktail of emotions brewing inside me, I stared at him, uncomprehending.

"What more do I have to do to make you understand that *you deserve to be put first?*"

My eyes prickled with wet heat. I couldn't even speak, struck mute by the turn this fight had taken.

His breath heavy, Azazel stared at me. "I've told you before, and I will tell you again—your safety is my first priority. *You* are my first priority. Do you truly not understand?"

I pressed my lips together, pain squeezing my chest.

"I love you more than anything," he said, the hint of a crack in his hoarse voice. "More than *anything*." He punctuated the last word with a hard swipe of his hand through the air. "And you being harmed in any way *hurts me more than anything*."

Lungs seizing, I blinked rapidly against the tears clouding my eyes.

"I would have been fine not seeing my mother," he continued. "Do I wish to see her again? Yes. I still love her, as much as the faded memory of her allows me to. Nevertheless, it would not have broken me not to visit her, even knowing she's alive." He paused, the only sound in the room the crackle of fire over his wings—and the pounding of my heart. "But do you know what broke me?"

My lips quivered. There was too much pain in my chest to draw a full breath.

"Coming home and finding that note of yours."

The sob that wanted to break free couldn't get past the knot in my throat.

"Knowing that you were in Lucifer's claws," Azazel went on, his voice as rough as gravel. "Spending the next days in the cold prison of my mind, imagining what he was doing to you. Not knowing how long he would keep you." He balled his hands into fists. "Not being able to do jack shit about it."

I sniffled and tried to find my voice. "He didn't hurt me physically. He couldn't. Lilith's power inside me prevented him from touching me with the intent to harm, and he couldn't even order someone else to do it for him."

He exhaled a shuddering breath and squeezed his eyes shut for a brief moment. When he looked at me next, the raw, painful relief in his gaze rattled me to the core. "Mephistopheles mentioned something like that," he muttered, rubbing both hands over his face. "I didn't know if he spoke the truth."

"He did," I said. "Lucifer couldn't lay a hand on me. And in the end, Lilith saved me from…" I trailed off and bit my tongue, realizing too late that maybe I should keep the psychological torture to myself.

His eyes glittered like broken shards lit by lightning. "From what?" he rasped.

I pressed my lips together.

"What did he do to you?" A quiet question, teeming with pain and fear.

"He made me watch a torture session," I whispered, "and scrub the glass floor in his entrance hall."

Azazel was silent while thunder rolled outside the window. I didn't have to elaborate. He knew me well enough to understand what that would have done to me. And it hadn't been too long ago that I'd puked all over Inachiel's freshly severed wings, demonstrating my soft heart and weak stomach.

He knew the way I was built, and I saw the exact moment when the realization of the emotional and psychological pain I'd suffered broke something in his gaze.

"Zoe," he said hoarsely, and then he was right in front of me, framing my face with both hands, laying his forehead against mine. "I am so sorry."

My heart jumped at his touch, so eager for his warmth, so starved for his affection. With a trembling exhale, I leaned into his hold. "I'm okay now," I whispered. I might still have nightmares about what I'd seen and felt, but eventually, time would dull the memories.

He pulled me to him—or tried to. I still clutched the damn fire extinguisher, and it bumped up between us. With a frown, he grabbed it and threw it aside, hauling me close again right away.

I melted into his embrace. The tension fled me on a full-body shake, and I grasped onto him with desperate need. I could feel the trembling of his muscles, the edge to his energy.

His voice was ragged when he spoke. "I died a thousand deaths imagining your torture."

"I'm sorry," I choked out, my face buried in his chest.

He squeezed me closer, then withdrew to clasp my face in his hands again, his eyes wild and pained. "I know you meant well. I know you thought you were just helping me see my mother, that you did it because you know how much she means to me." He shook his head, his thumbs stroking over my cheeks. "But you should have known that *you* mean more to me. I will always put you first. Not my mother, not my comfort, not anything nor anyone. I would rather bleed and break than see you hurt. Do you understand?" He gave me the gentlest little shake, his touch still incredibly careful and cherishing. "I need you to understand this."

I swallowed thickly. "I'm trying." Wetting my lips, I added, "But I need you to understand something, too."

His eyes darted between mine, his attention so acute it charged the air. "What, love?"

"That you deserve to be put first as well."

His brows drew together.

I laid my hand against his cheek, caressing him. "That you deserve someone who would willingly walk into torture for you."

His confusion fell away to reveal a glimpse at something raw, something unbelieving yet profoundly starved.

"You are worthy of a love so deep that it will bleed for you."

His fingers twitched against my jaw.

"What I did for you? I'd do it again. You say you'd rather break than see me hurt. Well, I'd bleed and break to see you happy."

"Zoe." A broken whisper.

His mouth crashed onto mine, his kiss equal parts claim and surrender. I responded in kind, my entire being pulled toward him, like a compass needle drawn toward true north. All the parts of me that had been shaken and shattered these past few days now righted themselves, mended in the benediction of his kiss.

He tunneled his fingers through my hair, his touch at once reverent and possessive. Fire licked through my veins, sparks of arousal buzzing all along my nerve endings. I jumped up and slung my legs around his hips, grabbing his shoulders to hold on. He moved one hand to my butt to steady me, the other sliding down to cover my breast.

"How partial," he murmured as he broke the kiss, "are you to these clothes?"

"Burn them."

"Good answer."

And with a squeeze on my breast, he lit my shirt on fire. I groaned at the delicious sting of heat that coursed across my torso, around my increasingly sensitive nipples, and then traveled south.

The scorched remnants of my clothes fell away a moment before my back met the mattress and Azazel rose above me in all his demonic glory. My hungry gaze devoured the sight of his massive bare chest—he'd conveniently incinerated his own clothes, too, it seemed.

"I thought you were patient," I said with a cheeky smile.

"Only for things that are worth taking time." He collared my neck with his hand, then slid it down torturously slowly, his touch becoming featherlight when he drew closer to my breasts. "And I'd rather take my time worshipping every inch of your naked body than spend it on peeling off your clothes."

I could only utter a sound somewhere between a gasp and a moan as he circled my nipple with his fingers before he cupped my breast and lightly bit the hardened bud. A zing of pleasure shot straight between my legs, making my hips buck off the mattress.

While he lavished my breasts with his attention, my hands roamed his broad shoulders, sliding to the point where his wings connected to his back. I stroked over the black feathers along the strong upper curve, then squeezed with both hands.

"Keep those wings out," I muttered.

A full-body shiver wrecked him, and on a spark of lightning all across the plumage, his illusion faltered and gave way to the black-and-white symphony of his true colors.

His stormy eyes met mine. "That spot is sensitive."

"I know," I drawled—and squeezed him again.

He groaned and bit my neck, pushing my legs apart with one knee. I arched into his touch as he cupped my mound and traced my entrance lightly. His fingers found me wet.

Ready. I was so ready for him, and I needed him inside

me. I didn't want him to leisurely worship my body as he'd promised. Right now, with my heart raw and open, with the memory of what it had felt like to be deprived of his warmth and love while I endured Lucifer's cruelty still fresh in my mind, I needed all of him.

"Let me feel you," I whispered, my lips seeking his.

The softest touch of his mouth to mine. "Always."

He traced his fingers down my inner thigh, leaving sparks of fire in his wake, and then grasped me under my knee to spread me wider. I moaned into his kiss as he slid his hard cock through my juices, coating himself in my wetness and rubbing over my clit. My pulse pounded in my core, my inner muscles clenching in anticipation.

When he pushed inside me, I arched against him in welcome, letting my head fall back on a helpless sound of pleasure. His wings trembled under my touch, my fingers still wrapped around the silken hardness of his sensitive arches. He trailed bites and kisses and licks over my exposed throat as he pulled out and thrust back in, as if he could barely restrain himself from devouring me quite literally.

Fire raged over my skin, sparks of lightning nipped at my fingertips, and deliciously dark power hummed all around me, while inside, a storm of pleasure was building. I'd wanted to feel him, and I'd gotten my wish—my senses were full of him, and only him. Everything else fell away, all my awareness subsumed by his powerful presence. His scent, his energy, his heat, his movements…his love, shown with every touch, every kiss, every caress.

I met him thrust for thrust, climbing higher with him while I sank ever deeper. Lust and arousal pulsed through me in quivering waves until I clawed at him with the need for release.

A hard push, a sizzling rush of his energy over my clit—and I came with a keening moan. He followed me over a moment later, bracing himself with one arm while he still held my legs spread wide with one hand under my knee, angling me just right for his final, powerful thrusts.

My eyes closed, I clutched him to me, our breaths mingling, our souls as fused as our bodies.

By the time my mind came back on track and I opened my eyes again, he was looking at me with a curious mix of smug and sheepish.

I blinked at him. "What?"

He just raised a brow and made a show of glancing around us.

At the incinerated room.

Wide-eyed, I propped myself up on my elbows and took in the smoldering damage. We were lying on what was left of the bed, all scorched and smoking, flames still licking at the last skeletal frames of the rest of the furniture.

"What—" I murmured.

He cleared his throat. "I may have lost control."

I gave him an incredulous look. "What about the sprinkler system? Shouldn't it have turned on?"

As if on—belated—cue, a sputtering shower of water started pouring down on us as the sprinklers came on with a belabored groan. My shriek of surprise veered straight into laughter, the ridiculousness of the situation too much after the roller coaster of emotions.

"Those sprinklers," I said between giggles, "are completely useless."

A grin lighting his eyes, Azazel angled his wings so the water wouldn't hit me in the face. "I think someone sabotaged the programming."

"What?" I stopped giggling. "Who would do th—" I broke off and sent him a dark look. "He wouldn't."

"What better way to demonstrate the continued necessity for his fire-extinguishing services?"

Ugh. "*Mephisto!*" I yelled at the top of my lungs.

I would absolutely kill that cat.

CHAPTER 29

Steam curled against my heated skin as I leaned back in the near-scalding water and closed my eyes.

"Open," Azazel said, and I obediently opened my mouth to accept the grape he offered me.

After the repeated incineration of our bedroom, we'd retreated to the luxurious bathroom in my old quarters to soak in the huge tub. Sunk into the floor, it was big enough to effortlessly accommodate half a dozen people, bordering more on a pool than a jacuzzi. Once, when I'd been in a particularly foul mood, I'd testily asked Azazel if it had indeed accommodated that number of demons at some point in the past. To which he, ever the smooth charmer, had reminded me he'd had this built only after I'd come to live with him and he'd relocated my quarters to be next to his.

No one but me and him had ever enjoyed this tub together, and the knowledge of it soothed some irrationally jealous part of me. Most days, I could easily deal with the sheer amount of time he'd lived well before me, and the number of lovers and experiences he'd had before I ever knew him. Sometimes, though, on days when my mind and heart were especially fragile, illogical insecurity would seep through the cracks and gnaw at my composure.

It was on those days when Azazel would handle me with unwavering gentleness, giving me the grace that I myself couldn't.

To be loved that much, through all my flaws and weaknesses…it was still so novel for me.

I now accepted the next piece of fruit he held to my lips, knowing that letting him hand-feed me soothed him far more than it did me. The past few days had scarred us both, and we needed to find reassurance in each other, in whatever form that would take.

While we were soaking in the hot water, I'd started telling him the tale of my sojourn at Lucifer's palace, filling him in on the details of what had happened, and when I came to the letter drafts I'd found, Azazel's gaze sharpened, tension hardening his muscles.

"He intends to ask for a pardon for her?"

I nodded, pushing a wet strand of hair behind my ear. "It's not clear from the drafts whether he actually finished and sent the letter, but judging from something Lilith said later, I think he hasn't sent it yet. I don't know if he completely abandoned the idea or if maybe he'll come back to it at some point…" I paused, my brow scrunching. "What I don't get is why he needs a pardon to have her healed."

Azazel tilted his head in question.

"Lilith alluded that it's in Heaven's—or more likely, God's—power to heal a broken mind. But why is it necessary for her to ascend to Heaven for that? Why not just heal her mind—I don't know—on Earth? And then send her back to Hell?"

"God doesn't come to Earth," was his simple answer.

I blinked at him in surprise. "What? Why?"

He shrugged. "No one knows. It's just a fact. God hasn't been to Earth since…" He trailed off, his expression thoughtful. "I actually can't remember an account of God having ever been on Earth. So if it's God's direct power that is necessary to heal a broken mind, the only way for Naamah to receive the required grace is to be in Heaven. I'm guessing it might also have something to do with being—and staying —near the source of all life. Maybe an instance of one-time healing wouldn't work, and she needs to be connected with the heavenly realm in order to stay healthy."

"Right," I murmured. "That makes sense."

Azazel's eyes darkened, his focus turning inward. "I'll go see her, then."

My heart skipped a beat. "Your mother?"

He nodded, the muscles in his throat moving as he swallowed. "There's no way to ascertain whether this is an ongoing plan of Lucifer's, which means I'll have to treat this as if it were." His eyes met mine again, faint lightning flashing in their stormy depths. "I can't very well ask him about it because it will, of course, raise the question of how I know. And he's shrewd enough to put two and two together, with your having just spent time in his palace, in personal spaces of his, and me suddenly asking him about whether he intends to have my mother pardoned and ascended to Heaven. This is undoubtedly something that few are privy to, given the sensitive nature of this information." His fingers drummed on the edge of the tub. "And I'd rather he not find out that you snooped and learned of this. Lilith's favor grants you some measure of protection, but we shouldn't push it. The less he takes negative notice of you, the better."

"I wholeheartedly agree," I murmured.

"So I'll have to assume that this pardon plan is still ongoing...and that my mother could be ascending to Heaven at any point, should Gabriel grant Lucifer's request." He took a deep breath and released it slowly. "Which means I might not have much time left to go visit her at all."

My heart ached on his behalf. I knew all too well what that felt like. Once Naamah ascended to Heaven, she'd be far out of Azazel's reach, much like my own mother would be forever lost to me when she died. There was a chance, of course, that Naamah might be able to visit Earth, and that maybe, just maybe, she'd be able to meet with Azazel and Azmodea once she was an angel and doing better mentally, but it might just as well go the other way. Heaven might restrict her movements and keep her from going to Earth, in which case, Azazel would truly never see her again.

I grasped his hand and squeezed it. "You should visit her as soon as possible."

He nodded, his face set in hard lines.

"Speaking of a visit..." I began, walking my fingers up his arm. "I may have agreed to accompany Lilith to Earth." Ducking my head, I bit my lip and squinted at him.

It was only after I'd arranged the meeting with Lilith that it occurred to me that maybe I should have consulted Azazel beforehand. It wasn't that I felt like he should make decisions for me, but he inarguably had more experience with politics and dealing with the subtleties of relationships in Hell, and he might have some insight or deeper knowledge that would be useful when it came to forging connections.

He tilted his head and regarded me for a long moment. "She wants you to visit Earth with her?"

"Yeah, well, it was kind of me who made the suggestion, because one of her handmaidens or whatever said that it would be good for Lilith, and I agree—she seems to be... happy whenever we talk and I tell her stories of Earth, and even Lilith herself said that apparently I woke her up from a long slumber and helped her jump out of the pot—"

Azazel looked distinctly confused.

"You know, the pot? With the boiling water? Never mind. Anyways, Lilith hasn't been to Earth in a super long time because she felt like it wasn't fair that she could go and Lucifer couldn't—at least, that's what she told me the one time—but we also think it might be because she didn't have a connection to Earth anymore and felt so out of touch, but then when she saw me, all of her interest in humans and Earth flared back to life, and so we thought with me as her guide, she'd be better able to enjoy a visit to Earth and—"

He covered my mouth with his hand, effectively interrupting my word vomit. "Zoe," he said, the hint of a smile playing about his lips, "it's fine."

I mumbled something against his palm, and he removed it from my mouth.

"No, I'm not mad," he answered my question. "In fact, I think this is a good thing."

"You do?"

"It's a smart, strategical move."

Well, butter my butt and call me a biscuit. I hadn't seen that one coming.

At my undoubtedly astonished expression, he elaborated, "You've just forged what amounts to an alliance with Lilith, the second most powerful being in Hell, and incidentally, the only one able to rein in Lucifer. You said she considers you a friend and has officially given you her favor and even rebuked Lucifer in front of witnesses for putting you in harm's way. On a smaller scale, she just did for you what Lucifer did for her when he established his rule—her power protects you." His smile was a tiny bit wicked. "And by extension, also me."

I raised my brows. "Oh?"

"From what you say, Lilith has made it clear that she values you and wants to see you unharmed...and happy. If Lucifer were to act against me politically, and if I lost my rank and status as a result, you would suffer as well because your standing is tied to mine. With a favor as strong as Lilith has given you, anyone who'd harm you—even by extension —would incur Lilith's wrath and displeasure, and that's something Lucifer especially will try to avoid."

My mouth hung open. I hadn't realized the full implications of all that had occurred...which was why Azazel's insight was so crucial.

"It's not entirely bulletproof," he added, giving me a stern look. "Having Lilith's favor doesn't mean you can strut around feeling invincible and act without regard for consequences. It's still prudent to stay off Lucifer's radar as much as possible."

I gave him a military salute. "Yes, sir."

"Save that type of address for later." His eyes held the slyest glint. "Your continued association with Lilith will be good, though. The fact that you're doing something nice for her, like being her guide on Earth, will strengthen the bond you have and thereby your standing. So, yes, I approve of that visit, and I'll come along as your escort."

"My...*escort*, hm?" I waggled my brows at him.

He splashed me with water for my efforts, and I giggle-shrieked and ducked. For the span of a few precious, light-weight moments, everything dissolved into a hilarious, ridiculous water fight that made my heart sigh with happiness.

"While you were away," Azazel said after we'd eventually called a truce and were snacking on fruit and candies again, "I seized another territory."

I drew up short. "Oh?"

"One of Inachiel's allies took umbrage at how I dealt with Inachiel." He popped a grape into his mouth and chewed. "So I demonstrated just how unwilling I am to listen to complaints from those who'd doubt my right to defend what is mine."

The beginnings of a shiver stole over my skin despite the heat of the bath.

"It won't be long now," he went on, offering me a piece of watermelon, "until I can claim the title of seraph."

I gave him a wan smile and accepted the watermelon. While I chewed, my mind scrambled to make sense of the sudden spike of dread I felt, the resurgence of the fear I'd felt all those weeks ago, triggered by the war interlude with Inachiel. Azazel and I had talked about it, but it hadn't felt resolved—deep down, I'd known there was something I couldn't see yet, couldn't name yet, and it lay at the heart of my fear.

Now, here in the bath, after my stay at Lucifer's and my conversations with Lilith, the realization of what it was rooted in crept up on me like some blood-soaked mist.

Noticing my no doubt stricken expression, Azazel grew still, his gaze sharpening. "What is it?"

I blinked and shook my head, trying to form into words what was haunting me. "Remember how you thought I was afraid of you? After the whole Inachiel wing massacre?"

He nodded, his silent attention searing me with its focus.

"I told you that I don't fear you," I said quietly, haltingly, navigating along my newfound clarity, "and it's true." I met his gaze, and every cell in my body felt electrified by the intensity of the contact. "But I fear *for* you."

His brows drew together.

"I fear for *us*." I licked my lips, my mouth suddenly dry.

"I didn't realize it earlier, but seeing Lucifer, watching him and Lilith...and hearing her talk about him..." I swallowed hard. "She said he was different when they first met. Not as cruel, not as callous. But when he brought Lilith to Hell and had to establish his rule and her rank as equal to his, the ruthlessness necessary to enforce her status and bring all the other demons to heel... Lilith said he had to kill parts of himself to achieve that." My voice dropped to a whisper at the last words, my lips trembling. "The softer, more vulnerable parts of him."

Azazel regarded me with narrowed eyes. "Go on," he said quietly.

"She also said that she'd grown numb over the millennia. To the point she barely remembered who she once was. What it felt like to be human, to have a human heart." I pressed my lips together, tight bands snapping around my chest, holding all that corrosive fear inside, to fester and spoil. "What if that...what if that is our future?"

"That is what you fear?" he asked softly. "That I will turn into Lucifer? That you'll grow numb like Lilith?"

I looked at him with helpless apprehension. "You said you'd fight your way to the top. That you'd leave a bloody trail of bodies on your quest to become powerful enough to make everyone respect my rank the way they respect Lilith's. That sounds an awful lot like what Lucifer did—what he had to do—in order to protect her by virtue of his power. He wanted to shield her from the cruelty of his brethren, but to do that, he had to become the cruelest of them all." I took a deep breath of the humid air. "I know you seek to rise in rank and power because you want to make sure I'm respected. But at what cost? What if the price for that will be the parts of you I fell in love with? Your spirit, your conscience, that core of kindness in you? What if I'll lose you, not to death, but to the slow erosion of all that is good in you?"

For an achingly long moment, he held my gaze, indefinable storms raging in his eyes. "Losing those parts," he finally said, his voice somber, "would be considered an advantage here in Hell."

A ping of hurt zapped my chest.

"But," he continued, "I find...that is one advantage I do not want to use. I would rather keep those parts of me...for the sake of keeping you."

I drew in a shuddering breath.

Slowly, he moved closer, the water sloshing around him, until he was right in front of me, and framed my face with his hands, his eyes glowing with fire and lightning. "There is no guarantee for anything in life," he spoke into the heated space between us. "No prediction of the future. But know this." He gently brushed his lips over mine. "I promise to fight to keep that side of me alive. Not only for your sake but also for my own. Because your love brings those parts of me to the fore...and I have never liked myself better than when I am with you."

I closed my eyes and slung my arms around his neck, love and fear beating in tandem with the pounding of my heart.

"And I won't allow you to become numb," he murmured at my ear. "Because it would smother all that makes you *you*. We'll keep each other in check, all right? Our fate is not bound to those who came before us. We can forge our own path. Together."

I nodded, my breath hot against the curve of his neck.

I wanted so desperately to believe it.

CHAPTER 30

Azazel went to see his mother the next day.

While he hinted that he'd appreciate having me there, we both agreed it was best for me to stay home, lest my presence provoke Lucifer. We didn't know whether Lucifer would actually be there during the visit, but we didn't want to chance it. The whole situation was charged enough as it was.

Daevi would accompany Azazel and Azmodea—whom Azazel had told about Lucifer's pardon plans, swearing her to secrecy—to lend the power necessary to enforce Azazel and Azmodea's visiting rights.

I kissed him goodbye and watched him fly out into the lightning-riven sky, regret heavy in my heart. I wanted nothing more than to be there for him during what had to be one of the most emotional and daunting moments of his life. I could only hope that everything would go smoothly, that he'd be able to reconnect with a part of himself he'd lost millennia ago.

And I wished for Naamah to be able to meet her children

with a peaceful mind, far from the dark torments she'd been struggling with.

With a sigh, I turned away from the window and toward the three-headed canine that had not left my side since I brought her back to our quarters sometime during the night. Azazel had told me Vengeance had been inconsolable while I was away, whining and howling incessantly. Nothing he'd tried would pacify her. She'd pace the rooms, scratching at doors, sniffing all the spots where I'd left my scent, all the while wailing at the top of her lungs.

It had gotten to the point where Azazel had been forced to put her back into the kennels, hoping that maybe her old handler, Hael, could work his magic on her.

Hael, for his part, had professed his expletive-spiked thanks when I came to pick her up from the kennels. Apparently, not even the hellhound expert of Azazel's estate had been able to soothe Vengeance in my absence. Her baleful howling had only stopped when I'd gotten close enough for her to sense me, and then there'd been no holding her back. She'd barreled right through the walls of her enclosure—the ones thick and massive enough to put a stop to a full-grown male elephant.

As Vengeance had virtually run me over in her enthusiasm to get to me, Hael had looked on with awe and a gleam of excitement in his eyes.

"You have to breed her," he'd said.

"Um, no, thanks?" I'd wrinkled my nose and tried my best to keep three lolling tongues from bathing my face in dog saliva. "I'm not into bestiality. Also, we're both female, and I hate to break it to you, but that's not how it works." I'd paused and wiped dog spit from my face, my brow scrunched in thought. "Although it *did* work in *Jurassic Park*. But only because the scientists were dumb enough to add the DNA of hermaphroditic species to the dinos, which made some of the females switch genders to male, which then led to the unplanned reproduction of the dinosaurs on those abandoned islands, but that's not gonna be the case here, right? I mean, I don't have hermaphroditic DNA—do hellhounds? 'Cause that might cause problems, I'm telling you. Better spay and neuter the ones you don't want to breed." I'd pointed at him with my finger.

Hael had closed his eyes and pinched the bridge of his nose. Somehow, I didn't think he appreciated my oral dissertation on reproductive issues among prehistoric reptiles in an iconic series of movies. Pfft, what a philistine.

"Vengeance," Hael had said with the long-suffering look of a beleaguered saint, "is the most powerful hellhound specimen I've come across in a long time. It would be a waste not to pass her genetics on to a new generation of hellhounds. So with your permission, when she is old enough, I would like to pair her with a promising male from a talented line."

I'd squinted at him, my breathing a bit labored since Vengeance currently sat on me, bracing part of her several hundred pounds of weight on her front paws. "Is overpopulation a problem here in Hell? I'd hate to contribute to an issue like that with breeding my dog."

Hael had shaken his head. "The hellhounds that roam the wild live and die according to the laws of nature, much like wolves on Earth. Birth numbers fluctuate depending on the resources available, and only as many hounds make it to adulthood as there is food to sustain them. The wild population is different from the hounds we keep here. We only breed as many as we can care for."

"Okay," I'd wheezed. "That sounds reasonable. If Venny wants some doggie action, she'll get some."

His expression sour, Hael had bowed and turned away, muttering, "Venny" under his breath.

After watching Azazel leave to meet with his mom, I took Vengeance on a grand tour of the grounds, catching up on playing with her. She was indefatigable. If only I could bottle that energy up and chug it down to get a boost myself, it'd be so much easier to get out of bed in the mornings.

I'd just returned to our quarters with a happily panting Vengeance in tow when I heard the door to the balcony from our bedroom—diligently restored by merihem after the "fire-splosion" from last night—open, and a moment later, I sensed Azazel's power in the other room.

He was home already? I checked one of the clocks in the living room. It had only been a little while since he'd left, and given the distance to Lucifer's palace, that meant he couldn't have spent much time there. With his mother.

My heart sinking, I rushed over into the bedroom, where Azazel sat in an armchair, his elbows on his knees, hands clasped, his head hanging. His energy touched me, a note of such devastated sadness in it that I physically cringed on his behalf.

"What happened?" I whispered, sinking to my knees in front of him and brushing some hair out of his face.

He took a heavy breath, his shoulders heaving with the movement. "It was a disaster." His voice was so, so rough. "When we walked into her rooms, and she saw us, she was lucid. I thought maybe it would go well. She recognized us even without introductions. Said she'd always know us, even if we weren't the children anymore that she last saw us as. Azmodea—she cried. She was so happy. But then…"

I gently stroked his hair, waiting for him to find the words.

"It was as if someone flipped a switch in her. She

changed from one moment to the next. Something…something in her eyes broke. She curled in on herself, sank to the floor, and started rocking. We tried to soothe her, but it only made it worse. She screamed and wouldn't stop. Every time we came close, every time she looked at us, she broke down even more. When she began tearing at her head—"

Oh, God.

"Daevi called for Lucifer. He was just outside the door, waiting. He went straight for Naamah and put her under."

"He—he knocked her out mentally?"

Azazel nodded.

"I thought you guys couldn't do that to each other."

He'd once explained that mind control wasn't really feasible among demons because their natural shields were just so strong.

"Lucifer can," was Azazel's simple answer now. "Apparently, that's how he's been helping Naamah through her episodes. Nothing else would work. No one else can do it but him. And he—" He wrung his hands, and a muscle ticked in his jaw. "He rounded on us when he'd made sure Naamah was safe. He was seething. Said this was why we weren't allowed to see her. Why he'd kept us apart. Something about seeing us…triggers her."

His words sounded like he had to press each of them through a grinder, hurting himself in the process. Tears pricking my eyes, I helplessly caressed his face.

"Daevi later explained that, in the beginning, right after her decline started in the wake of our father's leaving and after Daevi had taken us in, they were still trying to let us see her. I barely remember that part." He shrugged, his expression bleak. "But according to Daevi, Naamah could not get through a visit with us without having an episode. Alone or with others, she'd be able to go long stretches of time without an incident, but when she'd see us...she'd break."

His voice broke on that last word, and my heart along with it.

"So Lucifer decided it was best we shouldn't visit her anymore," he continued after a moment. "We weren't really old enough to understand. We kept asking for her."

My entire soul hurt imagining little Azazel and Azmodea, so desperately wishing for their mom.

"Daevi said...that it was easier to tell us Naamah had died. It stopped the questions."

Hot tears tracked down my cheeks. "It wasn't fair to you."

"No, it wasn't." He rubbed both hands over his face. "None of this is."

I threw my arms around him and pulled him close. "I'm so, so sorry."

He let me hold him for a long, long moment, in shared silence and pain. I almost didn't hear him when he eventually said, in a voice equal parts quiet and forlorn, "We will not go see her again."

And it broke my heart all over.

CHAPTER 31

The day of my visit to Earth with Lilith had arrived. Somehow, time had just flown by the past week. We'd been busy with regular day-to-day activities, another cringeworthy demon get-together with an undaunted ally of Azazel's somewhere in the middle, and before I could think much about it, it was time to fly over to Lucifer's palace.

Apparently, the hellgate we would use was right on the palace grounds, and I experienced a hot-blooded moment of envy that the demons living in Lucifer's estate could just easily stroll out into New York whenever they felt like it. Azazel's own hellgate close to his mansion led to Prague, which was super cool, too, but...it wasn't New York.

We met Lilith and her retinue in the courtyard around the hellgate. Azazel had instructed me to do the whole levitat-ing-out-of-my-body thing at home in his mansion, because he absolutely didn't want to leave my physical form behind in Lucifer's palace, no matter how much Lilith's favor might protect me. I couldn't argue with that, so we'd left my body in our quarters, being guarded by a vigilant Vengeance.

Now I stood in the torch-lit courtyard in my ghostly form, watching Lilith approach, also in her spirit form.

It was a weird kind of kinship.

Her retinue today comprised Destatur, Enaia, and two other demons I hadn't seen before, all armed, same as Azazel. Would she take all of them to Earth as her escorts? Wasn't that a bit of an overkill?

"Zoe," Lilith said with a smile, taking both of my hands in hers. Since we were both spirits, we could touch and feel each other—and no, my mind still couldn't process how exactly that worked. "How lovely to see you again. I must admit, I have not been this excited in a long time."

I couldn't help smiling at her genuine joy, her childlike anticipation of our trip. It radiated from her in warm waves, transforming her into a younger version of herself.

"Shall we?" she asked.

I nodded, and she let go of my hands and stepped up to Enaia, and the blonde demon gracefully lifted her into her arms. Destatur turned to the hellgate, an arch of dark stone inlaid with jewels that glistened in the light of the torches. She activated it with a series of glyphs drawn in the air, much like I'd seen Azazel do plenty of times when we went to Earth.

The hellgate turned on with a shimmer, the space between the arches on either side glowing faintly.

"I will scout ahead, my lady." Destatur inclined her head and then stepped through the portal.

A minute later, she came back and nodded at Enaia before once again moving through the hellgate to Earth. Enaia went in after her, carrying Lilith. The two other demons in her entourage followed, after which Azazel scooped me up and stepped through the portal as well.

The shimmer of the hellgate morphed to darkness, and

pressure pushed against me from all sides. Utter silence reigned, and then Azazel walked out into the light once more.

I gasped as he set me down on the sidewalk in front of a large stone staircase leading up to a building in neoclassical Greek style, with three huge archways flanked by Corinthian columns.

"Your hellgate," I said to an equally stunned Lilith next to me, "is right in front of the New York Public Library?"

My hot-blooded envy from earlier rushed back in full force.

"I didn't know," Lilith murmured. "It looks impressive."

"You should see the reading room inside."

A smile spread over her face like dawn's first light in winter. "I will."

Her eyes tracked from the library to the other buildings looming over us from the surrounding streets, and she had to crane her neck to take it all in. It was a splendid sunny day, New York showing herself from her best side. Sunlight glinted off the windows of the tall buildings standing sentinel on all sides, and the sound of cars honking and voices raised in arguments filled the air. Pedestrians hurried along on the sidewalks, precariously crossing the street between vehicles. The throng of people moving down on our sidewalk split around our group as if evading a clear obstacle, but without casting so much as a glance at us.

We truly were invisible to the humans bustling to and fro. But they didn't walk into or through us, instead simply skirting around the spot where we stood without even batting an eye.

"One thing," I said to Lilith as my gaze fell on an overflowing trash can nearby, "that's an advantage about visiting New York as a ghost is that you can't smell anything."

She wrinkled her nose as she followed my gaze. "I imagine it's an olfactory assault."

"It's worst in the heat of summer. Believe me, you don't want to know what baked trash smells like. Or human body odor that has been marinating in the same clothes without a shower for three days."

Lilith's face was the closest to a grimace I'd ever seen.

Okay, I wasn't really selling the human experience here. *Gotta do better.*

"But look," I hastened to say. "This here is Fifth Avenue, one of the most famous streets in New York, and it runs all the way to Central Park, which we'll have to visit, too. It's a huge park right there in the city, and when you're in the middle of it, you wouldn't believe you're in one of the biggest cities of the world, because it's so quiet and seems like another realm. And just down that way is Times Square, with these enormous billboard screens, but the best time to go there is at night when it's all lit up. And around the corner is Grand Central Station, which is, like, featured in *so* many movies and shows, partly because it's so damn pretty. And if we go down that way, we'll get to the Empire State Building, which has been around, like, forever, and you'll have an amazing view of the city from the top, although I guess for us it's not as crucial to be on top of a high building to get that view—I mean, we could just have our demons fly us around…"

Lilith hung on my every word as I morphed into a passionate amateur tour guide and underscored my explanations with lots of hand waving and arm movements, to the point that I resembled someone trying to tell the story of New York in interpretive dance. She studied the people rushing around us with such intense focus and fascination, as if she tried to memorize it all in order to write a paper on it later.

Her face was alight with joy, her lips parted on a smile, such life in her eyes. It truly did her good, being here. Seeing human life in all its facets. Feeling the vibrancy of modern civilization.

"All right," I concluded my preliminary exposition on nearby New York sights, "which one would you like to check out first?"

"Hm." Lilith tilted her head. "Let us walk down this avenue. I would gaze upon the sights along the way."

"Okay-dokay."

I grinned and was about to turn to lead the way when a whisper of power disturbed the air. Not demon power—but very, *very* similar.

Next to me, Azazel tensed in the same moment that a shadow flashed—right before a blade slashed through the neck of one of the demons in Lilith's entourage. His head rolled from his body, and the next second, he burst into sparks that dissolved on the breeze.

Behind him stood a specter of light, gleaming, silver-colored armor speckled with blood, red-smeared sword still raised from the killing strike, wings extended behind him.

White wings, pure as snow.

An *angel*.

What the ever-loving f—

Azazel pushed me behind him, and the remaining demons escorting Lilith crowded around her, blocking the angel's next strike.

Wings blotted out the sun for a second as more angels descended from somewhere high up, slamming down onto the sidewalk in a rustle of white feathers and clinking weapons.

Quick as lightning, the angels joined their vanguard and engaged our group, their numbers about the same as ours. Sunlight glinted off their blades and the polished, silver-colored metal of their armor, the air brimming with their power, as they advanced with single-minded focus. They slashed and hacked and swung their way toward Lilith.

Azazel spun and blocked an angel launching herself in our direction, and I half ducked behind one of the two big stone lions guarding the steps to the library, trying to get out of sight. I didn't have a weapon, but even if I did—this was a fight I could never win.

While Azazel kept holding off the angel, my eyes flicked to Lilith's group. They were fighting with both physical weapons and their magic, lashing out at each other with blows of power, shadows and flame against lightning and silver fire. Unperturbed by the supernatural battle raging in their midst, the humans in the area kept going on about their day, simply giving the battleground a wide berth without seeming to wonder why.

One of the demons dispatched one of the angels, decapitating him with a powerful strike, and the angel's body burst into sparks of light, which then dissolved in the air. But the demon didn't see the sword coming for his unguarded back. He jerked and fell to his knees, skewered by the angel attacker's blade. The angel pulled his sword out and then swung it at the demon's neck, severing his head. A moment later, the demon's body dissolved into particles of light that got swept away on a breeze, just like the angel's body had done moments earlier.

That left only Destatur and Enaia to defend Lilith—against three angels. Lilith was faintly glowing with some power of her own, but her face was terror-stricken, her ghostly body seemingly paralyzed with fear.

Right at that moment, Azazel rushed toward the group, having apparently defeated the angel he'd been battling with. One of the angels advancing on Lilith's entourage saw him coming and split from the group to engage him. Their swords clanged as they met in the air, both using their wings to elevate the fight to another level—quite literally.

Darkness and light clashed in the air, the sky flickering with powers beyond human capacity or notice.

But Azazel's intervention had evened the numbers a bit —only two angels were directly threatening Lilith now. She had a chance.

The largest of the angels, a male with shoulders as wide as Fifth Avenue, jumped forward, his sword raised high, his white wings flaring behind him...but instead of closing ranks to block him, both Destatur and Enaia stepped aside at the last moment, moving out of the way.

Too fast for my eyes to track, the angel's sword came down on Lilith, who stood frozen in shock. Everything hushed, the world standing still as the blade sliced clean through her neck, cutting her head off her body.

Her ghost form behaved just like a physical body would. Her faintly translucent skin split, and muscles and tendons separated as if she weren't made of spirit but of flesh and bone. The blade was able to touch her—like someone or something from Hell.

But that would mean...

My racing thoughts stumbled over one another as I watched in horror, in uncomprehending shock, how Lilith's head didn't roll from her ghostly body, but instead burst into a shower of light sparks that dissolved on the breeze, just like the rest of her spirit body.

She was gone.

Just like that.

One moment she stood there, and the next there was no trace of her left.

I watched it all as if through some weird lens, like I was seeing a movie. I didn't feel like I was really present. There was no way to make sense of it all.

Destatur nodded at Enaia, who took off toward the spot where the hellgate had spat us out earlier.

When one of the angels made as if to pursue her, Destatur barked, "No! She needs to tell him. How else is he supposed to know?"

The leader of the group, the one who'd killed Lilith, jerked his head at the angel who'd wanted to run after Enaia. "She's right. Stand down."

Enaia activated the hellgate and disappeared inside.

The angel leader swung his gaze to his angel comrade, and one side of his mouth quirked up. "But if you want to spill some more demon blood, feel free to assist me in killing *her*." He indicated Destatur with a nod.

"What?" Destatur took a step back, her eyes furious. "That wasn't part of the deal."

"The deal," the angel in charge drawled, "was for you to deliver us Lilith and allow us to kill her. We were to leave one of you alive in order to tell Lucifer, so he'd know she was killed by angels. No one said anything about leaving more than one demon alive. You"—he pointed his sword at her—"are bloody scum and should be wiped off the face of the earth and all the other realms."

"You will regret this." Destatur bared her teeth and raised her sword.

"You pronounced *enjoy* wrong," the angel shot back and lunged at her.

The other remaining angel launched herself at Destatur as well, rendering the fight profoundly unfair. With a yell of

399

rage, Destatur engaged them, spinning and twisting while she blocked their strikes. Impressively, she managed to take one of them down with a quick swing of her sword that decapitated the angel—the method of choice for killing either an angel or demon, apparently.

Now it was only Destatur against the angel leader, Lilith's murderer. And the unholy glint in his eye spoke to how confident he was that he'd best her, too. Destatur was wounded, bleeding from several injuries that obviously didn't heal well, while the angel leader seemed largely unimpaired.

He advanced on her with a mighty launch, pushing her back precariously—but he didn't see what I saw. Didn't notice how Azazel had taken out the angel with whom he'd been fighting, and how he now sped through the air on silent wings, sword raised for the kill.

The angel leader turned his head at the very last second. His eyes widened, his arm jerking back as if to ward off the new attack. But he never got the chance. Azazel's sword slashed through his neck with cobra-like speed, and then the angel's severed head and body dissolved in that sparkly way.

Azazel slammed to the ground next to Destatur, who turned to him.

"Thank you for that," she said with a smile—and rammed her sword into his chest.

"No!" I yelled and ran out from my hiding place behind the stone lion, stumbling over my ghostly feet in the process.

Azazel fell to his knees with a grunt, one hand spasming around his own sword while the other weakly groped for the handle of the blade sticking out of his chest. His movements were sluggish, though, and then halted altogether as he simply keeled over and crumpled onto his side.

"Splendid," Destatur murmured and pulled her sword out of his chest. "Makes it all the easier to take your head."

"No!" I screamed again and slid between her and him.

I didn't know what I was trying to do. I couldn't possibly hope to defend him.

But I wasn't thinking clearly. In fact, my brain wasn't quite there, half my attention focused on the bleeding body of the man I loved lying on the ground behind me, the other fastened on the traitorous demon in front of me.

The one who'd *engineered Lilith's murder*.

The heat of tears pricked my ghostly eyes. I glared at Destatur, who regarded me with something akin to amusement.

"Has your little human mind given up, dearie? Is this all too much for you? Never to worry. I'll relieve you of your suffering in a minute." Her smile was bloody. "Can't leave any witnesses, after all."

My thoughts whirled, scrambling to find a way out. Maybe I could stall her? She'd incapacitated Azazel with a blade to his heart, but demons woke up from that after a few minutes. If I could get her to talk, get her distracted, maybe, just maybe, it would be enough time for Azazel to come to and fight her. Perhaps I could coax her into a villain monologue? Was she arrogant and vainglorious enough to want to boast about her clever machinations in front of a nearly defeated enemy?

It was worth a try.

"Why?" I choked out, pinning Destatur with a hot glare. "You were her friend. She *trusted* you."

"Friend." Destatur sneered. "Lilith didn't have friends. She was far too *special* for that. Special and a fucking affliction for the whole of Hell." She spat to the side. "If it weren't for her, we would have won."

The gears in my mind turned in overwhelmed hyper-drive. "The war against Heaven?"

"Of course." Her eyes glittered hard. "If not for her, he would never have taken that deal. He'd have taken *Heaven*." She bared her teeth.

Oh, goody. She'd indeed fully launched her self-aggrandizing justifications for her nefarious actions.

"But through her," she continued, "he was shackled to Hell, keeping all of us on a leash when we should be the ones ruling Earth. But no more." She tapped her sword against her thigh, a self-satisfied smirk sitting upon her lips. "Any minute now, he'll hear the news that Lilith was killed by angels. Not by rogue demons—by agents of *Heaven*. His raging fury will be so swift, so mighty, he will snap the tethers that kept him in check and unleash the wrath of Hell onto Earth. As he should have done millennia ago. With Lilith gone, the deal with Heaven is null and void. He will be justified in his vengeance and usher in the last stand that will decide the fate of this world."

The apocalypse. Good lord, Destatur and her ilk wanted to start the *apocalypse*.

"But...but why did the angels help you?" I couldn't make sense of that. They'd been at each other's throats as much as they'd cooperated.

Destatur sniffed, a haughty sound that underscored her supercilious expression. "There are those on both sides who are not content with the status quo. Not all angels support the truce. Our plans for the ultimate outcome of Armageddon might differ, but it just so happens that our understanding of the means necessary to cancel the truce and initiate the end aligns. The angels who oppose the truce are convinced that they'll win when the war starts again." Her lips twisted in a smirk. "The more fool them."

I'd crouched down at some point, seemingly to lean on Azazel's prone body, when in reality, I kept checking whether he showed signs of waking.

He didn't.

And time was running out.

Destatur glanced at the spot where Enaia had disappeared through the hellgate, then back at me. "Enough chitchat, now." She swung her sword in a lazy circle at her side. "He'll be here soon, and you two need to be gone by then. Can't very well blame the whole thing on you if you're still alive to refute my claim, can I?"

"What? That's ridiculous. Why would anyone believe *we* had anything to do with this?"

"Oh, I don't know." Destatur tapped a finger against her mouth. "Maybe because you've befriended Lilith, getting her to trust you over the course of many, many months, to where you could convince her to do something she hasn't done in centuries—come to Earth. You know, incidentally, the only place where she could feasibly be killed by angels, which makes for the necessary motivation on Lucifer's part to consider the deal invalid and subsequently unleash Hell on Earth. Has your dear husband not been angling for more power for a while? Isn't there talk of him shooting up the ranks like a demon on a mission? And are he and Lucifer not alienated to the point they're trying to hurt each other however possible?" She tilted her head and regarded me with smug eyes. "Killing Lilith hurts Lucifer more than anything. And destroying the truce and then expanding Hell's dominion over all of Earth and Heaven opens up infinite possibilities of acquiring more power and maybe, ultimately, challenging Lucifer himself."

My mouth hung open. Holy shit.

"As you can see," Destatur purred, "I've given this extensive thought. By plausibly pinning the blame on you, I'll deflect it from myself, and when everything calms down and Lucifer is not completely out of his mind with raging grief anymore, he will not look at me for revenge. The culprits—that's you—will already be dead."

Fuck. Out of all the ways I'd imagined my life in Hell cut short, I would never have seen this one coming.

Destatur raised her sword, determination etched into her features. "Say goodbye to your pathetic existence."

Without taking my eyes off her, I groped for Azazel's sword behind me, my heart racing a mile a minute. I had to do something, anything. He still wasn't waking up. He couldn't help me. It was just me...and I was woefully incapable.

Just when my fingers touched the sword handle, Destatur spun and delivered a kick right to my face. The impact whirled me around and made me crash to the ground next to Azazel. Holyshitfuckdammit. Pain exploded in my head, my spirit body responding to Destatur's attack just like my physical body would. I couldn't see, my vision going blurry, pain throbbing in my jaw and nose where her foot had caught me.

"Now that you're so beautifully aligned," Destatur said, "how about I try to decapitate both of you at once?"

No! I wanted to scream, but the pain in my jaw wouldn't let me. Blindly, I reached out for Azazel. My fingers touched his fighting leathers, and I threw myself over him, clinging to him in what would be the final moments of our lives, despair lancing my heart.

We should have had eternity together. Our love should have lasted throughout the ages.

In those milliseconds while Destatur swung, I thought of how Azazel had only just found me, had only just begun to live his life with the person who made him happy beyond anything else. How he'd said I brought out the best parts of him. That with me by his side, he could defy the jaws of time and not fall prey to Hell's slow erosion of all that was good.

I thought of my own heart, so bruised and battered and slow to believe there was someone who'd love me so truly, so deeply, that they'd accept my flaws and put me first. I'd never get a chance to really grow into that belief now, and I'd never get to see where it might take me, take us.

I thought of Lilith, who'd just started to rediscover herself, who'd woken from millennia of numbness, only to be stabbed in the back by those she trusted, her light now forever extinguished.

Teeth-gritting, sorrow-soaked rage as I'd never known it rushed through me.

Something deep within me pulled tight with glowing force. A storm in the making, a reckoning to come.

The last sound I heard was the whirring of a blade through the air—before everything exploded in light so bright it blinded me.

CHAPTER 32

Destatur's strike never landed.

My pulse pounding in a ghostly echo of my real heartbeat, I lay there, draped over Azazel with panic tearing at my mind, and waited for the killing blow that didn't come.

Instead, I heard the clanking sound of metal hitting stone, like a sword clattering to the ground. Followed by a heavy thud, like a body collapsing.

Blinking away the blurriness over my vision, I lifted my aching head and looked behind me to Destatur.

To see her sprawled on the ground, spasming from some sort of seizure. Faint light glowed over her body— the same faint light that illuminated my own skin. Mouth agape, I glanced down at myself, at the shimmer of power coating me, having flowed from some inner source.

Lilith.

I could taste her essence, her energy, stored in that kernel of herself she'd gifted to me, now fused with my soul. All this time, I'd thought it useless as a power to be directly wielded. But now…now it had come to my aid, protecting me when I'd needed it most.

My gaze fell on the spot where Lilith had been killed, and my chest drew tight. Why hadn't it protected *her*?

Destatur twitched, and my eyes flicked back to her. I could dwell on the whys and the hows later. First, I needed to make sure we were safe. Who knew how long Destatur would remain stunned?

I was almost in a weird, dreamlike state as I dragged myself over to Destatur, grabbed her sword, raised it—and then brought it down on her neck. Blood sprayed my face and my hands and arms, and I blinked. Shit. I hadn't managed to completely sever her neck. It gaped about halfway open, tendons and muscles exposed, blood spurting from the large wound.

Destatur twitched and gurgled.

I realized how disassociated I was when instead of thinking, *Oh, God, she's still alive; I'm going to throw up*, my only thought was that I needed to do better because obviously that was not how one should behead a person. My brain, storage to random tidbits of knowledge, helpfully supplied me with the information that executioners of eons past had to train hard in order to be able to cleanly cut someone's head off their body and how it was seen as a disgrace to their profession if they couldn't manage it in one strike.

I mentally apologized to all executioners who had gone before me.

It was a lot fucking harder to decapitate someone than it looked.

After hacking unsuccessfully at Destatur's neck, trying to sever the last of the tendons and muscles, I simply rolled her over onto her front. This way, the still-attached part of her neck was on top, and it'd be easier for me to cut through it.

Such clinical thoughts. No emotion behind them.

There was no nausea, no scruples, no doubts or hesitation, only cold, detached understanding of what needed to be done.

Later, I would look back at this moment and shiver at the way my mind had completely disabled my feelings in order to protect my sanity.

Right now, though, I had a demon to behead.

I finally managed it, and Destatur burst into sparks of light, leaving only her clothes behind, like the other demons and angels who'd been killed. I marveled at the beauty of this kind of death. To dissolve into light and be swept away. No decaying body, no bones left behind.

With a start, I snapped out of my reverie and scrambled back to Azazel. He lay still, his usually dark tan holding a slightly gray pallor, the blood of his wounds fresh and glistening. He should have long woken by now. I remembered the times I'd seen other demons incapacitated by a blade to the heart—it'd normally taken only a few minutes for them to regain consciousness.

But Azazel was still out, and his wounds weren't closing.

Panic crept back in. My hands trembled. What was I supposed to do? How could I help him?

Maybe he wasn't healing because we were on Earth? I thought back to how he'd told me that demons drew their energy directly from Hell itself. What if he needed to go back to regain his strength?

I snapped my head up and stared at the spot where the hellgate was located, invisible until someone drew the correct sigils and activated it. Determination steeling my spirit muscles, I grabbed Azazel by his ankles, my back to the hellgate a few yards away, and pulled.

Oh, God, he was heavy. I barely managed to drag him an

inch before I had to take a break. The fact that his wings were still fully extended didn't make it easier to move him.

How could he be so heavy when he was, right now, invisible to the human world? How the fuck did that even work? And why was I getting a muscle cramp when I didn't even have a physical body at this moment, strictly speaking?

I turned around so I faced the hellgate and repositioned my grasp on his ankles. With a drawn-out grunt, I pulled and pulled and pulled, moving him inch by slow inch toward the portal.

"I never thought *I* would be the one to be dragged to Hell," Azazel drawled, his voice as raw as if caressed with a cheese grater.

I froze, dropped his legs, and spun around.

"Azazel!" I shouted and threw myself at him.

He winced and grunted when I landed right on top of him, but his arms wound around me, pressing me close as I buried my face in his neck. I breathed him in, and everything righted itself. My heart, so close to breaking, so full of concern for him, softened at the feel of him underneath me, awake and moving. *Alive.*

"I was so worried," I whispered as I peppered his face with kisses. "Are you okay?"

"Better now with you on top of me."

I drew back and gave him a gentle slap on his shoulder for that inappropriately funny remark. "Be serious," I said, heat pricking behind my eyes again. "You got skewered by a sword. And Li—" I paused to stave off the breaking of my voice. "Lilith is dead. We need to get back to Hell before Lucifer shows up."

Azazel's brows drew together, and he sat up with a wince. "What happened? The last thing I remember is

Destatur stabbing me, but I don't see her around anymore. I thought she was going to kill me."

"She was planning to." I gulped and then launched into a brief explanation of what had occurred, not just after he'd lost consciousness, but also the specifics of how Destatur and Enaia had been colluding with the angels to kill Lilith—something Azazel apparently hadn't really seen while he was locked in the fight with the angel.

"You killed her." His gaze held a gleam I couldn't quite place.

I shrugged. "It seemed like the reasonable thing to do."

The smile that broke across his face glistened like sunlight on ocean waves. "That's my girl."

His words caused a full-body shiver in me, even in my spirit form.

"You should have taken her wings," he said, his eyes crinkling at the corners. "Start your own collection."

"Uh, yeah, how does that work exactly? Shouldn't the wings also burst into sparks and disappear once the demon is dead? 'Cause that's what all their bodies did when they got killed." I waved around me at the nonexistent remains of the angels and demons.

"The wings stay if you sever them before death." He sobered and looked toward the hellgate's location. "We should get going. I don't want to be here when he arrives." He glanced at me as he rose to his feet, his movements a bit sluggish, his wounds still not healed. "From what you said, Enaia seems to have been in on the conspiracy, and she'll have told Lucifer that we were responsible. He doesn't know the truth yet. So if he finds us here…"

"We're fucked."

He gave a curt nod, then grabbed my hand and started walking away from the hellgate, limping slightly. Seeing him injured—actually injured and not healing right—kicked something fundamental in me out of balance. Azazel was invincible. Or at least, I'd somehow believed that, deep down. I'd just never seen him truly wounded. Rationally, I'd known that he could be hurt, and I'd seen him with minor cuts or bruises right after training.

But he'd invariably healed so fast. He'd never been impaired. Always, he'd bounced back quickly, and it had never been serious. Of course, none of the training fights had been intended to kill. Even with the battles he'd fought with other demons in Hell, there'd been the underlying understanding that there shouldn't be any casualties, because that would incur the wrath of their archdemon.

These fights here on Earth, however, were another matter altogether. When the angels had clashed with him or Destatur, it had been with the intent to kill. Take no prisoners, leave no witnesses, fight to the death.

And Azazel now showed the signs of it.

Watching him get stabbed through the heart with a sword, witnessing him fall and be out of commission, and now seeing him limping, bleeding from several wounds that wouldn't close—it did something to my mind and heart, something I was sure would leave scars that were to haunt me yet.

"Where are you going?" I asked him, throwing a glance back at the hellgate location—our only way back, right now.

"We need to find another gate." He kept pulling me along, limping down the sidewalk, while the humans, who were still oblivious to what had gone down in their midst, evaded us like a visible obstacle they didn't even glance at. "Do you really want to go through the hellgate at Lucifer's palace? Walk right into him, if we're unlucky?" He shook his head. "There are other gates in the city. We just need to find one, and then we'll go from there."

"Maybe we should fly?"

"I'm not sure I'm able to yet," was his quiet reply, and it made worry and fear explode in my stomach.

A rumble shook the ground.

Azazel halted—and the humans on the sidewalk paused as well, looking around. I felt it then, a wave of such dark power hushing the air that it raised all the hairs on my ghostly body and twisted my insides with primitive fear.

"Too late," Azazel whispered.

He yanked me to the side just as I glanced back at the location of the hellgate...where the portal now glowed, spilling inky darkness onto the pavement. Azazel pushed me into the tall bushes underneath the stone balustrade running along the elevated terrace in front of the library. Pressing me down and against the stone wall, he then folded his wings over us. I could barely see a speck of blue sky above.

A second later, another quake and roar rattled the earth, followed by screeching sounds—and an explosion of power that darkened the sky. Like the shock wave of a bomb, it hit us with enough force to flatten both me and Azazel to the ground. We landed with a grunt, half smashed into the bush next to us—which was on fire.

I blinked past Azazel's wings at the horrific scene playing out.

Everything was on fire.

Flames licked over the ground, over buildings, engulfing cars, buses...people.

Oh, God.

There were humans running away, burning and scream-ing, some of them on the ground, howling in agony. Trees stood ablaze, the flames reaching high up into an artificially darkened sky with churning clouds of light-streaked gray and red. Sirens blared in the distance. The air was filled with a cacophony of sounds of suffering...and deep, bone-chilling baying.

"Hellhounds," I whispered, clutching Azazel's shoulders. "Oh, God, he brought hellhounds."

And there they were, tearing out of the glowing portal along with a stream of winged warriors, their weapons at the ready. They all went straight for the humans.

Whoever wasn't burned to a crisp already now fell prey to the hounds, who chased them all down, snarling and snapping, or to the blades of the demons, gleaming in the flickering flames of the raging inferno.

I stared, shocked beyond understanding, at a kind of wholesale slaughter worse than anything I'd ever seen depicted in movies.

And then *he* stepped out of the hellgate.

Pausing with just the right significance before he slowly, deliberately, placed one foot onto the ink-and-flame-coated sidewalk, Lucifer then raised his head to the sky.

I flinched at the sight of him.

His hair had turned black.

Dark veins ran out over his skin from eyes of pure midnight, as if some shadow poison had taken hold of him. Black claws tipped his fingers, and his obsidian wings glowed with a red sheen as though coated in luminescent blood.

But it was his expression that truly gave me chills. Halfway between soul-splitting grief and feral aggression, he looked completely unmoored, utterly void of any capacity for reasoning.

I'd been scared of him before. This, here, seeing him like this…it redefined my understanding of terror.

He bared his teeth—canines elongated like fangs—and then unleashed a scream of raw, primal fury and anguish before he launched himself forward and joined the fray.

His demons and hounds bathed the streets in blood. They even tore into the cars and buses, ripping doors open and pulling screaming people out to die upon swords or fangs.

I jerked, my soul turning over at the merciless violence and indiscriminate brutality. So much death. So much destruction. And here we stood on the sidelines, unable to help. Because even if Azazel jumped in, what good would he do against this overwhelming tide of aggression? He was one against a horde of scores of demons and hellhounds. It would be like trying to hold back the rushing water of a broken dam with a two-by-four.

Light split the darkness of the sky in a blaze so bright it bathed everything in overexposed white for a moment.

Then, silver fire rushing in their wake, angels descended from the sky.

CHAPTER 33

Their wings gleaming white, they slammed down on the ground, one after the other, like some sort of coruscating missiles. Not missing a beat, they attacked Lucifer's forces within seconds. All over the place, angels engaged in combat with demons and hellhounds, pushing them back and drawing their attention away from the humans.

The Devil himself, for his part, seemed invigorated by the prospect of fighting Heaven's army. Diabolical joy mixed with grim-faced hatred tinged his expression as he threw himself into the battle, using both his powers and his sword to massacre his way through the ranks of angels.

And it couldn't be called anything else. It was mindless butchery as he slashed and hacked off the limbs of angels who were no match for him, skewering them with spikes of dark power, burning their wings with hellfire.

They fell like flies around him, bursting into embers of light.

What had seemed like a force of superior numbers now

dwindled down more and more, the angels taking significant losses.

And ever more demons streamed from the still-open hell-gate, an unending flow of reinforcements. Many of the new arrivals spread out through the nearby streets, pushing the battle toward the rest of the city.

Toward a population of millions.

My heart sank. So many. So many people whose lives would end today, caught in the fray of a supernatural war where they were little more than pawns and collateral damage.

My chest tight, I looked up as more streaks of light illuminated the dark maelstrom of the sky. About half a dozen angels landed with earth-shattering impact, their power giving me goosebumps on my ghostly skin.

Glowing gold energy wafted from them like mist on the water, their white wings shot through with gold and silver filaments. Their landing blasted nearby fighters to the ground, stirring the ash-flecked air into whorls of smoke.

"Archangels," Azazel murmured, pressing me back against the stone wall once more.

"That's good, isn't it?" I whispered back. "They'll be able to take on Lucifer, right?"

Azazel's wings twitched. "Only if the archdemons don't join the fight."

"They're not here yet?"

He shook his head, his expression grim. "You'd know it if they were."

As one, the archangels advanced on Lucifer, going straight for the biggest threat. His black eyes glowed with an inner fire as he met the challenge, his teeth bared in a grimace of a smile. The fight was a blur of black and white, silver, gold and red, the movements too fast for my eyes to follow as the deadly dance of archangels and Lucifer lifted into the sky.

Lucifer's power drenched the air, clashing with the magic of the archangels. The ground trembled, buildings shook. With a mighty crack, the asphalt of the street split. The quake that followed rattled everything around. In the surrounding buildings, the glass in the windows shattered and rained down to shower the ground in glistening shards. The middle arch of the library's entrance collapsed, the roof giving in and crumbling down.

Screams echoed from inside the building.

Up and down the street, in the air and on the ground, angels kept fighting with demons and hellhounds.

"We should go," Azazel said at my ear, his voice tight and urgent.

"But—"

"There's nothing we can do here. We can't help. The archangels are the only ones who could possibly bring Lucifer to heel, and when they do, you don't want to be anywhere nearby. What you've seen so far is nothing against the destruction they'll wreak to subdue him. We need to get away, find another hellgate or some safe place, and sit this one out."

"Okay," I whispered, my heart clenched in fear.

He extended his wings as if testing them. "I'll try to fly us out."

I nodded and let him pick me up, my hands trembling when I grasped his neck to hold on. Checking the way out, Azazel waited for a moment, then he launched us into the air.

His mighty wings had only beat a few times when something rammed into us. The impact made us careen wildly, and though Azazel tried to right his flight path again, it was no use, the impulse of the crash too strong. We slammed to the ground, Azazel grunting in pain, me being hurtled a few feet away.

My landing was a far less painful one than his, seeing as I didn't truly feel the impact in my ghost form. I raised my head to see Azazel already engaged in combat with an angel —probably the one who'd rammed him in the air.

Never mind that, technically, Azazel wasn't on Lucifer's side—he was a demon, and as such, all the angel saw was an enemy to be taken out. And it wasn't like Azazel could simply explain to him that he wasn't part of the killing brigade sent by Lucifer.

While Azazel battled it out with the angel, several dark shapes flashed past overhead. I craned my neck to watch how they dove for the tangle of powers that was Lucifer's fight with the archangels. Magic exploded from the newcomers, midnight lightning and hellfire flames searing the edges of the ring the archangels had built around Lucifer.

The ring broke apart. Three of the archangels faltered in their flight, and one hurtled down toward the ground, followed by a shadow-shrouded figure. When they landed on the street, the archangel scrambling to her feet, I could finally make out the exact shape and appearance of one of those newly arrived warriors.

Wings of red-streaked obsidian, his skin misted in dark power, the demon exuded such superiority and might that I had not a single doubt I was looking at one of the archdemons.

So they had come to join the fight.

I glanced back at the battle raging in the air. I counted about half a dozen archangels, including the one on the street, and maybe five or six archdemons. It was hard to tell, their movements so fast I could barely keep track.

Plus Lucifer.

I gulped. Those odds were not good. Lucifer alone equaled *several* archangels in power, from what I'd just seen. He'd held his own against all of them for quite a while before the archdemons showed up. Now that they were here? Chances that the angels would win this just got a lot smaller.

The air shook, the pressure of the magic so strong that it bent lampposts and dented the sides of entire buildings. Metal screeched, stone cracked, and more glass shattered as the buildings started to collapse under the strain of the powers at work here. Wave upon wave of magic pulsed outward from the clashes, each of them causing ever more damage.

They would destroy the city if this kept up. Already, I could see skyscrapers a block or so down from here shaking amid the pulsing waves of power. The buildings nearby crumbled more and more. Flashes of winged warriors— demon and angel both—zoomed through the sky, over and in between the buildings, fighting in the air above New York. I could only imagine what the situation was like on the ground in the surrounding streets. How far had the battle already spread? How many human lives had been lost?

This kind of destruction was eerily reminiscent of the fall of the Twin Towers on September 11, except back then, it had been a singular attack that had caused the chaos. As disastrous and deadly as it had been, it had been one strike—with two planes, of course—after which no new blows had come.

Now, though, it was an ongoing battle, with potential for so much more devastation… I had no idea how long this war would last. Days? Weeks, even? Or maybe…months? When I'd learned about the original war between Heaven and Hell, I'd never heard anyone mention a time frame.

What if this was just the beginning? What if, from now on, the world would burn and burn, while the angels and demons fought for supremacy, the humans merely a blip on their radar, an afterthought?

With Lilith gone and the deal with Heaven canceled, Lucifer had no reason to hold back anymore. He could go full force against his old enemies, and there were apparently many, many demons seemingly all too eager to finish what had started millennia ago.

As I watched, reinforcements came out of the hellgate, and I had no doubt that the same was true for the other hell-gates across the city. Lucifer had probably sent out some sort of general mobilization order through Hell, calling all of his demons to the fight.

And this time, they wouldn't let up until either they'd won the war, or Heaven had defeated them soundly.

Likely killing countless humans in the process.

My stomach turned over. Despair ate at me from the inside, desolation crawling across my soul.

A thought struck me at that moment. *The deal with Heaven canceled...*

Azazel landed next to me, whirling up dust and smoke and ash, apparently having won the fight with the angel. His landing was a far cry from the usual graceful touchdown he was capable of—a further sign of his injuries. I pivoted to him and threw my arms around him, relieved to see him in one piece, and for a brief moment, he folded his wings around us as he hugged me back.

"Let's go," he muttered. "Flying might be too dangerous right now. We may have a better chance of evading and hiding down on the ground."

He moved forward and pulled at my hand, but I

remained where I was, frozen by the idea that had just occurred to me. An idea that might just be our salvation...

"We need a new deal," I said, voicing part of my racing thoughts.

"What?" Azazel paused and turned to me, flames and swirling plumes of smoke in the background.

I blinked at him, refocusing my gaze on him as I struggled to corral my thoughts into coherent ideas. "The only thing that can stop this war now is a new deal, one that holds as much leverage over Lucifer as the old one. Lilith is gone"—I had to fight down the wave of shell-shocked grief about her sudden and violent death—"but what if there was another person who means so much to Lucifer that a deal could be struck with her well-being in mind? One that could force Lucifer to halt all fighting and agree to a new truce because he cares more about her than about winning against Heaven?"

"Naamah," Azazel whispered, his eyes wide.

I nodded. "For all we know, Lucifer never sent that letter. Heaven doesn't know he wanted to ask for a pardon for her." I squeezed his hand and stepped closer, my spirit form brimming with urgency. "But what if they knew? What if that would change everything? They're all fighting right now, yes, but what if that's just out of necessity, because Lucifer attacked Earth and they need to respond? What if most of them want to end this war just as much as we do? They just need a chance to broker a deal. This could be it."

Azazel's eyes darted between mine, the movement lightning quick and likely echoing the speed with which his mind ran through all the possibilities and ramifications of my suggestion. "We'd need to find a high-ranking angel who would be likely to support a truce."

"Gabriel?" He was the one who granted the pardons, after all.

"Maybe. Or Raphael." His gaze swung to the side, his brows drawing together. "From what I've gathered, he's always been a voice of reason."

"Is either of them here?"

"I think I saw them earlier, yes."

We both looked up toward the cataclysmic-seeming battle between archangels, archdemons, and Lucifer that still raged in the air above the street. They'd spread out some, with pairs of archangels and archdemons splitting from the main fight to duel it out alone, while at least two archangels were currently taking on Lucifer.

It was hard to make out individuals among the warriors, but somewhere up there were the two archangels we needed to inform about the pardon plans. They were our only hope. Sure, they needed to stop Lucifer from going ballistic for long enough to offer the new deal, but if anyone could do it, it was them.

Azazel's determined expression morphed to one of concern when he looked down at me again. "Zoe," he said, his voice tight, "I can't take you up there."

I pressed my lips together, scrunching my brow.

"I need to be able to maneuver fast through the air," he went on, "and that's harder to do when I'm carrying you. Not to mention I'll be distracted by trying to keep you safe, but in order to reach one of the archangels, I need to be able to take risks. That aside"—he framed my face with both hands, his eyes glowing—"I don't want you anywhere near those fighters. You've felt the waves of their power when they clash. I won't expose you to forces like that." His thumbs stroked over my cheeks. "I need you to stay down here, locate a good hiding place, and wait for me until I come get you again, all right?"

"How—how will you find me?"

"This here," he said, grasping my hand and laying it over his heart, "will always lead me to where you are."

Heat burned behind my eyes.

"Just make sure to hide well and far away from the fighting. Crawl into a wall if you must. Anything to stay out of sight, understood?"

I nodded frantically, my heartbeat stumbling in my chest. "Come back to me," I rushed to say, refusing to entertain the possibility that this might be the last I saw of him. "I'll haunt you if you don't."

"I promise." His eyes burned a path through my soul. "I'll come for you."

He gave me a quick, harsh kiss that spoke of the fear ravaging us both, and then he launched into the air. I watched him head for the clash of powers, worry fizzing inside me about how he could possibly make it through to one of the archangels without simply getting pulverized.

But standing here and stressing about him wouldn't help. The only thing I could do, the only thing I was *supposed* to do, was hide my ass. Evasion 101. I could do that.

Glancing around, I flattened myself against the wall of the building behind me. Could I not simply glide through that wall? Hadn't Azazel said as much? I was pretty much a ghost, after all, and I'd been walking through walls for a year now. Chances of me being spotted and vaporized by either an angel, a demon, or a hellhound *inside* a building were probably lower, right?

While fire raged across the street in front of me, the sky full of wings and blades and blows of power, I concentrated on moving through the wall. A heartbeat later, I was inside the building. Looking around, I recognized the shelves and aisles of a convenience store, completely deserted. Okay, good, I could work with that.

I gingerly walked around in search of an even better hidey-hole farther inside.

Overturned shelves and spilled groceries indicated there'd been a struggle here. My gaze fell on the floor— bloody tracks hinted that someone had been dragged around here, bleeding from a likely fatal wound. A moment later, I saw the source.

There, sprawled on the ground next to a shattered shelf, lay the broken body of a man. His stomach gaped open, intestines not just pulled out but more like entirely *carved out*. His head was missing.

I stood there with such eerie calm, so detached and unfeeling, that one might have thought I was shopping for groceries and couldn't decide which bag of potato chips to take home.

It was one of those moments again. Those disassociated moments when my mind apparently subdued my emotional response.

While unsettling, it helped me focus on what I needed to do. Find a better hiding spot, because obviously, this store here wasn't safe from attacks.

After a quick search, I hid inside a storage closet. Classic, I know. It was the best I could do for now.

I'd just settled in to wait when a shock wave like nothing I'd felt before rolled through the air, followed by a mighty roar. My spirit body trembled wildly, as if I were a leaf on a tree rattled by a forceful gust of wind. The earth shook, the shelves in the room crashing down. Cracking, rumbling, and snapping filled the air and my ears as the walls collapsed right over me.

CHAPTER 34

AZAZEL

"I promise," I said to Zoe, unwilling to acknowledge the possibility that this might be the last I'd look upon her. "I'll come for you."

And with a hurried kiss, I took my leave, lifting off into the battle-ravaged sky, my muscles screaming at me, my wounds pulsing with pain. I'd recovered enough to fly, but I felt the strain of my injuries with every beat of my wings.

I resisted the urge to glance back down to the ground, to where Zoe likely still stood watching me. Doing so would prove a distraction I could ill afford.

All my focus had to be on maneuvering through the air without getting engaged in a fight before I reached one of the archangels. Fear for her safety still clawed at me, and it went against every one of my instincts to leave her behind, unguarded, while I flew away.

But I had to trust that she'd hide herself well.

As long as she managed that, I'd find her again.

A flash to my right alerted me to an incoming attack, and I spiraled to the side to evade the strike. The angel who'd targeted me spun in the air, obviously aiming for another attack, but I closed my wings tight and shot down like a bullet, far away from my challenger in a matter of milliseconds. Once I'd put enough distance between us, I opened my wings again and soared higher on powerful beats.

I didn't have time for duels with common angels. The sooner I got close to one of the archangels, the better.

All around me, magic sparked as the highest-ranking angels and demons clashed again and again. Lightning threaded through the air, whirlwinds of fire whipped the clouds of smoke and ash, a heavy charge of electricity and heat pressing down on me. I scanned the pairs of fighters dotting the dark sky, and I zeroed in on a familiar face. *Daevi.*

My grandmother was here, likely called to arms by Lucifer's decree, now holding one of the archangels at bay.

Evading bolts of lightning, I shot forward until I'd reached the two warriors locked in battle over the crumbling remains of a once proud skyscraper.

With gritted teeth, I threw myself into the fight, attacking the archangel—Uriel? I wasn't sure—in order to buy the precious seconds I needed to get my message across to Daevi.

Lilith was killed by a group of rogue demons and angels in order to force Lucifer's hand and cancel the deal with Heaven, I spoke without preamble into her mind while we both fought Uriel. *But there is a way to end this. Lucifer wants a pardon for Naamah. Heaven doesn't know it yet. We must inform the archangels and suggest they strike a new deal to halt the fighting and reinstate the truce. Getting a pardon for Naamah is the only way to stop this war now.*

I saw how Daevi's movements faltered as I hurled this information at her, and it occurred to me that maybe she hadn't known about Lucifer's pardon plans.

Naamah was her only daughter.

How do you know this? Daevi asked as she blocked a strike from Uriel.

I'll explain later, I shot back while I engaged the archangel from the other side, drawing her attention away from Daevi for a moment. *There's no time now. Just trust me with this.*

Daevi didn't answer; she merely kept on fighting Uriel with grim determination.

Please, I added, swallowing my pride and the potent cocktail of emotions about the complicated relationship with my grandmother. *Help me.* Parrying a strike from Uriel, I added more quietly, *Help her.*

Achieving a pardon for my mother was not only a device to broker a new deal, but it was also the one way to maybe, finally, allow her shattered mind to heal.

Daevi's energy oscillated wildly, though it didn't slow her down, a testament to her strength as an archdemon. Strands of her gleaming black hair had come loose from her tight braid and now whipped around her face, her brown skin flecked with ash and blood.

Seconds ticked by while we both took on the archangel, keeping her busy blocking and responding to our attacks. The power Uriel kept sending out in waves and flickering lightning flayed open my skin, made my eyes bleed. I blinked the blood away, refusing to let up, at the same time fearing my plea was going ignored by Daevi.

If she didn't help me, I had no hope of reaching and informing another archangel. This close to one of them, I'd had to confront the bitter truth that their power would kill me if I engaged one on my own—I'd be dead before I ever got the chance to tell them about the pardon plans. The only reason I was still alive in Uriel's vicinity was the fact that most of her attention was locked on Daevi, the bigger threat.

The skin on my hands was completely flayed off. Blood glistening on raw muscles and tendons, I gripped my sword tighter as Uriel's power ate through my fighting leathers. My face burned.

This was not going to work. Daevi would not—

"Parley!" Daevi yelled and withdrew, holding her sword horizontally in front of her, ready to block but less likely to attack. White flames whispered over her wings, effectively making them look like angel wings for a few seconds.

My heart a drumbeat in my chest, I let up at the same time, flying back a few paces and raising my sword horizontally as well, flashing my wings to white.

Uriel hesitated, her own blade still lifted in attack position, her energy vibrating with an aggressive edge. The light of the fires exploding in the sky painted her ebony skin in shades of dark red and orange. Her face twisting, she hurled a bolt of lightning toward Daevi.

Daevi blocked it with her sword and a wall of hellfire but made no move to retaliate. "Parley!" she shouted again. "I swear to cease fighting in order to speak."

The rush of relief through me was only tempered by my anxious anticipation of Uriel's reaction. If she didn't accept…

"Parley," Uriel called out and raised her sword in the same gesture as she held her position in the air with mighty beats of her gold-dusted white wings. "I vow to rest all arms to hear you speak."

The corrosive power in the air lessened, the burning on my face subsided.

"Archangel," Daevi began, hovering in a respectful distance to Uriel. "I do not want this war. Few of us do. It is the work of a conspiracist group of demons who colluded with like-minded angels. They knew killing Lilith would push Lucifer over the edge. However, there is a way to stop this madness. Lucifer has been considering asking for a pardon for his daughter, Naamah. If Heaven lets her ascend, a new deal could be struck with him. We can end this war. I respectfully ask for your assistance. Let your brethren know of Lucifer's intentions to pardon Naamah, and use this knowledge to offer the Morningstar a new deal." Daevi lowered her sword to the side. "My grandson and I will retreat to give you leave."

She nodded at me and withdrew a few more paces, not turning her back on Uriel. I did the same.

Uriel remained hovering in place for a few seconds, the wind from her wings whipping her tight braids to and fro. Then she nodded once before she pivoted and launched herself higher into the air, reaching the outer ring of the main battle between Lucifer and several other archangels.

I kept scanning the area for stealth attacks by angels as Daevi approached me.

"A word," she said and signaled me to follow her.

We landed on the remains of a building jutting out into the sky, our backs protected by another pile of rubble behind us. Eyes the color of mahogany rooted me to the spot, and at once, I was a young demon again, tensing under the assessing gaze of his grandmother.

"It was a coup, then," she said, more question than statement. "Who was it?"

"Destatur and Enaia. Possibly more on our side. I don't think it was limited to those two."

She nodded and threw a quick glance at the still-raging

battle high above us. When she looked back at me, sadness darkened her eyes.

"She was merely a means to an end for them." Her jaw worked as she looked to the side. "She deserved better."

I inclined my head, well aware that Daevi had loved Lilith as well. They'd had a cordial relationship, untainted by jealousy. After all, Daevi had shared Lilith and Lucifer's bed many times over the millennia. Naamah was a result of one of those passionate meetings. As far as I knew, Lucifer had never been with someone else without Lilith being involved.

And while Lilith had never borne children, it was an unspoken understanding that each and every child conceived from those shared affairs was, in a way, hers as well. She'd always treated them as if they were her own.

"How do you know about the plans for a pardon?"

Daevi's question drew me back to the present. I quickly explained about Zoe's discovery at the palace, knowing Daevi would not censure Zoe for any snooping done. Not when it turned out to be the key to maybe ending this war before it ravaged the world.

Daevi's brows drew together, and she lowered her gaze. "He never told me." She shook her head. "I knew he was struggling with her condition, as was I. But I would never have guessed he'd go so far as to consider a plea to Heaven."

"Doesn't feel so good," I dared say in a targeted push, allowing my still-simmering hurt to make itself heard, "to be left in the dark about something of personal concern to you, does it?"

Eyes of rich red-brown flicked back to me. For a moment, she just held my gaze, the air charged between us. "You are justified in your anger," she finally said. "That is as much as I will say. Everything else has been spoken already."

I pressed my lips together and clenched my jaw. Daevi would not bend further, and I knew it would be a moot point to argue this anymore. She'd already apologized, she'd backed Azmodea and me when we'd gone to see our mother, and she'd listened to me now when I'd asked her to help deliver the message about the pardon plans. There'd be no further acknowledgment of the hurt caused by lying about Naamah for thousands of years.

Just then, a major explosion of power shook the air. Fire and lightning gripped the sky, spreading outward from the center of the fight high above us. A shock wave of energy followed, blasting us against the pile of rubble at our backs. Daevi threw up a wall of hellfire, blocking the worst of it with her own power, shielding me in the process.

I wasn't sure I'd still be standing if it hadn't been for Daevi.

When the dust settled, we looked out over a landscape of destruction. A crater gaped where streets and buildings had been before, right underneath the epicenter of the battle between Lucifer and the archangels. Everything surrounding the direct impact zone was flattened, buildings reduced to rubble, a wasteland of devastation, a tapestry of war.

And there, a few yards above the canyon ripped into the city, hovered Lucifer. Power dripped off him, palpable even from this distance, but it had lost its edge. His chest rising and falling with his rapid breaths, he lifted his head and looked upon the group of archangels holding their position across from him, their stances defensive but not threatening. Behind Lucifer, his archdemons lingered, watching, waiting.

For a moment, Lucifer closed his eyes, and a shudder went through him. When he opened his eyes again, a pulse of power went out from him, but this time, it wasn't one of violence. Instead, when the wave of energy rolled over us, his dark voice echoed clear in my head.

Cease all hostilities and retreat to Hell. By order of your lord and master, no more blood shall be spilled.

Out loud, he said, "A new truce has been decreed. I will uphold the terms agreed upon as long as you uphold yours."

An archangel I recognized as Gabriel spoke up. "We will await her arrival at our gates."

The breath I'd been holding left me in a rush, too many emotions tangled too tightly in my chest for me to make sense of in this moment. One, however, rose to the fore —fear.

Sharp, acidic fear for the one person who held my heart, my soul, my future.

Zoe.

"I need to go," I said to Daevi.

She nodded at me. "Hellspeed."

Turning my back on the historic scene playing out, I shot into the air, rushing toward the spot where I'd left her, anxiety curdling my blood.

That shock wave had been terrible, with enough power to raze entire city blocks. She'd been farther away from it than Daevi and I had, and I could only hope against hope that she'd come out of it alive.

I landed amid the ruins of what was once the building where I'd last seen her, my heart pounding fast. "Zoe!"

No answer. Smoke curled around me, sparks and flecks of ash floating on the breeze stirred up by my landing.

I pivoted on my heels, flying to the top of a pile of rubble. "Zoe!"

Nothing moved amid the debris.

I beat my incipient panic into submission so I could focus on the connection I had with her. Always, I'd felt her presence, a faint energetic bond between her heart and mine, forged in the moment we'd spoken our vows, strengthened over time as we'd grown into our love.

Without fail, it would lead me back to her.

My muscles tensing in concentration, I grasped for that connection, that bond, the pulse of her presence that I'd come to cherish so much, that had filled the darkest places in my soul.

I grasped—and felt nothing.

Because it was gone.

Without fail, it would lead me to her.

Without fail...unless she was dead.

I fell to my knees, and the anguish raging through me tore its way out in a scream that shattered the ruins around me.

CHAPTER 35

ZOE

I ducked and shielded my head with my arms, acting purely on instinct—it didn't occur to me until seconds later that none of the walls or objects would hit me in my spirit form.

When the rumbling stopped, the air full of dust and smoke and lingering power that seared my soul, I looked around. The darkness was so thick that I wasn't sure if I was caught inside a wall. But then my eyes adjusted, and I realized I was cowering in between huge blocks of stone and concrete.

The building I'd been hiding in was reduced to piles of rubble around me. Nothing remained of the convenience store, flames fanning out over the ground, silver lightning crawling across the debris.

I looked up at the sky, unable to fathom how a building

of several stories had been razed like this in a matter of moments. The amount of power that took…

Azazel.

My heart clenching, I searched for him—

A hand grabbed me by the throat and hauled me up in the air. I didn't need to breathe in this form, but it hurt like a bitch to be lifted by my throat. Frantically, I clawed at the hand that held me, and my gaze snagged on the person who had caught me.

On the *demon*, his black wings lit by sparks of orange flame.

My eyes widened as I took in the sharp cheekbones, the strong jaw, the eyes of emerald green. His brown hair pulled back in a bun, Inachiel glared at me with hatred twisting his features.

"You," he snarled, "took my wings."

My gaze flicked back to the beautiful display of black feathers and orange flame behind him.

"Oh, they grew back," he said, having noted where I'd looked. "Painfully enough to make me scream for hours and days." His fingers twitched against my skin, making me wince. "But I'd just love to share the experience of losing a few limbs with you. And now that I've got you in my grasp, I'll do just that." He pulled me closer, his face only inches from mine. "I will take you to Hell with me and hold you for ransom until all my titles and lands are restored to me, until Azazel bends his knee and submits to my authority. And while you're in my tender care, I will cut off your legs and watch you scream and suffer and plead for mercy. Let's see how much damage a Hell-forged blade can do to you in your spirit form."

Panic exploded in my mind. Fear rushing through me, I tried to grasp for that spark of power that had saved me from Destatur. It had worked before—it would work again, right?

Nothing happened. I couldn't grab that kernel of power inside me to wield it consciously.

Terror clouding my thoughts, I pawed at his hand and barely noticed how he pulled something out of his pocket. A small object, square and nondescript. A little box. I'd seen this kind of box before. From the swirling mess of my mind rose the memory of the moment when Azazel had released my father's soul onto Earth...from a box just like this one.

"You know what this is, don't you?" Inachiel wiggled the box, his smile edged with manic glee.

A soul transporter. Demons used it to store the damned souls they collected on Earth. It made it easy to carry a lot of them at once without being hindered or bogged down.

Goddammit, if Azazel had had one of these on him, he could have simply stuffed me in it and taken me with him while he tried to reach one of the archangels.

Instead, it was Inachiel who held the box, flipped it open, and then hurled me inside, compressing my spirit into a fraction of its real size.

My soul met the velvety black of the box, stifling, dull, and all-encompassing.

DARKNESS CHOKED ME.

Like a blanket of pitch-black energy, it lay heavy on me, its press on my spirit a constant push that seemed to condense me.

So this was "the box."

The impenetrable, unbreachable container used to carry damned souls toward their torture. Now used to carry me to mine.

I couldn't move. My ghostly body didn't even seem to exist anymore, all sense of dimension gone. There was no up or down, no left or right. No space outside myself. There was only the pulse of my soul, and the dull echo of my thoughts.

Panic raked me bloody inside my mind.

Disoriented, reeling in place, keeled over yet stuck, I tried to buck, to writhe, to claw and kick. I tried to scream and cry.

Yet no sound came. My spirit didn't move.

I was lost in darkness, and no matter how much I struggled, I continued to choke on utter stillness and the silence of my black prison.

I DIDN'T KNOW HOW LONG I'D BEEN IN THE DARK. TIME HAD NO meaning here, just like space.

I only knew, with increasing despair, that I was at my most helpless. Not even when I'd been lost in Lucifer's palace during the Fall Festival and attacked by a hellrat had I felt this powerless, this utterly crushed and insignificant. Back then, I'd had a dagger, and I had used it to kill the thing that had threatened me.

And even when I'd crouched on the glass floor of the Hall of Horrors, crying and puking my guts out, I'd known, deep down, that I had a way out. After all, I'd walked into my punishment of my own free will, and there would have been ways for me to walk out again.

Not this time. Not here.

I had no means of freeing myself. I had no way of fighting back. This box was specifically made to hold spirits like me. What chance did I have to find a way out? I had no power here.

No power...except the one gifted to me by Lilith.

I'd tried to grasp it again here in the box, only to find it impossible to consciously take hold of it and use it on purpose. It had saved me twice before, once by virtue of its nature when Lucifer hadn't been able to physically hurt me, and the other time when it had exploded out of me as I'd thrown myself over Azazel, thinking we were going to die.

Was that the key, then? Had it been my fear for Azazel, my feelings for him that had activated the power?

Driven by an impulse, I delved into the maelstrom of emotions connected to him. Beside my love for him, the affection for this man who had earned the kind of devotion I hadn't known I was capable of, there was my fear for him, my anger at being separated from him, my heartache and sorrow at possibly never seeing him again.

I dove deep, then gathered it all, balled it together, and used it to dig for the spark of power it might activate.

Nothing happened.

I wanted to sob.

How? How was I just so incompetent at this? Why couldn't I just wield this power?

If I'd had a voice in this bleak box of blackness, I'd have screamed my frustration, but alas, I still choked on silence.

My spirit vibrated with anger. I was so tired of being powerless. Of needing help, and rescue, of being on the lowest rung of the ladder, inevitably prey and never the

438

predator. Of always relying on Azazel to be my shield against a world that wanted to use me. I was so fucking fed up with someone like Inachiel waltzing up to me and thinking he could do whatever the fuck he wanted because I was weak and couldn't defend my own sorry ass.

I was so done.

Pressure built inside me.

I'd had it with these *fucking* demons and their *fucking* games and their entitled arrogance and their need for dominance and the fact that I was always on the other side of that *fucking* equation because...

I.

Wasn't.

ENOUGH.

This time, when I screamed, something cracked within me. Light spilled out of that fissure, and without missing a beat, I grabbed it.

Heat shot through me. My soul ignited.

I molded that fire, fanned the flames—and then blasted it outward.

The darkness of the box disintegrated.

CHAPTER 36

T he burst of light spat me out into another kind of gloom. I stumbled in the semidarkness until my ghostly eyes adjusted—however that worked in this form—and then I looked around, taking stock.

I was standing in a small cave of some sort, slanted walls of concrete or stone on all sides, with light filtering through cracks here and there. It looked like...like a half-collapsed room? I squinted at one of the walls. Yes, this seemed like it was a building that had come down due to an earthquake or something.

Or, you know, a cataclysmic event like Armageddon.

From somewhere outside, sirens blared in the distance.

There was a slightly bigger opening on one side, and as I tilted my head, I realized there were tracks of blood on the ground leading through the opening inside, like someone injured or dead had been dragged here.

My gaze followed the tracks to a dark corner—and I jumped at the sight of the body sprawled there.

His wings were shredded. His legs bent at an unnatural angle. One arm was missing, the other maimed.

And his face...it took me a moment. But underneath the blood and the strips of skin hanging off were the sharp cheekbones, the strong jaw...and when he opened his eyes, emerald green glared at me.

"How?" Inachiel rasped. "How did you—" He coughed, blood spilling from the wounds on his chest. "Come out?"

I balled my hands into fists, nausea and anger mixing in my stomach. "I remembered that I have some power of my own."

He coughed again, foam bubbling at his mouth.

"What happened to you?" I asked, frowning at his sorry state. He'd been more than fine when he'd stuffed me into the box.

"What's it look like?" Inachiel's eyes sparked with fury.

"Like you tried to fuck a lawn mower!" I snapped, my willingness to play stupid games at an all-time low. "Obviously, you had a fight with an angel or whatever, but didn't the deal go through? Is the war still on?" I tried to peer out of one of the slits between the walls of concrete.

Instead of answering, Inachiel just leveled a glare full of animosity at me, and I considered giving him a few good kicks to his mangled chest.

"Speak," I hissed at him. "Or would you like me to cut off your head with your own sword? I just recently acquired that skill."

"There is a new truce," Inachiel croaked after a moment.

My knees almost buckled with my relief. It had worked! The world wouldn't burn to cinders, no more humans perishing as collateral damage in a supernatural war. I thought of my aunt, living not far from here, and of Taylor on the other side of the world. Had there been fighting in Australia as well? Who knew if maybe demons had streamed out of all existing hellgates to wreak havoc on humanity? I had to find out if Tay was all right, if my aunt in Philadelphia had been spared.

"Lucifer ordered us to retreat," Inachiel continued, pulling my attention back to him. "Angels withdrew as well. Came a bit late for me, though. Last fight ended badly. I killed the fucker, but he got me good." More coughing. His entire body spasmed. "Dragged myself here to hide. Then the order to retreat came through. By then, I couldn't move anymore."

I studied him again. He wasn't healing here, due to being on Earth, just like Azazel hadn't healed right earlier.

Earlier.

I swallowed hard, my heart galloping in my chest. "How much time has passed? How long have you been here?"

Another coughing fit seized him, and I was about ready to shake him, too.

"A day?" he mused, his voice hoarse. "Two? I think there was at least one sunset and sunrise, but it's hard to say. The sky's still full of smoke and ash."

Two days?

I flinched, tunneling my hands through my hair and pulling. Two days! Oh my God, this was the longest I'd ever been on Earth in spirit form. Was I still connected to my body? Had I died?? How would I even know?

And where was Azazel?

I ran to the opening and peered outside. Ruins all around, sirens echoing over the piles of rubble, distant shouting from what I guessed to be first responders and cleanup crews.

I was this close to yelling Azazel's name when it occurred to me that maybe drawing attention to myself like this wasn't a good idea. Yes, the war was over and a new truce was in place, but that didn't mean there might not be some rogue angels or demons with less-than-kind intentions toward me—see exhibit A, currently dying in the cave-in behind me.

If I ran into the wrong sort of demon, one with a bone to pick with Azazel, and they recognized me as his wife, I'd slide right into the next messy situation.

All right, so…what? I'd just have to wait for Azazel to find me? When the clock was already ticking for me with regard to losing the connection between my body and mind?

Ugh, what other choice did I have? Maybe I could at least make it to the spot where we'd been separated.

I clenched my jaw and looked around. I had no idea where I was. I'd known my way around Manhattan from the summer I'd spent here as a teen, but these streets were now unrecognizable, only ghostly remains of buildings, broken and shattered stone, and metal jutting out into the cloudy sky like grotesquely huge gray teeth.

Wait. My gaze zeroed in on a scorched item lying amid the debris. I stepped closer and squinted at the green sign with the white letters on it, barely visible under the soot.

E 14 St.

I did some mental math, excavating the memorized map of Manhattan from the depths of my mind.

"What?" I exclaimed when I figured it out.

We weren't just one or two blocks out from the library where it'd all started—Fourteenth Street was almost thirty city blocks away from where Azazel had last seen me.

Shit. I'd have to make it there somehow. Chances were greater that he'd find me again in the vicinity of the battle center. I'd just have to be careful and look out for any marauding demons.

"Zoe."

The rasped cry from inside the cave-in made me pause.

Cautiously, I peeked back inside. Inachiel's eyes glinted in the faint light coming through the opening. He took a deep breath, his chest rattling.

"Don't," he said in a voice reminiscent of rusted metal breaking. "Don't leave me here to die."

I narrowed my eyes, my nostrils flaring. "The nerve of you. You kidnapped me to torture me and use me for ransom, and now that you're one step away from death, you have the gall to ask *me* for mercy?"

Red-tinged foam bubbled around his mouth as he implored me with bloodshot eyes. "Please. I beg you. Help me."

I glared at him, gripping the sides of the opening hard, still crouching at a distance to where he lay. "Tell me," I asked, a strange sense of calm washing through me, "what would you do in my position? Would you help your enemy —the one who wanted to harm you just moments ago—or would you let them die?"

I already knew the answer: no demon worth their salt would let an enemy live if the opportunity to be rid of them presented itself so clearly.

"I'd save them," Inachiel rasped.

"Bullshit. You'd revel in their death. Living with you lot has taught me that, if nothing else."

He shook his head, struggling to breathe. "You still have more to learn. When I save them, they will owe me a blood debt. An almost nonrepayable favor. What is worth more than souls in Hell?"

"Favors," I murmured.

"And do we ever break a vow?"

I lifted my chin. "No."

At least, not without consequences, and from what I'd

gathered, the magical ramifications for demons reneging on their word were severe.

"Save me," Inachiel pleaded. "Help me get to a hellgate. I will owe you my life. That is a rare debt to hold over a demon's head. Don't dismiss it too easily." He licked his lips, urgency threading his voice. "You need help, too, don't you? You're looking for Azazel, and you need to get home. I know where the nearest hellgate is. Once I'm in Hell, I'll be healing, and I can take you back to your estate."

I worried my lip, considering. Helping him move would cost me time. I still remembered how hard it had been to drag Azazel when he was unconscious. On the other hand, the way through the hellgate with Inachiel might still get me back into my body faster. Who knew how long I'd otherwise have to wait for Azazel?

Plus, the favor owed would be a big advantage.

"All right." I stepped inside. "I'll help you, for a blood debt and your assistance once we're in Hell."

He gave me a smile of red-stained teeth. "Thank you. Lucifer bless you."

"I'd rather he didn't," I murmured as I approached Inachiel. "Can you move at all? It'll be difficult to drag you. How far is the hellgate?"

With a wet gurgling breath, he heaved himself up into a sitting position, not an easy feat with only one arm and broken legs. "If you prop me up under my shoulder, I can take enough weight on my legs and give boosts with my wings to make the trek. The hellgate is only one block from here."

I eyed his wings. They looked like someone stamped confetti out of them. They didn't have enough feathers left to fly, but maybe they could really take off some of the weight if he flapped them.

"Okay," I said. "Let's go."

I ducked under his arm and half hoisted him over my shoulder, my ghostly muscles straining as I pushed us both off the ground.

The first steps were horrible, a mess of stumbling, lurching, and careening into walls until we'd made it out of the cave-in and onto the debris-strewn street.

"Left," Inachiel croaked.

"To the left, to the left," I sang under my breath, unable to halt my brain's singular ability to start playing songs on repeat after a one-word prompt. I was sure Beyoncé had never envisioned someone humming one of her songs in the aftermath of the apocalypse while dragging an injured demon back to Hell.

But hey, I'd rather focus on a good tune than on the fact that my soul might be separating from my body at any moment, or the uncertainty of not knowing where Azazel was and if we'd ever get to see each other again before I turned into a ghost forever.

"You," Inachiel huffed out, "are weird."

"Says the one who sleeps with an army of stuffies."

He tensed against me. "What?"

"Oh, unbunch your panties. I know, and I don't give a fuck. I'm just saying you shouldn't go around judging people for little eccentricities when you most certainly have some of your own."

His response was a wet croak that might have been a laugh.

We kept moving down what was left of the street, skirting around large pieces of the toppled buildings on either side. Every once in a while, I had to pause, not necessarily to catch my breath, as I didn't need to truly breathe in

446

this form, but I somehow felt exhausted nevertheless. Every step seemed like torture.

"How much...farther?" I asked as I strained to hold him up.

"It's over there." He pointed at what might have been the entrance to an alley, now a smallish opening between columns of ruins.

Okay, only a few more steps.

Finally, we stood right in front of it. I dropped him like a hot potato, unable to carry him any further. From his position on the ground, Inachiel drew the symbols in the air, and the hellgate activated with a shimmer.

My shoulders sagged with relief. It was almost over. As soon as we were inside, Inachiel would heal, and it wouldn't take long for him to be strong enough to take me home. And maybe we'd even find other help, depending on where this hellgate led.

Of course, there was the risk that it might belong to a demon who was at odds with Azazel, but it was still my best bet.

"Help me cross," Inachiel said on a rattle. "I can't make it on my own."

"Dude, I can't carry you anymore. I have no idea why, but this ghost form gets muscle cramps, and my legs feel like jelly right now. Best I can do is roll you over and give you a good kick."

Inachiel, lying on his back, stared blankly toward the sky. "This is beyond undignified."

I leaned down and patted his shoulder. "There, there. Thoughts and prayers. Now get ready. On three—one, two, *three*."

And with a grunt of exertion, I rolled him over, toward

the glowing hellgate, and then kicked him in his back to give him the last push to make it through the glimmering portal.

I can't say that it wasn't satisfying, in a way.

The hellgate swallowed Inachiel with a flash of light.

I was about to follow him when a shadow passed over me. The energy crashed into me before he did. Familiar, warm, vibrating with concern and relief and the acidic bite of fear, it engulfed me mere seconds before a large body tackled me to the ground.

I grunted from the impact, my fall broken by soft wings that had wrapped around my back, and then Azazel's arms crushed me to him with enough force that I'd have struggled for breath in my physical form.

As it was, I only hugged him back as the pent-up worry and adrenaline suddenly ebbed in a rush that left me dizzy. A sob broke from me.

"You're here," I whispered against his neck. "You found me."

He pulled back enough to pin me with eyes of churning clouds and lightning. "I promised I'd come for you." He laid his hand on my cheek. His fingers trembled. "I've been looking for you for days. I kept searching for you because I refused to believe you were—" He broke off, the muscles in his throat working. Instead of finishing his sentence, with the terrifying assumption that stood behind it, he claimed my lips in a kiss that voiced all he'd been through, all he'd felt.

My heart split open at the profound pain I tasted.

"I'm here," I murmured against his mouth when he withdrew. "I'm okay."

My fingers caressed the planes of his face, traced the lines of his lips while my eyes drank him in, his expression so raw and vulnerable, his heart laid bare before me.

448

"Let's go home," I said, feeling the press of time upon me. "Everything else can wait."

He nodded and pulled me up to standing, shaking out his wings. "This hellgate leads to a neighboring territory. I'll fly us home as fast as possible."

I wanted to say *okay* and hop up into his arms, but pain slashed through me. Doubling over, I cried out, feeling a ripping sensation deep within, like someone had taken a hold of my soul and yanked hard.

"Zoe!" Azazel's shout seemed to come from somewhere far away.

I staggered, feeling unmoored, unfastened, a tiny boat out at sea, drifting and spinning. Numbness took over where the pain had seared me before.

"What's happening?" I whispered, holding my middle, one hand over my chest...where I felt the distinct lack of something that should have been there.

A thread, or a bond, or a...connection.

I raised my widened eyes to Azazel, who stared at me with an expression of shock and disbelief.

"No," he said and shook his head. "No."

"Azazel..."

"No."

"Am I...?" I shivered despite the numbness spreading through me. "Has the connection between my soul and my body—"

"No." He kept shaking his head, as if the gesture could ward off the truth of what had happened. As if his denial could make it undone.

We both knew better.

"What now?" My voice came out high and woven with fear, the stirrings of panic scattering my thoughts. "What do we do?"

"I'll take you back home." He grabbed my hand, determination hardening his features. "Your body's still there. We can put you back, try to reforge the connection…"

"How?" Nausea crept up from my middle. I blinked against sudden wisps of darkness across my vision.

A muscle jumped in his jaw. "We'll figure it out."

He swung me up into his arms and marched toward the hellgate a few feet away. My sight winked in and out of darkness. The world lost color all around me for a moment, everything flashing in black and white for the span of a heartbeat.

I looped my arms around his neck, and my gaze fell on something on my forearm. I squinted at it. A crack? In my skin? My ghostly skin?

As I watched, it spread. One crack became a web of fissures. In one spot, a piece of my skin peeled off and fell away as ash, darkness pulsing underneath.

"Azazel," I whispered, horror seizing my soul.

He paused in drawing the sigils for the hellgate and looked down at me.

His face fell.

Raw, unfiltered devastation suffused his energy. "This is impossible."

"What's going on?" I fought to form the words, my mouth feeling weird, my thoughts skipping away from me.

He swallowed hard, his voice a harsh whisper. "You're turning."

"Into…what?"

His eyes, wild and pained, met mine. "A wraith."

CHAPTER 37

AZAZEL

"What?" Zoe's mouth fell open, her pupils enlarging and contracting as her gaze struggled to focus on me—more signs of her turning?—"I thought you said it would take decades. Why is it happening so fast?"

Her words sounded slurred, as if she had trouble forming them.

I shook my head and ground my teeth. "I don't know. Normally, it takes longer—but you're not a normal ghost. None of this is normal." Frustration and fear warred within me, my chest too tight to breathe. My mind still hadn't quite caught up to the devastating turn of events, my thoughts reeling. "Maybe it has to do with your soul being separated from your body because you stayed too long on Earth, rather than dying a natural death. Maybe it has to do with how we bonded, and how it might have changed you. Or perhaps Lilith's power altered you in some fundamental way."

All of them fair guesses, all of them born of trying to make sense of something that threatened to rip my very heart and soul from me.

None of them held a solution for this disaster.

Before my eyes, the marks of decay on Zoe's skin spread, her energy changing. A toxic kind of darkness whispered through her aura.

"Azazel," she murmured, her head lolling against my shoulder, "I don't feel so good."

Terror seized my thoughts. I couldn't think straight.

I, the strategist, ever so unflappable, swift of mind and never at a loss for ideas, stood there unable to move, incapable of formulating a thought other than *I'm losing her.*

My mind a wasteland of fear, I watched the signs of deterioration in her grow like visible cancer.

She was going to turn into a wraith, and there was nothing I could do. With the speed of her decay, even if I shot through the hellgate and flew home as fast as I could, I'd never reach her body in time, let alone have a moment to figure out how to even reconnect her soul with her physical form.

That would take hours, if not more.

Zoe didn't have hours—she'd be gone in a matter of minutes.

The woman I loved more than life itself would disappear, in her place a shadow of her former self, a malevolent spirit driven by instincts and pain.

And then the only merciful thing to do would be to end her pain.

I shuddered, icy claws of panic shredding me from the

inside while my mind still refused to process what was happening and help me find a way to save her.

I couldn't lose her.

I wouldn't survive it.

I couldn't fucking lose her.

In the periphery of my vision, color flickered over my wings. My illusion faltered, white feathers peeking through and weaving the tapestry of my heritage. Black and white, demon and angel, incongruously combined.

My heartbeat stumbled.

Heritage.

Angel.

An idea sparked in my ravaged mind. A plan as mad as it was desperate.

And yet, it was the only way out that I could see.

If he agreed.

Holding Zoe in my shaking arms, I closed my eyes and focused inward, pulling on the power worked into familial ties, bonds of blood that defied the rifts in relationships, persisted throughout thousands of years of estrangement.

As much as I might have liked to pretend those bonds had been severed, in truth they'd never disappeared, only lain dormant, suppressed.

I'd had no need for them.

I'd had no need for *him.*

Until now.

I spoke his name, tugging on those bonds, and called him forth in a summoning of age-old magic, the kind only accessible to relatives of flesh and blood. It wasn't the sort of invocation that would force an appearance, unlike using a true name.

It was a request, one that could be denied.

I waited, my only company my racing heartbeat and Zoe's weakening form in my arms.

She was getting worse by the minute. Already, I feared that her condition had progressed too far for her to be saved.

And still I waited, for what else was I to do? Either my madcap plan would work, or I'd hold her through her last moments of being herself, and then I'd see to her swift end.

I wouldn't allow her to suffer, even if destroying her would destroy me, too.

Pulling her closer, I pressed my forehead against hers, my heart in splinters.

A vibration in the air heralded his arrival.

My breath stuttered as I raised my gaze, as I watched his form take shape before me. Unique among his kind due to his duty and curse, he could move and manifest outside of laws of space and distance. He could traverse the world in the blink of an eye, split his attention between millions of places.

After all, the Angel of Death needed to be everywhere, all at once.

I studied him as he stood before me, the pristine white wings, silver lightning dancing over the feathers, the gleaming armor, the proud set of his shoulders…those features that, despite my not having seen him in two thousand five hundred years, were achingly familiar. Because they were a mirror image of my own.

"Father," I greeted him, my voice rough.

He'd come. I hadn't believed it until the last second. Hadn't thought he'd heed my call. Then again, I'd never tried to contact him before now. Perhaps his answer to my summons was born of an irresistible kind of curiosity. Millennia of silence, only for me to request his presence now.

Because he was my last resort.

"Azazel." He regarded me and the woman I held in my arms, his eyes of silver storms so reminiscent of my own. "Speak."

To the point. No polite intro, no inclination to chat. Not that I cared for any of that either. It wasn't the reason I'd called upon him.

"I need you to get her into Heaven," I said without further ado.

His gaze fell once more on Zoe, his expression unmoved. "She is not eligible. Her soul is slated for Hell." He looked at me and narrowed his eyes. "You were bonded. I cannot ferry her into Heaven when her soul still bears the mark of a bond to a demon. She would not pass the gate."

I resisted baring my teeth at him, old resentment rising to the fore. "I don't want you to ferry her soul. I want you to draft her."

Azrael blinked, his eyes widening in shock, an almost comical slip of his stoic mien. He caught himself quickly, though, his gaze turning flinty. "Surely you must be joking."

I clenched my jaw, the thought flickering through me that Zoe would have a quip for this situation and reply with a cheeky "I'm not, and don't call me Shirley." My heart fractured imagining I'd never hear her witty remarks and quirky repartees again.

I needed her in my life, needed her more than my next breath.

Which was why I was ready to beg on my knees in front of the father who'd abandoned me eons ago.

"I am," I ground out, "deathly serious. Ascend her. Please."

"She hasn't made a sacrifice. She's not a candidate for ascension." He slashed his hand through the air. "There are rules."

"It's in your purview to interpret those rules!" I shot back. "You're the Angel of Death. This falls in your jurisdiction—you can decide to turn her."

He opened his mouth to say something, but I cut him off.

"I have never"—my voice broke—"asked you for *anything*. You turned your back on us without a second glance, and I have not come to you for anything. For two thousand five hundred years, I have not had need of your help, your presence, your care. I have made no requests of you, though God knows I would have had cause."

He winced at that, revealing a glimpse of some long-buried vulnerability.

I hefted Zoe closer, my soul aching at how she kept slipping away from me. "But I am asking you this now. Help her. Please. Help her, and I will ask no more of you, *ever*."

Azrael examined me for the span of a few heartbeats, then he quietly asked, "If I do this for you, will you absolve me of my dereliction?"

I stared at him. In disbelief, in confusion, in simmering outrage. To ask me for forgiveness, after all this time, in exchange for saving the woman I loved.

To *negotiate* with me, when I had already *begged* him to help me.

The fury emanating from me made my wings tremble.

This, I knew well. Wrath, the heat of rage flowing through me, the urge to draw blood. This, I could handle.

What was harder to contend with was the hurt.

The corrosive ache of disappointment. The teeth-gritting anger at myself for even still having the capacity to be disappointed in someone who'd shown long ago that he was beyond hope.

I swallowed it all down, pushed it hard into the corners of my heart where I locked away the deepest pain.

This wasn't about me.

"You have my forgiveness," I grated out.

"Sworn in truth?"

I took a deep breath, my nostrils flaring. "I swear it on my mother."

He flinched.

Good.

A last, vindictive thought before I let go of age-old resentment, of a grievance held on to for thousands of years. Not a feat to be done in seconds, but rather the start of a process that would take a lifetime.

But I'd sworn it in truth, and I would not break my word.

Azrael nodded once. "Then I will ascend her. Lay her down and step back. I need space."

Gently, I placed Zoe's form on the ground, in a clear spot of pavement between the debris. Her eyes were unfocused, fine cracks spreading over her arms, creeping closer to her chest. She was running out of time. With trembling fingers, I pushed a strand of hair out of her face, then I backed up, giving Azrael the space he'd demanded.

He crouched next to her, and I reined in the protective impulse to lop off his hand as he laid it over her chest, right over her heart.

Closing his eyes, he murmured, "Rise to power, remade and reforged, bound in duty and privilege to God."

Below his hand, light gleamed. Magic threaded around us.

"Rise in glory, reborn and refined, in humble service to our Lord."

My skin began to itch. The white of my feathers glowed.

The light beneath Azrael's hand spread, engulfed Zoe's form...and erased all traces of decay on her skin, in her aura. Power charged the air, tasting both alluring and repulsive—

the opposing forces of my dual heritage wreaking havoc on my senses.

"Rise, angel," Azrael intoned and withdrew his hand, his voice vibrating with magic.

With a flash, the light pulsed through her. Zoe bucked, her back arching as she rose into the air as if pulled by a rope fastened around her middle. Power exploded from her as though every single cell had been shot through with divine energy that now poured from her in a fiery shower of sparks.

The light became blinding, and I had to shield my eyes from the glare, the heat of heavenly power scorching my skin.

When the energy lessened, the glow fading, I lowered my arm from my face and stared—at the newborn angel before me.

Her dark hair flowing in a phantom breeze, her eyes closed, features smooth as if in a peaceful sleep, she was at once familiar and yet not—it was still Zoe, though every line and curve of her face and body was now ethereally enhanced. Gone was her ghostly form, that echo of her earthly body she'd left behind in Hell. In its place floated a newly made, naked, truly physical body, crafted right from her soul, for that was the unique way angels and demons were created—our souls *were* our bodies. Unlike humans, we couldn't separate the two.

I couldn't stop staring at this new shape of her, at her glow of grace, the kiss of divinity evident in the silver sheen on her skin, the whisper of power in her aura…the sparkling white of her wings.

Her *wings*.

Awestruck, I drank her in, at once marveling at the stunning changes to her appearance…and grieving the loss of her imperfections. That scar on her right knee where she'd crashed the first time she'd ridden a bicycle. The fine white lines on the inside of her thighs, her skin showing how her body had grown into her own. That one toe on her right foot that was weirdly shorter than the one next to it.

All those little flaws that had made her beautifully human.

All of it had smoothed out, had been glossed over and "perfected"—despite the fact that she'd been perfect already.

Profound sadness filled me as I realized I'd never again see the version of her I'd fallen in love with. That I'd lost this part of her forever.

Though it was, of course, tempered by the relief of not losing her entirely. She'd live, and that was all that mattered.

The last glow of her change faded from her form, and all of a sudden, she fell onto the ground as if the power that had held her aloft had been switched off.

I jumped forward, ready to gather her in my arms, but Azrael moved into my way, blocking me with his body and wings.

"She is not yours any longer," he said quietly, his eyes as hard and cold as ore. "All bonds have been severed, all ties cut. You and she are now on different sides. She belongs to Heaven."

I pressed my lips together, primal possessiveness heating my blood to boiling. My power made the air glimmer.

"Even should you try," Azrael said in a low voice woven with warning, "she will not remember you."

My energy stilled. My breathing flattened. "What do you mean?"

"All newly made angels start with a blank slate. The change wipes their memory. No knowledge of their former mortal life remains." His features softened the slightest bit. "So I'd suggest you cherish the memories of your time together, for she has none left. The woman you loved is no more, and will never be again."

My gaze fell on Zoe, lying unconscious on the ground, her white wings draped over her naked form.

She will not remember you.

Tight bands wrapped around my chest, arrested my breath.

"You asked me to ascend her," Azrael said, speaking into the dull silence of my rising despair, "and now I ask you to respect her new life in the service of Heaven. You have to let her go."

I swallowed hard, my throat feeling like sandpaper, my eyes still on Zoe. My fingers twitched. "Allow me to say goodbye."

A moment, suspended in time, then he nodded and stepped aside.

I sank to my knees next to her, reaching out with shaking hands. The moment I touched her, an ache pierced my heart, right where the bond we'd shared had once originated. Like the phantom pain after an amputation.

I gathered her into my arms, pressed her close, and buried my face in her neck. Breathed in her scent, both familiar and new. Felt her warmth, the weight of her, how her body still fit against mine as if crafted for that purpose alone.

Steely resolve strengthening every beat of my bruised heart, I pressed a kiss to her neck and then whispered into her ear, too low for Azrael to hear, "I'll come for you, love. I will *make* you remember. You're mine, Zoe, and no power in the world or beyond can keep you from me. You're *mine*."

I laid her back on the ground only for a moment, only long enough for me to loosen the leather plates of my fighting gear, strip them off, and drop them next to me. I wore a tunic underneath, and I ripped it right off me and used the material to wrap it around Zoe's naked body, creating a makeshift dress. She was still so much smaller than I was that my tunic was large enough to cover her adequately.

Like Hell would I let my father carry her naked.

And when she woke, she'd be wrapped in my scent— even if she wouldn't remember me.

Yet.

I picked her up once more, rose to my feet, and then handed her over to Azrael, even though every single muscle and instinct within me protested the action. I wanted nothing more than to tear her from his arms and take her straight to Hell with me...only she wouldn't pass the gate. Not with those wings of gleaming white.

So I stood back, reining in the urge to claim her again, and watched how Azrael launched into the sky with her, my only solace the knowledge that this was not a farewell forever.

Because I sure as fuck intended to corrupt a certain newly made angel.

Thank you for reading *Till Heaven Do Us Part*!

I know, I know, it's a mean cliffhanger! *ducks and runs away* Zoe and Azazel will return soon in the final book in the *Infernal Covenant* trilogy, *Hell Over Heels*, which is set to release on April 26, 2024.

If you don't want to miss the release or any updates, be sure to sign up for my newsletter: https://nadinemutas.

com/newsletter/ Subscribers get an exclusive bonus scene for my books every month and are the first to hear about book news.

I also have an active reader group on Facebook where I usually post teasers of my work-in-progress and interact with my fans.

Much love,
Nadine

ALSO BY NADINE MUTAS

The *Love and Magic* series:

To Seduce a Witch's Heart

To Win a Demon's Love

To Stir a Fae's Passion

To Enthrall the Demon Lord

To Tempt a Witch to Sin

The *Infernal Covenant* series:

Hellishly Ever After

Till Heaven Do Us Part

Hell Over Heels

ABOUT THE AUTHOR

Nadine Mutas writes paranormal romances that are equal parts funny and spicy. She has won multiple awards with her books, but alas, no annual supply of coffee yet.

After majoring in subjects that were fun to study but less applicable for making a living with (Japanese, South Asian Studies), Nadine has turned to fully indulging her weird fantasies that people actually pay her to write down. You can usually lure her out of her socially awkward shell by striking up a conversation about languages (keywords: Indo-European family; relation of Sanskrit to Ancient Greek) and watch her geek out for the next hour.

She lives in Germany with her college sweetheart, beloved little demon spawn, and two infernal cats hellbent on cuddling her to death (Clarification: Her husband and kids prefer her alive. The cats, she's not so sure about.) When she's not writing, she can be found at the archery range, where shooting at things with sharp-tipped arrows has proven to be an excellent meditative practice.

Connect with Nadine:
www.nadinemutas.com
nadine@nadinemutas.com

Made in United States
Troutdale, OR
09/18/2024

22951621R00289